*To my wife, who reads every word,
even the bad ones.*

CONTENTS

Dedication	
Chapter 1	3
Chapter 2	28
Chapter 3	58
Chapter 4	76
Chapter 5	98
Chapter 6	118
Chapter 7	138
Chapter 8	155
Chapter 9	170
Chapter 10	186
Chapter 11	203
Chapter 12	219
Chapter 13	236
Chapter 14	264
Chapter 15	283
Chapter 16	301

Chapter 17	322
Chapter 18	338
Chapter 19	356
Chapter 20	381
Chapter 21	396
Chapter 22	412
Chapter 23	427
Chapter 24	445
Chapter 25	458
EPILOGUE	474
THE END	481
The Memory Mage	485

The Memory Mage Book 1:

Strange Addictions

By

T J Flaxman

CHAPTER 1

My name is Finley Chase, and I am an addict. It's a simple mantra but one I like to repeat to myself in times of stress. It doesn't so much relax me as remind me to keep my head. I'm also a mage, and as part of that demographic, I'm all too aware that we make up some of the worst drivers on the planet and that any sensible, forward-thinking practitioner, should let others get behind the wheel. Of course, there are exceptions to every rule.

I'd been trying to sleep. Any car journey spent conscious is a wasted one if you ask me. My driver had other ideas, however. She had gambled every amber, accelerated out of every corner like a rally driver and ground gear transitions with such ear-splitting regularity, I was beginning to think it was personal. I watched it all through lidded eyes and a slack-faced expression in the vane hope she would take pity on me. Instead, she attacked the curb with the reckless enthusiasm usually reserved for stunt drivers and people in rental cars when I decided enough was enough.

"Who are you again?"

"*Amber.*" said the teenager, her voice mockingly sweet as she thrust a foot against the brake. The vintage unlicensed cab came to an abrupt halt on a quiet residential street, lurching my body forward. I fumbled at my hip for the seatbelt and quickly returned the assortment of Tupperware and cardboard boxes back to their proper place.

"I thought it was Alice?" I said.

"She quit."

"Right." I said, rubbing my eyes. It seemed unfair I should feel this out of it when I couldn't have slept more than five minutes.

I heard the distinct sound of a makeup bag being rummaged through and sighed as the car started to roll forward.

"Amber, then. Could you please apply the handbrake before you do that", I said, doing my best to keep my voice polite. I looked at the pretty nineteen-year-old in the rear-view mirror as she applied another coat of cerise pink to her lips. The wheels rolled a foot backwards before she obliged. The ratcheting sound that followed made me wince as the wheels locked and the boxes containing my treasures teetered ominously before I steadied them for the second time.

Mages make the worst drivers, I reminded myself as I battled the urge to fire her on the spot and retake control of my vehicle.

"Go easy on her, alright, she's getting on", I said, touching a hand to a line of black duct tape where yellowing foam had started to spill from a break in the ancient upholstery. My 1973 Austin FX4 had its original Austin-made engine before they were bought out by Rover. She (for all cars of a certain age and character are most certainly a 'she') was a thing of subtle beauty. Thanks to careful maintenance and a little magic of my own devising, she was in reasonable condition with one or two minor exceptions. Vehicular restoration and maintenance was too costly for someone with my bank balance and the slew of careless drivers had done her no favours. The crumbling interior I could live with but the garish yellow bonnet on an otherwise uniformly black body among the dozens of scuffs and scratches was a constant thorn in my side.

Amber smacked her lips and tossed the cosmetic back into her bag before fishing for another. "Maybe, oh I don't know, think about paying me and I'll look after your stupid car."

"Pay you?" I repeated, the pitch of my voice betraying my anxiety surrounding the topic. Day one and she was already asking for money? She wouldn't last the week. "This is for your degree." I added, in more measured tones, "You can't buy this kind of life experience, let alone this kind of excitement."

She snorted.

"Would you prefer to spend your time working the tills at the supermarket?" She paused in her application of eyeliner to stare daggers at me through the rear-view mirror. When I picked up the antique at a motor fair in Soho I'd never imagined how often it would be used for this very purpose. Had I known, perhaps I wouldn't have braved the Underground and resulting panic attack to get it.

Still, I needed her just like I had needed every one of her predecessors, each of whom I'd somehow swindled into taking on an unpaid work experience placement. It wasn't that I couldn't drive – I had a current and legal licence – it was just better for everyone if I didn't.

"You sure this is the right street?" I asked, glancing out of the cab's tinted windows. Since I tended to travel with my most cherished belongings in the cabin with me, it was the one modern feature I was willing to tolerate.

"Positive", she said, with the confidence only a teenager with an internet-connected phone could muster. "It's the big one on the right. Number 57." she pointed, without looking.

I grabbed a post-it note from the box of stationery beside me and stuck it to the partition between the front and rear seats.

"How are you so sure? You saw him go in?" I asked, writing down the street name then adding the number 57 last.

"You mean you didn't see?" she asked in mock surprise.

"You know I was asleep", I said, stiffly.

She made a sour face at me through the mirror. "Oh that's right, how could I forget. You were half asleep when I drove an hour to your house to pick you up. You slept all the way back into London, didn't stir when I stopped for Coffee..."

"Well," I said, cutting her off and sensing she was only picking up steam, "shadow me long enough and you'll see just how tiring this work can be. Now *what* did you see?"

Amber wasn't talking. She continued to look unimpressed and began texting, so I waited. She wanted attention, but she wasn't cruel with it, at least not yet. A couple more days as my personal chauffeur might change that. I sat back and continued to wait. If I stayed silent she would crack. I had ten years on her; experience was on my side and all she needed at this point was someone to talk to. Thirty seconds, a minute tops, and she would tell me what I wanted to hear.

"Tell me!" I yelled.

She jumped and I felt both awful and, I'm ashamed to admit, a little proud. "Fine!" she said, like a stroppy teenager, which I suppose she was. "A man and a woman went inside just as we were pulling up."

"What did they look like?"

"She was thirty maybe, thin, though dressed like a complete tramp. He was old, like you, only in better shape. Must be loaded, I guess", she said, extracting an invisible trace of mascara from her eyelashes.

I took a moment to decipher Teenage Girl Goggles and recover from the insult. I wasn't made of stone, not even close. I guessed the woman was most likely in her early thirties given Amber's description. Thin I guessed meant attractive, particularly when combined with the tramp remark. He was old*er* but probably not *old, old*. I was 35 but could probably add five or six years to that on a bad day. She was just being mean because I lost my temper at her and I slept all the time.

I kicked off my shoes and put my feet into the legs of a pair of blue overalls as I studied the houses to either side of number 57. The road was quiet and the houses unremarkable. Terraced and a combination of white and London brick, there was little to differentiate one from the next. The opposite side of the street was largely occupied by high-rise flats and an recently remodelled play park. In front of the house almost directly opposite number 57 stood a skip filled with the remains of the old park including what appeared to be an old swing and a roundabout, both whole and in surprisingly good condition.

I turned back to number 57 and looked more closely at its exterior. It was showing its age more than its neighbours, both of which looked to have been painted in the last ten years, their windows more recently cleaned, their hedges trimmed. I could practically hear the estate agent in my head repeating phrases like "fixer-upper", "investment opportunity" and "good bones", all of which may well have been true, but I doubted any of those reasons had been the deciding factor in Greg buying the place. If it had, he probably would have told my client, his wife, about it.

I reached for the camera bag and paused, hearing Amber sigh. Feeling guilty about yelling at her, I stuffed the bundle through the partition at her. "It's point and shoot. Take as many as you can and – I can't emphasise this enough – don't be shy."

"What?" Amber said.

"I can't pay you, but I suppose I can try and make things more interesting for you. There's a park opposite. Find a good vantage point and fire at will." As part of the gentrification of the area an elaborate treehouse had been constructed at the centre of the Roman Road adventure playground, presumably to offset the high-rise flats ruining everyone's view.

"What if someone sees me?"

"Pretend you're bird watching." I smiled, enjoying the fact I had shaken that unshakable teenage confidence of hers.

I could see she was starting to blush – an unexpected but not altogether unsatisfying sight after her progressively colder attitude towards me as the morning had worn on. I suspected it had something to do with the realisation that my day job was, at least from her perspective, much less interesting than she'd thought it would be. It was the same with her predecessors; the shine wore off sooner or later. With Amber, it just seemed to be happening much quicker.

"Until now I sought to shield your innocent eyes from the realities of marital infidelity, but you took this job for a reason", I said, trying to keep my tone level.

"I'm not a perv!" she said, and for a second I thought perhaps I had just lost myself another driver. Instead she stared out the window for a moment then abruptly got out of the taxi with the camera. I smiled to myself, watching her disappearing behind a hedgerow.

I checked my watch: it was almost 3pm. Too late for a lunch hour rendezvous, so I figured their meeting had been planned in advance, which meant they probably had at least a couple of hours to enjoy themselves, perhaps longer. They would take their time, and Amber would have learned a thing or two about herself before they were finished.

I zipped up my overalls and slipped my feet into a pair of black Crocs which were as comfortable as they were disgustingly unfashionable. In my mind, I'm that fabled tree falling in the woods: it's only really embarrassing if someone's there to witness the fall. If all went to plan, nobody would see me, not even Amber through the telephoto lens.

I popped the lid off the transparent Tupperware tub to my right and examined my treasure trove of oddities. I glanced over the mix of cassette tapes, bound letters, postcards and frayed novels and reached for the dozen or so records neatly stacked on one side. I flicked through them as gently and as quickly as my fingers allowed. Eclectic to say the least: Pantera, Gina G, Elvis, Elton, another Elvis, ELO, Brahms and Spice Girls (the movie soundtrack), to name a few.

I carefully removed a 1954 original from

its sleeve, read the words *Bing Crosby* and *Try A Little Tenderness,* and smiled, dropping the ancient record (already scratched to hell) unceremoniously onto the seat without looking at it. Instead, I gazed eagerly at the faded blue ink on the cover sleeve cradled in my hands. With Amber out of sight, I savoured it like a prospector cradling a knot of gold, or perhaps more accurately, a crack-head with a big score. Even just reading the words I found myself smacking my lips and working saliva around my mouth, remembering the power they held. The confidence, the swagger old Bing had felt when he'd signed the message made my head swim.

Dear Jonny,

Try a little tenderness and if Lucy still don't forgive you, try a little more.

Yours,

Bing

I almost left the car right then and there as that sudden swell of confidence washed over me. Holding that record sleeve I could talk my way into, or out of, anything I wanted. It was my golden ticket. I stopped myself halfway to the door with a great effort of will. The Crocs, which Bing would never be caught dead in, helped enormously in this regard. I carefully folded the yellowing paper sleeve until it fitted comfortably in the breast pocket of my overalls, grateful for the dulling effect the separation had. I reached for my coat which hung from a hook above the passenger side door and transferred a tobacco pouch and a lighter to the seat in front of me. I undid the sticky tab and looked down at the contents. Among the wads of sweet-smelling tobacco lay strips of paper. I chose one about the length and width of my little finger and read the message.

I'll be watching you.

I gave a shiver and returned it quickly to the pouch. Selecting the right keepsake to draw on always reminded me of that scene in *Indiana Jones* where Indy had to pick the Holy Grail out from a line-up of similar cups. *Choose wisely.* When making magic, no truer words existed.

I rummaged a little more and found the one I wanted, reading the words a few times to get the feel of them. The taste of them. Compared to Bing, who's presence I felt like a physical weight at the slightest contact, the scrap I held offered very little and most likely wouldn't until I started consuming it to make magic. Had I held it with me for a few hours perhaps something of it would have seeped through into my psyche but I didn't have that sort of time and there were no guarantees. All I could do was repeat the words and hope my sense of the person behind them was accurate.

Even when you look at me, you don't see me.

I folded the slip of paper and got out of the cab. The street I stepped out onto was a quiet hamlet in greater London. The street was bordered by spindly trees and thick hedgerows. I crossed the road and walked purposefully towards the house Amber had pointed out, my generic overalls hopefully hiding me in plain sight from any curious neighbours. I walked around the rear of the house and stopped at the back door. I counted to a hundred in my head, my ear cocked for the slightest sound from inside.

After another minute, I dug my picks out of my pocket and coaxed the latch open in just under five minutes, which, given the age of the lock was a little disappointing. I could have popped the lock instantly with a little magic, but the line from the love letter I carried was, I suspected, ill-suited to the task and would have required more energy than I was comfortable forfeiting for the marginal gain in time.

I stepped onto the welcome mat and closed the door behind me, lingering in place where I stood like an awkward guest, uncertain whether or not to remove my shoes before setting foot on the kitchen floor. Experience told me the young lovers would have moved to the bedroom already, but I was not in any hurry and it never hurt to be sure.

A feminine giggle sounded from upstairs, confirming my suspicions and making my heart skip a beat at the same time. I dug out my tobacco and rolling papers and pressed the sentence, *"Even when you look at me, you don't see me"*, into one of the papers before bedding it in with an even line of tobacco.

I used as little as possible. I hated smoking, always had, but it was one of the safer ways to consume magic. I put the unfiltered death stick to my lips and lit it, echoing those same words in my mind. Feeling like the worst house guest imaginable, I inhaled deeply and held the putrid mix of tobacco, old paper and stale ink in my lungs for a ten count, like a pothead trying to savour his high. A playful scream sounded from above while I counted. It was quickly followed by the groaning of springs as Greg Thomas moved to the bed with his mistress.

"Even when you look at me, you won't see me." I said, quietly as I exhaled, the simple incantation sending unpleasant chills down through my body.

I started coughing. Not quietly, either. I didn't bother to cover my mouth as I doubled over, spat onto the kitchen floor and continued to hack away like a fifty-a-day, fifty-something, smoker. Thankfully the noise didn't matter, the spell had already taken hold. It was a bitter and brooding thing, unpleasant like a grey cloud, though not entirely unsatisfying in its gloom. It felt *Justified*.

I walked across the kitchen floor in my mostly-clean Crocs and pulled open the fridge. It was empty except for a half dozen eggs, some bacon, a litre of milk and a pack of Cokes. I noticed the Cokes were the pricier, glass bottled kind; a detail I was certain I wouldn't have noticed or acknowledged a few moments ago. I took one, oddly relishing in the satisfaction of tearing it from the cardboard packaging, as if that simple act of rebellion had somehow closed the class, financial and romantic divide between the owner's life and my own. The small sense of elation lasted roughly until the fridge door slammed closed.

Forcing myself to focus on the task at hand, I listened to the noises of the house: the occasional shift of springs or the indistinguishable murmurs and moans of lovers lost in their own little paradise. God, I hated them. Why couldn't I have this? Mr Thomas had it all, a beautiful wife, three kids and a second home where he and his mistress could meet in secret and share an afternoon of passion before drinking Cokes from individual glass bottles like film stars. It wasn't fair!

I was halfway to the kitchen drawers before I snapped out of it. *The first step to recovery is admitting you have a problem.* This is especially important for mages. You can't use magic without being affected by it in some way, that's just how it works. Sometimes it's a small thing like being a little overconfident, or in this case, depressed and jealous. Others can be far worse. The best mages learn to distinguish and compartmentalise their own feelings from those of whomever they are channelling. The real problem is, I'm an addict. All my kind are, whether they admit it or not. I can't stop using magic; doing so would probably kill me. Equally, if I use too much or the wrong kind, that would probably get me killed too. I find it best to think of myself as a functioning alcoholic. I know I have a problem, and I take various steps to manage that problem. But the problem never really goes away.

I spotted the bottle opener in the kitchen drawer but instead used the edge of the oak worktop to pop the cap off my Coke. I took a swig, sloshing the over-sweet liquid around to clear the ashen taste from my mouth and smiling maliciously to myself at the abhorrent table manners of the man I was smoking. Acknowledging that it was him and not I that was the cause of my current behaviour helped immeasurably in controlling it. When using magic of any kind it was essential to get a handle on who was driving which of your actions as quickly as possible. Mannerisms, moods and personality tics not your own could all present to some degree or another, but once you could identify them, you could encourage the helpful ones, entertain the harmless ones, and ideally compartmentalise and suppress the rest. It rarely worked so cleanly, but you were only in proper trouble if you missed them entirely.

I looked at the bottle of Coke again. This time another set of thoughts took me, these entirely my own. Certain people never leave you, the what if's and if only's. The ones that return to you years later through something as commonplace as a bottle of Coke sitting in a fridge. The cigarette wasn't helping. I recalled vividly how the mess of blonde hair fell across freckled shoulders and how heavy and cat like she slept the morning after she arrived, Cokes in hand, ready to cheer me up. Posh Cokes, that's what she had called them, only she had lingered on the "sh" sound in posh until I cracked a smile. Anyone else would have brought beer. Not Claire.

It's funny how mood can change perspective. At my most sober I would have described her as my first girlfriend, the one destined to fail due to our youth and lack of compatibility. Right then, under the influence of a depressed and lonely man, she was my first love and the one I would never get over. The one I should have fought harder for, if only I'd had the sense. The one all good clichés are written for. I considered the Coke then flipped open my Motorola's scuffed little LCD screen, thinking I would call her and we could reminisce. The sight of Bing's record sleeve poking out of my breast pocket and the Crocs in my peripheral vision acted like a one-two punch of pride and embarrassment and was more than enough to stay my hand.

I snapped the phone shut and tossed it into one of the deeper pockets in my overalls before commencing my search of the house. I checked every drawer and cabinet in the kitchen before moving into the living room. I alternated between taking measured pulls on my cigarette, just enough to keep the spell going, and washing the taste away with the Coke. I held both in my left hand while using my right to rummage through any paperwork I came across. At the bay windows at the front of the house I waved at Amber from her spot on at the top of the treehouse. She didn't wave back, nor did she offer any indication she could see me. It wasn't true invisibility of course, I wasn't channelling nearly enough magic to even attempt it, and it was almost as effective and significantly less costly to make oneself unnoticed, particularly if there were no angry pets or security cameras to contend with. My cigarette fashioned me with a cloak of sorts, one which radiated concentrated bland and until it burned down to its last embers, I was magically imbued with the power of being too boring to look at, too dull to comprehend.

Highly effective, though doing little to help my mood.

I took the stairs two at a time, unperturbed by the heavy creaking of the uncarpeted staircase beneath my Crocs. I glanced into the bedroom where Mr Thomas and his mistress made love on top of the covers with the curtains open for the whole world and Amber to see. I watched them for too long myself, feeling the twin pull of arousal and jealousy before managing to drag myself away. Images of their bodies writhing in pleasure clung in my mind as I pressed on to the next room.

Compartmentalise! I told myself. I was fairly confident the jealousy was all the cigarette's doing and I pushed it to one side as best I could. The arousal, on the other hand, was at least partly my own. It had been a few months and, mage or no, I was still only human. I stepped into the second bedroom, which Greg appeared to be using as a study. Documents were spread out in piles across the desk, floor and a foldout bed. Bank statements, solicitors' letters, invoices. They were all there. I read the first few lines of each letter and took pictures of any my client, *Mrs* Thomas, might find useful.

"Oh, Greg..." the woman called from the next room.

I started. I recognised the voice.

I went back to the doorway and ignored the tangled bodies entirely, and looked closer at the woman with the dirty blonde hair and the athletic long legs.

"Claire? What the hell!" I said, furiously. The weave of magic I had been absentmindedly maintaining fractured and broke away. The pair turned to me in unison and, seeing me, sprang apart. Claire dragged the covers around her and Greg stumbled to his feet on the opposite side of the bed.

"Who the fuck are you? Get out of my house!" Greg shouted. Glancing between the lit cigarette and the Coke in my hands his face seemed to be warring between incredulity and anger.

I took a breath, trying to steady myself. Claire refused to look at me, so I turned to Greg. "Greg, give your wife what she wants and I won't need to show her the pictures. If they come out in court, I doubt a judge will look too fondly towards joint custody."

"You mother..." Greg snarled as he started round the bed towards me, pausing only to extricate himself from the bedsheet around his ankle.

"Greg, don't!" Claire shouted, for all the good it would do.

I sighed, dropped my Coke and made a fist around the rest of my still-burning cigarette.

"*Carreg*", I said, muttering the Welsh word for stone and mentally weaving the heat in my hand to the intent of my spell. I winced as pain lashed across the inside of my hand as if I'd just closed my fingers around a candle without wetting them. I tilted my face slightly to the wall giving him an easy target and felt the wave of energy roll up my arm.

Greg's fist connected hard with the side of my jaw though he might as well have thrown a haymaker at the exposed brickwork above the fireplace. The cracking of bone against my jaw made my stomach turn over though his crying out of pain a moment later was not unsatisfying. He slumped back onto the bed, examining what I hoped was a broken knuckle or two.

Nothing but ash and an angry red line remained in my hand, the cigarette having incinerated the instant I drew upon it directly. The momentary rush I experienced, of drawing power directly through my skin, was gone. It was a reckless and unnecessary display really, foolish and an utter waste of a good keepsake. The stalker-cigarette had been a secretive and passive thing, ideal for stealth-based magic and utterly ill-suited to what I just applied it to. At that moment I didn't care, I was still too angry.

Confident Greg wasn't about to hit me again, I turned to Claire, still not quite believing she was really there. She didn't look even slightly abashed by my presence, the covers barely concealing her breasts and pale thighs. She continued to avoid my eye. I gathered up Greg's clothes which had been piled neatly in a chair opposite the bed.

"Go home", I said, stuffing the bundle into his arms and shoving him towards the door. I went to the window and waved to Amber, then pointed back at the taxi. She looked pale even from this distance. She stuffed the camera back into the bag and set off down the fire escape. Once I heard the front door slam and Greg climb into his BMW, I turned back to Claire.

"How long?" I asked.

"Why, are you worried about me?" she said, her voice teetering somewhere between playful and hurt. "I've not seen you in months."

I knelt on the bed beside her and turned her face towards me. She flinched.

"Show me." For a moment, I thought she was going to bite my hand but she just stared up at me with wide blue eyes like a hurt animal and slowly complied. I tilted her gently towards the light. Her gums were a dentist's nightmare: swollen and red, with blood spots on her back teeth.

"Fuck", I muttered to myself, staring deep into her eyes. "How long? Do you even remember?"

"A few days, not that long", she said, pushing

my hand away from her jaw and sounding like a girl half her age. "You're one to talk. Bloody hypocrite." She looked at the palm of my hand where a red line stood out among the ash.

"I was protecting myself. You know that's different." I said, though quietly I didn't entirely disagree. Eating and consuming directly through touch, both channelled a keepsake's power more quickly than smoking them. Each had its place, but equally, each could be misused and exacerbate our decline.

"Sure it is."

I shook my head, she didn't sound like Claire. "Well, where is it?" I looked around the room. A plate, the kind used to burn incense, stood on the mantel but I couldn't smell any on the air. That and the swollen gums told me she had been exclusively eating her keepsakes for probably a week or more. Most mages, myself included, rarely ate their keepsakes, especially when using the types of magic I suspected she had been using.

I found her handbag and rifled through it until I found what I was looking for. I withdrew a small leather-bound diary, the kind a teenage girl just leaving her pink phase might use to record her most secret and intimate of thoughts. I flipped through until I arrived at page which hadn't been torn out. It was near enough what I expected.

A secret crush, feelings of a sexual awakening. I bit my lip to stop myself from shouting at her. Passion and secrecy were like heroin to a mage – dangerous and addictive, particularly when eaten raw. I was furious but I kept my anger contained. Expressing it to Claire wouldn't help because it wasn't just Claire in there at the moment, and if she was this far gone she wouldn't listen to me. Not until I got her clean.

I turned to confront her, but she was already standing, one hand still holding the bedsheet up to her chest. The sheet was too thin, barely concealing the disciplined runner's physique she had spent years sculpting. I glanced down at her body, unable to stop myself, and felt a longing not entirely my own. I scratched at the ash in my hand, wishing I still had some power left to draw from. I dragged my eyes back to hers, expecting to see disgust and anger, only to find her face turned up to mine, her expression open and accepting. I gave my head a shake, giving the other party inside a shove, forcing his influence down a dark stairwell at the back of my mind.

Magic was always like that. Sooner or later the power burned out and you were left with the remnants and the difficult work of separating them from you. Isolation helped, but large groups were better. One other person to feed off and to be fed upon was almost always a disaster. She was so low right now, she just wanted to be held, and at that moment, there were too many parts of me happy to oblige. Her eyes were glassy as they searched my own. *That* was Claire. Her shame was gradually drifting to the surface, fighting to restore her control over the impassioned teenager.

Perhaps we could just lay down and hold one another, *he* told me. Perhaps it wouldn't spiral this time, perhaps we wouldn't need to make love or tear away at one another's spirit until there was nothing left. My inner stalker was already thinking of a dozen desperate questions to ask her. *Why don't you love me? Why did you choose him and not me?* He was already plucking at my memories, pulling our history from my mind and laying it before me like pictures in a photo album only tainting them through the prism of his fractured personality. Our first night together, the smell of her hair, the way she used to sleep with her head on my chest.

It was Bing that saved me, and not for the first time. Remembering the sleeve, I slipped a hand into my pocket and felt the touch of power like a cold slap in the face. I kept a finger on it while taking a step back and using his confidence to clear my head. I let out a deep breath and looked Claire square in the face. She needed me, but not in the way the shadow fogging my thoughts wanted her.

"Why don't you go take a shower and get

dressed?" I suggested.

She looked at my breast pocket and reached out a hand towards it, perhaps sensing what it held. She was more sensitive than most, but then again, Bing was my most powerful keepsake. He was my fail-safe and safety net. His previous owner had cherished him for over thirty years and If I treated him right he might last me another twenty. I caught her hand and squeezed gently, letting her finger touch the outside of my pocket before drawing it away. Even that briefest of contact with Bing's aura, was enough. Confidence alone would have been a problem, but there was more than enough pride there too to help her remember. It was enough, Claire had always been strong, she had just needed to be reminded of that.

I occupied myself by looking out the window of the bedroom as she gathered up her clothes and padded into the bathroom across the hall. I heard her run the shower and pretended not to notice how red her eyes were when she found me on the stairs drinking another of Greg's Cokes. I handed her a fresh one. Greg wasn't going to miss it.

CHAPTER 2

"I'm so sorry, Fin", Claire said.

"Save it for the meeting", I replied, not wanting Amber to overhear more than she needed to. Amber was still new to all this and must have been mortified when I brought *the mistress* with me back to the car. Amber hadn't said a word and I guessed she would be leaving my employ within the next few hours. I tried to read her expression in the rear-view mirror but I was carrying too much of my own baggage to get any sort of read on her. Claire was as much of a mystery, her eyes out of focus as she watched the human soup of the city pass her by and the cab inched through rush hour traffic at a snail's pace. I cracked my window and imitated her, finding comfort in the warm August breeze on my face.

I changed while we drove, and transferred Bing to my overcoat, wanting to keep him close if I needed him. Powerful keepsakes like Bing projected a certain aura. I hadn't yet drawn on him directly but his continued presence helped to level me out and keep my thoughts from tumbling too far down the rabbit hole of my stalker's overactive imagination. I could feel Claire watching me occasionally out of the corner of her eye. She needed to get clean. Not just her, I did too. When she wasn't looking at me, I was stealing glances at her. I had an entire wardrobe to change into stuffed into the back of that taxi, but she only had the clothes she had arrived in: a pair of short denim cut-offs, and a faded white t-shirt with a rainbow across the chest. I offered her one of my old shirts, which she took with thanks and slipped on. An innocent gesture only rather than curb my longing for her it seemed to only enhance it. She rolled back the sleeves and knotted the corners around her stomach so it hugged her across the hips. Something about a woman wearing your clothes was always appealing, a fact both I, and the stalker doing backflips around my skull, seemed to agree upon.

"Where are we going?" Claire asked.

"You'll see", I said evasively, hoping the answer was enough to keep her in the cab long enough for us to make it there. She already knew where we were headed. There was only one place to go once you had consumed magic. The addresses might change, but there was only one way to rid yourself of our passengers completely.

"So, how's business?" Claire asked.

"Could be worse", I said, the response something of a reflex.

"I envy you", she sighed.

"Why is that?"

"You are in control."

I snorted, unwilling to confide in her just how close I had been to abandoning my supposed control less than ten minutes ago. "You aren't?" I offered.

"No, I'm not. I might last a few months, sometimes maybe even a year or two, but sooner or later…" She shook her head.

I nodded. "Sooner or later", I repeated.

The taxi pulled to a stop outside a community centre next to a church. I held the door open while Claire climbed out, my eyes lingering on the long pale legs that preceded the rest of her lean frame.

"Ready?" I asked.

Claire stood with her arms crossed tightly beneath her chest, the muscles in her jaw taut, but she nodded firmly.

"Good." I slipped off my overcoat and tossed it onto the back seat, leaving Bing behind.

"We'll be half an hour", I told Amber, before heading in, Claire beside me.

There were familiar faces around the drinks

table, I nodded to the few I recognised and shook hands with the pastor leading the group. I took a Styrofoam cup and filled it with water and poured a black coffee for Claire. Once seated in the loose circle of uncomfortable chairs, Claire produced a *KitKat* and offered me half. It was an old routine of ours that felt too familiar, too intimate. She rested the chocolate on her bare knee as she ate a section at a time. I sipped the too-cold water, hoping to dull my fascination with the little smattering of biscuit crumbs and the smudge of chocolate that still lingered on her skin.

Slowly the ring of seats filled up around us. First timers were always the most reluctant to seat themselves if no-one else was seated, but were, conversely, always quickest to join once someone had.

"Good afternoon, everyone. I see some familiar faces and a few new ones. To the new, I am Pastor John, it's nice to meet you all." He looked around the group, his voice soft and welcoming. "Now first things first, this is a safe place. You don't need to use real names if you don't want to. There is no judgement here and everything we talk about should be treated with the strictest confidence and without judgement from any member, including myself. Now is there anyone who would like to start us off?"

I raised my hand immediately. Pastor John

looked at me and smiled encouragingly.

I stood, glancing around at each of the eleven members of the group. "Hello, my name is Finley. I am an addict."

"Hello Finley", the group chimed.

"Hi", I repeated, giving a thin smile. "I'm an addict, a user. Sometimes I can't help myself and I hurt people." Most of these people were habitual drug users or heavy drinkers, sometimes you could tell one from the other purely by their pallor or how bloodshot their eyes were. Claire and I were, at least to my knowledge, the only mages in the room. Just because our addiction was magic didn't mean we were above the process, however. In many ways, we were even more bound by its terms. I had to pick my words carefully; if I told a lie it wouldn't work and I wouldn't be able to start ridding myself of the second psyche dogging my emotional heels. Omissions were sometimes acceptable but in general, you had to respect the process for it to work. That meant offering the unedited, bare truth to complete strangers, an act that could be humiliating. Still, confession was good for the soul, so I tended just to clench my teeth and power through until I was done.

"When I use, I feel like I become someone else. Sometimes I like the feeling, sometimes I don't." I hesitated. "Last time it happened I watched two people having sex. I only saw them for a few moments but I loved knowing that they couldn't see me. It was just watching them though, and after all I could think was I wouldn't ever have that, that intimacy for myself, not really. How could I burden someone else with my situation?" It was the confessions of two people which cleansed me. I felt the other slip away with the mental equivalent of a deep, soul-shuddering sigh. I slumped back into my chair feeling exhausted and ready to sleep for a week. Amber was right, I did sleep a lot but confession was exhausting.

I returned to myself and realised people were applauding half-heartedly. I nodded a sombre thanks to the group and the pastor, then it was Claire's turn. She stood, playing with the buttons on the shirt I had loaned her.

"Hi everyone", she said with a half wave to the group. "I'm an addict too." She glanced at me. "I use to escape. I use because when I do, I get to feel what someone else does. It makes me feel special, better and more... connected than any other time in my life." She paused. "I hate where that leads me though. I encouraged the advances of a married man because I wanted to be wanted. I *needed* to be wanted. My work is supposed to help people, to help them with their problems. I'm the worst kind of hypocrite. I hurt my friend and when they tried to help me I hated them for it.

The worst part is", her voice caught, "I'm afraid not feeling that connectedness, that urgency, will mean I'll end up using again. Sooner or later".

I could see the diary leave her then. I wish I could say it was like a physical weight had been lifted but if anything, the opposite was true. Without the teenager's influence, without that shift in perspective, that carefree grace, all that optimism and playfulness evaporated, and with it the various mental walls that had given her reprieve from her own life. I reached out a hand to steady her as she returned to her seat. She didn't need it, but she nodded her thanks for the gesture. Once she was seated, I applauded with the others. As it died down and the pastor started speaking she leant over and whispered in my ear.

"What the fuck am I wearing?"

#

We listened to the other addicts speak in turn. A familiar thread wove its way through the fabric of each person's life. The final two were both alcoholics and both sober for over a year and struggling with the fact. Claire listened with rapt attention to them as they discussed the pressure they felt when reaching such milestones. We slipped out under the pretext of locating the toilets during the break and climbed back in the taxi. It was too late in the evening for a coffee so we opted for a quiet bar in Shoreditch where we could talk openly. I fumbled instructions to the place while Amber remained stoic, further strengthening my belief that she would quit the second we were alone.

As the taxi came to a stop I jumped out and held the door open for Claire eager to delay Amber's inevitable resignation.

"I've not been here in years." she said, smiling down the shady looking steps. "Is it still horribly overpriced?"

"I imagine so. Lucky for me you are buying."

"Is that right?" she said as her phone started ringing. She checked it. "Ah, I should get this. I'll meet you inside."

I headed down concrete steps to find a familiar steel door. I knocked and was promptly let in by a bouncer in a waistcoat. The place was quiet, the prices tended to keep it that way until later in the evening. I picked a stool at the bar taking in the scent of bees wax and bourbon.

I ordered two *Old Fashioneds* from a moustachioed barman and prayed Claire would arrive ahead of the bill. She didn't and I parted with a twenty pound note. I appeased my bruised wallet by watching the barman prepare our drinks.

"Whiskey or Bourbon?" he asked.

"What would you recommend?"

"If you like it smoky I would pick a nice scotch."

"Sounds good", I said, glancing at the door as Claire entered.

He retrieved a bottle of 12 year old Laphroaig from the wall behind him and mixed it with sugar and bitters before plucking a blood orange from a bowl on the bar and cutting a section of peel from the fruit. I watched the spray of oil as he twisted the peel and dropped a coil into each glass.

I nodded my appreciation to the barman, taking in the scent of citrus fruit and oak-aged scotch before taking a sip. Claire sat down on my right and took in the bar as I tried to recall the last time we had visited the place. Modelled after a prohibition era speakeasy, the place was dimly lit, the decor black and gold in the art deco design, and Claire had quickly fallen in love with it shortly after we met. She smiled revealing no trace of the conflicted feelings I had about the place.

"So, what happened? You were doing pretty well last time I checked. You liked your patients, things were good with Harold. What happened, he leave you? Run out of patients?"

"You know his name is Henry", she said.

I nodded but kept my mouth shut. She could

have ignored the slight entirely, as she had on more than one occasion in the past. The fact that she hadn't let it slide told me she felt guilty, and Henry wasn't responsible for her falling off the wagon. At least not this time anyway. I was relieved and disappointed at the same time. It meant she could go home.

"Stop it", she chided.

"Stop what?"

"Stop *that*. I can see your cogs turning, I'm a psychiatrist, remember? It's annoying. I'm not one of your clients, so don't treat me like one, alright?"

She was right, of course. She'd said 'client' but what she really meant was 'suspect'.

"I'm sorry, I'm just concerned."

"It's fine." She closed her eyes and let out a deep sigh. "Counselling was going fine. Better than fine, really. I had them writing down everything, I had a regular influx of good, steady material. Material I could trust. More than enough to keep me going and I was actually *helping* them."

"Then what? You got bored?"

Claire groaned, momentarily going limp with her forehead almost reaching the bar before rising again and pushing back her hair. "I don't know. I guess I must have, but I don't remember feeling that way. This woman brings in her seventeen-year-old daughter's diary, from her first marriage. In it is all this stuff about her dashing new step-father, the dreams she had been having about him. They were all so vivid. You know what it's like when they are that age. Everything new and exciting." Her eyes flashed and I saw an echo of the teenager return for just a moment. It meant she had used too much magic and would continue to have flashes of the other personality for at least a few more days. I dug out a pen from my pocket and placed it on the bar beside her along with a couple of napkins.

"Dangerous, is what they are. What would have happened if I hadn't found you?"

"I know, Fin. I'd end up empathically overwhelmed, die, and probably take poor Greg with me." She sighed. "Poor Greg." she took up the pen and held it over the napkin.

"Fuck Greg."

"It was hardly his fault."

"What do you mean? It isn't like you compelled him, is it?"

"God no", she said, her face souring. "I would never, besides you know I'm no good at the external stuff."

"Well good, so it was all him then. He chose to cheat on his wife, he could have just walked away."

Claire crossed her arms under her breasts and snorted. Even without the creepy stalker with me, I was still only human.

"I'd be more convinced if you didn't keep looking at my tits."

"Well wear a fucking bra!" I said, turning away. The barman raised an eyebrow at me.

"I'm sorry. I'm grateful too, for bringing me back", Claire said resting her hand on my arm.

"Good", I said, turning to her. "Anyway, looking isn't, you know, the rest of it. You might have tempted him but he decided on his own."

"I guess", she said. "So, the wife will get everything? That's what you said back at the house."

I turned to her. "I was just bluffing, needed to scare him to get rid of him."

"I think the broken hand did that."

"He didn't have to hit me." I shrugged.

Claire continued to look troubled.

"The wife wants half. Greg was hiding assets. Part of the reason she hired me was to figure out what else he owned and where he had stashed it. Anyway, the point is she still wants her kids to know their father."

"Really?"

"What can I say, Mrs. Thomas is a reasonable

woman."

"Well, I suppose that's something." She looked tired.

"Have you got somewhere to go tonight?" I asked, hoping it didn't sound like an invitation. I think.

She smiled at me. "I'll be fine."

"And call..?"

"Call my sponsor", she finished. "I will, as soon as I get home."

"Good", I said, clearing my throat. "Call me too."

"Of course." Her face lit up suddenly, and my breath actually caught in my throat. She kissed me on the cheek before pulling me into a fierce hug. "Thank-you, Fin", she said, still holding onto me. She was always a great hugger.

"Oh, and for the record, I wasn't staring at your tits."

"No?" she said, her voice ringing with amusement.

"I was staring at your legs", I admitted.

She snorted, slapping my arm in reproach.

"I've missed this." I said.

She paused, watching me with a wry look about her. "I've missed you too." she replied. Her phone started buzzing across the bar. "Sorry", she said, going over to stand beside the billiards table to answer the call.

I watched her, thinking about how little we had changed. I still erred on the side of caution, rarely saying exactly what I meant, while Claire spoke directly, always cutting to the heart of things. She also knew what I really meant; that I had forgotten how much I missed her.

"Fin, I'm sorry but somethings come up. I've got to go", she said returning to the bar.

"You need a lift?"

"Thanks, but you've done enough heroics for one day." She smiled.

"I suppose you're right." I nodded smugly, enjoying watching her roll her eyes as though wishing she hadn't drawn my attention to the fact. She glanced at our unfinished drinks then back at me. "If you're still in town in a couple of hours, maybe we can finish that drink?"

"You buying this time?"

"We'll see", she teased. "I'll call you in a bit." She kissed me on the cheek and left.

#

Four hours later I had four missed calls. They were all from Amber, none were from Claire. After she had left the bar I finished both our drinks then, slightly inebriated, ordered two more continuing to watch me phone. I dodged the first call from Amber but texted her immediately back and told her I wouldn't need her for another two hours. Amber called again around 8:30pm and again, I ignored her. By 9pm, with no word from Claire and pretending I wasn't watching my phone I finally tried to call her. I hung up when I heard her voicemail and swiftly departed in search for somewhere cheaper that didn't remind me of Claire.

A smart mage avoids alcohol, particularly in excess. We are addicts after all and as any addict would tell you, it's important to avoid potential triggers. This was part of the reason Claire and I started drinking at the speakeasy, the drinks were so expensive that we could rarely afford more than one.

I walked a mile lamenting the warm evening air and bold red sunset cascading off the windows of the high rises in the distance. The weather didn't suit my mood. I wanted the cold and rain and to know why I had been stood up. As confident as I was in this belief I continued to check my phone every five minutes as I walked. I paused briefly in another bar drinking a cheap whiskey but the evening crowd was out in force and their elation only soured my mood further. I caught sight of a blonde head of hair exit from across the bar and downed my drink before following after them. I texted Claire twice to find out where she was as I continued up the street. It was only when I checked the timestamp on my texts that

I realised what I was doing. I looked up, spotting the blonde stranger in the distance and turned immediately around and walked in the opposite direction. My stalker was still with me. Not only that he was taking advantage of my mood, drawing strength from it and pulling me down into his obsession.

"Sneaky bastard." I muttered under my breath, heading back towards Amber.

#

I spotted my taxi with the broken light and the yellow bonnet. I was halfway across the street when I saw Amber handcuffed in the back seat with a plainclothes policeman standing over her while another rifled through my record collection.

"I hope you have a warrant for that", I called across the street, trying not to let my drunken irritation show. I nodded to Amber as coolly as I could while they snapped the cuffs on me, read me my rights, patted me down, and pushed me into the back of a police car.

Amber didn't so much as look at me during the drive to the police station. She looked furious, I had kept her out past 11pm and spent the evening dodging her calls and ignoring her texts on the off-chance Claire showed up and could drive us back to my house.

#

Three hours later I realised the cell they had put me in was actually going to serve as an overnight cell too. Too many officers had been called away on more important business and my interview had dropped way down their list of priorities. A stoic but pleasant enough female officer came to check on me every hour and offered more cups of tea than any human could feasibly consume.

After I'd finished eating and paced around my cell for half an hour I started to feel claustrophobic. It took me another thirty minutes to realise my mistake. I was entering withdrawal. The physical symptoms had been cleansed by the meeting just prior to my arrest but the psychological ones could linger longer than this. I got the attention of the custody officer and request a pen and paper.

She returned forty minutes later and took one look at my pale sweating face and refused on the grounds she didn't think she could trust me with anything sharper than a soup spoon. Sooner or later I would have to get the words out somehow but I figured a police holding cell was not the best time to spend the night rambling to myself or scratching messages from the voices in my head into the wall so instead I burrowed into my blanket and tolerated the shakes and intermitted bouts of sweating.

Mercifully the keepsake wasn't an especially powerful one so the aftershocks from my passenger personality never lingered too long. I slept reasonably well after about 2am until just after nine. I accepted the offer of a shower and another round of toast and entered the interview room feeling tired and a little hungover but no less innocent.

The only thing Greg had on me was my physical presence in his home with no visible signs of a break in. Since he was still married and I was working for his wife, I was certain Mrs Thomas would side with me and the charges would be dropped. The issue of his injured hand was a bit sticky, but I was willing to bet that Gregg wasn't likely to even mention it. Male pride could be a powerful thing and after all, he had hit me.

I had once heard it said that, whether innocent or guilty, you should never talk to the police. The onus of proving any guilt is entirely on them, so why make their job easier? Most people feel compelled to prove their own innocence, however, and thus end up getting caught out in a lie. The only real reason I could think of to actually come clean with your interviewer is if they have some compelling evidence against you and you *have* to prove your case.

"Your full name is Finley Adam Chase, correct?"

"That's correct."

"You've been arrested on suspicion of breaking into a Mr Gregory Thomas's home." PC Harvey said.

"Was that a question?" I asked, contemplating the bubbles in my tea.

"Did you fight with Mr Thomas?" P.C. Harvey asked.

"No comment." I guessed Harvey was trying to get me to admit to being in the property.

"How did you gain entry to Mr Thomas's property?"

"No comment."

"You've denied legal representation for this interview; this led us to believe you were willing to cooperate with our investigation", he said.

"I'm sorry, but the way I see it, you don't have much of a case. I had permission to be where I was."

"In Mr Thomas's property?"

"No comment."

My interviewer was a middle-aged man with thinning blonde hair and enough loose skin to suggest he had recently taken the advice of a doctor after some medical wake up call or other. From the way his eyes lingered on my cup after I emptied four sachets of sugar into it, my money was on sky-high cholesterol. He looked at his notes then up at me and sighed, as if confessing would only help me at this point.

"Was the door open when you arrived?"

"No comment." I coughed and took another sip of my tea, feeling a dull ache forming in the back of my skull. I was growing uncomfortably warm even though I was certain the radiator behind me wasn't turned on.

"Why were you at an addicts anonymous meeting after you visited the property in question?"

"No comment." I put my hands under the table as they started to shake and took a breath.

"Are you an alcoholic? Habitual drug user?"

"No."

His eyebrows perked up at this. I wasn't quite sure if this was due to the deviation in my answer or the fact I was starting to sweat. Perhaps I had developed some facial tick I wasn't conscious of, it wasn't uncommon. Withdrawal isn't like it's shown in films and TV. Sure, you can sweat a lot and have any number of other flu like symptoms, but the teeth grinding, face foaming, begging and general desperation usually depicted doesn't do the thing justice. Symptoms vary person to person, and drug to drug.

At the physical level, things are pretty straightforward for a mage. Lucky even. You go to a meeting, you get clean, then you take whatever amount of time is required to deal with the comedown. Then rinse and repeat. Psychologically, things aren't quite so simple. It doesn't matter how few keepsakes you use, even one leaves a hole, a gap where another personality lived, however briefly. Sometimes they are so quiet in your mind, you barely notice they were there at all. Other times it's a relief to get rid of them, but again, it's rarely so simple. Even an annoying companion, can be missed once they depart.

It's the abrupt lack of connectedness that affects me most. When I'm using, there's another mind adjacent to my own, watching the world through my eyes like we are sharing a sofa and a bag of crisps, and our favourite soap is on. Even the slightest fraction of that other mind can provide insight and experience I wouldn't otherwise have, a contrast of opinion to commune, argue and reflect with. Humans are social creatures, mages are even more so. Isolate either and we become lonely. Keep us isolated and we become depressed.

I was taught to think of those we channel as neighbours rather than friends. They are there because they have to be, so it's best to have a good working relationship but anything more than that can get dicey. A neighbour will feed your cat and water your plants when you are away, but you don't take them to dinner or invite them to stay the night. You miss a departed neighbour, but you mourn a departed friend.

"Could I get a pen and paper, please? I'd like to write some notes." I could feel Harvey watching me more closely now. There was a certain eagerness, an anticipation to his posture now. I wasn't sure what I had done to warrant the extra attention. Perhaps he thought I was about to confess or maybe he was just that bored.

"Certainly, once we are done here. According to my records you dropped out of your university placement in your second year? I was never much for higher education, myself."

"That's right."

"And it says here you are now working as a private investigator? How long have you been doing that?"

"Almost a year."

"You're don't appear to have a license with the SIA?"

"That is correct." I said.

"You are operating without a license."

"Right." I said, taking another sip. The fact was new legislation for restricting private investigators hadn't come into effect yet, the politicians were still working out the specifics, or at least they were last time I checked. Licenses were issued for things like personal security,

CCTV monitoring and clamping cars, none of which I was involved with. I guessed they were fishing to find out more about my business in the hopes I would get defensive and incriminate myself in some way.

"What were you really doing at number 57, Hewlett Road, yesterday afternoon?"

"Sorry, client privilege and all that."

"And your client is?"

I remained silent. They already knew.

"I imagine that line of work wasn't quite what you expected. Deal a lot with divorcing couples?"

"Pretty much. Had a couple of over protective parents worried about their kid's drug habits and a half dozen background checks for a bank. Nothing too exciting."

"Is that why you left university? Lack of excitement?"

"No, too much of it if anything."

"Perhaps I should have gone. Was it the drugs then?"

I cleared my throat and gave my eyes a rub. "Something like that. Can we take a break?"

He glanced at the clock on the wall. "Why don't we give it another fifteen minutes. Now your father is Robert Chase, the author?"

"Yes. But what has that got to do with…"

"Must have been hard growing up under that shadow?"

"No comment." I said, finding it harder to focus on the PC's face.

"Don't get me wrong, I tried one of his books once. Does nothing for me personally, but the wife can't get enough of the stuff."

My hands were shaking so hard with the effort to contain my passenger personality I had to lean forwards to stop him from seeing them. I found myself staring at Harvey's notes and his messy scrawl. Just hearing the scratch of a Biro on the page was enough to make my gums itch.

"You two get on okay?"

"Not really, no." I said, leaping at the question. People want to be heard, want their story to be known and their reasons understood. The remnants of my lonely passenger was no different, he had done things he wasn't proud of. Judging by the scrambled thoughts bouncing around my brain, I guessed he had followed someone on more than one occasion. As much as he wanted to unburden himself before he disappeared from my mind completely, now was not the time. To keep him appeased it didn't matter what I said, I just needed to delay that catharsis for a few more hours and let out something, anything, and quickly via that lonely psyche gnawing at the back of my brain without it landing me in prison. I figured my dad was relatively safe territory. A lot of it he probably already knew so I continued before Harvey had a chance to ask anything more damning.

"Our relationship is hardly unique. We were close when I was younger and still *on track*, as he liked to put it. Thought if I had the brains then I had a duty to follow in his footsteps. We are mostly still on speaking terms because I've never admitted to him that I never plan to go back."

"Why not? Sounds like honest work. Plus, it might help keep your nose clean."

I ignored the double meaning, unsure if it had been deliberate. The constable seemed to be hinting at a drug addiction. "It just wasn't for me." I hesitated, sensing that wasn't enough of an answer to appease my passenger's guilt. It was all in police records anyway. "I had a bad experience. I'm sure you've already looked it up. A friend of mine was killed on a night out. He stepped into traffic."

"Were you driving the car that hit him?"

"God no, I was with my girlfriend. They never found the driver."

"Did you supply the drugs?"

"No, there weren't any drugs involved. It was just my idea that he go out in the first place. He didn't drink and went a bit overboard. I felt, I *feel* responsible." That wasn't the full story, but I couldn't get into the rest of it without talking about magic. Thankfully it seemed to be enough to appease my lonely companion, at least for the time being. I felt the tension knotting my shoulders ease and the dull throb at the back of my skull ebb away. Each successive breath that followed felt a little easier.

There was a rapid knock at the door then, the kind of urgent double tap you used when you needed to interrupt and didn't care about looking polite.

A striking tanned face appeared as the door was pushed open. "A word?" the woman said.

"Interview paused at 10:14am", Harvey said, before rising and following the woman out. "I'll only be a minute."

The anxious tugging at the back of my mind eased and I could think clearly enough to see how strange the constable's line of questioning actually was for a simple B and E. Perhaps Greg trying to inflame the charges to aggravated assault?

The pair returned ten minutes later, and together, sat down opposite, their faces neutral. "Interview resumed at 10:25am. PC Harvey is now joined by Detective Stone from CID."

"Detective?"

She offered an unconvincing smile. "Hello Mr. Chase. Sorry to have kept you. We'll have you out of here shortly. I just have a few more questions. You mentioned you were with your girlfriend at the time of the car accident?"

"That's right." Something wasn't right here.

"A Doctor Claire Parkes? Could you tell me how you became acquainted?"

"We used to date in college."

How long for?"

"Off and on for a couple of years."

"And now?"

"I guess I'd call us old friends."

"And when was the last time you saw Doctor Parkes?"

"Yesterday, we went for a drink at this bar called *The Back Rooms*. She left after fifteen minutes or so. A little before 7."

"Did you speak on the phone afterwards?"

I frowned. "I left her a couple of messages. We were supposed to meet up later for a drink but she never showed. Is she in trouble?"

"Did she say where she was going?"

"No, just that something had come up. She took two calls while we were at the bar."

"When was the last time you saw her in person

before that?"

"I'm not sure, a year or so ago, I think."

"Did you talk on the phone at all in between those two occasions? Text or email?"

"No, not that I can recall."

"What did you do after she left the bar?"

"I stayed for two more drinks. When I realised she had stood me up I went for a walk."

"Where did you walk?"

"I'm not really sure, I just walked." I said. "What's going on? Are you charging me with something or what?"

There was another knock on the door. The detective cleared her throat, stood up and exited for a minute while Harvey hit pause on the interview tapes. The constable sat staring at his notes, taking reluctant sips from what I assumed to be a skinny, sugarless coffee. Apparently the interview was over until she returned.

"Have you tried apple cider vinegar? Dilute a little in water and drink it through the day. Taste will make you long for that skinny coffee but it's supposed to be good for cholesterol."

"Vinegar?" the constable repeated, sounding sceptical.

"Apple cider vinegar", I corrected. "I had a client who swore by it."

"Oh?"

"I wouldn't go replacing your meds with it or anything, but might be worth a look. This is your health we are talking about."

The constable grunted, looking slightly uncomfortable, but nevertheless scribbled a note at the top left-hand corner of his notepad.

The smile slipped off my face when the officer returned. She was holding an A4 folder which she placed on the table in front of her with the kind of deliberate caution one usually reserved for the handling of firearms. Something felt off. Every mage has different strengths and sensitivities that help them channel their power. Some are stronger at internalising it, others are better at externalising it. Claire could internalise like the strongest of us but isn't up to much else. Me, I'm pretty much in the middle, a jack of all magical trades as it were, but definitely master of none. It was part of the reason I chose the work that I did. A varied skill set was a huge advantage in the field. One area I thought I was perhaps a slip above most was my intuition about people. All mages were empathic to a degree, it was a necessary prerequisite of our magic. *If you don't relate, you can't levitate,* as my father used to say. I just thought mine was little more attuned than most. Then again, perhaps all mages thought that – we weren't exactly short in the ego department.

As I watched Detective Stone, something in her posture or the set of her jaw gave me pause. Had her clothes and hair not been bone dry I would have been convinced she had just stepped out of an ice bath. I could tell by the lines beneath her eyes and the effort it seemed to take her to hold herself still and not recoil and flee from the room. Whatever had occurred in the moments since she vacated the stuffy windowless interview room had changed her demeanour completely. I felt it as keenly as the promise of pain; whatever she was about to say, I didn't want to see the contents of that folder.

"Mrs Thomas corroborated your story, you've been cleared of all charges regarding the break in", she said, her tone even. I should have been relieved, but the words sounded light and insubstantial beside the two tonnes of silence that followed. I glanced at the folder.

I cleared my throat. "What's going on? Why are you asking me about Claire? Those aren't my release papers are they?" The way her hand moved protectively over them told me it was something else, something worse. She seemed to steel herself, then stared me straight in the eye.

"I regret to inform you that Claire Parkes was murdered last night."

CHAPTER 3

I stood up abruptly then sat down again, closed my eyes and took five deep breaths. When I opened them again, the detective was still watching me. My eyes came to rest on the envelope.

"I don't... How?" I said, fumbling to find words and feeling like a jagged knife had been thrust into my side.

The constable cleared his throat, as if to remind everyone he was still in the room. Detective Stone shook her head. "This is an ongoing investigation. We can't reveal any information to the general public at this time. You are free to go. Constable Harvey will take you through processing", Stone said, getting to her feet.

I rose with her, almost tipping the table in the process. Harvey, to his credit, was quicker than I expected. He caught me in a vice-like grip just below my right bicep.

"I'm sorry", I said, spreading my hands and

relaxing to show I had no intention of fighting anyone. "Just... isn't there anything else you can tell me? You said it was a murder? Did you catch the one responsible?"

Detective Stone continued to stare at me, the envelope tucked firmly under one arm with the other held over the top of it. "We are not at liberty to disclose any information to the public at this time."

"Are you the lead detective?" I asked, taken aback by how impatient she sounded and hoping I might speak to someone else with an ounce more sympathy.

"I'm one of several working the case", she said, before reaching for the door. I spotted the gold band around the third finger of her right hand, and before I could stop myself I stepped around the desk towards her and was immediately blocked by Constable Harvey.

"Please, Detective", I said, drawing her attention back to me and extending my hand to her. "If there is anything I can do to help your investigation…" I kept my hand extended, trying to appear as non-threatening as possible with Constable Harvey standing over me. I was desperate now; the clarity and calm of a few minutes ago was lost. I could feel sweat prickling my back, though my skin was cold. Could she really be dead? I needed to know what had happened and if it was my fault. I had to know, I didn't care what it cost me.

Detective Stone reached across Harvey and squeezed my hand firmly. I gripped back, until I felt the warm metal ring beneath my fingers. Wedding rings generally go one of two ways when you draw on them. The problem is, they are useless without an engraving. Even a ring handed down over ten generations of happily married couples is useless without one. Even a boilerplate *Forever yours* will work wonders if the owner meant it when they had the engraving made. It's criminal when you think about it – all that potential, all that power, completely untapped.

Thankfully Detective Stone did have an engraved ring, only I hadn't anticipated just how powerful it would be. It wasn't hers exactly; I guessed she had a partner or lover, but not a husband, which made sense since she wore it on her right hand. Sensations flooded into my consciousness with such force that my eyes started to water. The ring belonged to her mother, who had married into an English family, and it had been her grandmother's before that. The hearts of each woman who had worn the ring bore into me with such force that it felt as if I'd pressed my chest against a furnace door. The phrase "good wife" flashed across my awareness and I felt anger at the very concept. Detective Olivia Stone,

Liv to her friends, little Livvy to her relatives, was the black sheep of the family. Liv had always prioritised her work with the police over her personal life. The mother had given her the ring when she turned thirty, hoping it would encourage Liv to settle down and start a family. Liv had worn it anyway in an act of defiance to her mother.

Liv jumped as I ripped my hand away, as if she'd received an electric shock from the half second of contact. My vision swam as I struggled to contain the sudden swell of energy jetting through me, far more than I had anticipated.

"*Cofio*", I whispered inwardly focusing only on the little interview room and stumbling as the world became impossibly clear. Everything my eyes touched throbbed into stark, almost painful clarity.

"Mr Chase?"

"I'm fine, just a little dizzy", I said, reflexively. I winced, closing my eyes as every freckle, crease and strand of hair was etched into my brain as if an artist had taken a compass to the back of my skull.

Unable to think of one of my Welsh incantations for the task as my mind soaked up and stored every detail of the room like a sponge, I muttered, *"Drop and open"*.

The good detective did as instructed, but

rather than the file spilling to the ground and scattering its contents as I'd intended, the file snapped to the door, as if held by a sudden and powerful wind. Before I could reign back my spell the envelope burst open. I ducked as paperwork and forensic photographs rushed over my head, caught by what could only be described as an indoor tornado. Each document and photograph slapped against the ceiling and stuck there, looming over me like some serial killer's trophy room. A rogue paperclip caught me in the shoulder with surprising force as each individual page from the main case file plastered the desk in neat rows, spilling onto the floor and walls when space was used up.

Within the space of a few seconds, every foot of the little box room had a document or photograph of some kind on it, each spaced evenly so as not to overlap another. With my suddenly enhanced sight and memory I quickly looked around the room, taking in everything I could. I left the forensic photographs until last. Each one would be seared into my brain in perfect photo quality definition until I managed a cleanse, so I put off looking at the bloody ragdoll corpses for as long as I could.

By the time Constable Harvey and Detective Stone bundled me out the door, my eyes were streaming.

#

"That air con's insane!" I said, pouring the last drops of power into each word, laying down a clumsy, hastily crafted influence spell over anyone within earshot. My eyes were still throbbing though the painful clarity ebbed away the moment I had stepped outside the interview room. What I had seen inside remained, however, and my mind continued to swim with images made all the more gruesome by my temporarily enhanced recall. Sentences from the chief medical examiner's report punctuated each bloody picture and I felt waves of such crippling nausea my knees started to shake.

all deceased expired from severe blood loss – possible mass suicide except for single named victim, Claire Parkes – body in tact... signs of a struggle... toxicity reports clean... blunt force trauma. CCTV footage is being reviewed... inconclusive... staff and guest interviews – ongoing...inconclusive... inconclusive.

I tried to make sense of the information, to process it and draw connections but it was like trying to hum along to one song while twenty more played over it.

Constable Harvey was my lifeline. The two of us walked the length of the corridor, his arm supporting me every step of the way. We stopped at a sturdy-looking door. While we waited for someone to unlock it from the other side, I put a hand out to steady myself against it.

"Bloody funding cuts. Everything's falling apart around here. Can I get you a water or something? I'm sorry, you didn't have to see that." He shook his head, looking sick, and even turned to glare at Detective Stone as she strode the length of the corridor to join them. She was clinging to the bulging folder with both hands as if it might spring open again any moment.

She stopped abruptly in front of us. Evidently, she had been out of reach from my last spell because her mouth opened and closed multiple times as if she wanted to accuse someone of something but didn't know exactly what. As I watched her my own anguish over the images were pushed aside as the sight of her brought the personalities of Liv's mother and grandmother to the fore of my mind. I embraced the momentary respite wholeheartedly. Little Livvy's brow used to crease in exactly the same way when she was a baby and she couldn't find the word she wanted. I wanted to laugh or maybe cry, I wasn't really sure which. The older of the two Greek women inside me was so proud of her little Livvy. I let those feelings wash over me. It was far from ideal, but the alternative was to think about Claire and I wasn't ready for that yet.

I fared pretty well until the three of us were waiting at a desk for my belongings to be returned to me. Detective Stone was still watching me closely while Harvey, *my rock*, filled out the paperwork for my release when I told him I wasn't feeling well enough to do it myself. I just needed to get out of there without saying or doing anything to implicate myself. I could see daylight through the window in the door beside me.

It was the look of suspicion on the detective's face when she caught my eye that did it. I couldn't stop myself.

"Your grandmother would roll over in her grave if she saw you staring at me like that!" I said, with every scrap of haughty indignation I could summon. One of the perks, probably the only perk really, of the moment after a mage has used magic and before they manage to cleanse themselves of it, is that they can throw themselves into another life for a time, walk in someone else's shoes and avoid their own. It was appealing in the same way people found watching soap operas appealing. Only it couldn't last; eventually you had to face your own reality again or sooner or later you wound up shouting at strangers with a faintly Greek accent.

The detective looked disturbed. She opened her mouth, closed it again, marched halfway up the corridor, stopped, then carried on until she was out of view. Harvey turned towards me very slowly with a look of utter disbelief.

"Sign here and you are done", he said, pointing.

I swallowed and did as the man suggested. As I signed my name I asked, as casually as if I were asking to borrow a pen, where I might locate the nearest arts and crafts shop. Even baffled and incredulous, Harvey didn't disappoint, delivering exact and easy-to-follow instructions to the town centre. I picked up the plastic bag which held my tobacco, keys and mobile phone, and offered him my hand, which he took after a shrug that said *"sure, why not, this can't get any stranger"*.

I thanked him with the sincerity and gravitas of a ninety-year-old Greek woman, waited for the door to buzz, then stepped out into breezy morning sunshine feeling sick to my stomach. I had been so grateful to Harvey as I said farewell, I had to fight an unusually strong impulse to cup the man's face in my hands.

Freedom tasted like an ouzo-soaked hangover.

#

I trudged into town and entered the first greasy spoon I came across. I couldn't face eating yet so I ordered a black coffee instead. The proprietor ignored me, the place was dimly lit and felt hostile and it suited my mood perfectly. I sat hunched over the table facing the wall and stared at the bitter steam rising from my cup. I did my best to avoid using internal and external types of magic in the same sitting. It was the magical equivalent of mixing beer and wine in abundant supplies. Drawing directly from a source like I'd done with Detective Stone's wedding ring was more akin to mainlining battery acid. Mercifully I had only taken a fraction of power otherwise the psychological after-effects could have been far worse. Still, the only way to undo my headache would be to continue using or find a group and start confessing some sins.

Once the world had settled around me I pulled my battered old Motorola flip phone from the plastic zip lock bag and dialled Amber's number. It took some convincing, but she agreed to come and pick me up. It turned out she had been released within an hour of our arrival at the police station the previous afternoon once she'd agreed to give a statement. I suspected she was curious as much as anything else; she wanted to know what had happened next. She wasn't the only one.

I drank half my coffee, told the owner I would be back in five and not to clear my cup away, then continued up the high street until I found the place the constable had described. It was really more of a stationery shop than an arts and crafts place, but it served my purposes just the same, so I decided not to hold it against him.

I purchased a hardback Moleskin notebook and a box of cheap pens, then returned to the cafe. The owner had cleared away my cup, so I ordered a fresh one, and set to work. In the space of a few minutes I had filled a dozen pages and showed no signs of slowing down. Each page of the police and coroner's reports were laid bare in my head. It was like transcribing the lyrics to a favourite song, every word was so well ingrained. Only rather than catchy rhymes about heartache, it was detailed scientific explanations, blood types, exceptionally dry procedural methodologies and blood spatter conclusions. I wrote for forty minutes straight, then went through and underlined anything I thought was significant. In truth, there wasn't much of relevance. I made a note of the hotel where Claire had been murdered, then started on the photographs. I tried to recreate one but I wasn't much of an artist. Having a photograph imprinted in your mind didn't mean you suddenly had the artistic talent to duplicate it. After two failed attempts, I started on a fresh page and made detailed notes on what I could see in each picture instead.

Again, it wasn't much to go on. The photographers had been focused mostly on the victims' wounds, their clothes, their unblemished finger tips and anything in the room that might have been used or touched by the killer to cause the damage. Finally, the image showing where Claire's lifeless body lay was all that was left in my mental scrapbook. I stared at it, making notes about the position of her body, the blood in her hair, the cleanliness of her clothes. I suspected that even after I got clean, this photograph wasn't likely to leave me anytime soon. I found myself wishing she could have just tried being different and going down the family route. Was it really so bad getting married and starting a family? If she had, surely this never would have happened.

It took me a minute to reconcile where that came from and I felt appalled with myself for polluting my own feelings over losing Claire with Mrs Stone's fears regarding her daughter. I thought of Detective Stone and realised this sort of horror was exactly why her mother had wanted her to start a family and retire from the police force. Pretty girls like Livvy and Claire were always a target.

I winced at the muddle of competing voices and grunted my frustration, flipping my notebook over and opening the back page. As the disembodied voices continued their monologues I scribbled down whatever they said as an endless stream of consciousness. Sometimes it wasn't words but a concept or expression which I continued to note down in shorthand.

...So many people, doesn't anybody work any more? Your cousin Kora still works and she has two children. Eye roll, sigh. Tut. What about Alex? I always liked him, remember those flowers he got you? He bought me flowers once, that was years ago.

He's married now. Well, exactly my point. Wait too long and all the good ones will be taken. Remember your aunt Sophia? Poor girl.

As the women continued to converse I struggled to distinguish their voices and isolate them by their specific tone. Olivia's was the easiest to pick out, almost always at odds with the other two. The difference between mother and grandmother was less pronounced, and would take more time. I would eventually need to be able to identify and isolate each of them in order to completely expel them from my mind. Lighter magic left a smaller imprint behind one that could usually be expunged by a simple confession. This was a different, and I had taken far more than I'd intended by channelling from Olivia's ring. Heavy magic use left a much larger psychological imprint, however, one that required days, sometimes weeks of cathartic expression to be rid of.

There was a meeting just south of the river starting in an hour and another at 6pm a little further east. As much as I needed to get rid of the Greek women plucking away at my mental resolve, I also wanted to see the crime scene with my own eyes. I wasn't quite sure what I expected to find that forensics would have missed, but if there was the slightest chance I could help catch whoever had done this to Claire, then I had to try. If I could make use of the lingering portions of Stone's psyche and investigative acumen, then all the better.

An idea occurred to me halfway down my fifth page, after a particularly long rant about young people today. I stopped writing Liv and focused entirely on the two older women, bundling them together on the pages of my notebook. Gradually the four of us split in two smaller parties, instantly restoring some order to my mind.

I could feel the impact Liv's more dominant position within the group was having on me. A certain analytical detachment took over more than once while I sat there and took in the little café's other clientele. I was certain it was her influence which brought my attention to laddered tights on one woman doing the walk of shame and a man sitting in the corner spicing up his morning brew from a hip-flask. The problem was keeping Liv separate from the others when I wasn't explicitly writing down their thoughts. Each time I stopped and turned my attention back to the graphic police notes in my moleskin notebook, it was a toss of a coin as to whether I would finish the page with cold detachment or recoil in horror halfway through the first paragraph.

I pinched the bridge of my nose and clamped my eyes shut, letting my mind drift aimlessly for a few minutes, a simple observer to the conflicted currents occupying my mind. Each time a thought occurred to me I would challenge it and, without writing it down, try to categorise it based on who I thought it originated from. Gradually I built up a picture of the three unique personalities and gave them a physical form. In my head, I invited each of them into a small but comfortable open plan apartment. I couldn't shut the door entirely on the two older women, they wouldn't like that and I lacked the mental energy to keep that up for any length of time. Instead I did what all good hosts do, I made them comfortable, encouraged them into a plush arm chair in the living room while Stone and I did our best to keep our voices down in the kitchen as we poured over my notes.

In my little mental retreat, Stone and I hunched over the table, the pages of notes and photographs piled neatly before us.

"I took Claire to the addicts anonymous meeting at around 6pm. We left at approximately half past, both of us clean. I was arrested immediately after and taken into custody." I said, keeping my voice low.

My part in the narrative was done, so I turned to Stone who flipped to the next page.

"At approximately 11.15am Claire and the others were found dead by the cleaner. Alarm was raised and police and ambulance were on the scene within fifteen minutes. No suspicious noises were heard prior to their discovery. Claire Parkes is presently the only named victim since she was the only one with any identification. Initial coroner's report indicates eight of the nine victims cut their own wrists. Ninth victim, Claire Parkes, appears to be unique in that the cause of death appears to be extreme trauma to the back of the head. No indication as to why the she was the exception. Injuries sustained to Ms Parkes indicate a brief struggle. Blood marks on the door are consistent with said injuries and the current theory is she arrived on the scene after the others. There was a struggle and someone, potentially one of the other deceased killed her before pursuing to kill themselves. The investigation is not ruling out another party being involved, however. Teams are reviewing CCTV for any suspicious persons arriving or leaving around the time of the murder. Cameras only cover the entrances and fire escapes so we cannot rule out guests. Initial reports set the times of death between 2300 hours and 0200 hours."

"What about hotel records?"

"No unaccounted for guests. The victims were not there officially. No sign of forced entry on the door but the tech used to secure them in that building is pretty dated and, I'm told, quite easy to bypass."

"What position were the others found in?"

"Sitting in a circle, each one with three long cuts from wrist to elbow."

"Three cuts?"

"Both arms, on every one of them."

"Is that possible?" I asked.

"I've never seen anything like it but we are waiting to hear back on that."

"I'm not privy to any more police intel, what you know now is all I'm likely to get. Tell me what you think?"

"Those cuts are too deep, too even, and too straight to have been done without some sort of assistance."

"You think it was Claire?"

"I don't know."

It was going rather well until Amber pulled up and honked the horn of the hackney carriage, breaking my trance and ushering everyone back to the forefront of my mind with a cry of *Young people today! No manners.* I bought her a latte and a croissant, then went out to meet her. As I handed her the coffee and the croissant she looked at me as if I'd truly lost my mind during my night in the slam.

"Well, you are looking a bit thin", I said, unable to stop myself. I recited the address of the hotel where the report said Claire had died, then got comfortable on the back seat between the reassuringly bulky boxes of records and closed my eyes. I heard Amber tut irritably before the wheels started rolling. I was asleep before we made it to the first set of lights.

CHAPTER 4

I sleep a lot. It might seem callous, particularly after what I had just seen, but the fact is it helps me find clarity. In my case, despite my best efforts to expunge them from my mind, the amalgamated personalities of Detective Stone's extended family continued to pull for influence over me. Sleeping, or getting as close to sleep as one could with Amber bumping and swearing her way across Greater London, was my best chance of not spiralling and landing myself in more trouble. At least that's what I told myself. The truth was, the smart move was to go and get clean, take a day or two to recover and talk myself out of this terrible plan. Unfortunately, although I was sober enough to realise going to the hotel where Claire was murdered the day after it happened was unwise, I was sufficiently affected not to care. As

I took a deep breath and tried to coax the Greek women lined up at the back of my brain to take a break from their mutterings of disapproval. It was indeed ridiculous to think I might just walk in and grab a key to the hotel room in question, not without some seriously heavy handed magic. The entire floor would be cordoned off, police posted at every lift and staircase.

The closer we got, the more anxious I felt. I must have seen a hundred films in my life which had a scene in them where, whether innocent or guilty, someone attempted to flee from a crime scene. I couldn't recall a single one, however, when someone attempted to sneak into a day-old crime scene. As we inched closer through lunchtime traffic towards the *Marriot Hotel* on South Bank, the phrase *returning to the scene of the crime* kept bouncing back and forth in my head like an unwelcome tennis ball.

I rolled a cigarette while we waited at a set of congested traffic lights. The lights cycled three times before we managed to push past them. In my little tobacco pouch I located the phrase *everything will be alright,* which I recalled cutting out of a letter from a house clearance in Brixton. It was tempting but ultimately dangerous given my situation. Certainly, it would calm my nerves but if the platitude had enough emotional force behind it, it could easily make me careless and stupid. Without the rest of the letter to hand, the only way to know for sure was to suck it and see. I continued digging until I came across *you'll get through this.* This too could have gone either way, the author of the letter in question could have been lying through her teeth at the time. Thankfully I recognised the blue tinted paper the woman had written on and, from previous experience, knew her to be something of a sincere realist. She had never led me astray before. I packed my little fortune in with the tobacco, cracked a window and took a handful of measured pulls, letting the magical energy pool in my centre. With minimal cognitive effort I could hold it there dormant for a few hours before it started to fade.

I stubbed the end into the cigarette tray in the door beside me and left the wrinkled remains in one of the grooves in case my nerves flared up again before we arrived. A little calmer, I started piecing together a plan to gain entrance to the building. I disregarded all the extravagant options immediately. Technically I could have disguised myself: grown a beard, enlarged my nose, darkened my hair, and maybe even put together a decent imitation of an officer's badge, but it was all a little high risk for my tastes. If my nerves flared up and a real officer challenged me, I might end up in a cell having to explain how exactly I managed to change my face without any makeup or prosthetics. Any changes I made to myself would wear off once I ran out of juice, after all.

Maybe I could talk my way into a room on a

nearby floor they hadn't blocked off and blast through a few walls until I found the right one. In theory I could do it quietly enough to not draw attention to myself, but once I started channelling that type of power, I probably wouldn't care so much about being subtle anymore. Doing so would also more than likely damage the crime scene and disrupt the actual investigation. My father would have called that the *Magician's Folly*. I think of it as *Mage on Bender*.

The point is, even with the best intentions going into a situation, once you start pouring something as addictive and emotive as magic into your veins, you can't fully trust yourself because you aren't just you anymore; there's a bunch of other folk rattling around in there too, fighting for a say. The more powerful you make yourself, the more vulnerable you become to those other voices and the harder it is to distinguish your own from the pack.

To tackle these shortcomings I advise all mages, young and old, to follow the old KISS approach: *Keep It Simple, Stupid.*

#

I stepped out of the taxi at the next set of lights and headed north east along Belvedere Road as per Amber's instructions. I never had much of a sense of direction; it was part of the reason I rarely drove myself anywhere. I wore a suede jacket over a white shirt and jeans, and a sturdy pair of leather boots with my *Alice In Wonderland* messenger bag slung across my shoulders. I held a protective hand over the bag as I walked, shifting it out of the path of oncoming pedestrians as if it was stuffed full of live grenades. In truth, it held an arsenal of an entirely different kind. A letter of apology from a cheating spouse, a snap-on bracelet from the nineties in a faded green and yellow combo, two mix tapes (both of which contained *Endless Love* as track 1, though I'm certain they were made ten years apart by completely different people), and a half dozen records. I brought the vinyl along too just in case I ended up getting searched. No reason to make myself look even stranger.

My heart dropped into my stomach at the sight of two uniformed police officers marching towards me. One of them caught my eye and for a moment I thought I caught recognition on his face but a moment later they turned into a Pret and I continued on, sweat pricking my forehead. Part of me expected the alarm to go up, to be tackled to the ground and the cuffs slapped back on me. Less than a minute later, however, I arrived at the hotel entrance, through a set of revolving doors and passed a French concierge talking animatedly with three more officers and a handful of journalists.

A dozen or more guests milled around the reception desk, several of whom glanced at me with a distinct mix of anxiety and suspicion, before averting their eyes towards the knot of stressed police officers. I suspected all the more senior officers would be on the fifth floor where all the excitement had been. Everyone left in the foyer was for controlling the media and taking contact details from guests who probably hadn't seen anything. A balding, sturdy looking man in a grey suit and charcoal overcoat finished speaking with one journalist as another popped up, blocking his retreat. His face was flushed red and his eyes seemed about ready to pop out of their sockets, an illusion only enhanced by the too-small shirt collar and tie pulled suffocatingly tight into his thorax. I took up a position at the back of the little crowd of journalists to buy myself some time to pick my target.

Listening to the questions being asked, it was clear the police had done a good job of keeping a lid on the details of the murder. Either that or the rumours the media had heard were too strange to print. I couldn't help but feel for the man. An impossible murder and the media breathing down his neck. I stood patiently behind the cameraman as another journalist tried to shove a microphone under his nose. I turned away and scanned the crowd looking for a more suitable target among the black and white uniforms, as the journalists continued to fire questions at the beet red officer.

"This is an active crime scene. A formal statement will be made to the press in due time", the Inspector said in well-rehearsed monotones.

"Why has the fifth floor been cordoned off?" the reporter interrupted.

I started. To my immediate left was a man eating a sandwich from the packet. I would have assumed him to be just another journalist except for the fact that he was facing me.

"You look lost?" he asked, his mouth half full of a ploughman's sandwich. I could smell the pickle.

"I don't know, are you with them?" I asked, gesturing to the crowd.

"Oh no, I'm no journalist. I'm Officer Price", he said, returning his sandwich to the packet, and offering me his hand after wiping it on his jacket.

I shook the offered hand. "Fin Chase, I'm here to see Detective Stone. She said I should come by", I said, vaguely.

I had prepared for the rejection, I'd even drawn in a little extra power from Bing to use in persuading the man. This was an active crime scene after all; I shouldn't be here. He would have surely tried to pass on the message then have an officer drive me to the nearest police station. Instead Price looked me once up and down. "Well you are in luck, I'm just finishing up my lunch break. Let me finish my sandwich and we'll see if we can't find her."

"Alright, thank you", I said, retracting the magic I had been ready to release, with no small amount of difficulty. It was like trying to suppress a particularly loud sneeze.

"Thompson," he called behind him while I winced with effort, "is Stone still upstairs?"

"*Static*", I whispered, feeling the flow of energy leave me in a sudden rush.

"What's that?" Price asked.

"Hmm?" I said, shaking my head innocently as if I hadn't uttered a word.

"Getting some sort of interference, sir", Thompson said.

Price took the radio from Thompson and tried himself. The walkie crackled and fuzzed convincingly enough.

"Want me to run up and get her, Inspector?" Thompson offered helpfully.

Inspector? I swallowed, my mouth suddenly feeling very dry. Price's jaw tightening for the briefest of moments was the only sign of his irritation. So brief was it, that a moment later I was certain I had imagined it.

"I can wait", I suggested, hoping to get away from

the man who had deliberately hidden his rank.

"Nonsense, follow me", he said, loping past the reception desk and through a set of double doors which were held open by two more uniformed officers. Heavily polished wooden floors gave way to a two-toned brown carpet which reminded me of the bloody clumps in Claire's hair. I closed my eyes as we stepped inside a lift flanked by two more uniformed officers and prayed I wouldn't have to live with these memories for much longer.

When I opened my eyes again I realised we must have stepped into a service elevator, given the lack of upkeep and dated interior. It made sense that they would restrict access to the fifth floor on the regular lifts and post officers in the stairwells in order to keep the rest of the hotel running. The lift moved so slowly, I didn't register we were moving at all until I saw the digital display switch from 1 to 2 in a wink of LED lights.

"I'm Chief Inspector Price, Mr Chase. I'll need to search you and your bag before I can let you see the Detective. It's just procedure", he said.

"Of course", I said, feeling like I had just walked into the world's most obvious trap. I slipped off my messenger bag and handed it to him. "It's just some records and books and things. Junk really." I shrugged, feeling guilty for insulting my treasures.

He took a look inside, flicked through one of the books, saw me watching him, perhaps a little too closely and set the bag down in the corner.

"Arms up. Anything sharp? Any weapons of any kind?"

"No nothing like that", I lied. I raised my arms and he patted me down thoroughly. My heart plummeted as he removed my most powerful weapon from my coat pocket.

"Careful!" I said, as he unfolded it. "Sorry, it's just that's an original sleeve."

"Huh." he looked confused. "An original you keep folded in your pocket?"

"It's a luck thing. I'm kind of superstitious."

He flipped it over then returned it to me.

"My bag?" I asked, folding the sleeve but keeping it in my hand.

"It'll be safe there. You can have it back later. So, what is it you have to tell Detective Stone?" he asked, still facing me. Several things slid into place as I studied the open, even kindly expression on Price's face. It was a face cultivated over years in the force, a face to unburden yourself to. He thought I had come here to confess to the murders; that was the only reason he was willing to provide the special treatment.

I swallowed, "I'd really rather wait and talk to her".

"Understood. She's a fine Detective. Young, determined. If it was me, I'd probably want someone like her to talk to as well. I mean, you could do a lot worse." He gave a hollow bark of a laugh and smiled at me in that way men do sometimes when they turn to their friend after an attractive woman passes them on the street.

I didn't smile back. This, just like everything else he had said or done since the foyer, was designed to put me at ease, or to take the measure of me, and it had worked, every last bit of it.

The doors swung open behind the Chief Inspector but he didn't move. I tried to focus on the knowledge that I was completely innocent, but that seemed irrelevant beneath the weight of his gaze. I could feel he wanted that confession all for himself; it had probably been years since he'd had the opportunity to really lean on a suspect. I thought of the friendly, sandwich-eating officer I had met downstairs and struggled to reconcile that with the predator that had backed me into a corner and blocked off my only means of escape.

I looked over his shoulder at the vacant corridor beyond. Halfway up I could see another officer seated outside a door which had strips of police tape across it. The vivid photographs of the deceased flashed through my mind and I felt my stomach knot.

"I don't see her", I said.

"No? I'm sure she's here. Come on."

Before I knew what was happening, the Inspector led me up the bland corridor with the same awful carpet I was quickly growing to hate. Dotted with military precision at intervals of ten paces, a vase with paper flowers stood on a plain plywood table or a painting of a famous London landmark stood out in watercolours upon wallpaper so nondescript it was instantly forgotten.

"Sir?" the officer outside the one open door said as we drew level with him.

"Stone?" the Inspector asked.

I took a step closer to Price, even as every part of me screamed to turn and run. I looked through the open door at the heavily stained carpet beyond, where a team of forensics appeared to be hard at work gathering DNA on cotton swabs.

"She's with the little boy", the officer replied, glancing at me.

"What little boy?"

"You not hear the radio? Stone took him to try and find his parents. We figured they must be staying on the fourth floor since six is closed for the refurb. She'll be back in a minute."

I was barely listening, my eyes glued to the muddy brown stain burrowed into the loop pile carpeting.

"Quite a sight, isn't it? In my twenty-five years, I've only ever seen one other this bad", Price said. "Folks, could we have the room for just a moment?"

The forensics team filed out looking a little confused, then Price held the tape up for me and we went inside.

"Careful", Price said, catching my arm and making my heart rocket into my throat. "Only step in the marked areas. If you contaminated the crime scene that would be very bad."

I rooted myself to the spot and did my best to ignore all the signs of death and focus on Price. "Should I be allowed in here?"

"What do you mean? You looked as if you couldn't wait to get in here a moment ago?" he said, incredulously. "I figured we could wait for Stone, you could get a good story out of it too and I could get away from the tabloids for a few minutes." He sighed. That part at least seemed genuine. "You have no idea how persistent they can be. If they don't get details of the victims, they will run a story about how the police are wasting tax payers' money having ten officers standing around doing nothing. You'd think I could just take those officers away, hide them out of sight up here, but then they have a story about how incompetent we all are in handling a murder investigation. The trick is to give them nothing interesting enough to print. Making murder dull seems to suddenly be a big part of my job."

"You don't like being Chief Inspector", I observed.

"You could say that."

A silence hung over the room for a moment and the Inspector stared at the blood-soaked sheets hanging off the bed, as if seeing them for the first time. "The fact is, we haven't got much to go on here. Nobody heard a thing, DNA contradicts blood spatter, and blood spatter throws our timelines out the window. No IDs back on the other victims, we are looking into missing persons but it'll be days before we turn anything up."

"Nobody heard anything?" I asked.

"Not a peep. Neighbour says he and his wife are light sleepers, even had their rooms switched once to get away from a couple playing their TV too loud the night before. Never heard a thing. Truth is, we are getting desperate. Unless we get a miracle witness or the DNA turns something up, it'll be early retirement for me. Don't suppose you could loan me some of that luck of yours?" he laughed, humourlessly, as he glanced at the record sleeve still clutched in my hand.

My hand holding Bing was shaking so I put it back into my pocket and drew on him properly, letting a trickle of power flow up my arm.

"I can't give you my luck, but maybe I could offer you a fresh pair of eyes, some..." I feigned a cough, using it to mask the word *mewnwelediad*, "fresh insight?"

"That's right, I heard you were a private investigator. Well, I'll take any help I can get at this point. So, what do you think?" he asked.

I looked at the layout of the room, feeling my mental focus sharpen to a razor point. "The room was found exactly like this?" I asked, my own voice sounding distant and muffled. That was really how the spell worked. I wasn't powerful enough with internal magic to make myself literally more insightful or more intelligent. The spell worked by enhancing those sensory and cognitive elements I believed would affect my ability to process information while similarly turning off or tuning out those other senses or parts of my mind which could cloud those abilities. Consequently, while my eyesight and sense of smell improved, my hearing reduced. My sense of taste switched off entirely. Uttering the Welsh word for insight was really just a placeholder for a dozen little changes I wanted made.

"Except for the removal of the bodies and a few

pieces of evidence", Price said. His voice barely registered, echoing dimly at the back of my mind.

I continued tracking my eyes over the scene. Wherever anything had been removed, including one of the bodies, a small coloured cone had been placed, marking the location. With some of the cones, a numbered photograph had been placed inside a clear plastic envelope of whatever evidence had been removed.

The room itself was large but unremarkable. More family room than suite, with a double bed against the opposite wall and a large sofa bed to my left next to the window with two comfortable chairs in faux brown leather. Two camp chairs had been removed to allow access into the room and replaced with more little cones and photographs in their stead. All the seating had been repositioned to face into the centre of the room and pools of blood were focused around each chair. The already murky red carpet did an admirable job of obscuring the worst of it, the eye immediately drawn to the bed where I guessed two or even three of the mystery guests had emptied their veins staining the bottom half of the white bed sheets. An office chair lay on its side a little behind me, spatters of blood on the legs and still more on the desk behind it.

I invited the small part of Stone that remained

to the forefront of my mind, welcoming her analytical detachment. The positioning of the chairs, the nature of the injuries sustained by most of the victims suggested some sort of mass suicide. At the very centre of the room lay a little yellow cone with a picture of a single razor blade attached to it. The precision and consistency of the victims' injuries suggested that they took it in turns to cut themselves open and watch each other bleed to death. The thought of being handed a razor blade by someone bleeding out sent a shiver through me. I spotted black and grey spots of ash on the carpet, which Liv and the police guessed to be part of a ritual by fire. It would have been cut and dry, neat even, had it not been for Claire. Death by trauma, and found outside the circle. The most obvious conclusion, was that she was there to assist the others. That would certainly go some way to explaining how every one of them had managed to make three long cuts on both arms. If she got cold feet halfway through and was killed for it, how did the final victim or victims make the final cuts alone? The answer was they didn't, there must have been someone else present.

Liv took a step back in my head and I took up the reigns, fighting off a wave of nausea in the process. This was my first real crime scene, after all. I suspected the only reason I hadn't thrown up yet was the fact that I couldn't accept any of it as being real. It was just paint, a crude exhibition at the Tate modern designed to provoke.

I inhaled deeply taking some comfort from the scent of singed paper that lingered in the air. It took me a moment to realise the scent was far too strong for the little power I had drawn from Bing.

"This fire ritual, it never triggered the alarm?" I asked.

"No, they are Type 3 alarms, they detect heat not smoke. I guess whatever they were doing in here didn't produce enough to trip the alarm."

I stared at the little smudges of black and grey on the carpet and felt my throat constrict. The smoke produced from mage fire would set off a smoke alarm but it was relatively heatless. I looked at the cones with images depicting the other victims and spotted a handful of other numbered cones which had no photographs attached.

"That's the victims' belongings. They don't bother tagging every item so we just put them in the file." Price said, watching me. He handed me a blue binder with more of the same plastic envelopes containing photographs. Each one was colour and number coded for easy reference. The first one I came to showed a Sainsbury's shopping bag which had been flattened and the contents laid out upon it. A half dozen second hand novels, a sleeve from a CD mix tape, a stack of bound letters and two VHS cassettes. I skipped to the next page and found more of the same. Every item contained some handwritten message or other, and by the time I'd finished flicking through the album I suspected the killer and his victims had all been mages.

Price's eyes were still fixed keenly on me, almost eager, and that same sense of nervous excitement struck me from within and realisation dawned on me like a cat stuck between headlights. I had played right into Liv's trap. She and Price thought I was involved. Though they couldn't yet prove it or place me at the scene my alibi was weak, I had been bar hopping alone for most of the night, not to mention I had left messages on Claire's phone trying to find out where she was. I should have been suspicious when Liv offered no objections to me coming here. Innocent people have no desire to visit a brutal crime scene where their friend was murdered.

My spell wavered and I shivered as the photographs of Claire flashed through my mind before I could push them away. I needed time to think, away from the stench of death and the threat of imminent arrest I had stupidly fallen into. I turned to the grizzled inspector and studied the man. To the casual observer, it could have appeared that he was simply an escort, standing a respectful distance away, waiting patiently for my assessment of the scene. Had it not been for the fact that he had been watching me like a hawk for the last few minutes without comment, I might have believed it too.

He wasn't just fishing blindly, he had a good reason to suspect me now, having seen the contents of my Alice in Wonderland bag. If I wasn't before, I was now certainly the prime suspect in a multiple homicide. Liv had encouraged me here to confess and Price had allowed me up to the hotel room to watch my reaction to the scene. Unbeknownst to either of them they had paired up against me. The mere fact that I was willing to step inside this hotel room was surely suspicious. I could see the inevitable conclusions forming behind the inspector's eyes. Price might have believed I had come to confess when I first arrived, but I could see plainly that notion had left him the longer we had stood together in that room. He thought I wanted to see the results of my own carefully-constructed plan first hand. Not to mention to appease the psychopath's ego and let them know who was behind all this death and chaos, even if they could never prove it.

The last of the spell's power bled away. I felt sick, like I'd been on a ten day bender.

"Nothing to report?" Price said, scratching his beard before rubbing a hand over the top of his bald scalp. "Come on, let's go and see if Stone is finished on four."

We left the room and walked back towards the lift. The forensics teams all avoided looking at me.

"Maybe retirement won't be so bad. I can watch all my old films again", Price said, as he pushed the button for the fourth floor.

"You like westerns", I said, my diminishing insight turning the question into a statement that bordered on an accusation.

He tilted his head to the side and studied me for a moment.

"Eastwood fan?" I asked.

He nodded. "For my fiftieth birthday the wife and I turned one of the kids' old rooms into a home cinema. Ridiculous flat screen, leather recliners, surround sound. Nothing too expensive, but you get the idea. We spent two hours figuring out how to work the thing, then fell asleep halfway through *The Good, The Bad, And the Ugly*."

"Leone was a genius. I always liked Dirty Harry though", I said.

"Great film. Still a Western too by all accounts", he said, as if expecting me to contradict him.

"Still a man with a code", I said, nodding my agreement. I could see Price's taste in films cut to the heart of the man. He had always thought of himself as a man with a code, but he hated feeling like a politician; he longed for the Old West way of doing things which I guess explained why he was willing to bring me onto an active crime scene.

"So, which are you?" he asked as the doors rolled open on the fourth floor.

"Hmm?" I muttered distractedly, as I spotted Detective Stone halfway down the corridor. She crouched down beside a blue backpack, removed something and rose in one lithe movement.

"The good, the bad, or the ugly?" Price said.

I opened my mouth and pointed in confusion at the smoke pouring from underneath the door beside Olivia. Before I could utter a word of warning, blood fountained up the lift interior beside me.

CHAPTER 5

My first thought was how wrong the gunshot had sounded. Perhaps muffled by the thick carpets or just tainted by all my previous exposure of firearms coming from films and TV, I felt cheated and unprepared. The first shot took Price in the abdomen. At the sight of blood my hand instinctively flew into my coat where Bing lay in wait. I started to draw on him when the second gunshot sounded taking Price in the shoulder and sending him careening into me.

We both went down in a mess of blood and a tangle of limbs, the control panel flashed into view with its dim amber lights before my vision was obscured with smoke billowing up from my pocket. We hit the deck and I threw out my hands desperately mashing blindly at the buttons on the control panel.

Price had thrown himself across me when the gunfire had started, his weight still driving me into the floor. I felt something pinch in my forearm as more gunshots echoed up hallway. I snatched my hand back from the panel as the lift doors started to rattle closed but a sturdy black shoe appeared between the doors halting their progress.

A flash of panic sent a shock through my nervous system, spurring me to action. The inspector let out a cry of pain as I wriggled free from beneath his limp weight. I put my back to the lift doors as the opened, threw one arm around the back of my head and grasped the waist of my coat in the other and covered us both with the thick wool as best I could.

"Gwehyddu Dur", I said, releasing Bing's magic into the coat. I felt the wool turn rigid in my hand the instant before the sound of more gun shots hammered against my eardrums. This time, in the close confines of the lift, the bullets sounded exactly as I thought they should. I held my eyes closed and felt each strike like a whip crack against my back and side. If I wasn't already lying down the force of each bullet as it struck my enchanted coat would have been enough to floor me. As it was, I gritted my teeth and curled into a tighter and tighter ball as I waited.

The gun clicked empty and I rolled onto my back, painfully winded and gasping for air. My eyes met the detective's, her eyes wide and watering as she stared down at Price's bloody form. With shaking hands she dropped the magazine release and reached slowly into her pocket.

Still struggling to pull sufficient air into my lungs, I struggled onto my front and pushed myself up onto hands and knees. Listening to myself wheeze I pulled my *Alice in Wonderland* bag to me from the corner of the lift and withdrew a copy of *Eat Pray Love* in time to see detective Stone slide a fresh magazine home.

As if performing some sadistic slow-dance, she cocked the hammer with the same measured deliberation as I buttoned up my coat. If her eyes hadn't been screaming I would have thought she were savouring the moment. I was still kneeling but managed to get one foot up in front of me to help brace myself. I let the sleeve hang over my hand before raising it to my shoulder such that my head and face were hidden as she took aim at me.

"Gwehyddu Dur", I repeated, linking the spell from my coat directly to the copy of *Eat Prey Love* in my hand. She fired off successive rounds, each one striking my coat just above my bicep, and each one taking a large bite out of the novel in my hand, large sections of which exploded apart in a shower of ash as my coat absorbed the impact of each shot. She emptied the magazine, leaving me with just the spine of my novel intact and a throbbing arm.

Again the pistol clicked empty, Stone dropped the firearm, turned and started calmly walking back up the corridor where the smoke was thickest. There was no urgency to her movement, though I thought I detected a tension across her shoulders, as if her entire body was shrieking in silent horror.

"Liv?" Price whispered, his voice hoarse. He was clutching his bloody abdomen and staring in bleary-eyed disbelief.

I pressed my hand to his chest and closed my eyes. I scoured my mind for something that might help him, some way to stop the bleeding, but my mind was blank. *"Be calm"*, I whispered, letting the last of the magic I held flow out down my hand and into the Chief Inspector. He slumped back, his breathing instantly growing more even. I pressed his hands against the gunshot wound in his stomach and told him to keep pressure on it. It was all I could do for him; the lift was already starting to fill with smoke.

Staggering to my feet, I pushed the button for the lobby, grabbed my bag and stepped clear to let the lift doors close behind me, stranding myself on the fourth floor. I made a beeline for the closest fire alarm but a wave of nausea struck with enough force that my vision tunnelled and my strength faltered. I tried to call after Olivia but my voice was weak. It was as if I'd spent the last two days in bed with stomach flu.

I pulled another of the paperbacks from my bag and tore out the first page. I stuffed it whole into my mouth and started drawing a steady stream of power in to myself as I chewed. I didn't bother to read the message but it tasted like misspent youth and a teenage crush. The Greek women still rattling around at the back of my consciousness bristled like hens.

My nausea abated as quickly as it had arrived and my strength gradually returned. I pulled the fire alarm and hurried down the hallway after Liv.

"Liv!" I called, the smoke filling the top third of the corridor. "Olivia, where are you?" I called, crouching down where the air was still breathable. The maternal parts of me continued to scream at me to hurry.

She was slumped beside the door, head turned away from me, her body obscured by the rolls of smoke billowing out from beneath the door. I tried to lift her but her left hand was latched onto the door handle in a death grip. I could hear the flames licking up the other side of the door. The heat from it, even with a solid door between us, was oppressive, and the lack of oxygen was making it harder to think.

I dropped to the floor, getting as low to the ground as I possibly could, and tore out two more pages from the novel, rolling them into a cone like a child's paper trumpet. The trumpet in one hand and the rest of the novel in the other, I used my body as a conduit between the two. I focused clearly on what I needed and in a flash the book crumbled to ash before my eyes, the power it held surging through my body like a thunderclap and down into the rolled pages. I pushed it into my mouth and started breathing through it. Smoke was sucked up through the end but only clean air met my lungs as it passed through the cone.

My bag of tricks was already half gone, but I wasn't done yet. I retrieved the last novel, ripped out two fistfuls of pages and willed inhuman strength into the muscles of my arms and hands. It took three attempts before the handle tore away from Olivia's hand. I lifted her easily onto my shoulder and made it to the stairwell before the spell failed me, and her limp body seemed to triple in weight.

I was breathing harder through the enchanted paper trumpet, an effect I guessed was due to the diminished oxygen in the smoky corridors. The enchantment could filter out any trace of the smoke, but it couldn't create the oxygen out of nothing.

I kicked open the door to the stairs and collapsed onto the other side, dropping the detective with far less decorum than I would have liked. To the relief of what felt like Liv's entire ancestral line, she coughed and spluttered as her back hit the ground.

"Help!" I cried, knowing police must have been

stationed here just moments ago. There was no answer. I put the trumpet cone to Liv's mouth. She tried to bat it away; I persisted.

"Breath through it. Trust me", I said, now struggling for breath myself. The smoke was spreading much quicker than I would have thought possible.

She looked at me through heavily lidded eyes, but did as I suggested. Her eyes stopped swimming and I saw the memory of what had happened hit her like a slap across the jaw. "I... I shot you. Didn't I?" she said, looking at my chest for bullet holes. To my surprise, I had in fact been shot, though the bullet had only grazed my forearm.

"Guess I should be grateful your aim sucks", I croaked, noting my own juvenile tone through the fog.

"Price?" she said, more to herself than to me. She looked both confused and faintly ridiculous with the coned paper sticking out the side of her mouth, like a school girl pretending to smoke. She shook her head and gathered herself, any trace of vulnerability gone a moment later. Little Liv vanished and in her wake stood Detective Stone.

"We need to get out of here", she said.

The stairwell door slammed into my back as I reached to help her up. "Finally", I said, expecting to see a police official or a fireman, ready to escort us to safety.

Instead, a thirteen-year-old boy in an oversized hoody and baggy shorts stood frozen in the doorway. He stared at me for a long second, before rushing me and bowling me over with surprising strength. I got my feet under me just in time to see a Fitness First backpack disappear round the next flight of stairs. I was halfway down the first flight when fire erupted up through the stairwell to meet me. I fell back as the two flights below me were similarly consumed. I gritted my teeth against the heat and retreated up to the relative safety of the floor above.

"We'll have to get to the roof", Liv said, starting up the next flight as she looked down at the flames.

I reached for my bag, but it was gone. I must have dropped it when the boy had barrelled into me, because I could see the Alice and the Hatter bubbling and melting away on the stairs below me.

The fire continued to spread unnaturally fast. As I watched, the flames caught on the bland wallpaper and lashed up the walls as if they were soaked in petrol.

With some effort we managed to put a floor between us and the fire. Passing the eighth floor, it soon became apparent that Liv was in far better shape than me. She came back for me twice and took my arm to help speed me along, as if I were an invalid. We passed the trumpet cone back and forth between us, but by the time we reached the upper floors it became obvious she was handing it back to me far more quickly than I returned it to her.

By the time I reached the top floor, my bruised ego in tatters, she was already at the top of a ladder, her top half obscured by smoke. I heard her pounding on what I guessed to be a hatch or trap door which opened out onto the roof proper.

"It's locked", she said, after recovering her breath through the paper trumpet. "We need something to leverage it with." I mentally kicked myself for leaving my lock picks behind with Amber.

"What kind of a lock?" I asked.

"A padlock, why?"

"Climb the ladder and hold onto it", I said.

She looked at me like I was insane but did as I asked, taking a deep breath and holding it before stepping back onto the ladder.

"Give me your right hand and pull with your left."

"Okay, I'm pulling", she said, impatiently.

"There's no need for that tone", I said, irritably. "I'd think you'd be a little more open-minded given what you've seen today."

"Sorry?" she said, unconvincingly.

"On three, pull with everything you've got", I said, clasping the fist she still held tight around the door handle in both of mine and drawing steadily from her grandmother's wedding ring. I drew in power, held it for one savoured breath, then folded strength back up through her body.

"Three!" I said.

I heard the snap of something metal followed by a sharp intake of breath, and then she must have thrown open the hatch because a backdraft of fresh air flooded down past me, and the flames on the floors below doubled in height.

"Move it!" she said.

I threw myself up the ladder and slammed the hatch closed behind me. Sucking in deep, mostly clean lungfuls of air, I tried to get my bearings but enormous black clouds were pouring from the structure on all sides. Sounding much too far away, I heard the distinct wail of sirens interspersed with the honking of car horns and the shuffling of busy traffic.

"I can't see a thing", Liv said. "The fire shouldn't have spread this quickly."

"I think this fire had some help."

She turned the paper trumpet over in her hand, squeezed it a little and looked down the end. "This is just paper? How is this possible?" The indignity in her voice told me she wasn't just talking about the paper trumpet.

"It's enchanted", I said. There was no point in denying it now.

"Like magic?" she said, shaking her head. "Is that why I can't let go of this?" she asked, holding up the door handle her body still refused to release.

I winced. Angry red blisters were visible where hand met handle. Her knuckles were bone white and her arm was shaking from what I assumed to be over-exertion.

I nodded.

"This is insane. You're telling me you're a wizard?" she said.

"Sort of. But not like the one causing all this", I said, raising my chin defiantly in a gesture that didn't belong. I flicked through the fragmented personalities in my head looking for the owner but came up empty.

"Well", she said, taking a cautious step closer to me as the pocket of clear air we stood in shrank, "prove it and get us off this fucking roof".

I took the magic trumpet back from her as the wind changed, immersing us both in acrid black smoke. "Awfully bossy for someone who just tried to shoot me." The quipping teenager lodged in my mind after consuming the paperback was starting to annoy me. "The fire crew will be here any minute." I added, the statement ringing false to my own ears.

Liv starting coughing so I handed back the paper cone and took stock. We had Liv's wedding ring, what remained of Bing's record sleeve and fourteen floors to traverse before reaching safety of the street below.

"Well?" Liv coughed, when I didn't answer. "Can't you fly us to safety or something? Summon your broom? Conjure a fucking dragon?"

"That tone isn't helping, Olivia", I said, flatly. I only just managed to stop myself from adding the 'young lady'. Liv's grandmother was doing backflips in my head. Apparently, she didn't approve of her little Livvy cursing.

My eyes were streaming to the point I could no longer keep them open against the fumes. Panic started to set in when the heat of the fire reached us. As the heat intensified my carefully fleeting control over my passenger personalities evaporated. We held hands like frightened children and pressed our bodies lower in a futile attempt to find air.

A combination of self-doubt, smoke inhalation and withdrawal hit me like a speeding train. The words "fucking dragon" kept repeating in my head as the smog grew denser, cutting off our air and prematurely blocking out the sun. I could barely see my own hands on the concrete roof. I removed Bing from my pocket and reached through the darkness for Liv's hand. I could hear Liv coughing beside me, and used the sound of her suffering to anchor myself and the two Greek women in a singular purpose.

"Get ready to hold your breath", I said, rising as I clutched the record sleeve and opened the floodgates wide. Bing ignited in my hand, the full power of my most prized keepsake gathering like an electric storm at my centre. I gave Liv's hand a reassuring squeeze, thrusting the other into the air like a holy man crying out for the intervention of some deity.

I could have called down lightening, raised mountains or wrecked cities, or at least that's what it felt like. Instead I summoned the air itself. A whirlwind cut through the smoke above us forming a column of breathable air, driving back the darkness.

The record sleeve's history darted across my mind with a vibrant lucidity I'd only caught glimmers of before. I could smell the leather of the ancient and sunken chair beside the record player. I could hear the pop and crackle of the vinyl as the needle dropped into place and the song washed over me. I felt the coils of the headphone cable as it wrapped around my fingers and the satisfaction that little ritual brought me every time it was performed. It was Friday nights in with the wife, Sunday afternoon's watching my daughters play on the shag pile rug at my feet while I nursed a scotch and reflected on my life, all the while cradling that record sleeve and admiring the message old Bing had signed all those years ago.

Since I'd acquired the record, I had referred to it as Bing: Bing's confidence, Bing's swagger. I realised now, this wasn't where the keepsakes true power resided. Certainly, it was Bing himself that had written the message, but surely he had written dozens, hundreds of the like over the years. No, the true power was with Jonny, the owner of the record, and how he had cherished that message, how it had been his source of confidence and driven him to live a life, simple though it may have been, courageously.

Judging by my current frame of mind I guessed a lifetime worth of Jonny's confidence would equate to a few hours of intolerable arrogance and a smattering or two of poor choices. Nonetheless it was powerful, and power was what I needed.

"Are you… are you doing that?" Liv cried over the wind.

I beamed at her, my hair whipping about my face. I held an image in my mind as the black smoke coiled and congealed in front of me. I didn't let go of Liv's hand as the mass of smoke continued to swell, the fire fuelling my creation. A thick torso formed first, then a long forked tail which cut the air like a whip. It took an enormous amount of concentrated smoke to make the beast solid. I willed the particles to compact tighter, layering them one on top of the next.

"Climb on", I said, pointing to the sweeping, slightly opaque mass, with points like shark fins sprouted from its back.

"Is that…?" she said, reluctantly stepping forwards.

"You wanted a dragon", I said, grinning like a mad man. A large saddle blossomed from between two of the pointed scales at the centre of the creatures back. I stepped forwards, pressed my hand against the saddle and felt pillow-like resistance. I quickly climbed on and motioned for Liv to do the same. She hopped on behind me and we both held on as wings sprouted from just in front of my knees, each indistinct and ghostly limb sucking smoke in like thickening tendrils. Slowly, the tips of each wing grew more distinct, sharpening talons and rendering flesh from nothingness. The beast's body turned steadily darker until it was the colour and texture of tar. Riding the wave of energy flowing through me, I touched the beast's back and the wings started beating downward even before they were fully formed. With each progressive beat they grew stronger as they gained greater purchase on the air. Tendrils of silver-grey poured from the tips of its talons and the edges of each wing as if the creature's very body were indeed aflame.

Liv caught me tight around the waist and I clung to the saddle, digging my heels into the dragon's flanks as it lifted up onto stocky hind legs. I watched the dragon's talons leave the ground and couldn't help but feel a swell of awe at my creation as we took to the air.

The beast snorted a deep nasal growl across the city and rolled its head. Then, without any further warning, it pivoted its body and dove lithely over the edge. We dropped twenty feet before levelling out and soaring across the street below. The exhilaration of flying, of cool clean air whipping my hair back as my magic propelled us across the sky was undeniable. I glanced down at my hands and watched the last trace of ash blown from my fingers. Bing had left the building, but what an exit. We left the fire behind us and emerged from the smoke, the city coming into sudden relief.

At a mental nudge the beast dropped lower and rolled left at the end of the street, where an enormous building blocked our way. My eyes met those of a cyclist who only just managed to stop himself before riding into the back of a taxi. I encouraged the beast beneath me with a nudge of my will, and at once it spread enormous jaws wide, let out a screech and spewed a funnel of smoke across the bridge as we flew across it.

As we reached the end, the beast pitched up and turned in the air, still gushing smoke from its nostrils, and turned back the way it came. I ducked low against the creature's back and picked a spot on the bridge where the smoke was the densest.

We came in fast, the dragon's body pitching vertically as we came in to land. I heard the scratch and grind of metal as talons slashed into car roofs before its thick legs crashed into the top of a mini bus. The bus lurched forwards onto the front two wheels and the dragon let out a snarl of fury, turning its massive head from left to right. Then, in an explosive rush of soot and smoke, the dragon exploded and we dropped to the roof of the bus in a tangle of limbs and several groans of pain.

"Shit-a-brick, what the hell was that?"

I dropped to the pavement, managed to stumble, bumping into the bonnet of a mustard yellow hackney carriage, on my way to the pavement. I collapsed sideways across it and threw up into the drain. When I came up for air the mustard taxi was still right in front of me, which made me heave again. Once there was nothing left, I rolled onto my back and stared at the sky, listening to Detective Stone as I watched the dissipating smoke drift apart against the blue sky. In my mind, Smokey (for what else could I have called my dragon?) had just flown off seeking his next adventure, and the little drifting rings left behind were all that remained. I started to well up at the thought of never seeing him again.

I realise it was overly-sentimental for a creature devised entirely of my own imagination and existing for barely forty-five seconds, but I was an emotional wreck and horrendously hungover, at least in the magical sense.

"A fucking drone?" the cockney driver said.

"We are doing everything we can to locate the owner. The police will call you when we have his insurance information", Olivia said.

I heard footsteps and then she was beside me, her shadow falling pleasantly across my face. As I managed to get her into focus I found myself staring up at her, silhouetted like an angel. Her hair looked much better down and the smudges of soot on her nose and forehead were strangely humanising.

"Jesus, you look like shit", she said.

"You look like a chimney sweep", I said, smiling a little until my stomach rolled unpleasantly, as if in protest to any other part of me experiencing the slightest respite. "I need to get to a meeting."

I closed my eyes for a moment as Liv stood and looked up and down the street. "Traffic is gridlocked here, we won't make it ten feet. Think you can walk to the other side of the bridge?"

I honestly wasn't sure but decided trying was better than lying in the gutter all day. With Liv's help I got to my feet and started walking with my arm over her shoulder. My body felt twice its normal weight, but as long as I had Liv's help and I didn't move my head too much, I seemed to be just as capable at feeling awful upright as I had been lying down.

"What's wrong with you? Do I need to take you to a hospital?" she asked.

"No doctors", I said, sounding like an irritable drunk from a bad film. "I just need to get clean. I need a meeting."

"What do you mean by a meeting?"

"AA, NA, SA, SLA, anything with an A in the title. I'd take an OA at this point."

"OA?"

"Overeaters Anonymous." I grunted.

"Right."

I glanced at her profile and immediately regretted it. Not only did the world start spinning unpleasantly, but the budding irritation I had been cultivating towards the good Detective immediately blossomed into anger and sadness. I felt as if I hadn't seen her in months, but the relief at seeing she was well was overshadowed by my anger and disappointment that she hadn't contacted me sooner.

"Why are you staring at me like that?" she asked, her brow furrowed.

"You should call your mother", I said, voice cracked with emotion.

CHAPTER 6

The next time I opened my eyes I was lying on the floor of my cab staring up at Detective Stone's shoe as she flicked through my record collection. "That isn't mine, it belongs to a friend", I croaked, as she picked up *Spiceworld: The Album*.

"Good, you're awake", she said, keeping her voice low and touching a hand to her throat as she continued. "I'm supposed to inform you that if you start to feel dizzy or nauseated we should take you immediately to a hospital."

I grimaced feeling a pang of guilt for hogging the bewitched paper cone. My throat was sore, but more akin to the effects of a bad head cold than the bag of razor blades Liv seemed to have swallowed. My guilt evaporated a moment later when my stomach lurched and I almost fell back onto my face.

I tried to focus on my watch but the effort made my head swim. Instead I glanced out the window at the passing traffic.

"You've been asleep for two hours", she said and even at a whispered croak, she still managed to convey her disapproval at the fact. Judging by my sore throat and hazy vision I was fairing little better. "I called the station while you were out."

"Oh?" I said, dragging myself into one of the fold-down chairs and nearly toppling over as Amber made a sharp left in too high a gear.

"Chief Inspector Price is in a medically-induced coma. He suffered some brain swelling as he fell apparently, and with the blood loss from the gunshots they thought it was his best chance given his age."

I swallowed. "What does that mean?"

"It means he is having the best treatment possible", she said, her tone short.

"I meant regarding the investigation."

"Oh, that's the funny part", she said in a tone that suggested no amusement. "They put me in charge. There are more senior officers obviously, but they said I was the most familiar with the investigation. The truth is, nobody wants within a hundred feet of this, particularly now we don't have a crime scene. You seem better?"

"A little. It comes in waves. Until I get myself to a meeting, though, I won't be myself."

"I don't really understand why we needed to come here and not the hospital, but your driver was persistent. There's a meeting starting soon apparently", she said, handing my Motorola flip phone back to me.

"So, you called Amber?" I said, pocketing the device and keeping my voice low.

"I did", she said, sounding guarded. I watched her glance to the driver's seat.

"She isn't like me", I said, in an even lower register.

"And thank god for that, fucking cheapskate", Amber replied.

I grimaced at the volume of her voice as we pulled into a health club car park.

"How long?" I asked, looking through the hatch at Amber.

"Twenty minutes."

My first thought was to set the alarm on my phone and sleep until the meeting started, but one look at Liv told me she needed some answers.

"Come on, I need some fresh air", I said, opening the door and slipping out into the dim glow of late afternoon sun. I grabbed my coat and held the door for her as she climbed out after me. I dug out the half-smoked cigarette stub from earlier, which I lit and inhaled. The little trickle of power flowed across my body like a gentle ocean tide. I closed my eyes for a moment to savour it, then started walking towards the tennis courts.

"I'm guessing you have some questions for me?" I said.

She watched the smoke rise from the end of my cigarette for a few seconds then turned to face me. "Did you have anything to do with those murders?"

"No", I said, firmly. "Claire was a friend. We looked out for each other when things fell apart. Yesterday was the first time I'd seen her in almost a year, though. She'd been doing well. It was just happenstance I bumped into her when I was working a case."

"She was…"

"A mage, yes", I said.

"That's what you call yourselves?"

"I guess. Wizard sounds a little too dramatic and magician makes it sound like we do card tricks. Some people differ, but generally we go by mage."

"Okay, mage it is", she shook her head. "So how does it work?"

"Magic?"

"Yes. *That*. Can you do anything? Read minds, punch through walls, raise the dead, shoot lightning out of your…?"

"Christ, straight into it then", I said, cutting her off. "Well I can't read minds, I could probably punch through a wall under the right circumstances, and the lightning thing sounds unlikely, though, frankly, I've never tried. Oh, and what was the last one, raising the dead? You could animate practically anything with enough power and a strong enough will behind it."

She continued to stare at me as if she were trying to decide which of us was insane. I took another pull on my cigarette. "Okay, you don't believe me yet, that's fine. I'll tell you this anyway so when you do, you have a bit of context." I paused to take another pull. "The first thing to understand is everything to do with magic has a price. I can't just wave my hand and make things happen. I need a source to draw from, something imbued with powerful emotion. The stronger the emotion, the more energy I can draw. That energy can then be used to make changes in the physical world."

"Like the file in the interview room?"

"Exactly, it all has a cost. Moving something small like the file for a few seconds is easy. You might have noticed a little smudge of ash on your finger afterwards. Drawing from a source literally burns away a part of it. Making lightning or raising a zombie, would take huge amounts of power to get right, more than any mage is going to be comfortable parting with."

She was quiet for a moment in thought. "What did you use to do that? The file, I mean."

I blinked uncomfortably. "Your grandmother's wedding ring. Just a tiny bit of it, mind, and a little bit more to crack the padlock earlier", I added, hoping the knowledge that it had been used to save both our lives might offer some comfort.

She turned her hand over and looked at the wedding band, her expression guarded.

As she turned her palm to face me I realised the door handle had finally come free and in its wake an imprint of the design lay seared into her palm.

"Jesus, your hand", I said, wincing.

"Forget it", she said, slipping it behind her back. "Look if this is true, and you haven't just drugged me, how is it people don't know about this, about you? It sounds like there are enough of you that it would be public knowledge."

"Well we tend to lead pretty quiet lives, keep out of the news. It's sort of in our nature."

"We just rode a dragon through the centre of London, or did I just imagine that? Christ, did I? I'm actually losing the plot." she shook her head.

"In fairness, it was made entirely of smoke. I doubt anyone spotted us through all that fog. Even if they did then I doubt they would have believed their eyes." I smiled.

"You are awfully confident all of a sudden."

"Oh well that's Bing for you", I shrugged.

"Bing?"

"Bing Crosby. It was his 1954 EP I channelled to make the dragon. Well the record sleeve at least, or more specifically the message he wrote on it. It was perfect for a confidence boost or some flashy magic like the dragon. The written words are like a conduit; as long as there's some strong sentiment attached to the object it will bind, and I can use it to do magic, not to mention reap the benefits of his swagger for a while. Without a written message we can't do anything with it." When she continued to look confused, I took another little pull on the cigarette and pushed a little clarity into my mind. I was finding it difficult to string more than a few words together without getting impatient or going off on a tangent, a side effect of my fatigue and the half dozen personalities bouncing around my brain.

"You are channelling his emotions? *Bing Crosby's* emotions, right now?" she asked.

"A little of Bing, mostly Jonny, the owner of the record he signed though. Bing made the initial bond by writing the message, but Jonny cherished it for most of his life after that, effectively pouring his heart into it. That imprint remained until I consumed it this afternoon."

"Consumed?" she repeated.

"Yeah, just like it sounds. Doesn't have to mean

eating it though. Smoking it gives a steady release, that's the easiest to manage. You can also eat it, which has a bit of a delay before suddenly hitting you. Or you can draw on it directly like I did with the Bing sleeve. That's generally only for when you are in a pinch though."

"So that's why you seem so different from this morning? What happens to you when these other people take over?"

I could see where she was heading. "They don't take over, as such. It isn't like I'm possessed or anything. Frankly it would be simpler that way. No, I'm still here, along with Bing and everyone else I've channelled since I last got myself clean. They just have an influence, a voice. Think of it like we are all sharing one emotional entity. They can pull me in different directions, reduce or increase my inhibitions, make me more conservative or liberal, but it's still my mind they are affecting."

"Do you experience their memories?"

"Sometimes I get flashes. Usually when I first draw from a new keepsake. Everyone is different though."

"Keepsake?"

"That's what I call them. Basically, anything with a powerful emotional message written on them. Books, mix tapes, letters, record sleeves. Anything really."

"Wedding rings?" she said.

I swallowed, but kept silent. People tended to have polar reactions to discovering you could gain some insight into their deceased relatives' thoughts and feelings. Either they wanted to know what you knew, or they wanted to run away and never think about you again. I figured a woman like Stone fell into the latter camp.

"Look, I get that this is scary, but you don't need to be afraid of me. Most mages, all mages I've met in fact, don't use their magic to hurt people. Occasionally we slip up, but most of the time we only hurt ourselves", I said, turning away to face the broken line of addicts entering the health club reception.

"Don't be afraid of you? A five-year-old boy just told me to shoot you and I did it without raising an eyebrow. Now you tell me you could do exactly the same to me using nothing but my grandmother's wedding ring?"

"I just want to find who did this to Claire. You can ignore or disbelieve all the magic parts if you want, but just believe that." I said, keeping my voice firm. I could see she wasn't entirely convinced, at least not yet. She had been guiding the conversation to keep me talking.

Liv pursed her lips then sighed. "Even if we do somehow manage to find this psychotic little delinquent, assuming he was somehow the killer rather than some third unknown psycho controlling him, how do I even go about convicting them?"

"Haven't you ever heard of falsifying evidence?"

"I'm serious!"

"I wasn't joking. We might have to cross some lines here. I've never heard of a mage being capable of this sort of thing. In the heat of the moment would be one thing, but these murders were methodical and planned carefully in advance. I can't even imagine how that is possible for a mage. Until now I didn't think it was."

"What do you mean? Anyone can kill someone under the right circumstances, why not one of you?"

I frowned. This was all new to her, so I tried not to rise to the insult. "Because", I said, summoning as much patience as I could, "magic doesn't happen without an emotional connection. Going on a killing spree using magic would be like trying to rip out your own heart and beating someone else to death with it. Trust me, Livvy, you wouldn't get very far."

She looked as if she was about to hit me. "Don't *ever* call me that."

"I'm sorry", I said. "It's the calm in the tobacco. It stops me throwing up but also makes me careless sometimes."

She turned away from me, examining the red marks on her injured hand.

"Here", I said, stepping closer to her and holding out my hand. "Let me take a look at it."

"It's fine", she said, shortly. I persisted and she reluctantly held her hand in mine, palm upwards.

I returned the cigarette to my lips, inhaled deeply, watching the orange embers flare as I rested my other hand gently on top of her injured palm. I felt her try to pull her hand back but I kept hold of it, pushing energy through from my lungs, down my arm and into her blistered hand, willing the burns to ease, the tight tender skin to loosen and the pain to fade.

I opened my eyes after a moment and let go of her. "It's not much but it should help with the pain a bit."

She held her hand up, opening and closing her fingers. The flesh was now pink rather than red and the pattern from the handle had faded a little too.

"Could you help Price with this?" she said.

I shook my head. "It is technically possible to heal with magic but it requires an enormous amount of power and it's only really effective on simple injuries like that. These days the sciences are much better equipped than magic for anything more than this."

She looked disappointed. "This is insane."

"You still don't believe me?" I asked, amused.

She opened her mouth but managed only to shrug her shoulders instead. What else was there to say when your worldview was being rewritten in one afternoon?

I dusted the ash from my palms. "I should head inside. I'll be a little more tolerable once I've cleared my head. I won't be long."

"No problem, I've got some calls to make. Mind if I use your cab?"

"Be my guest. I guess we'll be working together, at least until you have me committed."

"Or Price wakes up and has me arrested." She glanced towards the health centre then back at me. "Is that a mage thing, or are you actually a sex addict?"

#

"*Fucking hell*, Amber", I groaned once I'd slammed the door of the taxi and checked the list containing the times and locations of that week's various addict meetings across the greater London area. "There was an AA meeting half a mile away starting ten minutes earlier."

"There was traffic, you prick!" she shouted back.

'Which road?"

"Oh, didn't you see it?" she said, her voice soaked in mock surprise. "Maybe because you were passed out on the fucking floor again!"

I took a deep breath. "Fine", I snapped. "Could you drive us away from here? Quickly."

Detective Stone pocketed her iPhone and glanced towards the health centre. "Meeting go alright?"

"Fine", I said dismissively. Stone continued to stare at me, however, and I figured I owed her a little more than that. "I don't particularly want to get into the details, but for the cleanse to work I have to be honest, and being honest means telling the truth. Telling the truth without getting yourself kicked out of a sex addicts meeting when you aren't actually a sex addict is troublesome to say the least."

"Dirty fucker", Amber muttered as the taxi pulled forwards.

I took another deep breath and slid the partition closed behind me. It didn't matter, it was done now, and I was firmly back in control.

I turned back to Liv and watched her eyes linger on the wedding band on her right hand. She looked almost regretful for a moment, but it was gone a second later. "I called Price's wife. He's stable and they will prep him for surgery first thing to remove the bullet still in his shoulder. I had a thought regarding the boy but I don't know enough about all this to be sure."

"Go on?"

"Well everyone who left the building had to stay with the fire crews, say their name and what room they were staying in to make sure everyone made it out, and every guest was accounted for and ticked off against a room number."

"Right? Don't tell me they gave their real names?"

"Even stranger, he didn't make it out of the fire."

I felt sick. "They found a body? I'd guessed he was being compelled by the actual killer to destroy any evidence he left behind but..."

"No, the building was in pretty good shape so the fire crews were already able to get in and do a sweep. No sign of any bodies, so they must have made it out somehow, but there were enough police at the exits keeping track of everyone that they couldn't have just walked off. Could they have, you know, used magic to make themselves invisible or something?" she lowered her voice when she said the word 'magic' and 'invisible'.

"I've never heard of anyone managing true invisibility", I said, recalling my own mixed efforts the day before. "There are just too many variables to consider. Disguises and distractions can be nearly as effective but generally you need a lot of power or a very specific type of keepsake.

It's not easy, but given he was channelling enough power to flatten me, then in the next breath summon fire to engulf an entire stairwell, it's possible."

"What are you thinking?" she asked, studying my expression.

"It's just... I'm struggling to imagine being so well resourced. If he had enough power on hand to stage these murders and get away clean, then locate and compel a child mage into torching the hotel, and still have enough left over to control you... Even if I consumed everything in my collection I don't think I would have enough for a quarter of all that."

"You think the killer might have some money then?"

"If not wealthy then he has some serious connections. Keepsakes aren't always expensive, it's mostly the amount of time it takes to come by them."

"Go on, this could help me build a profile", Liv said. "How do you come by this stuff? Charity shops and antique fairs?"

I smiled. "You've decided to believe me then?"

"Answer the question." she said.

I frowned, she didn't believe me, at least not yet. "Antiques fairs are okay; charity shops occasionally turn up something good. Auctions, garden and car boot sales are always good too. Older generations wrote more letters than we do. Many of us pick a career where we have easy access. Claire was a therapist so had her patients keep diaries."

"What about second hand jewellery stores, gold exchanges?"

"All good, but that tends to be your more high-end stuff. Remember it has to be engraved or written on in some way, otherwise it's useless."

She frowned. "Couldn't you just buy a bunch of old wedding rings and get someone else to engrave them?"

I shook my head. "You could, but the sentiment would have no connection to that first family so it would lose all that potential. They need to be the ones to do the engraving really. It needs to be their heartfelt sentiment. It only grows stronger if the sentiment is carried on down the family line. Take your wedding ring for instance, you are feeding it all the time, whenever you're feeling powerful emotion. Especially if you are thinking about your mother or grandmother. Since they both wore it through most of their lives, it has a huge amount of their feelings buried in it too."

"And the size of these keepsakes is irrelevant in terms of the proportion of power they can hold?" she asked, rolling her thumb around the wedding ring on her finger.

"Right. In fact, that was probably what the bag was for. I saw you crouch down over a backpack. Did you see anything else in there when you went for the gun?" I said.

She thought for a moment. "It's a bit of a blur to be honest. A couple of books maybe? I remember it was heavy, I said as much when I carried it to the lift for him. You think they were stuffed with these keepsakes?"

"Probably."

"And the gun", she said, her eyes drifting.

"It wasn't you that pulled the trigger."

She cleared her throat. "So, someone could have spent a lot of money acquiring these things quickly or he might have just been storing up all these trinkets all his life waiting for the right occasion to use them? So, old or possibly wealthy?"

I thought for a moment. "I'd say wealthy is probably the more likely of the two. Every mage I know stocks up on keepsakes, that's something we all have in common."

"Why is that?"

I considered her. This wasn't a piece of information I particularly liked sharing but I needed her to trust me. The truth was it was a miracle she hadn't arrested me already, there was certainly enough circumstantial evidence to suspect me. "We can't stop using magic. Ever. At least not completely. A few days, maybe a week at most. If we did, it would kill us. As a result, most of us who aren't desperate or chasing the dragon have a rainy day stash or two somewhere."

"Oh."

The upward pitch of the way she said it told me she didn't really grasp what that meant. It was understandable, it was easy to fixate on the flying through the sky dragony parts, over the cravings, vomiting and mood swings, even if the latter was far more frequent than the former.

"How much of your stockpile did you use yesterday then?"

"About half, enough to have lasted me four or five years."

"Ouch."

I looked out the window at a mother and son entering a supermarket hand in hand. "How old did you say the boy was?"

"He looked around five, maybe six. Why?"

I shook my head. "I can't make sense of it. You are sure everyone that came out of there was accounted for?"

"As sure as I can be", she said, shortly. "There were hundreds of witnesses, not just the police and fire crews. Not to mention forensics are already pouring over the surveillance footage from both entrances."

"I have to see it", I said.

"That isn't going to happen. I can't just take something like that out of evidence mid-investigation."

"They won't know what to look for. I will."

"Look I'm going to have to get back to the office. I've been gone for too long already."

"Can't you just tell them you are chasing down a lead?" I said, dismissively.

"That's what I told them I *was* doing, but I'm supposed to be leading the investigation now, not chasing down hunches with a self-proclaimed sex addict." She looked exhausted as she said it.

"Seriously?" I said, my own voice growing in volume. "I'm your best hope of catching this killer. You would have…"

"I know that!" she shot back, cutting me off. "Could you pull over please?" she said, her voice straining to be polite when she addressed Amber.

"Wait, you're leaving now? You don't believe me? You think you imagined it all?" I said.

"It doesn't matter if I do or not. I have to go, I have a fucking job to do!" she shouted.

The taxi pulled to a stop between a

carpet emporium and a red, white and blue Underground sign.

"Fucking bureaucrats. What about Claire?" I said.

She stopped with one foot out the door and half turned. I saw the look on her face. It was as if I'd slapped her. Then without a word, her face hardened, she slammed the door and jogged towards the underground steps.

I watched her go, then sat back in my seat.

"Ow! What the hell Amber?" I said, switching seats to get away from her and rubbing my ear frantically.

"The lead she was chasing was you, idiot. She has to go and convince them that you, their one suspect, is innocent, and they have to keep looking."

I was so shocked by both Amber's level of knowledge regarding the day's events and her insight into the detective's frame of mind, my mouth hung open.

"Oh", was all I could think to say.

CHAPTER 7

The hour drive home was a sombre affair. Feeling foolish and self-absorbed, as if I'd been smoking teenage hormones for the last twenty-four hours, I didn't say anything as Amber dropped me off at my house in Berkhamsted. I felt some small measure of relief when she said she would pick me up at the normal time tomorrow, and that I should pull my head out of my arse and get to work. I decided it was good advice.

I unlocked the three heavy locks to my front door and scraped my way inside. Behind the door lay a stack of old newspapers as high as my shoulder, with the crosswords cut out. Beyond that were cardboard boxes of newspaper clippings, cassette tapes and CDs, scratched and naked. The lids on each box wouldn't quite close as a little more was added to the discard piles each day. Anything magically useful was extracted with surgical precision by my own hand and the rest was recycled, sold or binned. I picked up the post from behind the door. Three letters and two padded manila envelopes from the eBay fairy.

I pushed the bundle under my arm and angled my body sideways to make it through to the living room and kitchen. The smell of day-old pizza mingled unpleasantly with the thick musty scent of old newspaper. I tossed the bundle down on the kitchen counter and cracked the window behind the sink which overlooked the little garden. I took a deep breath, letting the smell of overgrown grass and a gardening deposit I was never getting back wash over me before turning to the counter where the house phone sat.

As much as I had been dreading it, I found myself disappointed to find no messages on my house phone either. Perhaps Claire was already in the hands of her killer by then or perhaps she hadn't really meant to call in the first place. Maybe it was just one of those things you say like *let me know you get home safe*, but rarely actually mean.

I stood in the middle of the living room staring at the dusty curved screen of my old CRT TV. I'd meant to buy a new one when the digital thing happened but I hadn't bought a stand for either the old or the hypothetical new one yet, so it seemed pointless to do so. A box of VHS tapes with words like "Thomas and Louise's wedding - DO NOT TAPE OVER" printed in thick red letters sat beside the TV on the dated shag pile rug. I found myself longing for the sweet leathery solitude of my Austin taxi's back seat. The sofa was piled with more boxes, though these ones were plastic rather than cardboard and stuffed with old records too scratched to listen to. I couldn't bring myself to move them, or myself, towards the dusty sofa. I had meant to buy a vacuum or hire a cleaner when I moved in. That was eighteen months ago.

It was strange to think a house bursting at the seams with the loot of a hundred lives could feel so hollow. When my home offered me no comfort I searched my mind, eager for the return of another voice, another perspective to take my mind off things. Given the amount of magic I had used I should have been inundated with the aftershocks of those other psyches but there was nothing. Resigned to what I hoped was a temporary isolation, I headed for the bedroom, stomping my feet on the thickly carpeted stairs as I went, as if to remind myself I was still there. I undressed and lay down on the bed thinking about how empty the house felt.

I wondered, if I had invited Claire back here instead of letting her go home, would she still be alive? Perhaps she would have stayed a few days while she recovered from falling off the wagon. We would have gone to meetings together and talked about things. She would have ridiculed me about the state of my living conditions and perhaps teased me until I swore to clean up the place and buy some proper furniture.

Exhaustion eventually got the better of me and I fell into a fretful sleep where Claire and I were walking around Ikea looking at boxes of old cassette tapes and laughing about how long it would take us to assemble one. They even came with little packets of dust to sprinkle over each box like sugar.

I slept an hour before waking. I sat up and swung my legs off the bed, unwilling to lose Claire or Ikea yet in the folds of further sleep. I looked around the little bedroom, my eyes barely making it to the door before I started to cry. Mages cry a lot. Take in the heartfelt sentiments of others and mix them up with your own emotional baggage and it's impossible not to get at least a little glassy eyed.

This was different though, this was all me, alone, and these were deep sobs, the kind that shook your shoulders and reminded you of a time when you were still young enough to cry from skinning your knee but old enough to feel ashamed of the fact. Claire was gone and I could have helped her. Had I invited her back here or not interfered at all back at Greg's she would probably still be alive.

Still clinging to the dream of us in Ikea, I studied her face. I wanted sympathy, words of comfort, but my picture of her blurred or she turned away any time I tried that expression on her. She quirked a half smile instead. Even in my own head, she knew me too well, offering what I needed to hear rather than any false comforts I might want her to say. I recalled her voice as reliably as if she were in the room beside me.

"Self-pity was never a good look on you," she said.

#

I slept most of the following day, ignoring my doorbell when it rang at 9 and again at 11:30am. When I wasn't sleeping, I ambled around the little house peering vacantly into the fridge, the silent house phone or at the powered off TV, contemplating but not quite managing to summon the effort to eat, listen to my messages, or turn on the TV.

Around noon I had a cluster of aftershocks hit me. I was sitting on my sofa watching the dust drift across a sunbeam when Stone's mother and Bing returned, manifesting themselves in a powerful sense of shame at my living conditions. I immediately threw open all the windows to air the place and in minutes I had retrieved every cleaning product from the depths of the cupboard beneath the sink and spent the next three hours cleaning the house, pausing only to expel the occasional sneeze and to write a few pages of their thoughts whenever my hands started to shake.

About five o'clock I found a bunch of old photos

and lingered over any that contained Claire, as if seeking some sort of recognition from her younger self. I continued in this vane for several hours until I stumbled across a picture of my sister standing with her elbow resting on my head. We both held ice creams and were smiling. I closed the album soon after and returned to the safety of my bed.

Depression is a funny thing. As a psychiatrist Claire dealt with depressed people all the time. Once we had discussed a news piece about a woman who had committed suicide by jumping off a bridge into M25 traffic, killing a family of three in the process. I had expressed my anger at the selfishness of the woman, suggesting she should have simply overdosed or slit her wrists. Claire had told me that my suggestion implied the woman was capable of rational thought at the time and the fact was depression could be all consuming. A person in that state couldn't function properly, couldn't imagine a tomorrow where things might improve, or how others might feel if they were gone from the world.

#

On the second morning I awoke to the sound of loud knocking on my front door. Assuming it was Amber or a delivery man, I headed down in my boxers and a dressing gown. I pulled open the door poised and ready to tell them to piss off, only to discover my client, Mrs Thomas standing on the threshold.

"I left you several messages Mr. Chase. Get up and meet me on the corner in fifteen minutes," she hissed, her nose wrinkling. "In fact, make it 45 minutes. Take a shower, Mr. Chase. I don't want that smell in my car," she said coolly before turning away. The scent of cherries and summertime lingered in her wake, cutting through the fog of my melancholy. This, coupled with the woman's intrusion into my domain, set my mind on edge: a shot of much needed caffeine firing across my synapses. It was the third distinct perfume I had detected on her which made me wonder if she had different scents on different days of the week or maybe she wore different perfumes for different occasions.

I closed the door and darted back up the stairs to my bedroom and watched her hasten out of the cul-de-sac like a fox out of a hen house. She wore tight grey yoga pants, a hoody with large dark sun glasses and a headscarf which made her look like a cross between Audrey Hepburn and, well, Audrey Hepburn on her way to yoga. The estate was still asleep, but Mrs Thomas kept her handbag clamped under one arm, her eyes fixed dead ahead, as if she expected the alarm to be raised and the paparazzi's to dive out from behind a wheelie bin at any moment. The side of my mouth quirked at this, until I realised her fears were not so farfetched.

I sniffed myself before taking the woman's advice and heading for the shower. The hot water helped but not nearly as much as Mrs Thomas herself. Her simple and unlikely presence crashing into my home forced me to think beyond my own bubble of self-pity. I had obligations and a client who was depending on me.

As I stepped out of the shower and towelled off I thought back to the Bing-smoke-dragon. It had been so long since I'd used so much magic in one go, literally years of supply vanished in a puff of smoke, that I had failed to anticipate how it might affect me. I had managed to get myself clean quickly enough but there was always a dip, a comedown after any use. This one just happened to be far bigger than any I could remember, but it made sense-the bigger the highs, the bigger the lows. I should have anticipated it or at least recognised the signs. The realisation didn't make me feel better, quite the contrary, it made me feel ashamed. I had sat and done nothing for two days while Claire's killer walked free.

I dressed quickly and went to the kitchen. The milk had turned so I made porridge with water from the tap instead. I found the remnants of a bottle of honey, unscrewed the lid and poured in some boiling water before adding it to the mix.

It was over-sweet but there was plenty of it.

I switched on the radio, then sat down at the kitchen table and ate quickly. I reached for the phone intending to call my sponsor before I noticed the blinking number 3 on the phone dock.

The first two messages were from my father, which I quickly skipped as soon as I heard his voice. The third was Henry. He sounded sober but he'd left the message a little after 4:30am and his voice was off. Colder than usual, his speech stunted.

Hi Fin, It's me. We need to talk. Come by the flat. Today. It's important.

I half dialled Henry, then Amber, then my sponsor, as a series of half formed plans occurred to me and were rejected. Henry I owed a face-to-face, not a phone call. Amber, I probably owed an apology to but, again, I would deliver that in person once certain she was still in my employ. Finally, my sponsor would take at least an hour, assuming I could keep him on the phone and he didn't insist on meeting in person. That was time I couldn't afford, and what good would it do? I needed resolution, not sympathy. I glanced at the Ikea lamp behind the TV.

I settled the phone back in its cradle, grabbed my coat off the newspaper clippings by the door and headed out into the street. The cul-de-sac was still quiet except for a man in pressed suit trousers, shirt and tie, loading a suitcase into the back of an Audi. I nodded a silent greeting and he nodded one back, though his was too knowing, conspiratorial even. I dwelled on this as I passed him, wondering which of my neighbours he must have believed me to be sleeping with. I emerged out onto the road just as a silver Jaguar pulled silently to the curb beside me. Mrs Thomas wound down the window and glared at me over her glasses.

"Well get in then", she said.

I walked around the rear of the car. Out of habit I checked the back seats for any other passengers before climbing in beside Mrs Thomas.

"Good morning", I said, warmly. She was my only paying client, after all.

"Mhmm", she muttered, checking her blind spot before pulling away. "You missed our rendezvous. When you didn't turn up I thought you might have gotten cold feet."

"I'm sorry. Something came up. I couldn't get away."

"Yes, I heard about my husband's whore."

"Claire wasn't a whore", I said, through gritted teeth.

She glanced at me. "So, you did know her?"

"You could have just asked. I wasn't going to deny it."

"Then you see my problem?"

"Not really."

"Photographs of Greg bedding this woman will draw me and what remains of my family into all this unpleasantness. Your connection to this woman means your photos are no good to me now."

"You didn't drive all the way out here just to tell me that."

"No. I want to know how you are going to fix this?"

"And I suppose you have some thoughts on how I should do just that."

"Hire a different woman. Get this new one to seduce him too and then take your pictures. It shouldn't be too difficult, knowing Greg."

I looked at her. "You think I hired Claire? I didn't know that's who your husband was seeing until I walked in on them. She's a psychotherapist, not a prostitute."

"Frankly I don't care who these women are."

"*Woman.* There was only one", I said, not entirely sure why I cared to correct her. I certainly didn't care about Greg Thomas's infidelities.

"I know my husband, Mr Chase. Regardless, I'm still not of a mind to care either way."

I didn't believe her. I didn't care how "over" a marriage was, she was still crushed even if she did hide it better than most of my previous clients. One of the greatest emotional hurts anyone could suffer was being made to feel, in some way, less. That "less" could present itself in many different ways: less adventurous, less attractive, less young, less interesting. The problem was the "less" part didn't really have a finite answer. Mrs Thomas had no doubt dwelt on all of these things, as most people did when their spouse ran off with someone else. Some of these imagined shortcomings were easier to accept than others, however. In this case, it was far more favourable for Mrs Thomas to believe her husband was a serial skirt chaser than to entertain the idea that he had just fallen for someone else.

I adjusted in my seat and looked across at her. Her skin was flawless, her hair tied back in a neat bun though she wore no makeup, which told me she was most likely heading to a class once she was done with me. I knew Mrs Thomas to be forty-six, though she could have easily passed for late thirties, a feat I attributed to her rigorous health regimes and yoga five mornings a week with tennis on the weekends when the weather was fair. Her figure had lost some of the fullness associated with the twenty-somethings in glamour magazines but what had replaced it was just as attractive. She had grown leaner, more athletic, her face thin but not at all to the point of looking gaunt or unhealthy. What she had lost in blushing innocence she more than made up for in sharp wit and a good dose of no-nonsense moxie.

She caught me looking, so I turned to glance into the back of the car. In the footwell was a yoga mat beside a handbag large enough to carry a change of clothes and a towel. From memory, I knew she always carried several pairs of footwear in the boot of her Jag. It was a quirk she and I shared, minus the Jag.

"What is it? Are we being followed?" she asked, looking over her sunglasses into the rear-view mirror.

"No, we're fine. I was just wondering where we were headed. Off to yoga this morning?" I asked.

"My mornings are not what you should be worried about, Mr Chase. Think what the lawyers would make of it once they got their noses into this?" she said, pulling into a multi-storey car park. We went up two levels then she pulled into a vacant space and switched off the engine and turned to me. I could see a tension in her I hadn't noticed before, a knotting of muscles across her shoulders as if she were anticipating a bucket of cold water down her back at any moment.

"Don't you see what could happen if Greg's lawyers put all this together? I hired you to follow my husband. Now his mistress, who you knew, has been murdered hours after you fought him."

"I didn't hire her and I certainly didn't fight anyone."

"It doesn't matter, it will look like you did, and they will think I told you to."

In the six months I'd known her she looked genuinely afraid for the first time. "He could take my children from me." She reached behind her seat and retrieved a Tupperware box. She popped the seal and showed me the stack of fifties inside.

"Will this be enough?" she asked.

I blinked at her. "For what?"

"To hire another one."

I sighed and looked at the plush leather interior of the car dash. "You know the worst thing about gathering evidence of other people's indiscretions?" I said, "Everyone believes you are capable of the same things and worse."

"You are right, don't tell me anything. Just take the money and take care of it", she said, pushing the box into my lap.

I stared down at the box for a moment, smelling the lemon-scented washing up liquid I guessed she had scrubbed it with before setting off to meet me. "Jennifer, what is it you want?" I asked. "What do you want to come out of this?"

"I told you before. It hasn't changed."

"You want primary custody of your children, and

for them to still see their father regularly, and half of all his holdings."

"I just want what's fair."

"He betrayed you, you don't want more than that? To see him punished for what he did?" I could see a flash of fire light her eyes for a moment as she gazed unseeing at the static needle on the speedometer.

"Why are you asking me this?"

"Just say it out loud."

"Fine, yes. I want to punish him. He deserves it. He doesn't just get to walk away and leave me. I want to humiliate him, break him. Make him doubt everything he is and beg me to take him back." She had started quiet and calm but by the time she was finished, her chest was rising and falling heavily like she was already half an hour deep into a spin class.

"We used to laugh at people like this", she said. "Now I'm one of them. I comforted Linda when George started cheating on her. I was *there* when Christine left Mike. I was bloody... winning!" she said, struggling to find a word that would fit.

She glanced at me, embarrassed, then at her knees, then turned and stared out the driver's side window.

"You aren't weak or small for feeling any of that", I said.

She snorted. "Thank you. It doesn't change anything though. I still feel like shit."

"Actually, it changes a lot." I took the lid and resealed the box of money and handed it back to her. "I'm not hiring anyone, I won't need to."

"What do you mean?"

I paused as if I was doubting whether I should say anything at all. She was right, Greg's solicitors could piece this together the wrong way and if the police got involved when no other suspects were available, I was certain I would resume my top spot on their radar. Mrs Thomas's only priory was to her children. If she thought that her custody over them was in jeopardy I had no doubt she would throw me under the bus and jump on board with everyone else. I needed to resolve this quickly. Sometimes people just needed a little push, it didn't always matter in what direction, they just needed a nudge to reaffirm their position. For my own piece of mind I needed to know she was serious and wasn't about to get cold feet.

"Look", I said, "why don't you just take him back? You probably planned to again somewhere down the line, right? You could be a family again."

She started trying to say something but I cut her off.

"Yes, he strayed a little, does that make him a bad father? Didn't he always provide for you?"

She turned her head very slowly towards me, her jaw set.

"Are you out of your mind?" she said, her voice low but controlled. "This is the second time I know for certain this has happened. There was probably more. He started moving money around, hiding things from me, as if he knows what's coming."

"And what is coming?"

"A fucking shit storm", she said, spitting the words. The venom behind them made me recoil in my seat and an idea struck me as I considered just how terrifying this woman could be. "Why are you smiling?"

"Think you can you have those divorce papers ready by tonight?"

CHAPTER 8

I outlined my plan to Mrs Thomas; she listened with sceptical attentiveness as if I were a builder pitching a garish new kitchen design. She was reluctant, but ultimately willing to try my approach. I was still determined to find the one responsible for Claire's murder but my bout of depression over the last two days had tempered my desperation and exposed the cracks in my previously reckless approach. The fact was whatever step I took next could further incriminate me. I thought I had Liv on side for now, but if the investigation was going as poorly as I suspected it might, she would have a hard time convincing her peers of my innocence for much longer. My connection to Mrs Thomas and her husband only complicated matters. If the police decided to press Greg I was certain he wouldn't hesitate in suggesting my involvement. Similarly if the police spoke to Mrs Thomas, and she voiced her belief that I had hired Claire to sleep with Greg, then I would be in even deeper waters. Selling Finley Chase the private eye as a serial killer might be a hard sell but Fin Chase the pimp would be a much easier leap. I needed to get them on the same page and a swift and relatively painless divorce agreement was the best way to do that. To do that, I would have to move quickly and be willing to crush Greg while he was mourning Claire. I didn't much like that part of my plan, but the alternative could be prison.

We left her Jaguar and made our way towards the steps leading down to the street. Sensing a growing awkwardness, I hung back at the top of the stairs and watched her go on without me. She muttered a goodbye and continued on alone. The sound of her echoing footsteps fading sounded oddly melancholic to my ears. I couldn't say exactly why. I certainly felt a little abandoned, though I had already come to terms with the knowledge that I was nothing more to Mrs Thomas than an employee. A useful employee, at least for the next few hours, but an employee nonetheless. It was an occupational hazard. Rich, well-bred socialites were never entirely comfortable with me. I'd never really understood why – they were the ones doing the hiring after all. If they didn't like it, they could simply stop paying my invoices and never see me again. I was viewed as something of an uncomfortable necessity in their lives. Someone had to dig up the dirt.

I didn't love the snooping part of the job but I'd

be lying if I said I hated it. Secrets are an exciting currency even to the regular PI, let alone one with the dietary requirements of a practicing mage.

I entertained the idea of rolling a cigarette to give myself some immediate purpose, but her footsteps had faded to nothing by the time the thought was fully formed. The idea of pretending I was Humphrey Bogart at the end of *Casablanca* was much more satisfying than the reality of said execution.

I sped down the steps, got my bearings and texted Amber the address of a charity shop twenty minutes away. Amber was already there when I arrived, the old Austin pulled up in a loading bay with her hazards on. Amber yawned into the back of her hand then waved sleepily with the other.

I held up a finger to indicate I would only be a minute, then headed into the shop.

"Are you open?" I asked of the teller, checking a phantom watch I had forgotten to put on.

A woman in her fifties with a sincere-looking face glanced at the clock on the wall. "Close enough", she said, smiling.

"Thanks."

I headed for the nearest stack of books and started working through them methodically, checking the first and last few pages for any inscriptions. I was well-practiced at the art, and made it through two display tables and the bargain basket before I was noticed.

"Anything I can help you find, love?" the woman asked. Her tone was a little too accommodating, as if her first customer of the day had a crippling case of OCD.

I turned to her and gave my best bumbling *this-is-so-silly-but* face. "I'm a bit of a collector; I don't suppose you have anything with an inscription in, or perhaps some notes? Anything like that really?"

She cocked her head at me and smiled. "Ah, you are one of *those* are you?"

I smiled. "That obvious?"

She laughed, "Just a little. It's fine by me, gets rid of the stock nobody else wants". She started moving back behind the counter and lifted a sturdy looking bag-for-life stuffed full of novels beside the till. "Some people don't mind a little graffiti of course. Personally, I think it adds a little character. Anyway, I said I couldn't hold them and I stand by that, but he was buying so many I just started bagging them up when they came in. Saves him cracking all the spines on the best sellers like you just were. You are welcome to take any you want, it's just not cricket otherwise."

I smiled at her and flicked through the first two books at the top of the heap. I skimmed the messages; all fairly generic, but not without use. "These are perfect", I checked her name badge, "Janet. How much for the lot?" I asked.

"Fifty pounds", she said, without blinking.

I blinked, my smile frozen in place. "Oh, I see. I thought you said this was stock nobody else wants?" I said, bouncing my head and checking the titles of the next half dozen in the heap, then reaching for my wallet.

"Well, we price based on demand you see", she said, wincing as if it hurt her to even contemplate such things.

I thought of the Tupperware box stuffed full of fifties that Mrs Thomas had attempted to force on me. "I'm afraid I don't have much cash on me at the moment", I said, digging through the contents of my wallet and frowning at the *CASH ONLY* sign Blu-tacked to the till.

"Well, like I said, I can't hold them. It would be unfair to the other customers, but there's a cashpoint about a ten minute walk away."

"It's fine. I'll take a couple now and try and come back later for the rest. I have to get to work."

"Certainly, anything you like, they are £3.75 each", she said.

I nodded, lifting out each book in turn and

checking the titles. I selected four paperbacks and one bright yellow children's book in hardback. I double checked my selections to make sure they all had inscriptions and I wasn't being fleeced twice in the same transaction, then paid and left with my wallet empty.

"Best to hurry back. Who knows how long I'll have these for", the shameless teller called after me.

"Thanks, I will", I said before pausing in the doorway. "You have many people come in asking for books with inscriptions?"

She let out an amused snort. "You'd be surprised. They are hardly beating down my door, but I have my regulars."

"Any more than usual in the last few months? Just curious how much competition I have in the area", I smiled.

"Oh well", she laughed. "I don't think you have too much to worry about. It tends to be the same handful of faces that come in every week or two."

I climbed into the back of the Austin and gave Amber Henry's address. As we sped away, I put the armful of books to one side and lay back thinking about what Janet had said.

#

"Oh, Mr Chase, it's time to wake up now", someone was calling me. Amber, only it didn't sound like

her, the voice sweetly musical. I gradually came to and was surprised to see Amber's flip-flopped foot bouncing in front of me. She was sat facing me in the fold-down chair, reading one of my new purchases, *Pride and Prejudice*.

"*Wakey, wakey, Fin*", she chimed.

"Are we there?" I asked, pushing myself into a sitting position.

"Finally", she sighed, "I've been trying to wake you for ages".

'Why didn't you shake me or something?" I said, noticing she was at least a chapter deep.

"Well, you seemed upset last time. Thought I'd try the softer approach." She twitched her nose as if she were addressing a baby rabbit.

"Uhuh", I murmured. "Well, wait here, and don't get any jam or anything on that book, it's a classic."

"Yes, boss."

Boss? I studied her for a moment before retrieving two more of the overpriced novels and stuffing them into the side pockets of my coat along with my tobacco. Amber remained where she was.

"You've never called me 'boss' before?"

"I wouldn't get used to it, I was just teasing", she muttered.

"You are still here."

"Right? Where should I be?"

"You know I'm the suspect in a murder investigation?"

"Yeah, so?"

"So, shouldn't you be more concerned or angry at me? I got you arrested! You could have thrown me under the bus with the police."

"You didn't kill anyone." She shrugged.

I smiled at her. "I'm growing on you, aren't I?"

"Fucking weirdo", she said shaking her head and disappearing behind her book.

As I vacated the larger seat and clambered out of the cab, Amber stretched out fully, her face buried in her new book. I walked along the High Street, passing two curry houses and a burger place. It had been so long since I'd been in Claire's flat, I walked straight past it without recognising it. The Istanbul Kebab house, I remembered, had moved or gone bust and a chip shop had taken its place. I doubled back and found the door with the chipped green paint and rang the buzzer for flat three. It took several minutes before anyone answered.

"Hello?" Henry said. He sounded hungover even through the static of the intercom.

"Henry, it's me."

"You better come up." The door clicked, and tugging it both ways in quick succession, I was granted entry into the musty hallway beyond. Takeaway menus littered the floor beneath the stairs. Henry was stood behind his flat door, peering out through a crack about the width of his ears. It was just wide enough for me to make out his face, a cow print slipper, and an open dressing gown showing too tight, bright red underwear.

"You're alone?" he said.

I didn't like the coldness in his voice, I took my hands out of my pockets as I reached the top of the stairs, just in case. The memory of being in a bedroom with a mostly naked, very vulnerable Claire just hours before she died tied my stomach into knots.

"Yeah, just me", I said, keeping my voice level and a good two paces between us.

He nodded to his slippers, then kept nodding. He sniffed, swung the door wide, his dressing gown falling all the way open, and embraced me. "You're a good friend!" he cried. Then he really started to sob. "Better than I deserve."

I got my arm under his and around his back and guided him back into the flat as he continued to sob. As the door closed behind us, the volume of his cries seemed to double.

"I should have been stronger. I should have

listened!" he said. I rubbed his back lamely and tried hushing him.

"It's all my fault!" he cried louder, over my hushing.

A thumping came from the wall behind the sofa.

"*Oh fuck you*, Mrs Cho!" he said, instantly regaining his composure and banging his fist against the wall an equal number of times before throwing himself back on the sofa. His mottled blue dressing gown flapped wide like a cape on the worst-dressed superhero imaginable. His bare, slightly flabby, exceptionally hairy chest jiggled for a good second and a half longer than the rest of him. It was oddly mesmerising.

"When did you hear?" he asked, pawing blindly at the coffee table, where a generous measure of whiskey on the rocks sat precariously just out of reach.

My eyes flicked between his belly and the glass. It was like trying not to look at the sun.

"Two days ago", I said, trying to focus on his face. "They had me in custody just after it happened."

"Jesus fuck!" His eyes snapped to me as if I'd just called his mother something unforgivable. "They didn't think you had anything to do with it?"

The sudden look of concern on Henry's face was touching. It would have been more so if he had paused, even for a second, in reaching for his elusive drink.

"I don't know, maybe."

"Fuck, well I'll vouch for you", Henry said. "Anything you need, man."

"Right, thanks." I couldn't take it anymore. I stepped around the coffee table and sat down, retrieving the glass a moment before it tipped over. I sniffed it.

"Apple juice?" I said, passing it to him.

"It was that or vodka", he shrugged, as if that explained everything. When I continued to stare at him he half snorted, half sobbed. "Whiskey is what you drink when you are depressed about a woman. Vodka is what you drink when you are upset about your country. I ran out of whiskey, so apple juice was really the only option." He sat up and slumped heavily back into the sofa, his gut hanging over his underwear as he stared down at the ice rolling around the bottom of his glass.

"Henry, what happened? How long was she gone?"

"What do you mean, she didn't tell you?" Henry said.

"No. Two days ago was the first time I've seen her in months. Last I knew you were still living together."

"Huh", he said. He looked out the window, then

went over to the writing desk beneath it. On it sat an old typewriter, a laptop computer and a stack of crumpled paper. He licked his thumb and turned the pages, laying them face down until he found the one he wanted. Then with a surprisingly impressive feat of sleight of hand, a biro appeared which he used to draw a line through a paragraph of text.

I sighed and went over to him. "What's that?"

"A letter to Claire", he said, downing the apple juice and wincing as if it burnt his throat. "Aside from drinking, it's the only way I know how to deal with it. She was with someone else, wasn't she? I thought it was you. Sorry."

I thought he was going to break down again, but instead he stuffed the pages of his letter into his pocket and put his hand on my shoulder and squeezed. "How are you holding up anyway?" he asked, with such sincerity and attentiveness I considered the question for a moment before recovering from what I can only describe as conversational whiplash.

It was always like this with Henry. He was no mage, but he could talk like no other. He also knew all about mages; Claire had confided in him years ago and introduced him to a few of us. He was a writer by trade, mostly periodicals but also a handful of novels. Most mages tended to gravitate towards someone expressive like

Henry. Charismatic, creative, good with words. On a practical level, it made sense to be with someone like that, someone you could feed off. But there was more to it than that. When it worked, it would work beautifully. You could never be quite as in tune with another person as you could be with a mage. We could literally put ourselves in our partner's shoes, feel exactly what they felt. It was like the most intense couples therapy imaginable. It was a slippery slope, though. Drink too much of the proverbial Kool-Aid and the lines would start to blur, you forgot to separate them from you. After that it's only a matter of time before things turn south when you finally figured it out again.

"Enough, Henry", I said, firmly. "You need to tell me what happened. When did Claire leave? Do you know where she went, who she was staying with? Have you any idea who might've done this to her?"

He sighed. "She left about a month ago", he said, and for a moment I thought I might get some specifics out of him. "It doesn't matter. She's gone. Left us both for good this time." He lifted the empty glass to his lips then lowered it again when he realised it was empty.

"Henry", I said, just as the phone started ringing. I glanced at it on the windowsill behind the typewriter. A number eight shone from the charging cradle in red LEDs. "Have you checked your messages?"

He groaned. "I don't have the energy for all that."

"All what?"

"The family, police all that. It's too much. Since Mrs Parkes told me what happened I've been incommunicado."

"Claire's mum told you about the murder?"

"Yeah, why?"

"Then when did you speak to the police?"

"Are you joking? I told you I can't be dealing with all that. They'll blame me for it. Claire's mum said as much. They always look at the boyfriend first."

"So, you thought avoiding the police was the way to deal with that? That's probably them, Henry. They are probably getting a warrant to turn this place upside down if you haven't even given a statement." I looked around, hoping there was nothing too damning. "Don't you get it? This makes you look guilty."

"Don't be daft, I was here when it happened."

"Were you with anyone?"

"Of course not", he said, indignant.

The phone stopped ringing for a second, then started up again. This time it was accompanied by a heavy banging downstairs.

I rolled my eyes, stepped over towards the door and opened it, as heavy-booted footsteps came charging up the stairs.

I wedged the door open and walked back over to Henry, who was starting to panic. He picked up an empty whiskey bottle by the neck and drew it back like a club. I snatched it from him, clipped him round the ear and put the bottle back on the table, out of reach.

"Henry, you are fucking innocent, so stop acting guilty", I said, putting my hands on my head and interlacing my fingers.

Henry mimicked me, though he started to cry. "What if I am guilty?" he said sadly. "What if it was all my fault?"

Before I could offer any comfort or chastise him for saying something so stupid, armoured men with riot shields stormed into the room and tackled us to the ground.

CHAPTER 9

"Hello, Detective", I said, as I was lowered into an armchair, my hands cuffed behind my back. Henry was similarly restrained, only he was slumped on the sofa sideways looking utterly morose.

Detective Stone didn't reply immediately. She was standing at the centre of the room dividing officers into pairs and sending them off into different rooms of the flat to start searching the place. Two more had already started going through the kitchen drawers and the several bookcases which framed the living room.

She finally came over to me. "Mr Chase, have you got any weapons on your person? Any sharp objects?"

I shook my head. "Nothing like that, no, unless you're worried about getting a paper cut."

She nodded and proceeded to empty out my pockets onto the table while another officer did the same with Henry.

"Careful with that, I've not typed it up yet", I heard Henry saying.

I looked over as the officer leafed through the pages of Henry's crumpled letter. "Err ma'am?" he said waving her over. He was barely onto the second page.

My heart dropped like a stone as I considered what Henry might have said in that letter. I watched her read through every page.

"Book him", she said.

"Henry Pullman, I'm arresting you on suspicion of murder…" the officer started.

"Fin?" Henry said, in a small voice as they took him out of the room and down the stairs.

Detective Stone came and sat on the edge of the coffee table. The room was empty now except for the two officers rummaging through drawers in the kitchen and another standing by the door talking into a radio.

"Why are you here?" she asked. I could tell by her tone that my presence here complicated things for her. She looked tired.

"He called me this morning. He sounded like he was in trouble. I didn't quite realise how much trouble. I'm sorry, I assumed he had already been cleared of any suspicion. I figured he would be the first person you went to."

"There was a delay with the warrant and he

refused to speak to us otherwise."

"What was in the letter?" I asked.

"An apology. Reads a lot like a confession though."

"He didn't do this", I said firmly. "He's not capable of it."

"You mean he's not..?" she glanced over her shoulder.

"No, he isn't."

"Well it doesn't matter, I have to follow the evidence on this. We have more than enough to question him with. Did you know he was following her? He admits it in the letter."

"Jesus", I sighed. "I didn't, but I guess it doesn't surprise me."

"You are mentioned in here too."

"Yeah, he scribbled something out when I told him it wasn't me she had run off with. What did it say?"

"He says that he would understand if it had been you, the two of you always looked out for each other and that he wouldn't have stood in the way if that's what she really wanted."

I looked away as my eyes started to sting. I cleared my throat until I was confident I could trust my voice again. "Are you arresting me or can I get out of these handcuffs?"

She dug out a set of keys from her pocket and I turned to the side so she could unlock them.

"Did he give you anything?"

"She left about a month ago, that's basically all he told me before you lot came barging in."

"He didn't leave us much choice."

"No, I know. I'm sorry, It's fine really. It's good the police can clear him of any involvement. You might actually get some sense out of him once he calms down a bit."

"You're sure he couldn't have done this?"

"Positive. The reason they've been together for so long is because he doesn't get jealous. Whenever Claire fell off the wagon and disappeared for a week or two, he never got angry."

"Sounds implosive to me", she said.

"Trust me, I know it's strange, but their entire relationship is a sort of functional co-dependency. If he got to keep her the rest of the time, he could forgive her when she slipped. It was why they worked so well together."

She must have read something in my eyes or my tone because she asked, "And she and you didn't?"

"Right. Mages don't pair well together. It's like having two alcoholics trying to take care of each other", I said. "Can someone else interview

Henry? I'm going to have a talk with Greg Thomas, you should be there."

"We've already spoken to him. His alibi is airtight and we can't see any motive."

"I don't think he had anything to do with the murders, but he might know more than he realises. Do you know where he is staying?"

#

Detective Stone gave me the address and we drove separately, me with Amber in the Austin, and Liv in a black BMW. She didn't want to give her department any cause to worry about her judgement. Taking a former suspect to interview another potential suspect was hardly standard procedure, after all.

I had another bout of aftershocks on the journey across town. I noticed it more quickly this time as even with the windows open and the wind blasting through the cabin my skin started to prickle with sweat. I started writing before the shakes took me, allowing the endless stream of dialogue to flow out and onto the pages of my notebook. It read something like a transcript of a recorded conversation between six different people. I tried to mediate and give everyone room to speak but the result was still a disjointed mess where voices competed and talked over one another. I caught sight of Amber looking at me strangely in the mirror and guessed my facial expressions were flipping between whoever was the active speaker at the time. I slumped down lower in my chair to hide myself from view.

Amber pulled in behind the Detective's car and I got out and went to the boot of the Austin and pulled out a pair of running shoes. While I changed, Liv came around the side of the taxi, her arms crossed against the chill in the air.

"Anticipating a chase, or is that another mage thing?" she asked as I finished tying my laces off and pulled off my overcoat.

"Just a precaution", I said, slipping the cigarette I had rolled on the drive over onto my ear.

"Okay, ready?"

'Yes", I said, following her up a gravel driveway leading to a spacious group of modern flats. The Detective rang the buzzer and waited.

"Hello?"

"Hello, Mr Thomas. It's Detective Stone, we spoke yesterday. I just have a couple more questions for you", she said into the intercom.

"I already told you everything. Please just leave me alone."

"It will only take a minute, sir", she pressed.

There was a pause, then the door buzzed and clicked and we climbed the stairs to the top floor.

I examined the spotless landing, noting the lack

of any post or even a single takeaway menu. The carpeting was new, the walls painted a metallic grey. I decided the effect could have been cold and industrial, but due to some cleverly-placed lighting, the complex felt minimalist and clean.

I was warm in the face by the time we stopped outside flat five. Beside the door sat an expensive road bike.

"Know anything about bikes?" Liv asked, looking at the frame.

I thought for a moment. "Not today, you?" I said, pulling out my phone and taking a picture for Mrs Thomas.

"Enough to know I'm looking at about six months of my salary," she said.

I pocketed my phone just as the door swung open.

"You! What the fuck is he doing here?" he said, backing away a little.

I did my best not to smile when I saw how bruised the knuckles of his right hand were.

"This is an associate of mine. Mr Chase is helping with our investigation", she said, with a placating gesture. "We all just want to find out what happened and do everything we can to find the one responsible."

"Helping? He broke into my house", Greg said, staring at me as if I might attack him.

"Actually, your wife granted me access. But I'm not here about that, the divorce can wait", I said, off-handed.

"We just have a few more questions. We'll try not to take up too much of your time. Can we come in?" Liv said. She seemed to have a knack for diluting tension.

"Fine, as long as it's quick, and he keeps the hell away from me. I was about to take a ride to clear my head."

"That is quite a bike you have there."

"Thanks, with everything that has been going on, I've only taken it out once since I bought the thing."

Greg walked us down into a sunken living room space with a large brown leather corner sofa taking up one half of the square space. Opposite, and mounted onto the wall, was a large flatscreen TV. Speakers were also mounted in recesses in the ceiling. It was the perfect bachelor's den. The entire apartment was open plan, the immaculate kitchen and granite work surfaces sparkled from across the room and brushed steel implements hung from hooks above an industrial-looking oven.

"HD?" I asked, pointing to the TV on the wall.

He looked at me as if I was making a joke. "Yes, now can we get on with these questions please?"

Liv gave me a warning look and we both sat down on the sofa while Greg took the chair.

"When did you meet Claire?" I asked.

"We've been over this already", he said.

"Please, Mr Thomas."

"Fine. We started seeing each other about a month ago."

I nodded. "How did you meet?"

"My wife and I have been having some problems for about a year. Claire was my counsellor, for about two sessions six months ago."

"You only went twice? Why did you stop?" I asked.

"I didn't think I would get anything out of it, no matter how long I went. I was too uncomfortable the whole time. I didn't see her again until about two months ago. We started going to the same gym. Things just happened."

I looked around the flat and realised the place wasn't just new, it had recently been cleaned. I could smell the Pledge coming off the floor speakers behind me. "When did she move in?"

"About two weeks ago."

"Where are her things?"

"In bags in the spare room. I couldn't look at them any more."

"So, the other house? Where I saw you two days ago?"

"We were getting ready to move there. This place is a rental, just temporary, until I got my affairs in order. Now... I don't know what I'll do."

"Regarding your divorce, you mean?"

"I suppose so, yes", he said, rubbing his face. "I guess I didn't really think about it."

"You have two girls?" Stone asked. Her voice had grown a little harder.

He shook his head then rose from his chair. "Let me get you something to drink", he said, walking into the kitchen.

I watched him cross the room, then I turned to face Liv. "Does he seem any different than when you first interviewed him?"

"Not really, but he is probably in shock. Not everyone cries", she said. I thought of Henry and hoped he was alright. He was probably already in an interview room but there wasn't anything I could do for him but try and find the real killer.

"Ask him about his wife for me? I suspect he won't take kindly to my asking."

"Do you love your wife?" she said, as he returned with two glasses of water. He and I both blinked at the bluntness of the question.

"No, I don't. What do you want me to say? She's

a great mother, always makes time for the kids, puts them first. I respect that, it's why I stayed as long as I did. But without the kids, there's nothing between us, hasn't been for months, years even. She knows that, even if she won't admit it."

"What's she like?"

"Direct, a little cold sometimes. Very determined. She's more in love with her position in life than she ever has been with me."

"You make her sound like a bit of a gold digger?" I said.

He sat down his face turning a little harder as he appraised me. "Who exactly are you to be working with the police anyway? I've not seen any ID."

"Please, just answer the question Mr Thomas", Liv said.

"Fine", he said, nodding to Stone. "I wouldn't use those words exactly, but yes. She always wanted to be rich. Marrying me got her that wish. She's never worked a day in her life. It's not her fault exactly, but it's hard to have any sort of perspective if you've never washed a dish or met a deadline in your life. You know she spends two hours at the gym every day while I'm at work?"

"You're jealous?" I said.

"Wouldn't you be? When I was at home I used to

leave the house at seven and get home at seven. I'd spend time with the kids in the evenings and weekends when I didn't have to work. It doesn't leave time for much else." He looked at us both. "I can see you are both thinking I'm that typical rich prick. In your shoes, I probably would too. But tell me, what's the point in having money if you never get to enjoy it? Jennifer loves Yoga and I love biking. Jennifer does Yoga every single fucking day. She'll sit in traffic for an hour just to get to a class. That bike out there, I bought it six months ago and I've only taken it out once. You think that's fair?"

"I think half of all your assets and joint custody of the kids is more than fair", I said.

"Half?" he laughed incredulously. "I'll throw every last penny on a pyre before I give her half of everything."

I nodded. "Fair enough, I promised her I'd pass on those terms."

Stone frowned at me.

"Did Claire start acting any differently over the last few weeks? Was there anywhere she went regularly, anyone she met up with?" I asked.

The mention of Claire's name sent a sombre chill back through the room. "We both took some time off from work. We spent pretty much the entire time together."

"What sort of things did you do together? Where did you go?"

"We did all the things we couldn't do when we were in work. Went to the cinema at two in the afternoon, got drunk, spent hours reading books in coffee shops. Slept late, all that stuff."

"No time spent apart?" I asked, inwardly sighing at how far she had spiralled so quickly.

"I think she went into the office maybe once a week when I went to see the kids. That's about it."

"Her office? Do you know why she went in if she was on leave?" Stone asked.

"I'm not really sure, I never asked. I think she was feeling guilty about all the time she had off."

I nodded to Stone; it was worth looking into. I had assumed she must have come into contact with someone new in her final hours, but maybe the killer had been someone she'd met at work.

"When you went shopping, did you go to many charity shops? Second hand books, vinyl, anything like that?"

"Actually, we did at first. I think she liked the character of those places. But she seemed to lose interest after the first couple of weeks."

"You can't think of her mentioning anyone new in her life? Anyone at all?"

"I've been racking my brain since the first

interview, but no. Sorry. I don't remember her mentioning anyone."

Stone and I exchanged a look, confirming we were both out of questions.

Greg walked us to the door and promised to contact Liv if he thought of anything.

I walked with Liv down two flights of stairs then stopped. "Ah I left my tobacco. I'll catch up", I said, jogging back up the stairs.

When Greg opened the door I stared at him for a moment before speaking.

"I touched the cigarette on my ear and took in the smallest touch of power I could. "Hear me out", I said, and his mouth slowly closed. "You are right. Half of everything does seem unfair. But she's a good mother, raising *your* children. You said so yourself. And you did cheat on her, humiliate her."

"What the hell is this?" he said.

"Just hear me out", I said again, letting a little more power into the words. It wasn't enough power to force him. I deliberately hadn't brought nearly enough with me to do that. I just needed to be heard. "Do you really want to fight her on this? Even if she doesn't get sole custody, she could still turn them against you."

"She told you to come here and threaten me?"

"No, and I don't even think she would do that, at

least not deliberately. But she could make it very difficult for you to see them. Push the workaholic angle hard enough and suddenly you are an unhealthy influence in their lives."

"She has some fucking nerve."

I could see he was getting ready to slam the door in my face. The subtle weave of magic was already broken and my words were only making him angrier. This was going to be a messy, long divorce. They were both too proud for it to be otherwise. One of them had to back down.

"Even if you keep your job after all this murder business blows over, have you considered what your prospects will be like?"

He froze mid door slam. "What? I had nothing to do with it."

"Right, but there are no other suspects at the moment. If the newspapers catch wind of the fact you were sleeping with her, they could run with it for weeks. Months even, if the actual murderer isn't found."

"You'd go to the papers? Tell them I was with Claire?"

I could see the same fire in his eyes when he'd swung at me two days earlier. I was out of keepsake; it would hurt me a lot more than it would hurt him this time.

I shook my head. "No, I won't."

"Bullshit."

"I won't need to, Greg. Your wife and her solicitors will figure it out on their own."

"If they ruin my reputation I'd be worth nothing to her. Fifty percent of nothing..."

"Is nothing. Which is exactly what she would be getting anyway if the settlement went your way."

"She wouldn't do that to me. She's cold, not cruel", Greg retorted, though his words lacked conviction.

"Maybe not, but what about her solicitors?" I shrugged. "Look what it boils down to is a percentage? Twenty? Thirty? Is it really worth all the effort? If you sign those divorce papers today, then it's in your wife's interest to stand by you through all this."

His entire body seemed to wilt before my eyes. His shoulders dropped half an inch and he stared through me as if I wasn't even there. "Think of your kids. What's best for them. She's expecting you at six this evening. Just go see her and be willing to talk", I said, before turning and walking away. I felt like I was going to throw up.

I felt even worse as I turned onto the next flight of stairs and found Stone sitting on the bottom step with her back to me. I reluctantly followed her down the stairs and out to the cars.

CHAPTER 10

Liv didn't speak until we were both seated in the back of the taxi with the partition firmly closed.

"What was that?" she asked, folding her arms across her chest.

"I was doing him a favour."

"By blackmailing him? I'm a police officer, I can't just ignore things like that."

"It was hardly blackmail, barely even a threat. I was merely voicing an opinion, that things would go much better for everyone if he followed my advice. There was no coercion."

"You have a vested interest in your client who is paying you to do a job. He could press charges."

"He could, I doubt he would get anywhere with it though. My contract with Mrs Thomas will terminate once the divorce papers are signed. If I personally wanted to benefit, I would have said nothing and dragged this out for as long as possible."

"You didn't force him? You know, *compel* him?" she asked.

I was momentarily surprised by her use of the term until I recalled the shooting. Being forced to shoot someone against your will was probably one of the worst uses of Compulsion magic imaginable.

"No, I didn't force him to do anything. I encouraged him to hear me out, but that's all."

"Could you have? Forced him, I mean."

"That's not the right question."

"What? Why not?"

"Physically, yes it's possible in the same way that you could pick up a gun and shoot someone. If you are asking me if I *would* do that, then no, not unless it was life or death."

I was eager to discuss the interview with Mr Thomas but I could tell whatever was on her mind needed confronting now, so I waited. Liv's eyes cast around the inside of the cab as if she were looking for the right words for something. Her eyes came to rest on the nickel-plated ashtray embedded in the door.

"How are you not rich?" she asked.

I was so wrong-footed by the question my mouth hung open while I tried to put a context around the question. "You mean, why don't I just walk into a bank and demand they hand over all the money?"

"Right, maybe not by a bank heist but there must be a hundred ways you could do it. High stakes poker or blackjack games, things like that? Couldn't you just convince them you were getting twenty one all the time?"

"Sure it's possible if you had enough power, and you were clever enough in your execution. Security cameras and things like that can be tricky, and anything involving modifying memory is always unreliable and dangerous, but there are ways, sure."

"So why aren't you ruling the country, or at least driving around in a more expensive car? Are all mages serial underachievers, or moral elitists? I don't get it."

I considered her for a moment, frowning.

"What? Why aren't you saying anything? Did I touch a nerve?" she said.

"Relax, it's just a big question. I want to do it justice. Okay, so let's assume I'm flat broke and decide I want to make some money."

"Imagine that?" Amber snorted.

I frowned listening to the muffled beeps and chirps of Amber's phone through the partition as she played some game or other. "Let's say I decide to steal Amber's phone, only she keeps it in a locked box I cannot get to without the use of magic. Okay?"

"Sure."

"Now tell me, would you ever steal?" I asked.

"No, not unless there was no other option to feed myself or someone I loved."

"Pragmatic and reasonable answer", I said. "Now if you did decide to steal within the criteria you just described, would you ever have any doubts about it, do you think?"

"Probably, but if it was within that scenario, I doubt it would stop me."

"Right, so level-headed, sensible you. The you on basically nine days out of a ten, would happily steal that phone to feed your family. So, you start channelling, but suddenly you are not just you anymore. There's someone else there too. Perhaps you ripped a page out of teenager's diary and consumed that. Now suddenly it's you and this other girl trying to steal. Now the girl's father is so strict, she's terrified of being found out. Suddenly you are fighting yourself and are reluctant to take the phone."

"Sure, but I'm guessing you pick more carefully than that? You could easily use something from someone you knew wouldn't have any qualms about stealing."

"Right, in which case you would probably get away with the phone."

"So far it sounds like you are agreeing with me?"

"Right, I am. But the phone isn't nearly as valuable to a mage as the keepsake, in that scenario."

"Because you need them to survive?"

"Exactly. It's possible, it just isn't very likely. Sure, if I had to steal the phone for money to feed someone else, then I could do it, no problem. Odds are the magic could be better utilised elsewhere to meet the same goal, though."

"Ok, so that explains petty crime. What about something bigger?"

"Well it's just like regular crime: the bigger the payoff, the bigger the risk. To really cash in takes a lot of power and even then it's never risk-free. The greater the power you channel, the more of those other personalities step in. You could end up killing someone in a panic, or running out terrified before you've even stepped inside the bank. It's a risk I've never known any mage to take. I'm not saying it doesn't ever happen, it's just difficult and not likely."

"What about politics?"

"Mages never make it far in politics. We'd be in and out of addiction groups too often for it to go unnoticed. That tends to leave a bad taste in the mouth for voters. I know a few who have dabbled in big business though. Closers, barristers, people like that. But to my knowledge they rarely pull the magic card. When they do it's usually directed internally for a little confidence or charisma."

"Why not, surely they could win any case or close any deal they wanted?"

"In a courtroom, convincing an entire jury without looking suspicious in front of the judge? They could if they had enough power, but it would be like a diabetic selling off the next five years of their insulin supply in order to win a single professional victory. Technically possible, but I can't see it happening."

"What about buying Google for a hefty discount then?"

"Compelling every one of their ten, I think, board of directors to sell up and drawing enormous attention to yourself in the process?" I shrugged. "Plus I'm fairly confident either Page or Brin is a mage. I reckon they'd have some pretty substantial safeguards to that sort of magical tampering."

I watched her eyebrows rise up her forehead and I thought she had added a few more pieces to the puzzle. I couldn't imagine having your world view quite so completely and utterly shattered. It must have been like growing up Christian or Jewish and finding proof that the Jedi had been right all along.

I busied myself with checking my phone messages as she sat in thought for a few more moments. Dad had called again while we were interviewing Mr Thomas. I made it through the first half of the message this time, before cringing and hanging up.

"So, where to next?" I asked.

"It's thin but the only lead we have is Claire's office. The staff have all already given statements though, so I'm not sure what good it will do. After that I'm out of ideas until the labs come back."

"Any luck identifying the other victims?"

"Not yet. Definitely not any of the staff; they've all been accounted for. The full toxicology report should come in today. Maybe that will give us something. Have you had any more thoughts on the magic side of things?"

Beside me, in the Tupperware box holding my dwindling record collection, sat the moleskin notebook with my detailed notes. I hadn't opened it again since my pen left the page but the details of what I had seen were still fresh enough in my mind to chill me to my core.

"Still working on it", I said, rolling my phone over in my hand. "If Claire's office gives us nothing then I have a source I can call to help on that side of things."

#

We made it across the river in good time, and arrived just before the early lunch crowd started filling up the streets. The BT tower sat looming like some giant alien relic; its unforgiving chrome aesthetic made me think of an enormous subterranean robot from the eighties rising just high enough out of the sewers to give the more modest brown stones of London a thick-knuckled middle finger.

Claire's practice was located a little south of Regent's Park, just off Baker Street. Amber mounted the curb as if she were pitching to get air time before breaking hard, indicating and pulling the Austin to a stop on a set of freshly painted yolk-orange double yellows. The freshness of the paint, and the fact I had a high-ranking police officer in tow, made the illegality of it twice as satisfying. It almost made up for her total disregard for things like tyres, a clutch and brake pads.

Amber seemed to be hoping to get under Detective Stone's skin. I caught her peering out at the detective with a malevolent grin as though she expected Liv to object to the repeated parking violations and questionable road etiquette. Liv said nothing, but then it *was* London, and she had more pressing concerns.

I glanced up at the wall of nondescript office

space then lowered my head through the passenger side window of the taxi.

"Go get some lunch. If you don't hear otherwise, meet us back here in an hour."

Amber glared at me in that aggressively bored way teenagers of a certain disposition seem to keep on hand as their default expression. I beamed at her then followed Detective Stone up to the office block's doors.

To the right of a reception desk sat two turnstiles, beyond which stood an uncarpeted wide staircase and a single set of lift doors. The receptionist, a man of stocky build, faded tattoos and advancing years, quickly revealed himself to be not a receptionist at all but a security guard. The distinction was made instantly apparent by the surly manner with which he greeted us after he was forced to look away from an episode of *Highway Interceptors,* which was unfolding on a fifty-inch television mounted on the wall behind him.

"Who are you here to see?" he said, tapping the mute button on the remote. The sound of tinny sirens cut out immediately.

"The psychiatrist's office", I said, quickly skimming the list of company names and logos on the wall behind the guard.

"June and Silver Practitioners", Liv added, beating me to the punch.

The guard all but rolled his eyes. "No appointment then? You need an appointment so I can sign you in."

"I'm Detective Stone", she said showing the man her ID. "My associate and I will need to speak with their team."

"Oh, right." The guard wheeled slowly to the other side of his desk, leafed through several pages in a binder then dialled a number on his desk phone.

"Hello, got a Detective Stone here wanting to come up." He cleared his throat, and turned to Stone. "Have you got a warrant?"

"No, we don't need one to ask questions", Stone said.

"Nah, they don't", he repeated down the phone. "Right, thanks." He hung up.

"You can't go up without a warrant because they have clients in at the moment. One of the doctors will come down once he's finished with a patient. Have a seat."

I went over to the sofa and immediately made myself comfortable, stretching my arms out across the backrest. Stone remained standing while the guard un-muted the TV and resumed watching his show.

We waited for the remainder of *Police Interceptors* and almost an entire episode of *Cowboy Builders* before anyone showed. I was just reading the disappointing conclusions regarding a family still chasing eighteen grand from a bodged loft conversion when the doctor arrived. He came down the stairs at a jog and smiled apologetically.

"I am so sorry to have kept you both waiting, I was with a patient. I'm Doctor Silver", he said, shaking our hands in turn once he had pushed his way through the turnstile.

"We were hoping to ask you some questions about Claire Parkes?" Stone said.

"Of course, we were all devastated to hear the news", he said. "Just awful. She was such bright light around here." I felt my throat go dry at the Doctor's kind words. He sounded genuinely crushed about Claire.

"Is there somewhere we can talk in private?" Stone asked.

"Sure. We can't really take you up to our offices, but the third floor is empty and they have a boardroom we can use." He turned to the security guard. "Harry, could we have two visitors passes please?" his clipped tone, marking his disapproval of the TV.

Harry grumbled but pulled two red lanyards from a drawer and handed one to each of us. The clips hung empty and I saw a flicker of annoyance cross the Doctor's face, but he recovered his smile quickly enough, and led us towards the stairs. He glanced at the lift as we passed but made no further comment.

Once we were out of earshot of the guard, he immediately started apologising about Harry, their new old security guard.

"He's ex-Navy. We were having so much trouble finding a decent receptionist with enough wherewithal to challenge people from just going upstairs, the building owner eventually just hired him behind our backs." He shook his head. "Anyway, how is the investigation coming along?" he asked as we arrived on the third floor.

Silver walked us past a deserted reception desk with a logo behind it which looked vaguely pharmaceutical, and through the centre of an open office space which looked as if it ran the length of the entire floor. The third floor was entirely devoid of furniture, with the exception of the occasional broken or unwanted office chair. Littered across the sky-blue carpet every ten feet lay a phone plugged into a socket in the floor.

Doctor Silver walked us across the gutted floor and into a glass-walled conference room. This was furnished, though the decor looked as if it hadn't been updated since the mid-nineties or late eighties. I sat down in one of the high-backed, faux leather executive chairs and was surprised at how comfortable I was looking out over London. The three of us took up one corner of the large oval conference table.

"I'm not sure how much further help I can be, but I'll do anything I can", he said, smiling.

I smiled back, finding it difficult not to soften a little. Doctor Silver was clearly devastated by Claire's death, but it wasn't just that. His entire demeanour projected comfort and safety. He wore khakis and an old, rather than vintage, suede jacket, over a white shirt and black jumper. His hair was dark brown and shaggy, though he was immaculately clean shaven and wore understated glasses. The combination could have come off as a little pretentious, like a San Francisco barista, but somehow he made it work. Even Stone looked at ease around him, flashing the occasional smile, her body turned towards him as they spoke.

"So it says in your report that Claire was taking a leave of absence since July 24?" she said.

"That's right. The work can be pretty challenging at times. No-one is immune. I think she just needed a few weeks to regroup."

"And she never came in during all that time?"

"Hmm nope, we spoke on the phone, but no, she never came in. I'm sorry, that's all I can really tell you."

I watched the two of them, a part of me inwardly smiling as they mirrored one another in a bouncing head nod. Stone seemed to give herself a slight shake as if suddenly remembering something.

"And did she have any new patients we should be aware of? Did she mention anyone particularly challenging before she went on leave?"

"None that I'm aware of, I'm sorry. Once the warrant comes through of course you can have copies of all her case files."

"I understand. We should have it by tomorrow, all being well."

"Great, great." His voice lifted slightly and he cleared his throat.

"Well, thank you for your time, Doctor. I think that's all we have for now", she said.

"Oh, please call me Steven", he said, smiling more broadly at Stone.

"Okay, thank you, Steven", she said, her cheeks flushing by the tiniest degree. Had I not been so relaxed and watching the two of them with such idle fascination, I would have missed it entirely.

Good for you, I thought sitting back into my chair, running my hands deeper into the armrests.

"Anytime, and if you have any more questions or anything you have my number right?"

Stone flicked through the pages of a note pad. "I have you on 020..."

"Oh, that's the main work line. We have our own receptionist but she only works Tuesdays and Thursdays. Any other time you'll get Harry. Who knows where you might get redirected to." He raised his eyebrows, to show what fun that would be for us and we both laughed. It felt good to be laughing again, but at the same time, some part of me flinched at the sound.

"Here, I'll give you my mobile. Call me anytime, I always keep it on me", he said.

"Except during sessions?" I said.

They both looked at me as if they had forgotten I was there. I almost had myself.

"Right, of course", Steven said, smiling. "Well I should probably be getting back." He glanced at the clock on the wall.

I smiled back, I couldn't help it. *I couldn't help it.*

"Actually", I said, as we all stood to leave. "would you mind if I got a copy of that number too? Just in case I have some questions later on." I dug into my pockets as I skirted around Stone and stopped beside Steven and started emptying my pockets onto the desk. I found a pen and a clean napkin which I handed to him.

"I can give you a copy? I have it here", Stone said, looking irritated by my rudeness.

"It's fine", Steven said, smiling again at Stone. "Anything to help the investigation."

I smiled again. My mouth was starting to hurt, I was smiling so much.

He leant over the desk and wrote out the number.

"Oh, could you write your name too, I don't want you getting lost among the others", I said, grinning like an idiot.

"No problem", he laughed, companionably. "Here you go." He looked up reluctantly. "Now I should really be getting back to it."

I took the napkin from him in my left hand, then extended my right which Steven shook. His hand was clammy.

"Thanks for this."

"Anytime", he said, blinking.

"*Datgelu...*" I said pausing as I struggled to recall the Welsh word for truth, "*...gwirionedd.*" The meaning of the words wasn't important, nor was my butchering of the accent. They could have been in any language or not spoken aloud at all. Using them simply gave clarity to the intended reaction. The napkin flared, engulfing my hand in fire just as I punched Steven squarely across the jaw. Steven fell onto his back looking up at me. He wasn't stunned, he was terrified. He started pushing himself back away from me. He only stopped when he reached the glass wall.

"Oh god, you are one of them!" he cried, pressing himself into the wall.

"Jesus Christ, Fin! What the hell?" Stone shouted, rushing forwards.

I caught her arm. "Give it a second", I said, watching the look of shock dissolve into confusion.

"What was that?" she said, looking down at Steven.

"Magic. Someone put a spell on him to distract us." As I said the words, terror unlike any I could remember clawed up through the pit of my stomach like a frozen hand, extending slowly towards my heart. "Someone upstairs", I said, looking up at the lowered ceiling, feeling tears gathering at the corners of my eyes as my whole body started to tremble.

CHAPTER 11

Liv rolled Steven onto his belly, planted a knee into the centre of his back and handcuffed him. I shuddered, focusing on the Doctor and forcing myself to recognise that the fear I was experiencing wasn't my own, but Steven's. It didn't help; I could feel the room closing in around me. I felt suffocated, as if the air in the room was thinning. I wanted to run, get away from that office block, but my feet wouldn't move.

"You're hyperventilating. Sit down", Liv said, pushing me back into a chair. I couldn't find enough strength to object. I continued staring at the doctor as he wept into the carpet, muttering incomprehensibly. It sounded like he was begging for his life.

He hadn't tried to run. The thought stuck me as odd, given how scared we both were. I wondered if whatever magic that had made him so endearing to us had also dulled his sense of fear. But why stay? He had been by the exit just minutes ago; he could have escaped whatever waited above.

Another wave of panic shook me and my vision tunnelled. My voice failing, I mimed smoking a cigarette to Liv. She started searching my pockets. She found my tobacco and started rolling me a cigarette. I saw her stuffing the phrase, *You make me better than I ever thought I could be,* into the papers before licking the paper and sticking it down. She pushed one end between my lips and lit the other.

"Liv", I choked, the tension in my frayed nerves easing a fraction. "We have to get upstairs."

"You look like you can barely stand", she said, retrieving her phone from her pocket.

"We need to get up there now. I think... I think his daughter's in danger. It's why he didn't leave when he could have", I said between gasps. I failed again to get my feet under me.

I continued to inhale deeply as she dragged Steven to his feet.

"What's up there? What the hell is going on here?"

"My daughter, I can't reach her", he said.

I felt every sobbing word like he was voicing my own worst fears. I pulled harder on the cigarette, holding the smoke in my lungs for five seconds before exhaling. My strength gradually returned and my hands stopped shaking.

"Where is she?" I asked, getting to my feet. My voice barely shook when I spoke, as borrowed courage hardened against the panic.

"In the lift. I don't know how he did it... Please let her go..." he became incomprehensible. I started noticing details I had missed before, which the spell had kept hidden. The sweat around his collar and the crumpled jumper, the faded remnants of ash across his knees.

Liv led the way as I pushed Steven after her, his wrists still cuffed behind his back. The doctor recoiled each time I touched him.

"Listen, I'm not like him, alright. I don't hurt people", I said firmly. He was too far gone to believe me, he just cowered and marched after Liv.

I forced him to keep pace with Liv as we passed the empty reception desk and continued up the stairs to the fourth, then fifth, floor. The fifth floor was split between a solicitor's firm and Claire's psychiatric practice. We took a left after the stairs and pushed cautiously through a set of double doors and into a large but comfortable reception area and waiting room. The floor was littered with piles of plastic multi-coloured files lying open with wads of paper next to a large shredder. They had the same sky blue carpet as the vacant office two floors below, only instead of desk phones there lay chequered lines of bin bags stuffed to overflowing with shredded clumps of paperwork.

Steven turned immediately to the left wall, where a desk had been flipped on its side. It took me a second to realise it was wedged between the lift doors, a heavy chain wrapped around its centre as if it was weighted there.

Steven approached the desk and put his ear to it. "Honey, can you hear me? Stephie? It's Dad!" Steven called through a narrow crack.

"Daddy?" A quiet voice echoed back.

"Jesus Christ." Stone stepped up to the wedged desk and peered down. "It looks like she's tied to the chain a few feet down. I'll call the fire department." Stone pulled out her phone.

"No, he said she would fall if we called the police."

She looked at me then back to Steven. "What else did he tell you?"

"He.. he said if I shredded every document in here he would come back and free her." He shook his head.

"How long has she been stuck down there?"

"Since this morning. Please, you have to leave and let me finish before he comes back." The doctor pleaded. "You don't understand, he can... do things. Impossible things." He hesitated and looked towards a closed door across the room.

The name on the frosted glass read Doctor Terrance P. June.

Stone went over to the door and opened it. She looked inside, her eyes fixed on the floor and lingered there. After a moment she pulled the door shut and returned with the same look on her face I had seen when she'd interviewed me at the police station.

Steven was staring at Liv as if he hadn't quite believed what was on the other side of that door until the look on her face confirmed it. "I don't know how..."

I swallowed past the bile in my throat. "Forget about that now. What else did he tell you to do?"

"He left a number and said to call if any more police showed up. I called him an hour ago when you first arrived. He said to get rid of you and he would come by and free Stephanie."

"Where is the number?" Liv asked.

Steven pulled a scrap of paper from his jacket and handed it to her. She took a small plastic evidence bag from her coat and let him drop the phone number in before sealing it and pocketing it.

A scream echoed up the lift shaft as individual chain links un-bonded themselves and clattered to the ground until only a single line remained across the back of the desk.

"Please, just go!" he begged.

"What about the lift doors on the floor below?"

He shook his head. "I tried that, they won't open. It's like they've been welded shut. He said if I tried to pull her out, the chain would break. I didn't believe him," he said, pointing to a pile of individual chain links. I noticed three separate groups within the pile. Each of the broken links looked as if they had been prised open with a crow bar, one by one.

I sucked hard on the remains of my cigarette and forced clarity into my mind.

"Please..." Steven said, the word feeble as if he was losing all hope.

"I need him," I said. "Un-cuff him." I pulled a pen from my pocket and a piece of blank paper off the floor and pushed it at the Doctor once the cuffs came free.

"Start writing. Write about how much you would do anything to save her. Mean it."

"What?" he stared at me in utter disbelief.

"I can use it to help her but you need to start writing now", I said, pushing him towards an empty desk.

"Do it", Stone said, urging him on.

I dropped to my knees beside the broken chain links, retrieved two of the rustiest links I could find and started rubbing them together over another sheet of paper.

"What can I do?"

"Keep him writing. Get him to focus on saving his daughter, keep him away from despair. Convince him we can do this."

She went and stood beside him and started talking to him in a low, calm voice.

I lifted the piece of paper holding the copper shavings and poured them carefully into the palm of my hand. I felt Steven staring at me after something Stone had said. She kept talking, and I saw his jaw harden before he continued writing.

Liv handed him another sheet of paper and nodded to me. I swallowed the last stub of my rollie and pooled every drop of power into my hands, compressing it into the copper shavings as I approached the desk.

"*Give me sight*", I whispered into my cupped hands. I blew gently across my palms, watching a stream of red-gold flow into the gap between the lift door and the sideways desk. I held my eyes tightly closed for a few seconds until a picture started to form in my mind as the cloud of copper expanded into the elevator shaft. In my mind's eye, anything the cloud touched started to flicker and burn like a minuscule firework. Slowly the picture gained depth; first the four walls with Stephanie at the centre, swinging slightly.

I urged the rust particles higher, revealing more of the car above. I swallowed. The lift car was barely recognisable. The four corners had been crushed inwards as if a giant had attempted to crush it into something resembling a sphere. Above it I could see a single fraying wire holding it in place above Stephanie, like a conker at the end of a thin shoelace.

"Fuck", I muttered, willing the cloud towards the lift doors below Stephanie. Steven had been lucky he hadn't been able to pry the doors open. They hadn't been welded shut, but they had been wedged closed around a heavy piece of metal, the end of which was joined to another chain which ran past Stephanie and up to the crushed lift car twenty feet above her head. I guessed the killer had rigged it so it would drop the instant the doors below were opened or the desk was removed.

"Stephanie, I'm a friend of your dad's. I know you are scared, but be brave, okay? We are going to get you out in a minute."

Perhaps sensing the fear in my voice, she sniffed.

"I bet it's dark down there? Can you see anything at all?"

'It's too dark", she said, between sobs.

"Really? You mean you can't see the fireflies?" I

added, urging the rust shavings to pair up and rub against one another until they glowed like a tiny orange flame.

Stephanie sniffed and then said, "I think I see them?"

"Good girl. Now, can you watch where they are going?" I called, binding more of the little sparks together, lighting the way towards the lift doors on the floor below.

"I see", she said.

"Okay, now keep your eyes on that point, that's where your dad and the nice lady Detective will be in a few minutes. They are going to catch you. When the doors open, be ready and reach for them, okay?"

"Okay, I'll try."

"Good girl", I said, trying to stop my voice from shaking. The part of Steven's emotion I had consumed, that overwhelming sense of fear, was still there, but there was also such love and pride in that girl, more than I had ever known for anyone in my life.

Liv and Steven finished and joined me by the desk. "Will this work?" she asked.

I took the two pages and skimmed through the first. "The lift doors on the floor below aren't sealed, but they are jammed, and booby-trapped. You will be able to pry them open, but wait for my signal."

They both nodded.

"I need something I can use as a rope when the chain breaks."

"I started trying to make one out of some work shirts but they aren't strong enough", Steven said.

"Get them."

While he was gone, I took the first page of Steven's letter and consumed a fraction of it, pouring inhuman strength into my hands. I climbed onto the receptionist's desk and pushed aside one of the lowered ceiling tiles and eyed the network of steel crossbeams which held it in place. Clasping the crossbeam in both hands, I twisted and pulled until the joints snapped apart.

A dozen more precise breaks and three hard pulls, and half the ceiling crashed to the floor in a cloud of debris.

"Help me clear away the floor tiles. I just need the metal", I said, coughing.

Doctor Silver paused in the doorway looking shocked. I went over to him and took the dress shirts, suit jackets and trousers from him and set to work binding them together. "Help her clear away the tiles", I said, pouring more magic into me as the fabrics began to bleed together.

The Doctor did as I asked immediately, avoiding looking at me as his clothes started to melt into one seamless, narrow piece. I finished the rope and tied a loop in one end, and started threading it through into the lift shaft.

"Stephanie, can you put your head and both your arms through this rope and pull it tight around you?"

"I can't reach", she called back.

I fed more into the shaft until I felt her catch it on the other end.

"Okay", she said after a minute.

"You have the loop around you nice and tight?" I called.

"Yes, sir", she said.

I smiled, and gave the end a little pull, feeling the reassuring resistance of a small body at the other end. "Good girl", I called back.

I handed Stone the end of the rope and walked over to the grid of steel, feeding more power into my veins and ripping apart sections of steel with my bare hands until I had a dozen pieces, roughly fifteen feet in length. I could feel both Steven and Liv watching me from beside the lift. I did my best to ignore them as I set about crushing and pinching the ends of each bracket of steel into a point and dropping them in two equal piles either side of me, facing the lift.

"What the hell are you planning?" Liv asked.

"It's the only way I can think of to save her", I said. "When those doors open on the fourth floor, the lift car up on sixth will drop. If we remove the desk, the car will drop. We have to do both at the same time. I'll catch the car, you two catch Stephanie."

"Are you sure about this, about him?" Steven asked, looking at Stone.

"He can do it", she said firmly.

"Here", I said, reaching out to touch each of them on the shoulder.

"What are you doing?" Steven asked, recoiling.

"I'm just feeding you both a little extra strength so you can get those doors open."

"I'm sorry, it's just that's what *he* did. All he did was touch my arm and I couldn't move. I just stood there and watched as he... did all this."

"Trust him", Liv said.

I held my hands up again. Blinking anxiously, Steven finally nodded. I touched my hands to each of their shoulders and poured strength into them.

"Once you've got her, get away from the lift as quick as you can. I don't know long I can hold it for", I said, taking the end of Stephanie's life line and tying it off around my waist.

"This is insane. What if we can't get the doors open?" Steven asked.

"You will, trust me." I glanced around the room for the nearest fire alarm. "As soon as you hear that alarm or a big crash, you get that door open and grab her, okay?"

Steven looked at the rope around my waist, then nodded. They headed for the stairs. I counted to a hundred, then crumpled the rest of Steven's singed letter in my hand and reduced it to ash, feeling a lighting storm of energy gather in the pit of my stomach.

"Ready, Stephanie? It's about to get very loud, but don't worry, it's all part of the plan."

"Okay."

"Can you still see the fireflies."

"Yes, I see them", she replied.

"Alright. Here we go", I said, taking careful aim as I braced myself, one arm pressed against the wall, the other hooking behind the desk. I let energy flood into my entire body, until every nerve and cell was alight with it, then, in one sudden movement, I tore the desk free and hurled it across the room in an explosion of wood and metal. The desk crashed into the wall and the fire alarm started blaring just as Stephanie started to drop and the rope around my waist snapped tight.

The chain exploded into a shower of ash the moment the desk was removed. I kept my eyes fixed on the dark opening and threw my hand out behind me like a javelin thrower.

In the back of my mind I felt the twelve makeshift spears rise into the air behind me, as an ominous creaking echoed from above. Channelling every last drop of power, focusing on protecting my daughter no matter what, my hand shot forwards. Like Zeus himself, streaks of white lightning and a roar of wind ripped through the air around me and speared the falling lift car through the centre of its crumpled metal doors. The car halted, pinned in place against the opposite wall as a great thunderclap cracked through the room. For a moment I thought my plan had worked, but slowly, inch by inch the lift cart continued to descend.

I watched helplessly as one by one, the makeshift spears bent and snapped, and the lift continued its descent. I heard Stephie scream and I rushed forwards, but there was nothing I could do, I had used up every ounce of magic I had. I didn't care, I reached for the spears, planning to hold onto them. Even if my flailing strength only bought her an extra half a second, I would do it. Before I caught hold, the last three spears snapped and the lift plummeted.

I don't remember being hit by any debris but I was on my back the next moment, wheezing through a thick cloud of dust. I rolled to my feet and stumbled to the stairs, squinting through dust which hung like a dense fog in front of my eyes. I felt a slight pull around my waist and realised the rope was still secured around my waist, the other end trailing uselessly a few feet behind. I refused to consider what that might mean. I hurried blindly down the stairs, feeling my way. I was shouting, but barely heard my own voice. The impact had deafened me. The fire alarm was a distant hum, and worst of all, I could hear no voices, no cries of anguish or cheers of celebration. Had I failed? Had she fallen?

I lost my footing as I reached the fourth floor, and tripped before I managed to catch myself. I was halfway to the open lift doors when a strong hand caught my shoulder and wheeled me round. Liv was shouting, her eyes glassy, her hair grey-white with dust as she pulled me away from the lift and back towards the stairs. She pointed and through the fog I saw them. A little doll-like child rocking in her father's arms.

I stammered, unable to find the words. I felt hot tears tracking down my cheeks. My heart almost fell out of my chest when I finally saw her move. She hugged Steven back, her eyes open and alert. I moved to join them as relief washed over me, but Stone stopped me and put her lips to my ear.

"She's fine, but she isn't yours, Fin."

I choked back a sob and turned away as the truth of her words crashed into me. I took a step towards the banister then slumped down onto the stairs. But without anywhere else to look, I watched them together. I found myself rocking in time with Steven as he continued to cradle his daughter as if she were still two years old. I knew better. If asked, Stephie would say quite matter-of-factly that she was seven and three quarters. Even though she was the youngest of Steven's three kids, her mother would say she was by far the bravest. I agreed.

CHAPTER 12

The fire department arrived swiftly and extracted us from the building and within an hour I found myself sitting on the curb halfway down the street breathing into an oxygen mask every once in a while and brushing dust from my hair and clothes. Dozens of paramedics, uniformed police and fire crews milled around, seemingly doing nothing but talking to one another. My mood had plummeted since the excitement of the last hour had faded and I found myself alone, craving a glimpse of a child that did not belong to me. The distinction between Steven's feelings and my own had grown clearer as the minutes passed, but no matter what I did, I couldn't hide from that hole in my chest.

I glanced up as a shadow fell across me.

"How are you doing?" Liv asked.

"I've been better."

"They will let us leave soon."

I nodded, fixing my eyes on a pot hole in the road. "Did anyone question Steven about the man that did this?"

"They have. We even have a picture, though it's low quality." She held out her phone. I looked down at the image of an unfamiliar ordinary looking man carrying a rucksack across one shoulder. The picture was indeed blurry but he didn't look like a killer.

"Steven was sure this is the guy?"

"He gave us a description first before we showed him the picture from the security cameras. The description was basically a perfect match, and he confirmed it again when we showed him the photograph."

"*Basically* perfect? So, there were some differences?" I said.

"There's always a margin for error. Memory can be fickle under high pressure conditions like that. It's a wonder he didn't describe him as seven feet tall with horns given what he's just been through."

"It might be important."

"He just said the man looked younger to him than in the picture. But the picture is very low quality and the timestamp matches perfectly with when Doctor Silver said the man left here this morning. We are trying to get hold of a better one from the surrounding CCTV cameras."

"Steven said he was coming back."

"Don't worry, the photo has been distributed to uniformed and plain clothes police in the area. If he shows we'll get him", she said.

I suspected she was thinking the same thing I was, but I didn't voice my doubts. Whoever this man was, he was too dangerous and too clever to get caught so easily. "What about the shredded files?"

"Cross-shredded. It will be days, probably even weeks, before we get anything useful out of the information."

I looked up at the broken windows on the fifth floor, watching dust steadily billow out across the street. "Why didn't he just burn it?" I asked. "He had the opportunity, he was there this morning. The place was quiet. Why go to the effort of getting Steven to do all that when he could have just torched the place like he did with the hotel?" I asked.

"He didn't want us to pick up this link he had with Claire. He's covering his tracks so we don't make that connection. He must have been one of her patients."

"I suppose that must be it", I said. My mind felt tired as it churned sluggishly through the revelations of the past hour. "But why risk letting

Steven identify him?"

"Maybe they met outside of the office and the Doctor never saw him before today? Even if he was a former patient it's possible it was just so long ago he didn't recognise him or the killer only came in a couple of times."

"Maybe", I said, feeling the start of a headache breaking at the base of my skull. "But if he has this child mage under his control, why come himself?"

"Well this wasn't an active crime scene, perhaps he thought it was less of a risk for him to come here than to the hotel."

Something still didn't feel right to me about the fire. "Can you trace the number Steven gave you?"

"It's a mobile number. The phone is switched off and probably already sitting in a bin somewhere. We might get something if we can trace who sold it, but I'm not holding my breath."

"I'm sorry", I said.

"What for?"

"For second-guessing you. You are a Detective, and you are humouring a two-bit private eye. I'd probably still be in custody if you hadn't intervened."

She pushed her lips into a thin line. "What you did... Fin, she would have died."

I glanced at her, then stared down at my shoes.

"After the lift dropped you were calling out to her like she was your daughter. Is that really what it feels like?" she said.

I could hear the pity in her voice. I didn't say anything, not entirely trusting my voice. Any sort of outburst now could land me or Liv in more trouble. The last thing I needed was to undermine her judgement in me by breaking down in front of two dozen police officers.

Three medics wheeled out a coroner's bag on a stretcher.

"Is that the other Doctor?" I asked.

"Doctor Terrance Paul June."

"How did he do it?" I asked, remembering the cut wrists of his last victims.

"Initial verdict is severe blood loss through multiple lacerations across his body. We are talking hundreds, maybe thousands of cuts", she said.

"Made with what?"

"From the looks of it, paper."

"Paper cuts?"

"That's what it looks like to me, but forensics are confused by the timeline again since Steven said he arrived just after 9am with his daughter, but Doctor June arrived at 8:55am. They are saying it would take at least an hour to make all those cuts one at a time, not accounting for the time it would take to drug or otherwise subdue the victim. I guess with magic…"

"It's possible. Brutal, and wasteful, but possible."

"What do you mean by wasteful?"

"I don't know how he is able to kill these people with magic without being emotionally crippled by the act. But he could do this by making himself stronger and breaking their neck. It would be quicker and cleaner and use far less power in the process. Either he has some enormous supply of keepsakes, or he is determined to make a point with these killings."

"Or both?"

"Or both."

I watched Doctor June's body getting loaded up into the back of an ambulance.

"Strange isn't it?" Liv asked, watching me. "Why kill June if his goal was the destruction of those files, why not force them both to do it? If he planned to come back, he could have killed them both at the same time if that was his plan all along."

The thought hadn't occurred to me. I had simply tuned out, fixed on a single point in front of me which just happened to be the back of the ambulance June's body now occupied. I cleared my throat, considering the question but I had no answers for her. None of it made much sense to me and I could see no pattern emerging except an unrelenting desire to punish his victims.

"It's like he's experimenting", I said. "Almost as if he's a new mage."

"Could he be?"

"I don't think so, I've never known one to manifest that late in life. It's always been in the early teens. Maybe a little later, but not by much." I felt a twinge of something at the back of my mind: a half-formed thought taking shape in a cloud before collapsing into vapour.

"You don't sound certain."

"Sorry, I'm not certain of anything right now."

I bowed my head towards my knees and stared at my shoes, feeling morose and utterly useless. I didn't want to see the look of disappointment or frustration on Liv's face. I wasn't helping, I was simply muddying already disturbed waters.

After a moment I felt a finger poke me in the wrist. A little girl I had never met was standing cautiously beside me with a blanket wrapped around her shoulders. She had a sweet face, big brown eyes and curly hair which spilled out over her shoulders.

"Hello Stephie."

She rolled her eyes and glanced back at her father

who was standing a little way back, "Only my dad calls me that", she said, though she sounded amused rather than upset.

"Oh, I'm sorry", I said, the lump reforming in my throat. "What should I call you then?"

She thought for a minute with a finger pressed against her chin and her lips pushed out to the side in thought. "I guess Stephie is okay." Then she smiled and held out her right hand. "Thank you for the fireflies."

I shook her little hand and nodded. "Anytime, Stephie."

Then she ran back to her father. The doctor gave me a weary nod before returning to the officer standing beside him.

"What's the official story?" I asked, looking up at Liv.

"About what happened? More or less the truth, with most of the weird parts removed."

"And you're okay with that?" I asked.

"Not really, but I can't see any other choice."

"I can't wait to see what the newspapers make of this one."

"I think they will push the heroic father's rescue, rather than the deranged killer rigs elaborate death trap angle. That's how we've pitched it anyway." She stepped away as another officer arrived. They spoke briefly then she nodded.

"You can go find Amber now and get yourself cleaned up. I'll need to get a statement from you at some point, but it can wait until tomorrow."

"What will you do?"

"I've got to talk with the fire marshals and speak to Doctor June's wife when she arrives. How long will it take you to get back here? I could still use your help here."

I looked at my watch. It was a little after 3pm and I had no idea when the next meeting was or how far away it would be. "Too long", I said. "Can you spare five minutes?"

"As long as it is just five minutes."

I waved her towards me. She sighed and squatted down beside me, putting an arm around my back and helping me up. I felt immediately faint, and clung to her shoulder until my vision cleared and the nausea subsided.

"Like Cantonese food?" I asked, directing her towards a restaurant across the street from us.

"Not sure I've ever tried it to be honest."

"Me either. I just hope it's authentic." I sighed.

"Is that important?"

"No, just less embarrassing."

We entered the Cheng Po Palace and were immediately shown to a table for two. I did a quick head count as we were handed little plastic menus. A Chinese family of four sat across from us speaking in Mandarin, and a twenty-something couple sat directly behind Liv poring over a map of London. The only other customer was typing on a laptop in the far corner of the room. Seven customers plus Liv, and two more waiters was plenty.

"Quiet", I said to Liv.

"Probably has something to do with the massive dust cloud outside."

"Right", I said, distracted. I needed to get my head on straight.

"What are we doing here, Fin? I need to get back to work, not drying up your hangover or whatever it is with chow mein."

"Relax, we'll get it to go", I said, feeling my stomach roll unpleasantly as I looked at the dishes on the menu, each of which had a little colour picture beside it.

"Jesus, are you going to throw up?" Liv asked inching away from me.

"I'm fine", I lied.

As the waiter came over, I spouted a random list of numbers off the menu and asked for it to go. He made notes on a little pad and disappeared into the kitchen.

"Right", I said pushing back my chair and

standing. "Excuse me." I called loudly to the larger room. "Excuse me, I would like to say a few words. Everyone?" I waited until the family of four had stopped talking and everyone was turned to face me. I smiled at the father who appeared to be out with his three sons. The ages between them were spaced such, and the resemblance so strong, I thought they could have been a family of nesting dolls. Liv stared at me as I tried to determine if the thought was racist. I decided not, though I probably wouldn't voice the thought to anyone else.

"Thank you, I won't take up much of your time." I took a deep breath and began. "I just wanted to tell you all, that I am an addict", I said, speaking loud enough for everyone to hear me. "Today I used again, in front of a child. A little girl. I was so... under the influence I actually thought she was my own daughter. I realised, while I was thinking that, I would do anything for that girl. *Anything.* Even hurt people or myself. I think I scared someone I respect, and I'm afraid they will think less of me now that they know what I am, and what I'm capable of. It's not very often I get to be completely honest with someone."

I swallowed and exhaled slowly, twisting my head to either side. The nausea and the shakes were quickly subsiding. "Thank you, everyone." I smiled, feeling instantly better, and sat down. The sweet smell of deep fried duck was suddenly extremely appealing.

"That counts?" she asked.

"It does."

The Chinese family rose and filed past, the youngest and smallest first. He grinned at me. The father came last and patted me on the back as he drew level with us. "Good for you mate, get it all out."

The oldest son ahead of him had stopped to watch and started laughing.

"Figures", I said, turning to watch them file out. The image gave me a thought.

"The picture of the killer, did he look familiar to you?" I asked.

"No why?"

"Can you show it to me again?"

She brought up the picture on her phone and turned it towards me.

"That wasn't a child at all." I said.

"Who? At the hotel?"

"It was one man, the killer, just a younger version of himself. He used magic to reduce his age. Each time we saw him, he was just a little bit older."

"You're serious?"

"Yes. Dammit, I should have thought of this sooner. My does does it all the time, just never to this extent. Steven said he looked older in the photograph you showed him than in person, right? He did it again this morning on his way out of the building in case we got a picture of him."

"You can do that?"

"Yes, it would still require a lot of power to keep it up for any length of time, but less than taking control of another mage and giving them instructions that specific. He reduced his age to take control of you and start the fire, then walked out the door as an adult guest of the hotel."

"So, is this him now?" she asked, looking at the picture again.

"I doubt it. My guess is we are looking for someone older."

"So you are saying he could walk out of that office looking thirty and by the time he reached the end of the street he could be silver haired and bearded?" Liv said, she looked concerned.

I nodded.

"He's playing with us", she said. "He showed his face deliberately. He's just handed us a killer we won't ever be able to find."

My takeaway order arrived and was dumped unceremoniously on the table in front of me. Before I could say a word, Liv grunted and pushed her chair back. She was out the door and halfway up the street before I'd managed to locate my wallet and pay.

I jogged to catch up with her but pulled up short as a man in his late fifties with a thin crop of spider's legs hair and a perpetual frown intercepted her. I didn't catch what was said but I knew a talking down when I saw one. After exchanging brief words, they both turned to face me, Liv's expression was guarded. The man started towards me in a bulldog stride.

Sooner or later every mage worth his salt becomes a student of body language to some degree; it helps us to attune ourselves better with the emotions of others and to identify creators of suitable and useful keepsakes. It also helps us to pick out the problematic and the dangerous. The boss who smiles constantly, speaking positively about everyone in his office, but whose eye twitches whenever someone cuts him off mid-sentence, or the academic who pinches his own thigh so hard it makes his eye water whenever someone answers a question before him in class.

"Chief Inspector Riley" said the bulldog, extending his right hand to me as he stepped in just a little too close to be comfortable. It was a classic intimidation tactic, both overly familiar and invasive, while his tone was clipped but pleasant. He spoke a margin above a whisper, conspiratorial, as if he had just exchanged a secret and now it was my turn. It was a well-honed mix designed to wrong foot a person, and I found myself wondering just how many suspects had fallen victim to it.

"Finley Chase", I said, switching my takeaway bag from my right hand to the left, to free up my hand for what I guessed would be an overly firm handshake.

"Quite the hero", he said, clasping my hand tightly. "If not for you we would be looking at two murders here, and not one." A raised inflection teased the end of the statement into a question.

I nodded but said nothing, forcing myself not to glance at Stone. The silence stretched as we both waited for the other one to speak.

I felt for a second he was about to slap cuffs back on me and my takeaway would be ruined, but then his face split into a slow smile. "Stone will take you wherever you need to go. You've both had quite a day, take some time." He gave me a knowing nod, then walked away.

I went over to Stone who led me up the street where a line of officers had sectioned off the street. We crossed under a line of police tape and continued until we located the Austin with the rusted bonnet.

"What was that about?" I asked the moment the door clicked shut.

"Riley is taking over."

"Can he do that?"

"He's my senior officer."

"You don't seem upset? Isn't this bad?"

She reached forwards and took the takeaway off me and started tearing into the prawn crackers. "It was hardly unexpected. I was only running things while the investigation was in the toilet. With a photograph of a viable suspect they are more than happy to step in. Manhunts are easy. Even if they lead nowhere, it's an easy spin with the media."

I got the impression she was actually pleased by this turn of events so I merely grunted my irritation on her behalf.

"It's fine, my new assignment is going to be much more beneficial to finding the killer."

"He reassigned you?"

"Yes. Now I'm to keep tabs on you, follow you wherever you go. Make sure you don't get yourself into any more trouble."

"I'm still a suspect then?"

"Afraid so", she said, pulling the lid off the chow mein and dipping a cracker into the steaming noodles before taking a bite. "The fact is, there isn't anything tying you to either crime. Well, except for the fact you keep showing up at the scene. To be honest, I think he just wanted us both out of the picture."

"Shit", I said. "So no access to case files, evidence or update reports?"

"Nope, at least nothing official. He made it quite clear I was to keep away from the investigation from here on out." She put her hand into her bag and pulled out two thick files, followed by the notebook I had seen her scribbling in whenever we had discussed magic over the last few days. I saw her hesitate, then reach her hand into her coat pocket and present an evidence bag containing a scrap of paper and a phone number.

CHAPTER 13

"You took that from evidence?" I asked, staring at the slip of paper in her hand.

"Yes, can you use it? Steven said the killer wrote it himself by hand."

"Christ", I said, working through the implications of what she had done. Words like 'obstruction' and 'tampering' came to mind.

"It's fine", she said, her voice a little too high to be entirely convincing.

"You stole evidence?" I said.

She took a deep breath before speaking. "The killer wore gloves when he wrote it so there are no fingerprints to check for. I asked Steven to copy out the number again in his own handwriting; that is being submitted in evidence instead. He also agreed to lie and say he wrote the number down himself."

"What about handwriting analysis?"

"It doesn't matter. Even if that did lead the police

to the killer, they still can't convict him when the evidence contradicts itself. *You* are my best chance of catching him. So, can you use it to find him or did I just break chain of custody for nothing?"

"Maybe", I said looking closer at the scrap of paper without offering to take it.

"Maybe? Can't you do your thing on this and find out who he is? Find out where he is, or where he might be going next?"

"It's just a number", I said, shaking my head. "I might get something faint, a hint of emotion. Chances are it wouldn't be enough to find him."

"Anything is better than nothing", she insisted.

"I'm not sure about that", I said, cringing at the thought of willingly taking on whatever delusional and hateful emotions that could lead a person down this path. I took two Biros out of my coat and used them like chopsticks to take the scrap from her, still not wanting to touch it with my bare fingers. "There might be another way. We'll need a stalker though."

"A stalker meaning…?"

"A *stalker*, you know, one who stalks? Their keepsakes are the best for tracking spells."

"Any ideas?" she asked.

I shook my head. "I think I know where we can find one." I turned in my seat and slid the partition open. "Amber, head for Dad's office. It's already programmed into the sat nav." I watched her flick through the menu painfully slowly. "It's under D, for Dad", I said.

"No shit, Sherlo..."

I closed the partition, muffling the rest of the insult, passed the scrap of paper back to the detective and reached for one of the unopened containers of Chinese food. We ate in silence as the taxi sped across London.

"You should really start paying her if you are going to keep treating her like that", Liv said.

"Says the woman devouring her share of dinner."

She paused with a prawn cracker heaped over with so much chow mein, the noodles ran as far as her Fitbit.

"Her's is the chow mein?" she asked, thickly.

"Mhmm, it's her favourite. I can't stand the stuff." I lied.

Liv replaced the lid on the carton and returned it to the white plastic bag before snatching the tub of ginger chicken from my lap.

I ate what was left on the plastic fork, slipped the fork into the pocket of my coat then lay back and tried to sleep.

It was only a short drive however, and the traffic was steady. Just as I was dozing off we pulled up to the Life Sciences block at the University College, London.

"Fin, we're here", Liv said, stepping out.

I followed her, yawned and passed Amber the bag of Chinese food which she accepted without comment.

Lush grass framed a broad pathway leading up towards the library. I led the way up through the centre of the courtyard, between two grand alabaster pillars and in through the double doors. We entered an intimidating and stately reception hall before turning left up a hallway.

"You father works here?" Liv asked as I got my bearings.

"He teaches a creative writing course", I said. We walked down a half dozen more corridors, the polished hardwood floors giving way to more modern hard-wearing carpets, white washed walls and cork noticeboards. We finally came to a sign which read "Prof. Robert Chase".

"Come", a pompous voice replied as I rapped on the door.

I opened the door and stepped inside.

"You know you would do us all a favour if you showed up only slightly late, or not at all. Honestly, forty minutes, there really isn't any..." My father turned away from a circle of eight students, all but one of whom I noticed, was female. My father sat with his legs crossed facing the centre of the group, his glasses poised between thumb and first finger as if I had interrupted him mid-gesture. He wore a tweed blazer over dress jeans, a faded black Metallica t-shirt and a pair of fine brogues which looked as if they had never left the safety of his office. It was the uniform of my cultured and charismatic father, every item carefully selected. Even his hair I suspected was the result of deliberate styling to look just the right amount of effortless.

There was more going on than clothing and an expensive haircut, however. Robert had never disclosed his real age to me, but I knew he must have been in his late fifties. The man sitting before me looked no older than forty, but the kind of forty you associated with vigour and 5am runs and whatever the hell *clean eating* meant.

"Hi", I said, taking in the familiar scent of sandalwood and good scotch. It served a pleasing contradiction to the over sweet tones emanating from the contingent of attentive looking students competing for attention.

"Oh, it's you", Robert replied. "Class, please forgive the interruption. I will only be a moment. I must speak with my son."

I thought I could see a few hearts melting at the news that Robert Chase had a son. The most stunned of the bunch put their heads together and immediately started whispering to one another. Another, wearing black nail polish and an electric blue streak through otherwise raven black hair, rolled her eyes at this and started writing in a notebook. Now that I looked for it, every student had an identical diary-like notebook: an impromptu gift from my father no doubt.

"How do they look?" Robert said, when he was standing right in front of me.

"What?"

"The class, when I announced you were my son?"

"Oh, fine. Utterly indifferent", I lied.

Robert pursed his lips and raised his eyebrows in an unconvincing imitation of a fatherly, I-know-when-you-are-lying, type face. It didn't suit him. "So ungrateful!" he sighed, as if it couldn't be helped. "Honestly, you would think the sheer volume of student taxi drivers I've sent your way would be enough to earn me an ounce of respect. How many is it so far this year? Ten? Twelve?" His voice dropped an octave and continued in little above a rumbling whisper. "I could really use a second opinion here, my boy."

"Fine", I said, looking over his shoulder at the group. "The doodler keeps looking over. Dr. Marten's hasn't looked up from her pad, but she's pretending not to listen to the gossiping blondes, they giggle every..." I stopped when I realised he was no longer listening. He was staring in alarm at Liv who had been propping the door open behind me.

"Done with that are we? Right." I said, turning to introduce Stone. He continued to stare, open mouthed at her. Eager to curtail whatever chat-up line or otherwise inappropriate remark he was considering, I added, "Dad, this is Detective Stone. With the police."

"A... A detective? And so young?" he said, extending a hand to her.

She frowned for a moment, her expression guarded. "Mr Chase, is there somewhere..."

"Call me Robert, please. You aren't one of my students", he chuckled nervously, as if the very suggestion was somehow amusing. I cringed. If he thought the fumbling professor bit was going to get him anywhere with Stone he was sadly mistaken. I frowned at him, surprised by his poor read on her. Perhaps he was genuinely unnerved by a police presence.

"Right. Robert, is there somewhere we can talk, it's quite important. Your son is helping me with a murder investigation."

"Murder?" he repeated, stunned.

"Yes, murder", she repeated, loud enough for the closest student to hear her. "Is there somewhere we can talk in private?"

"Oh… of course." He said, recovering himself. He turned to his class and dismissed them. I watched as he bid farewell to each student in turn, every one of them was treated like an old friend, his attention utterly intent on each of them, even if it was for only a few seconds. It was the kind of treatment that few would experience outside of therapy or a lover's arms, and it was no surprise that each one of them lapped it up. It was like watching magic, I could see the change as it occurred. My father's light fell on each student and faces would brighten and backs would straighten.

"Jessica, *fine* work today. Emma, have a look at *Dead Souls*, I really think you'll enjoy it. Ryan, I will see you for a pint and some chess on Thursday, I hope? Good man! Everyone, I want your thoughts on anything you are reading. What it makes you think, and more importantly what it makes you *feel*, and as usual, hand written submissions only, please."

I noted several over-the-shoulder glances back at my father as they filed out. I counted at least three crushes in the making, one who was probably infatuated and two more who saw him as the father they never had.

"Tell me that was a mage thing?" Liv said, once the girls had filed out. "It's for getting keepsakes right?"

I made a face, but was excused from answering her question by my father's interruption.

"Oh ho?" he said, beaming from his perch against a dark mahogany desk. "So you know? My son must be quite enamoured with you to share our most closely-guarded secret."

"Actually, a mage forced me to gun down my boss while Fin got in the way. I don't think he had much choice but to confide in me after that."

My father glanced at the television in the corner of his office. "You mean a mage did that? I heard about the strange murders at that hotel, it's not possible."

"I've seen his handiwork myself. He's definitely a mage, though I don't know how exactly he is pulling any of this off. That's why we are here, we need your help to find him. No one has a better collection of stalker keepsakes than you."

"You're going after this maniac?" he shook his head. "You aren't even with the police, Adam."

"Adam?" Liv asked.

"It's just what he calls me when I'm disappointing him", I said, dismissively. "Dad, they need our help. I didn't think it was possible either, to kill like this, at least not on this scale. But it's beside the point, somehow he has managed it. One of *us*."

"He'll run out of steam if he hasn't already. There's no way he could keep it up, he'll be overcome with guilt and turn himself in."

I shook my head. "It's been days since the first murders took place."

"Then he'll be about ready to turn himself in. He's probably held up somewhere crushed under the weight of his.."

"He killed Claire", I said, practically shouting over him.

My father's face fell. "I'm sorry, son."

I opened my mouth to apologise for the outburst, to claim my loss was negligible compared to Henry's or her parents, but I didn't mean it. He looked at me with such pity, it was all I could do to keep standing. Finally, I cleared my throat and added "He trapped a little girl in an elevator and almost crushed her earlier today. He isn't slowing down. Now will you help us?"

"Is this your influence?" he demanded of Stone, his bluster instantly restored. "I've been trying to get him back here to finish his doctorate for years, now suddenly Adam finds his fire." He finished holding a hand up to his heart as if he were grasping at a fire in his chest. "So be it. I will assist you."

I rolled my eyes at the dramatics.

My father invited us to sit within the circle.

"Judging by your expression, Detective, you have questions my son has been unable to adequately answer."

"How does nobody know about you? Government, the police, the media?"

"To answer that adequately, we would have to explain a little about our history. To put it bluntly, we have none. I don't mean to suggest we are a new development in human evolution, of course. What I mean to say is that no record, book or document exist which reference us and our nature directly."

"You can say this with certainty?" Liv asked.

"Absolute certainty, yes, because I, nor my son, nor any human or mage I've encountered has been able to make mention of our gifts directly via the written word. To the best of our understanding, we are bound by some ancient magic which prohibits such a transfer of knowledge."

"Why?"

"To castrate us", he said, his voice betraying a bitterness I hadn't heard in years. "To stifle and handicap us, thus ensuring our methods and knowledge cannot spread as quickly as they, presumably, once did."

"Why handicap your knowledge at all though? Fin told me that mages could be born to non-mage families? Wouldn't they be a far greater danger to society than an educated mage?"

"He is quite correct, though that danger would more than likely be contained to the individual or to those closest to them. A well-trained mage, or a network of such mages… well who knows what devastation we might cause?"

"I get it, a Hitler or Stalin with a mage's ability to compel an enemy."

"That's the theory." I said.

'But how has not being able to write down your history stopped you from public recognition?" she asked.

"Well, in short it hasn't. Mage's never stopped communicating, we have been quelled to a degree certainly, but we found other ways. A hundred years ago we were heathens burned at the stake for sharing our lore. Today we are considered entertainers, internet phenomenon, urban myths, or…"

'Writers of best-selling fiction." I added.

My father pursed his lips but reached across his desk and handed Olivia a copy of his first book.

"*Spectres of the Half Moon?*" Liv said, reading the title. "I thought you couldn't write about your magic?"

"We cannot write about it directly. There are one or two loopholes, however. What you hold in your hand is one of many works of fiction which elude to our nature."

She flipped it over and read the blurb, doing her best to keep her expression politely interested.

"Not to your taste?" Robert smiled.

"I never really understood the attraction to vampires and werewolves." she shrugged.

My father put his hand on his heart as if he'd been physically struck.

"Ignore him. The point is we can use metaphor to write about magic." I said.

"With vampires fighting zombies?" she said, her eyebrows betraying her scepticism.

"What better metaphor could there be? They each are a reflection of our condition."

"Vampires drink blood, zombies feed on brains, and werewolves go on a killing spree once a month?"

"Broadly speaking, yes, but you are missing the deeper levels", Robert said. "Think of them each as a cautionary tale. We feed on human emotion, their passions and intellect. We are dependent on them. The word zombie stems from the 8th Century Kongo word *nzambi* which translates as 'spirit of dead person'. If we take on too much and we become unrecognisable, perhaps even monstrous. Feed too little and we will become like the dead walking."

"Ok, I think I get the idea, but what actually happens to you if you go without for too long or you use too much?"

"Go without and we will fall into progressively worsening withdrawal and eventually die. Consuming too much is a little more complex. We run the risk of being overwhelmed by one of these other personalities. Once we can no longer distinguish our own voice from that of our passengers, then we can no longer cleanse ourselves completely."

"And when this happens, when they are with you, you hear their voice in your head? They can tell you things?"

"More or less, though the frequency, the manner and detail of the experience will vary depending on the keepsake."

Liv met my eye then looked quickly away. For the first time since we'd met, I saw real vulnerability there.

My father, presumably mistaking her silence as awe, continued, "I realise it can be quite a remarkable thing to discover that we have the ability to commune with the ghosts of the past."

"Dad, stop now. She gets the idea."

"What, I'm hardly bragging, son. The good detective asked to learn more about our people. There is no sense in downplaying our abilities or we may mislead her into a false belief."

"I said *enough*." I could see Liv's stoicism starting to crack. Whether atheist or of some faith or another, the reality of this new perspective had repercussions to dozens of people previously at the fringes of society. Psychics, mediums, palm readers, fortune tellers and spiritualists who previously lacked credence with most of society could no longer be so easily dismissed. As an officer of the law it was troubling, but as a woman with a complicated relationship with a mother and grandmother, the latter of which I was confident had now passed, this could be world shattering. I, a virtual stranger, had channelled both women after all and what did I know about their inner most thoughts that she did not?

She was quiet for a moment longer, my father too seemed to have cottoned on to his error in judgement and was watching her with some concern.

"Adam, what did you do?" he said, turning to me.

I sighed. "Nothing I could have avoided."

"How does the werewolf fit in?" Liv asked, interrupting whatever reprimand my father was about to try and deliver.

"The werewolf is there to remind us that there is no cure and that even with the best intentions, sooner or later the beast will rise up again."

"You're telling me Dracula and every other book about vampires or werewolves like it were written by mages?" she asked.

"Some almost certainly were, others were perhaps just imitators building on the lore. That is part of the problem. Much of my life has been spent dissecting works of fiction which add to our hidden history among the thousands of others which are simply there to be entertainment. You mentioned Bram Stoker's *Dracula*, do you recall the book and how it is written?" My father asked, approaching a bookcase and retrieving a worn copy of the text. I could see colour coded tags sticking out from dozens of pages.

"It's been years since I read it but it's told through a series of letters isn't it?"

"Curious, don't you think?" Robert said, opening the text.

"I am all in a sea of wonders. I doubt; I fear; I think strange things, which I dare not confess to my own soul."

He flipped to another page.

"Even if she be not harmed, her heart may fail her in so much and so many horrors; and hereafter she may suffer--both in waking, from her nerves, and in sleep, from her dreams."

"Sounds a good deal like the aftereffects of using magic doesn't it?" he closed the book and passed it to her. She read a few more passages to her herself while my father looked on, clearly pleased by her interest.

"Remember my friend, that knowledge is stronger than memory, and we should not trust the weaker." she recited.

"A fine choice, that is the very quote which encouraged me to write my first novel." he smiled.

"I don't understand?"

"If we trust only memory - only that information passed on to us from our families and friends through the other mages we directly come into contact with - then we are limiting ourselves to just one way of thinking and one way of using magic. *Knowledge,* in this context I take to mean what other mage's have managed to bury within fiction. Do not trust the weaker – memory, trust in knowledge. I took this as a call to build on his work and write my own books for the modern mage."

I cleared my throat and they both looked at me.

"You disagree?" Liv asked.

"My son has a slightly different interpretation of the quote." he said, though he looked pleased.

"I interpreted it to mean that we should distance ourselves from those we channel. Trust in their knowledge and ability but not their memories which are more likely to corrupt us."

"How do you mean?"

I hesitated. "Well for example, when I channelled your ring back at the police station, I had you in my head afterwards or at least a version of you. I thought you were on my side, but you tricked me. Encouraged me to visit the crime scene, and effectively incriminate myself. I think you were hoping I would confess."

"I don't really know how to respond to that. Sorry?"

"You're forgiven." I smiled.

"So those other minds you carry, they can work against you too?"

"Exactly. Memory should not be trusted."

"I'm guessing all these quotes are open to different interpretations like that." she said. "You said before you couldn't write anything more specific than this? How exactly does anyone stop you?"

"Try it and see for yourself. The same spell will stop you." Robert said.

She opened her notebook then hesitated, looking at me.

"It won't hurt or anything." I said.

She put pen to paper and scribbled a sentence down then leaned back in her chair, away from the notebook. "What should happen?"

"Any second…" my father said.

The page started smoking and in seconds the words she had written were obscured as if a hot brand and been pressed into the page. The smoke cleared a moment later and Liv came back into view, looking startled and confused.

"Seriously?" she said, staring down at the royal coat of arms showing a chained unicorn and lion framed around the royal shield. "That's the royal coat of arms?" she said.

"Similar, only much older. Notice anything off about the shield?"

"It's hard to tell", she said, turning her head to the side and studying the charred remains of her page. "It's not split into four. It's just the three lions on the shield. Who's crest is that?"

"Richard the Lionheart, about eight hundred years ago. Our best guess is that sometime between 1198 and 1369 this spell was cast and it's been going strong ever since."

"How?"

"We have no idea. We suspect that whatever methods they used back then to create this spell was exactly the sorts of knowledge they wanted to hide from future generations. Ever wondered why we still have a monarch?"

"Right, enough of the history lesson. We'll be

here all night if we get any deeper into your work."

"*Our* work!" Robert hissed.

"Right, but nevertheless I don't think a discussion on the Crown Jewels or what may or may not be written on the back of the Magna Carta is going to help us find the killer."

"You seem tense? Who did you last channel? I've told you once I've told you a hundred times, you need to screen your sources better, son."

"I'm fine." I said, through gritted teeth.

He squinted at me suspiciously. "You don't sound fine, my son usually has more manners. Who else is in there?" he said, turning my face from side to side. "Have you seen him writing in his notebook today?" he said, turning to Stone.

"Err no?" she said, awkwardly.

"Tell me you aren't suppressing your aftershocks?"

I sighed, pushing his hand away, and doing my best not to lose my temper. "I'm sorry I interrupted you, alright? I've not had any aftershocks yet today. Now enough stalling, where is this keepsake?"

"What keepsake?" he said, evasively.

"The keepsake to track the killer? You do still have one?"

"Oh", he said, scratching the back of his head. "Well I might have recently sold most of my more choice wares. A lecturer's salary leaves a lot to be desired you know? But, I think if you open that door you might find someone writing just what we need."

Stone got up and paused by the door before opening it and scanning the corridor beyond.

"Well... any young admirers?" Robert smiled.

"I don't see anyone", Liv said.

"Hmm." Robert looked momentarily confused. "Ah, the weather is mild", he said, moving to the window and peeking through a gap in the blinds. "There we are. Almost a full house too", he said, waving us both over and sounding very pleased with himself.

"You think they are waiting for you? They could just be enjoying the sun?" Liv looked out through the blinds, before shaking her head and stepping away to let me see.

"You've managed to convince them all to keep a journal?" I asked, counting off five of my father's students dotted around the green below, all of whom were hunched over writing into those same notebooks and glancing up at the entrance every few seconds.

"It certainly appears that way", he said, producing a small pair of binoculars so quickly I suspected this wasn't the first time he had spied on his students from that window.

"Have you noticed any of them following you around? Any notes, threats, anything?" I asked.

"Jess and Ali I've caught dogging my heels a couple of times but I'm not convinced it's an obsession, more of a game between the two of them. Nothing serious or concrete. The occasional note along with an essay, but nothing out of the ordinary. Enough to keep the old dog going of course, but ill-suited to our mission, I think", he said, his voice filled with a disappointment I suspected had more to do with his ego and nothing to do with the investigation. "Had I known you would need this I would have started paying closer attention and moved up my timeframes. It's still early days."

"Wait, so you encourage them to stalk you, over what period? Months?" Liv asked. She sounded appalled.

"Of course, my dear. This is how you cultivate the more specialised magic. The longer the better", Robert offered reasonably.

"Liv, it's not as bad as you think", I said, cutting off the argument before it could take root. "We need this if we are going to find the killer."

"Right", she said, tersely. She turned away from the window and withdrew her phone to check her messages.

"Fair enough. So how do we pick the stalker out from the crushes?" I asked.

"Patience, my boy. Let's wait a little while and see what happens when I don't appear."

"Alright. You keep watch. I need to talk to Liv." I waited until she was off the phone and went over to her.

"They have just released Henry", she said, before I could get a word in.

"Is he alright?"

"He's upset. But it was fairly obvious he didn't have anything to do with this. A neighbour confirmed he was in his flat. The two argued through the wall apparently?"

"Sounds about right. Good, thanks for keeping track of him for me." I watched her eyes harden on the back my father's head. "Look, we could be waiting a while. Go ahead, ask."

"Let me get this straight. He charms the pretty girls into liking him. Then he convinces them to write journals, effectively seduces them, and then steals their journals to sell on to other mages to make some extra money?"

"More or less", I said.

"That's disgusting. I should be arresting him, not asking him for help."

"I know it sounds bad when you say it like that,

but - and I can't believe I'm defending him - but he is actually one of the best at what he does."

"That makes it better?" she said, her voice rising.

"I mean 'best' as in, morally good. He has a surprisingly strict code of ethics when it comes to all this."

She looked at me as if I were insane.

"He never uses magic to directly affect someone else's feelings towards him. Right, Dad?"

"Never", Robert said from the window. He sounded insulted. "There is no greater intrusion than to force your will upon another person. Manipulating someone's emotions directly through magic is an unconscionable abuse of power."

"So, they all have a choice is what you are getting at?"

"Exactly, and he only goes for students over twenty-one, and never encourages them if they are unbalanced. Right?"

"Certainly not. I get them the help they need if I suspect anything of the sort."

"Is that before or after you steal their property? Where do you even draw that line? You can't know what they are thinking." Liv said.

"Actually, I can! You forget I grade each of their hand-written papers every week. I'm not just their teacher, I'm their councillor and confidant. I know them."

"How much do you charge for their diaries once you've stolen them? Do you bill by the page or is it a lump sum?" she asked.

"For the families, I charge nothing. For everyone else, I'm happy to let the market decide.", he said, his voice had lost its edge now, and I felt my own chest tightening.

"What families?" Liv asked.

"Let's go get a drink from the vending machine", I said, grabbing Liv by the arm and leading her outside.

"What families?" she repeated, as soon as the door closed behind us.

I put a dozen steps between us and my father's office before answering. "Dad only sells the less powerful diaries, the ones that won't work effectively for tracking."

"The spell for locating something?" she said, confused.

"Or someone", I added.

She paused, her frown softening. "He uses them to locate people who have gone missing?"

"Missing children."

"How many has he found?"

"Four", I said.

"So few", she asked.

"It takes a very specific kind of keepsake for the spell to work effectively for any length of time. The further away they are, the longer the spell needs to last, you see."

"How long has he been doing this?"

"Since I was a teenager, after my sister went missing."

"She...?"

"...never came home. Dad nearly killed himself trying to find her. Eventually he had to give up the search." I continued on to the coffee machine, not letting her finish the thought, and jabbed blindly at the buttons until something resembling coffee poured into a plastic, caramel-coloured cup. I hadn't spoken about my sister for years. I found myself startled by how quickly the carefully constructed wall I had built around that part of me could come down.

"What was her name?"

"Belle", I said, sipping the too-hot coffee and grimacing at the flavour as much as the temperature.

"Was she a mage too?"

"No, but that isn't unusual. It isn't always hereditary. We aren't really sure why", I shrugged.

"What happened to her?"

"I don't know. Dad tracked her across most of the country before she crossed the channel into France, he ran out of keepsakes somewhere along the border to Luxemburg and had to come home. That was about twelve years ago, she'd be thirty-two in October. We still don't know if she ran away or..." I swallowed over the lump in my throat. "Dad kept looking for a few years, honed his knowledge of location spells to something of a fine art, but the further away she got the harder it was to even get near her. It isn't like plotting on a map, the spell works by literally pointing the way like a compass. Eventually it became too much for him."

What about your mother?"

"What about her? She's a mage, but she left long before Belle disappeared."

"Divorced?" Liv asked.

"No, they are still technically married. She just left. I've not heard from her in about ten years. Last I heard she was living somewhere in the States."

"Belle never contacted you?" Liv asked.

I shook my head. I could see the police cogs turning behind the sympathetic expression on her face and the inevitable conclusion reached by anyone with even a fleeting knowledge of missing persons' statistics. She was probably dead but that wasn't something I could say out loud, nor did I have the strength to try and confirm that suspicion one way or the other.

"Wait, your father calls you Adam? As in Belle and Adam?"

I snorted. "When the *Beauty and the Beast* came out in the nineties he became obsessed with it. Started calling me Adam the moment we left the cinema. He was convinced the writer must have been a mage claiming it was the perfect metaphor for our condition."

"Tame the Beast and the prince will shine through, sort of thing?" Liv said.

"Something like that", I sighed. "Are we done?"

"Hold on. I have a couple more questions for you." she said.

CHAPTER 14

"What's with the Welsh?" Liv asked. "You use it for your spells right? I figured you would use Latin, like in…"

"The language is irrelevant", I said, cutting her off. "It could be anything, French, German, nonsense words, whatever. Using a second language, one you don't usually speak, is perfect for establishing mental connections for shaping spells. Often a spell isn't just one action, but a combination of several working together. You bind whatever number of changes you want to make to a word or phrase. Then whenever you say that phrase again you are focused on it. Sort of like a mental shorthand."

"Can you do it without saying a spell? What if you want to do something that you haven't done before?"

"That works too but it's less efficient. Fine for small things, but anything big you are likely to burn through your keepsakes quicker than you would otherwise."

"Like the smoke dragon? I'm guessing you didn't have a prepared spell for that?"

"No, I didn't. Thankfully that keepsake", I hesitated, the loss was still pretty raw. "Bing, was all confidence and showmanship. He was suited to something flashy and off the cuff like the dragon. For that sort of improvisation I didn't need a verbal spell."

"You still haven't answered my question. Why did you pick Welsh?"

"Oh, well dad uses Latin. He was something of an elitist about it."

"So you rebelled?"

"It was a phase", I shrugged. "Are we done?" I said, glancing at my watch. Almost forty minutes had passed us by as I answered Liv's seemingly endless string of questions.

"I have one more. You can't write your own keepsakes right? But if your father is a Mage too, why don't you just make them for each other I mean? Surely that's an endless supply?"

"Ah, well that's an interesting one. Keepsakes written by other mages do work, just not very well. There has to be genuine sentiment there."

"He's your dad?" she said, frowning.

"Right, of course, but he's also a mage. If he writes a letter knowing I can use it to make a spell then there's a conflict, an agenda, and the purity of the message is diluted."

"Which what? Dilutes the magic?"

"Exactly. It's pretty ineffective most of the time unless he's feeling particularly sentimental. Doesn't happen very often." I paused, watching her. "You still have more questions?"

"Of course. You said it wasn't hereditary? Does that mean you could grow up not knowing you are a mage at all?"

"It happens, but you soon figure it out. Usually you draw power from something by accident and that sets you on a path of experimentation which will inevitably manifest in all manner of colourful ways. Usually it hits in your teens, rarely later."

"But how do they know to cleanse themselves?"

I shook my head. "They don't. If they are lucky they don't spiral too far before stumbling into another mage. We teach them what we know when we do. Show them how to get clean, teach them to manage the addiction. That's how I met Claire. Her parents knew nothing of mages, they just thought she was a troubled teen going through a phase. She ended up getting sent to this after school thing. I was there the first time she got clean." *And the last,* I thought.

Liv opened her mouth to speak but something in my face made her hesitate. The stoic investigator vanished as if she'd just caught herself falling into old habits. I guessed whatever question she had been about to ask would come later. I could see it was hard for her to switch off from it. I recalled Claire telling me something similar the day she died. I could see the detective's mind working now too, figuring out the best way to approach a topic without scaring off the perp.

"Has a new mage ever approached you like that?"

"I've picked up one or two when I spot the signs. If they are really new to it, you'll see them coming a mile off."

"I'm not so sure about that." she said, looking out the cafeteria window.

"What do you mean?"

She shook her head. "It doesn't matter. Come on."

She led the way back up the hallway to my father's office. We arrived to find Robert and Henry standing at the window, both holding binoculars up to their faces with one hand, and a slice of pizza with the other.

"Henry?" I said, as he turned and grinned at me.

"Hi, Robert called me. Said you guys needed my help."

"You brought pizza?" I said, finding myself grateful he had at least located a pair of jeans and a passably clean T-shirt before coming here.

"Perfect food for a stakeout", he beamed. His smile faded as Liv entered behind me. "Detective. Help yourselves, there's plenty more", he said, coolly, before turning back to the window.

"Is this a good idea?" Liv muttered. "Letting him get involved like this?"

"I can hear you", Henry said. "Look, I just want to be anywhere but home right now, but if you really want me to go, your share of the pizza was ten-fifty."

"It's fine, actually", I said. "I have some questions for you anyway. This saves me tracking you down later."

"Perfect, well I'm glad that's resolved", Robert said.

"How are we looking out there?" I asked.

"We are down to four!" Robert announced like a commentator reporting at the races.

"Ho ho!" Henry laughed, "I think someone's losing his touch."

I eyed the pair of them for a moment.

"Have you two done this before?" Liv asked.

"Well, once or twice, perhaps", Robert said.

"When Claire left, I started coming by. We'd just talk sometimes, but this ended up being much more fun", he shrugged.

"It's fine", I said, mostly to Liv, who seemed like

she had more to say on the matter.

She looked at me, sighed, helped herself to some pizza and went over to the window.

I sat down within the circle of chairs and sipped my coffee, hoping the caffeine would at least give me a little more focus. I gave up after two sips and instead used a pizza chaser to cleanse my pallet of the foul-tasting stuff.

Liv left the window after a few minutes and joined me within the circle. She sat with her legs crossed to my right with a second slice of pizza resting on a napkin on her knee. I stared at it for a moment thinking of Claire, and how we had shared a KitKat the day she died. I remembered the little smudge of chocolate on her leg and felt profoundly guilty all of a sudden. I glanced at Henry as though he might turn on me any moment and start yelling. He didn't; he and my father seemed to be making wagers on which of his students would drop next.

I considered the coffee but instead set it down on the chair beside me along with the half-eaten slice of pizza.

"What's wrong?" Liv asked.

"I was just thinking, this was how they were found isn't it? In a circle like this?"

She nodded, then pulled out the little pad she had been using to make notes on and looked at me expectantly. I realised she had been waiting for this, waiting for me to be ready to go over that first murder with her. I had been too hurt and too preoccupied with tracking the killer down that I had forgotten that Liv had a case to build and a conviction to make if he was ever to see justice.

"We should go over the murder. Henry, if you don't want to hear any of this you should go now."

"I'm staying. It's why I came", he said.

Liv nodded and went around the circle placing a piece of paper onto each of the chairs and positioned more still on the desk and floor, totalling the nine victims. The one closest to me on my left read CLAIRE. To my right read JOHN DOE - 6ft2, 160 pound male. The list went on. Three unknown females, five unknown males and Claire.

Liv described the scene and summarised the timeline as best as the MET Police had been able to determine. I listened with a vague sense of déjà vu, recalling the Liv in my mind going over the very same details.

"We have no idea who the other eight victims are, none were carrying any identification and did not appear to be guests at the hotel. Nobody was unaccounted for after the fire and no one has contacted the hotel looking for them, at least not yet. We think the killer took their IDs with them to delay the investigation. The strange thing is, nobody has come forwards to identify them."

"What about Claire?" Henry asked.

"Claire was the exception," I said, thinking aloud. "If she hadn't been there at all, what would the police have thought about those deaths?"

"Without any other evidence they would have been put down as some sort of ritualistic suicide. The cuts are strange, but we would have had nothing else to go on and the higher ups would have been eager to put it to bed."

"And the fire would have eventually been attributed to you."

"Yes, along with the shooting."

"She was compelled by the killer to shoot her superior officer and die in the fire." I added, noticing my father's face. I turned back to Liv. "What are you thinking?"

"I'm thinking Claire was never supposed to be there. I think she showed up during or just after the event and found our killer either assisting or, more likely, causing their deaths. There was a struggle, and this person lashed out and killed her. The fact that he bothered to take their ID means he cares about being discovered."

"But you said he left Claire's ID behind?" Robert asked.

"That might have been a mistake", Liv said.

I stared at her. "You think the killer felt guilty?"

"It's possible, or perhaps he just panicked when she showed up unexpected." she said.

"Makes sense." Henry nodded.

She glancing at each of us. "Any thoughts on the *other* side of things?"

"My guess is he used compulsion magic to force them to cut their wrists." I said, feeling disgusted with the thought. "Then returned the following day, reduced his age and compelled you to shoot Price before starting the fire."

"What?" Robert said, shaking his head. "Impossible."

"What makes you say that?" Liv asked.

"It's too much. I don't care how gifted the mage, just one of those spells would be enough to flatten a person for a week or more."

"What if he wasn't getting clean, what if he just kept using? Fin suggested that it might be possible if the killer was well resourced." Liv asked.

"Indeed, far better than any mage I've ever encountered. It isn't just power though, the type of keepsakes are important too and their emotional compatibility to one another. One psyche second guessing the others could undermine their motivation to kill anyone. I cannot fathom how anyone could source enough to last them through two murders let alone this many."

She nodded and made a note.

"Any news on the hotel?"

"They've cordoned off most of it so they can check the extent of the damage. After we got away from there, they got the fire under control pretty quickly. They won't be having guests anytime soon but structurally it should be fine. The foyer, conference rooms and basically anything below the forth floor were basically untouched and as they were before the fire."

"Any events planned? Anything that will need to be moved on account of the fire?"

She flipped back through her notes. "There was a wedding the weekend before in the smaller reception rooms, but nothing booked during the time of the murder."

"No cancellations or last minute rescheduling?"

"Nothing within a few days of the murder", she said, flipping over more pages. "The only thing in the diary for the conference centre this month is a self-help seminar due to start this weekend but that looks like it will go ahead since the conference centre was in a different part of the building from the fire."

"What sort of self-help?" I asked.

"Positive thinking and self-actualisation. It's

called…", she flicked through more pages. "The actualised self, or something like that."

"The Positive Self?" Henry said.

"Yes", Liv confirmed, once she found the right page.

"How did you know that? I've never heard of them before", I asked.

"I'm not sure, maybe I got one of their flyers or something", he shrugged.

"Did Claire ever mention it?" I said.

"I don't know, maybe?", he offered, unhelpfully.

"It could be important."

"I'm sorry, maybe it was just a lucky guess? The police turned the flat upside down, if there was anything there with it written down, they would have found it right?" he said, directing the question at Liv.

"They would have made the connection. I doubt it's relevant, the murder was a full week before the conference. Guests wouldn't have started to arrive that early."

"Mages might have", Robert said. He came and sat down within the circle, leaving Henry to keep watch at the window. "A conference like that can be a pretty good draw for a mage on holiday."

"Really?" Liv asked.

"I know it must sound bizarre, but with a

little careful planning and some well-chosen keepsakes to fuel us through the stay, it can make for quite the party." His eyes turned skyward and to the left as if he recalled something I was certain I didn't want to hear the details of.

I heard Henry mutter, "You dog!"

I cringed and turned to Liv. "The idea is they can use the conference to get clean. It's a way to manage themselves and ensure they stop when they mean to."

"Sort of like flying to Ibiza to get smashed for a week knowing you have to sober up for the flight home?" Liv said.

"Sure, if Ibiza had some alcohol prohibition laws making it difficult to get any more booze than what you brought with you."

"It's a difficult path to navigate", Robert said. "Most mages who do this often struggle to limit themselves to just one trip a year once they get a taste for it."

"What's it like?" she asked, looking at me.

My father and I started speaking at the same time. He smiled at me, and I cleared my throat. "You go ahead, this is really your area of expertise."

"Well it isn't all about sex, if that's what you were thinking. Certainly, there are many who go just for that. Sex, when you are channelling something appropriately attuned, can be extremely intense and immensely satisfying." His eyes bulged a little as he said this. "In fact there are people who make their entire living in trading such keepsakes."

"There's big money in pleasure, always has been", Henry said around a mouthful of pizza.

"I get the idea. What else?" Liv said.

"Well then there's healing."

"I didn't think mages could heal very well?"

"Oh not physical healing, you are quite right about that. Channelling the emotions of someone else who has overcome something traumatic you are suffering with however can be enormously cathartic. Imagine a father struggling to get over the loss of his wife and being unable to see beyond it. It can be like fast-forwarding your emotional recovery several years. Even if it lasts only a few days, that time can be integral to his recovery. Being told a pain will ease eventually is very different than actually feeling it for yourself."

"How do you know which conferences to attend?"

"Well, Mages don't function well in very large groups. Things can escalate if there are too many of us gathered at once. The allure of so many keepsakes in one place can make you a target, too. Tight knots of twenty, perhaps thirty are the most common, I would say. I've certainly never seen a gathering of more than fifty."

"How far do they travel?"

"How far would you travel for a holiday like that? They will come from all over the world if the circumstances are right."

"The other victims could be from anywhere in the world if this is why they were meeting", she sighed, turning to a fresh page and making more notes.

"I can understand the others, but Claire had just gotten clean", I said. "She was headed home. I don't know why she would have been there. You don't end one bender to immediately start another one."

"Are you sure she was clean?" Robert asked.

"I was there, I watched it happen. She went right after me."

"She could have lied, you know it's hardly unheard of." My father lowered his voice sympathetically and added, "You have been known to have a little bit of a blind spot when it comes to her."

I frowned, but didn't dismiss it out of hand. Certainly, the Claire I knew would never have lied to me like that, but then people changed and I hadn't seen her in over a year.

"Oh fuck, we are down to two", Henry said. "Just the goth girl and the frumpy boy left."

I recalled the boy in question and thought it was a bit rich coming from Henry but I didn't mention it. I was still recalling that afternoon with Claire. I had never even considered the possibility that she had lied during her confession just to get rid of me. I didn't believe she would, but then I didn't want to believe it. I glanced at Liv and reminded myself that she was the actual detective, methodical and objective. Or as objective as she could be, dealing with a subject as strange and subjective as magic. I wondered if I was actually helping her investigation. Certainly, I could consult on the possible uses of magic but in all other areas, I was biased. Especially when it came to Claire.

I took another slice of pizza and joined Henry at the window. I peered down at the two remaining students through my father's discarded binoculars. We stood together for a minute listening to Liv ask my father more questions about broader mage culture. My father was in his element and slipped comfortably into teacher mode.

"She wouldn't lie to you, Fin", Henry said. "I knew her as well as anyone, and she just wouldn't."

"Maybe", I said. "I'm not sure I can trust my judgement on this, though."

"Trust me. Doubt everything else about what happened if you have to, but you two have been through a lot, together and apart, and you've still always been there for each other. Don't start questioning that now."

I nodded, remembering Greg's statement about Liv's whereabouts in the weeks before her death. "Did Claire mention any new patients? Anyone high risk, anything like that?"

"No, nothing. She didn't exactly give me details about her patients though. Occasionally she would say if she had a particularly bad day but I'm certain I would have known if she was seeing anyone really troubled", Henry said. "She seemed fine before she left."

"You're certain? We heard that after she disappeared she still went into the office once a week. The only reason I could think of her doing that is if she had a patient on suicide watch, or something like that."

"Oh, well she was probably just going for a session herself."

"Claire was having counselling?" Liv said, from across the room.

"It's not unusual, most people working in mental health do it."

"But once a week seems a lot, when did that start?" I said.

"About a year ago. I think she was having a pretty tough time with one of her patients back then."

"Did she say that?"

"Not in so many words - she couldn't talk about her patients directly - but I noticed things. I figured she was about to run out on me again but instead she told me to keep a closer eye on her over the next few weeks. She took some time off and was really low for a while, but we got through it."

"That's when she started talking to someone at her office?" I asked.

"Yeah, she gave me his number just in case. Doctor Summers, I think his name was?"

"June? Doctor June?" Liv said.

"That's the one. Knew it was seasonal", Henry said.

"Can you remember exactly when Claire took that time off?" I asked, turning to Henry. He was still standing at the window, his head resting against the window pane.

Henry thought for a moment. "I think it was late March, maybe the first week of April. Why is it important?"

"We think the killer might have been one of her patients during that period. It had to have been someone connected to their practice", Liv said.

"Can you get a list of names?" I asked.

"The digital records were all destroyed before we got there", she said.

"But they still have the shredded hard copies? That will help them narrow down the search, surely?" I asked.

Liv pinched the bridge of her nose. "The police have a photograph of the killer leaving the crime scene. They will be throwing all their resources into the manhunt now. I doubt they have even started looking at the paperwork."

"They didn't get any patient files after Claire was killed?" Robert sounded appalled by the lack of effectiveness in the London police force.

Liv for her part seemed unaffected by the slight. "We wanted to", she said, "but we were still waiting on the warrant to come through. It would have been a higher priority if we weren't trying to identify the other victims. I still don't see how they fit into this. If it was a former patient of Claire's, why not go after her when she was alone?"

"Henry, did Claire keep any notes anywhere other than home or at the office?"

"Hmm, maybe? We have a lockup in Brixton", he said, scratching the side of his head. "We used it mostly for a couple of sofas and lamps and stuff after we moved in together, but now that I think about it I feel like I've seen some boxes of files in there too."

"Has she been there recently?" Liv asked.

"I wouldn't say recently, but within the last five or six months. She could have dropped off some more files."

"We should get over there and take a look once we are done here. How's it looking?"

"Still a two-horse race", Henry said.

"Ok, let's speed things along a little. Hedge our bets, as it were", I said.

CHAPTER 15

"Can't you just go up to them and ask for their diaries?" Liv said, irritably. "Blank their memories or make them think it's yours? There must be a quicker way."

Robert and Henry both laughed.

"Why is that funny?" Liv asked.

"There are other ways, but I'm running pretty low on keepsakes right now, particularly since the dragon incident", I said.

"Did you say dragon?" Henry grinned. He had been like an excitable puppy since I suggested my plan to relieve the two students of their property. At the mention of a dragon he looked positively giddy. "You have to tell me about this."

He and Robert were rifling through an Ikea wardrobe in the corner of the office stuffed with a dozen dress shirts, jackets and variety of expensive looking shoes.

"Here", Robert said, holding up a grey shirt and a jacket. "This will match your colouring nicely."

"Perfect!" he said, beaming.

"What part of this plan requires you to dress up?" I asked.

My father rolled his eyes at me and Henry began pulling off his t-shirt. I turned to Liv, who was clearly having second thoughts.

"There must be a quicker way", she said.

"I'm open to suggestions, but without you playing the police card, I can't think of a way that doesn't require some seriously invasive magic, which frankly we can't spare given what we are up against." I thought of the bookshop with the overpriced bag of keepsakes ready to go and wished I had gone back and paid the woman's inflated prices.

"What about Robert? You really think he sold all of his keepsakes?"

"I wouldn't put it passed him. Teaching keeps him in a pretty steady flow so he tends to run things pretty close to the bone sometimes. I'm sure he has more stashed away but we should keep as much in reserve as possible."

She eyed me suspiciously. "We aren't confronting him. Once we find him, we just have to follow him until we have enough evidence to pass on to the team in charge of the investigation."

"Right, but better we go in prepared. You've seen

what he can do."

She didn't say anything but continued to watch me as Henry pulled on a suede jacket over a shirt that was two sizes too small for him, the gaps between each button opening to reveal his hairy belly. Mercifully the jacket buttoned easily across his stomach, covering the worst of it.

"Alright, ready?" I asked.

My father and Henry both looked genuinely excited by the prospect of some mischief. My father rubbed his hands together and even exhaled into his hand to check his breath.

"You realise this is ridiculous, don't you?" Liv said.

"What? Three grown men and a police officer conspiring to steal a teenager's diary? Yes, I'm quite aware."

"Come on, you are ruining it", Henry said, doing a surprisingly good imitation of an emoticon sad face.

"And they are both twenty-two, thank you very much", Robert added.

"Fine, just try not to enjoy this too much", I said, holding the door open for my father.

"See you soon." Robert winked before squaring his shoulders and striding down the hallway.

I sighed and followed him.

"Did you really sell off your keepsakes?" I asked as we took the stairs.

"She has you questioning your own father?" he asked, sounding more amused than hurt. "What can I say, I saw a good opportunity and was given a very good price. How was I to know you would need my help? I suppose you could have returned one of my many calls, but then hell would have frozen over so where would that get us?"

I started to apologise but he interrupted me.

"Game face, son! Here we go", he said, pushing the handle of the fire escape and stepping out into a cool summer evening. We crossed the courtyard path before veering left towards the girl sitting cross-legged on the grass in her dark red Dr. Martens.

She looked up as we approached and I noticed a lipstick tone that matched perfectly with the colour of her boots.

"Victoria, would you care to join my son and I for a quick drink?"

"Oh, alright", she said, smiling. I thought I saw her blush a little bit.

"Good, good. So this is my son, Finley", he said.

I smiled. "You can call me Fin", I said, shaking her hand.

"Okay."

"Ryan, you must join us too. I want to go over our last chess match", Robert said, calling across the field.

Robert gave me a more formal introduction to Ryan, and we too shook hands.

"Finley here used to be quite the chess player in his time, nowhere near our standards of course but a solid player nonetheless." As we headed off campus, my father leading the group, he was like a conductor leading an orchestra. Any awkwardness there could have been between this unlikely procession was quickly quashed by my father's relentless charm. He wasn't obnoxious or performing, he just excelled at picking up social cues and anticipating conversational lulls long before they ever presented themselves. He drew connections between the three of us, digging through our lives for threads of common interest like some savant seamstress.

Within minutes my nerves about the plan evaporated as I quickly found myself absorbed in a discussion with Victoria about the works of Japanese director and animator Hayao Miyazaki, whom we both shared a love for. Robert had interrupted me asking a question about Victoria's classes to pointedly ask her about a pin in her hair I hadn't previously noticed. I recognised it instantly as belonging to the enormous furry creature from *My Neighbour*

Totoro, and instantly fell into a comfortable back and forth.

"I think *Castle in the Sky* was the first film of his I ever watched, but *Mononoke* has to be my favourite. What about you?" I said.

Victoria nodded, as if these were acceptable answers to her. She held an almost rueful smile as she considered her answer, as if it was a question she had given a great deal of thought to. "*Totoro* was first for me, but I'm not sure I could pick a favourite. Maybe *Mononoke* or *Spirited Away.* Now the important stuff; subtitled or dubbed?" she said, as if she were asking me if I thought Jesus was a good guy or not.

"Definitely subbed. The dubbed versions of the later stuff is solid, but the voices never feel quite right for me."

"Way too Disney", she added, with an approving nod of the head.

We arrived outside a pub and my father ushered us inside. At barely 5.30pm the place was just starting to fill up with the evening crowd, though thankfully there were still plenty of tables free.

Robert directed us to the nearest one and negotiated the seating arrangements so that Victoria and Ryan were sat beside one another, facing us across the table. The tables ran four horizontal rows from the windows in end to end groups of three or four. The bare floor boards and wood panelled walls gave the pub a dated, raw quality that reminded me of my own university days.

I tried to guard my expression, knowing any visual sign of nostalgia shown to my father would be swiftly used against me and my life choices.

"Miss it?" Robert asked, immediately. He had been watching me, with a slightly smug expression. He could always tell what I was thinking. "You know you could come back?"

"One day, maybe", I lied. It was old ground for us and the reason why I skirted his calls as often as I did.

I expected more, but my father nodded and busied himself making two trips to the bar, returning with three dark ales and finally a Guinness and black for Victoria. We clinked our pints together and the conversation quickly split off; my father discussing a series of books I hadn't read with Victoria while I started on graphic novels with Ryan.

"*Superman: Birthright* had a nice take on the origin story", Ryan said.

"I've not read that one. Was that Mark Waid?" I said, glancing back at the door.

"Yeah, you can tell he really loves the character",

Ryan said.

"What about Alan Moore?"

"I liked *Whatever Happened to the Man of Tomorrow* to be honest though, I think he's good but kind of overrated. I didn't get *The Killing Joke,* at all, but then I always liked Barbara Gordon as Batgirl", he added, reasonably.

"Really? What about the ending?"

"Yeah", he cringed a little. "I didn't like Batman laughing with the Joker. It looked cool, but I thought it was a bit of a limp finish after what happened to Barb. Batman doesn't laugh."

I stopped halfway, and returned my pint of bitter to the table and stared at him. "You don't know?"

"Know what?"

"The ending, when the laughter cuts out? Batman kills him, he breaks the Joker's neck."

"What?" Ryan's eyes went wide.

"Honestly, you don't see it, but it's heavily implied. The laughter cuts out suddenly remember? Right after Batman reaches for his throat. That's the *Killing Joke*." I felt an enormous amount of satisfaction at seeing the shock in his face.

"How did I not see that? I'll have to reread it when I get home."

I smiled, glancing across at Victoria and my

father, who were deep in conversation. They were both smiling a lot in that indulgent private way, people who are intimate often do. They were discussing *Quadrophenia*, a film I had never seen.

My father was right, I did miss it. The campus, the lifestyle, the conversation. I had been a private investigator for nearly a year. It had started out as a temporary hiatus, but after a few months I realised I had become too comfortable in academia, too accommodating of my addiction. I had been blessed with a father well versed in magic, but this had blinded us both to certain things.

My disagreements with my father were both philosophical and personal. We agreed, at least fundamentally, that the mage's duty was to better the world and to help those around us. Beyond this very simple concept, however, is where our beliefs differed. He believed I should follow in his footsteps, pick a ladder and climb my way to the top as quickly as possible, then branch out and help those around me. He felt a mage's first duty was to himself and his kin.

I agreed with this to a point, but this presented me with several problems. For one, it meant being dishonest. Not the type of lying one does here and there, I mean the kind you build your life around. It meant leveraging my power to get ahead, to subtly influence our peers, make ourselves smarter, giving ourselves any and all edge our magics might afford. It wasn't easy, cheating like that was a commitment you couldn't pull off half-heartedly.

That was where I faltered.

I was twenty-three when the cracks became apparent, twenty-five when it all fell apart. A mage needs friends, and I had one of the best. Ian was honest, loyal and more studious than anyone has any right or reason to be. He also wrote copious handwritten notes in preparation for any big exam which he passed on to me without hesitation. On a regular diet of Ian's castoffs I was his equal in all areas of study, with one crucial distinction. While he spent every evening pouring over books I was doing what my father had taught me, out making friends, establishing contacts and getting girls to write down their phone numbers on napkins.

I convinced Ian he needed to get out and make some more friends. *It's not just what you know, it's who you know*, I told him. Ian died a little over fifteen hours later after getting drunk enough to step into traffic. His mother passed on some letters he had written which mentioned me. He never resented me, he was just grateful to have a decent friend, but then he never knew I had cheated him and stolen every one of his successes for myself.

I know it wasn't my fault. Who wouldn't encourage a sheltered friend to join them on a night out? Still, innocent men hide nothing and I hid everything. It was how I had been taught and therein lied the problem.

Robert had spent so many years perfecting his life strategy for me, so much time agonizing over his own moral imperatives before passing the results on to me, he had forgotten how important the agonizing part was. He had lines he would not cross, lines hard won, reinforced and cemented in place through a lifetime of struggle. Mine, I soon discovered, were simply not robust enough to stop me speeding out of control towards them. I was a man drinking to build courage and never quite finding enough of the stuff.

A few months out of higher education I gained some perspective. I had needed a change and Claire had suggested working as a PI. She had been joking of course, but I had liked the idea and run with it.

"Are you alright?" Ryan asked.

I looked up suddenly, realising I had been silently staring into the bottom of my pint glass. "Yeah, fine", I said, doing my best to smile. "Just missing the student life a bit." The wave of nostalgia had hit me harder than I thought it would. I took a moment to dig through my emotional baggage for the source and realised the driving force wasn't me. Doctor Silver was making a gradual return. Minds seek commonality, and my lack of children had meant Silver had been forced to dig deeper for it.

"Oh yeah? I've no idea what I'm going to do next year. What sort of work do you do?"

"I'm in security." I said, immediately. The PI conversation was not one I felt like having, not with Doctor Silver pushing for greater mental real estate. I pulled a biro from my coat pocket and reached for the wooden block at the centre of the table which held the napkins and menus.

"Are you guys wanting to eat? The food is better than the beer", Ryan said.

"Oh yeah? Uh maybe", I said, spotting Henry's entrance out of the corner of my eye. He made a show of stretching as he yawned before moving to the bar like he was re-enacting a performance of someone who had just finished a long day at the office. He was sweating profusely, though thankfully he made no move to take off the borrowed jacket. I opened a menu and scribbled Silver's thoughts down between the small plates and the starters as my own nerves flared up in response to Henry's.

"Yeah, beer is better round at *The Lukin*, but this is closer", Ryan said glancing at my father with a wry smile, as if he expected him to argue otherwise.

I nodded, returning to the menu. My heart skipped a beat as I read the name of the pub off the menu. *The Fitzrovia Belle.* I silently cursed my father, blinking back unwelcome tears as I realised the name alone would be enough to draw my father here.

"What's good?" I asked Ryan, over the menu as I struggled to expel enough of Silver to regain composure. Henry slid into the seat directly behind Ryan and Victoria and set down his pint beside a leather messenger bag before withdrawing *Terrifying Tales* by Edgar Allan Poe. I almost expected him to produce eye glasses and start smoking a pipe as he opened the book and drank a quarter of his pint in one pull. He casually turned in his seat and hung an arm over the back of his chair and gradually started reaching for Ryan's backpack.

"Burger is always a safe choice", Ryan said.

"Hmm", I said, bobbing my head as if considering. "How are the salads?"

"I've not tried them to be honest. Hard to mess up leaves though", Ryan shrugged, glancing at the bar.

"Yeah, I guess. Hey, it's my round. Help me navigate the ale list?" I said, feeling the prickling at the corners of my eyes starting to ease.

"Sure."

We both rose and headed towards the bar discussing *The Dark Knight Returns*. I glanced back at the table every few seconds, seeing Henry sweating hard, his thumb so firmly pressed up against the inside of the book's spine I was certain he had yet to turn a page. The look of pained concentration gave way to relief, and he clumsily stuffed the book into his own bag before letting out a deep breath. From across the bar I saw a drop of sweat fall from the corner of his eyebrow into his victory sip.

"Pint of *Frequent Flyer*, please", Ryan told the barman.

"Same, and a *Guinness* and black, please." I said, continuing my outpour of emotion onto the back of a beermat.

"You and your old man are a lot alike." Ryan observed, watching my scribbles as we waited on the *Guinness*.

I paid, and returned to the table. Just as I went to put the pint of *Guinness* down, Liv knocked into me, turning the glass and spilling the contents into Victoria's lap. She leapt up, sliding her chair back suddenly.

"My apologies, miss", Liv said, raising a hand in a placating gesture towards Victoria as she turned to my father, ignoring me completely. "Mr Robert Chase, I'm going to have to ask you to come down to the station with me."

"What? Why?" he demanded, rising from his chair. My father continued to look outraged as Liv did her thing.

"Sir, I will arrest you if I have to", she said, she was gripping his arm as if she meant it.

There was a flurry of movement behind Victoria as Henry reached for her bag. I stepped into Ryan's path, blocking his view of Henry's nervous hands. My breath caught in my throat as Victoria started to turn, reaching behind her for her bag.

Liv saved us at the last moment by slamming my father's face down into the table. "I'm arresting you on suspicion of fraud. You do not have to say anything unless you wish to do so though it may harm your defence if you do not mention when questioned, something you later rely on in court."

Robert grunted as she slapped on the cuffs and dragged him out through the front door while the rest of us looked on, stunned by the blatant act of police brutality.

We stared after them in awe. I waited for Henry to give me the nod then turned to Ryan and Victoria.

"I better go with him. Really sorry about this, I'm sure we'll get it all cleared up", I said, as Henry disappeared into the crowd at the bar.

"Yeah, of course. It was good meeting you", Ryan said.

"Will Robert be alright?" Victoria said, pulling a wad of napkins from her bag and dabbing vaguely at her jeans as she continued to watch the door.

"I'm sure it's just a misunderstanding. Take care, both of you", I said, then noticing how Ryan wasn't watching the door at all, his eyes fixed in an entirely different direction. "Ryan, make sure she gets home alright, yeah?" He started, as if I'd accused him of staring. I shook his hand then followed after my father and Liv.

Amber was parked right around the corner, and in moments we all piled into the taxi and drove away. My father sat beside Henry, both of whom were laughing like musketeers. My father even seemed to be crying at the fact that he was still in handcuffs.

I grinned at the pair of them.

"So how did we do?"

"Jackpot!" Henry said, grinning and pulling out the two diaries from his bag and fanning himself with them.

I took them and started skimming through the pages as Liv took the handcuffs off my dad, whose laughter had subsided enough for them to begin recanting the scene we had just left.

"Such deft hands, you should have been a pickpocket", Robert said, patting Henry on the back once his hands were free.

I snorted, and even Liv cracked a grin at that, though she shook her head while doing so.

"So, any good?" Robert asked. "Or has this old dog truly begun to lose his touch?"

"Well Victoria is definitely a fan", I said, surprised by some of the content. "She knows your schedule pretty well, there's even some letters in here too we should be able to use."

"Just a crush?" my father said, sounding disappointed.

"Afraid so. Ryan however…"

"*Really?*" Liv and Henry said at the same time.

"Ah ha!" Robert grinned. "It wouldn't be my first male admirer."

"Not exactly", I said reading a few more pages. "He likes Victoria, but knows she likes you."

"Oh, Jesus", Liv said, rolling her eyes.

"I know, but he's following Dad to figure out why she likes him. Pick up some tips sort of thing. He's pretty familiar with your work schedule too."

"Will that still work?" Liv asked.

"Not on its own, but the two of them combined might be enough. Dad? you're the expert on this?" I handed the diaries over to Robert who peered down his nose at them as if he were marking an essay.

"It should suffice", he agreed.

"Are you actually sulking?" Liv asked.

I smiled but cut off the argument by sliding open the partition and calling through to Amber.

"Amber, can you take us to Brixton, please?" I said. I nodded to Henry, who squeezed through the partition and passed on directions.

When I turned back around, Liv was staring at me.

"Just in case", I said.

CHAPTER 16

We made it to Claire and Henry's lockup on the east side of Brixton a little after 7pm. Two rows of garages ran the length of the street beneath two blocks of run-down high-rise flats. A chill had crept into the air since the sun had set and I felt myself shiver as I stepped out of the cab.

We were standing at the garage door before Henry remembered he didn't have the key on him. Thankfully I had my picks in the taxi and I fussed the lock open in a little under a minute.

"Easy pickings eh?" Henry whispered. He had changed back into his t-shirt, giving all of us an eyeful in the process, and had been scanning the street playing lookout as if we were committing another crime.

"Padlocks are easy", I said, knowing it was the kind of brash statement Henry would enjoy.

He beamed and slid the garage door up before clambering over a sofa and disappearing into the back of the dark recesses of the garage. Liv fiddled with her phone and it lit up like a torch, filling the garage with white-blue light.

"Thanks", Henry called, as he stumbled knocking over a lamp. "I think this is it", he said, sliding two sturdy cardboard boxes across a dusty leather sofa towards me. I pulled the lid off the first and flicked through the top file.

"This is it." I passed the first box to Robert and the second to Liv.

"We need to drop her home before we do this", Liv said.

"Who?" I asked, distractedly.

"Amber."

"Oh right", I said. "We'll drop her off once we are done here. Are you alright driving?"

"You want me to drive your car? Why don't you drive it, you have a license", she said.

"Legally I can, but mages make really awful drivers."

"Some more so than others", Robert added, raising his eyebrows at me.

I cleared my throat. "It's a sensitivity thing. Mage's are very susceptible to the influence of other drivers. It's just safer if we don't."

"I don't mind driving", Henry called.

"No", Robert and I said in unison.

"He actually doesn't have a license", I added.

"Less of a risk than either of you."

"It's still illegal."

"Oh that's where we are drawing the line is it?"

I considered him for a moment – he had a point.

"*I'll* drive", Liv said, walking to the taxi examining the contents of the first box in her arms.

There were four boxes of patient files in total, which we stacked into the already cramped confines of the taxi. Henry extracted himself from the garage and presented me with a final Tupperware box. He handed it to me before dropping heavily off the arm of the sofa onto the pavement beside me.

"Are you sure about this?" I said, looking down through the clear plastic lid at the treasures within. I could make out a stack of letters atop a dozen or so scuffed romance novels. This was Claire's rainy day supply, her backup in case things got desperate.

"That's everything. It's not much but if it helps catch this guy, its better in your hands than mine", he shrugged.

"Thank you."

Henry gave me a sad smile as he turned away and closed the garage door. It struck me then just how much grief he must have been carrying. He needed this. It wasn't just about being out of the flat that they had shared, he needed closure. She had left him a month ago, but he didn't know if they would have reconciled or if she had left him for good this time. I felt selfish and ashamed of myself for not realised it sooner. He acted upbeat so much of the time it was easy to forget we were both grieving.

"Henry", I said, as he closed the padlock on the garage door. "Claire was coming back, you know that right? It wasn't the end for you two. It was the addiction that led her away, not you. But she was clean, and she was coming home. She told me so herself."

When he turned, I thought for the second time in as many days he was going to hit me. But his lip trembled and he put his arms around me in a fierce brotherly hug. I let him lean on me for a few moments, until my neck started to hurt, then I patted him on the back and pushed him off.

"You're a good dude, Fin", he sniffed.

"Come on, we should get moving."

He nodded and we climbed back into the cab, my father turning to me the moment the door closed, a disapproving look on his face.

"Fin, this poor girl tells me you aren't paying her for her time as your personal chauffeur?"

"It's an *unpaid* internship", I said, looking around me for support. Liv avoided my eye and my father continued to frown, though his eyes twinkled with mischief. I turned to Henry who sniffed and wiped his eyes on his t-shirt. "You can't buy this kind of life experience", he said.

"Tight fisted fuckers", Amber muttered.

My father's eyebrows shot up his forehead and he bit his lip to stop himself from laughing.

I did my best to avoid Amber's eye. "Can you drive us back to your house? We'll take the taxi on from there."

"What? Why?" Amber said, looking at me in the rear-view mirror. Her eyes narrowed. "Where are you going?"

"Somewhere dangerous, which is why we are taking you home", Liv said.

I rolled my eyes, "Don't tell her that!" I said, incredulous.

"She has a right to know what you are getting her involved in, Fin."

"I concur", Robert added, his voice stern and unnecessarily pompous, though by all other accounts he seemed to be enjoying himself.

"They have a point", Henry said, reasonably.

I shook my head. "It's not that, she'll want to come if she thinks it's going to be interesting."

"I'm nineteen, not nine. Besides why would I want to hang around with a bunch of old people?" Amber replied, sounding bored.

My father cleared his throat. "I like this one, son. Wherever did you find her?" he said.

Knowing full well he was my one and only source of free labour, and that I was in no position to complain, I opted to keep my mouth shut.

Amber slid the partition closed and muttered something that sounded acutely like *'fucking wizards'*, though with the partition closed it was hard to know for certain. She put the car into first and pulled away smoothly, mounting the curb as she pulled a U-turn and headed further south down Brixton Hill.

In the cramped confines of the rear cabin, we each took a file from the first box and started leafing through Claire's meticulously handwritten notes and quickly gave up when lack of light and Amber's driving got the better of us.

The evening had closed in by the time we reached the Domino's Pizza and turned left onto Cricklade Avenue where Amber lived. Amber pulled into a permit-only bay and switched off the engine before gathering her assortment of cosmetics and returning them to her handbag.

She got out and slammed the door without so much as a goodbye, and made her way up the little path to her front door without looking back.

"Such an enterprising young girl", Robert said, smiling as he turned a page in his file.

I got out of the taxi, holding the door open for Liv as she climbed out behind me. I was just finishing a stretch, working out the kinks in my tired muscles, when Amber stopped in front of me, hand on her hip looking sour, as if she was about to do something unpleasant.

"What?" I asked.

"You can come in and use the kitchen if you want to read or setup that spell of yours", she said.

"Uhh, spell?" I said.

"That partition is plastic, not lead, you muppet. I've heard most of what you've been talking about."

"Really?"

"Mhmm. I saw that man try and punch you yesterday too, remember? I was certain he was going to flatten you. Glass jaw like that..." she said eyeing my chin and shaking her head.

"Right", I said, suddenly feeling careless and vulnerable.

"I saw the news last night about the hotel, and where I picked you up earlier was right where that girl and her dad were attacked. You are really chasing a killer?"

"Yeah, we are. I'll understand if you want to quit. It might be best to take a break until this is over. I'll still give you a good review for your work placement."

"Bloody right you will", she shrugged. "I'll think about it. So you coming in? Mum won't be back for a bit and Granddad won't give a shit."

I looked back at the others and could see them each struggling to read under the same flickering bulb in the back cabin.

"That would be great", I said, but she was already at her front door.

"Fine, but I'm not making any fucking tea", she said loud enough so that half the street could hear.

"Fair enough."

We filed in through Amber's front door, each of us carrying a box of Claire's old case files. A man in his eighties sat so well ensconced in a threadbare arm chair facing the TV, none of us noticed him until Henry blocked his view of the TV and he started to grumble. Amber gave Henry a shove out of the way and the old man quietened instantly as his view of *Homes Under the Hammer* was restored. We left the old man to his show and settled around the dining table.

"So, what do you need for this spell exactly?" Liv

asked. She remained standing a good two feet behind the closest chair, as if she expected it to burst into flames any moment. Henry, on the other hand, sat down and tucked his feet under the table, looking eagerly between us. He had always been fascinated by magic.

"Not much, a shoelace or a bit of string and a nail, or pen to use as our compass. Anything like that will do", Robert said. My father produced the two journals and stacked them neatly on the table in front of him.

"Is that it?" Henry said, he seemed disappointed.

"You were hoping for fireworks?" Robert asked.

"Maybe not fireworks, but something a little more spectacular. I thought this was the serious stuff?"

"It'll be plenty impressive if it works", I said. "Amber, do you have any screws or nails? We only need one."

Amber exhaled heavily out her nose before going to the kitchen drawers and rummaging through them. Liv stepped forwards and retrieved the scrap of folded paper from her pocket. She carefully unfolded it and placed it on the table between us.

My father unbuttoned his sleeves and rolled them up his forearms. I looked up as a breeze touched my face and spotted Amber propping the back door open with a bin while Liv watched her out of the corner of her eye with her eyebrow raised. She glanced at us then reached over the sink and pushed open the window.

"If anyone requires the bathroom, now would be the time to go", Robert said.

"Why?" Henry asked.

"We don't know how far away the killer is, or how long it will take us to get to him. Once we start hunting him we will have to keep going or the magic may wear off before we reach him."

"Oh, we can't just drop a pin on a map or something?"

"Afraid it doesn't work like that. It'll be more like a compass, only this monster will be *our* true north", Robert said. "You are certain he wrote this?" He peered down at the number without touching the paper.

"That's what we were told", Liv said.

"Good. If he is as aggressively active as you say, he shouldn't be too far. What time is it?"

I checked my watch. "Almost eight. Roads should be clear enough."

Liv took the lid off one of the boxes and started going through them, as Amber dropped a ball of string and a box of screws onto the table before retreating to the kitchen.

"Thanks, Amber."

"Want some help?" Amber asked Liv.

Liv blinked at her. The rest of us turned to look equally nonplussed in her direction.

Amber blushed. "Sooner you find what you are looking for, the sooner you can fuck off out of my house."

"Pick a box. We are looking for any patient records between February and April last year. Just mark them with a star when you find one."

Amber nodded and grabbed a bunch of files from the same box and started reading. The pair of them leant against the kitchen counter, frowning into their respective files. We each took it in turns to use the bathroom before returning to the kitchen table.

"Adam, pay attention. I'll need your help with this", Robert said. "Yours too, Henry."

Henry sat up a little straighter and nodded.

"Why does he keep calling him Adam?" Amber asked.

"A little quiet, please", I said, avoiding looking at Henry, who was smirking.

"I'll tell you later", Liv whispered. She too sounded amused.

I picked up the roll of string and untangled it before cutting a section about a foot long and tying it around one of the longer screws in the pack Amber had provided.

"Alright, now Henry, if you would be so kind as to hold our compass over the piece of paper holding the phone number" Robert said.

I passed him the bit of string and the screw after checking the knot was tight. He rubbed his fingers against his thumbs before taking it from me, his face serious.

"Now Henry, all you have to do is remain perfectly still with the screw dangling just here", Robert said, guiding his hand. "Just a little higher. There, perfect. Now whatever happens, just hold that position until I tell you, alright? The phone number might burst into flames or jump around a little but don't panic, and don't move. It's all completely normal." he said.

"No worries, I've got this", Henry said, cracking his neck like a prize fighter going through his warm-up routine.

Both Amber and Liv glanced up from their files at the mention of fire. Liv's eyes darted across to the fire blanket above the stove and then to the back door.

"Very good." my father said, handing me one of the diaries.

"So if nobody needs the toilet, I think we are…"

"I need the toilet", the old man croaked behind

me. I turned, in my seat and regarded the old man. He looked confused, as if he couldn't remember where he was.

"Then get off your arse you idle old prick", Amber said.

The old man's face broke into an enormous grin, then he belted out a hearty laugh watching our faces. "Fuckin' vegans", he said, still chuckling to himself and shaking his head.

My father blinked then grinned. "Well if we are all quite ready, let's begin."

A silence fell over the kitchen as my father and I both focused on the phone number lying between us. We both rested a hand on our respective diaries with the other, fingers splayed, in a barrier either side of the phone number.

I pressed my hand into the first page of Ryan's diary and began to draw in power from it. My mind returned to my all-too-brief conversation with Victoria. What had seemed like a positive exchange at the time suddenly left me feeling embarrassed and childish. Why had I brought up those films in the first place? She must have thought I was such an idiot. I felt my cheeks start to redden at the memory. Why didn't I try to talk to her again, invite her to the bar? My dad was way too old for her anyway.

"Steady, son", my father said, as I felt the lick of heat rolling between my fingers.

I blinked, keeping my eyes focused on the phone number and eased back a little, calming the stream of power flowing up through me.

"Still with me?" my father asked.

"Yeah, just getting past that initial anxiety", I said.

"First hit is always the hardest." Henry said.

"Right." I gave myself a mental shake, reminding myself and the anxious part of Ryan of the task at hand. I returned my focus to the piece of paper between our hands and it started to twitch ever so slightly, as if a tiny insect was moving beneath it.

"Alright, I'm ready", I said, gripping the diary tighter.

"Excellent. On my count, son. Everyone, it's about to get very smoky in here but don't worry, it will dissipate quickly, nothing else will burn except the diaries, such is the nature of mage fire."

"On three?" I asked.

"Just like last time. One!" he said.

My hands started to shake as I pressed down into the ashen core of the diary.

"Two."

I accelerated the process. Drawing in more of the diary, half of it was spent already, a steady stream of smoke billowing around the dining table. I held the energy in the centre of my chest before pushing it down my arm and through my trembling fingers. The phone number lifted off the table, held by the sheer concentration of magical energy pooling beneath it.

The centre of the diary burnt through completely and the magic it had held thundered through my body like a powerful electrical current and out through my fingers, sending the scrap of paper higher until it was an inch away from the dangling screw. It hovered there as our wills aligned. *Find them,* I said inwardly. *Find who did this. Guide us to the one responsible. Take me to the one who killed Claire!*

"Three!" Robert said. As he said the word I shifted my attention to the dangling screw, only it was gone; obscured not just by the rising smoke but by sudden explosion of white. Thick foam sprayed over the table, the diaries, Henry, Robert and myself. I recoiled in shock, turning my head away from the source beside me. As the smoke cleared Amber's grandfather stood over us holding a kitchen-sized fire extinguisher.

"Where is the compass?" Robert asked, wiping foam from his face.

I looked around, and though Henry's arm was still suspended above the table, the string and screw were nowhere to be seen.

"Fucking hell, Grandad", Amber cried, as I started wiping foam from the table in search of the missing compass.

"Well excuse me for trying to stop the house from burning the fuck down!"

"It wasn't on fire!"

"Where'd all this smoke come from then?"

My father lifted something from the floor and held it up. The screw hung from the string, swinging back and forth and pointing in no particular direction.

"What the fuck is going on in here?" a woman shouted from the doorway.

I was too angry to respond. I slumped back in my chair continuing to watch the screw.

"You can put your arm down now", Robert said to Henry quietly. "We failed."

I glanced at him; he was still holding his arm extended over the table.

"I can't", he said.

"Grandad just had a funny turn, that's all." Amber said.

"I did not have a…"

"QUIET!" I shouted, the room fell quiet as everyone looked at me. Everyone except Henry who was still looking at his arm, motionless above the table, a bewildered expression on his face.

"Henry, can you move your arm?"

"Erm…" he thought for a moment, the muscles in his jaw tightening. "No?" he said, baffled.

"Can you move anything? Try and stand up?" my father asked.

Henry blinked and rose from his chair though his arm remained extended, pointing directly at the TV.

Henry smiled after a moment. "I think your spell worked", he said, turning the rest of his body one way then the other until his own flexibility and the immovable right arm stopped him. "I'm the compass!"

"We have to move", I said, as the others stared at him. "Hurry, Liv you're driving." I grabbed the keys off the table and tossed them to her.

"Dad, the files. Amber, sorry about this. I'll pay for the damages", I said, rushing around the kitchen gathering up boxes with Liv and Robert. Amber piled a second box onto the one already in my arms.

"I'm holding you to that", she said, seemingly indifferent to her mother and grandfather shouting at one another. He was still holding the fire extinguisher and mercifully took the bulk of the angry woman's wrath.

We hurried for the door, stopping only briefly

to help Henry fold himself through the hallway and out onto the street. He still managed to take the skin off his knuckles even with the help of several of us pushing and contorting him.

"This feels so weird", Henry said.

Liv had her phone out and was walking alongside Henry. "He's pointing almost directly west", she said.

"Ok good", I said, piling in the back.

Henry climbed in the front passenger side, his right arm extended across the dashboard. Liv climbed into the driver's seat and started the engine while my father and I scraped foam off the files and tossed them in the back, before getting in ourselves.

I gave Amber a wave as Liv gunned the engine and we pulled away. Her face in the dim light from the open front door was unreadable. I hoped she didn't call the police, or worse, the university. I felt distinctly as if I had missed something, misjudged or underestimated her somehow. I had rarely seen her whole face, having, for the most part, seen only a portion of her scowling features in the rear-view mirror. It felt like I was seeing her again for the first time.

Amber disappeared as we reached the junction at the end of the road and a cry of pain brought me back to the present. Liv had started to make a left turn when Henry's possessed arm swung across the cabin and smacked her across the forehead.

"I am so sorry!" he said.

"In the back", she said, thickly, slamming her foot on the brake.

Henry climbed in the back with me, and Robert graciously accepted the safety of the front seat without hesitation. Henry sat in the back opposite me, pointing off to his right.

"Alright, go", I said.

It took some careful negotiating on roundabouts, but we gradually got the hang of it, yelling out directions based on Henry's position on a clock face.

"Two o'clock... Three o'clock... Now four", I said, ducking under Henry's arm as we swapped seats.

"Right turn coming up", Liv called back.

Henry and I prepared ourselves as the cab slowed, clasping our left hands and switching back to our original seats.

"Okay, one o'clock... twelve... now eleven."

"Alright, Robert keep an eye on that compass. I'll keep heading west towards the M4. If you stop pointing in the same direction then we know we have gone too far", she said, putting her foot down.

"Still west", Robert repeated in a bored tone every few minutes as Henry and I continued to swap seats whenever we made a turn and he needed to rotate his arm the opposite way. I could feel the magical hangover gradually starting to kick in. My initial excitement gave way to anxiety the further out of the centre of London we went. I found myself starting to sweat and grow more nauseated at the constant seat switching and Ryan's subtle pull on my emotions.

My father looked far better by comparison. Once we escaped the winding roads around the more residential parts of London and we had to turn less often, he rested Liv's phone in his lap and used the backlight to pick through his own tobacco pouch. He cracked a window, pulled out his pipe and lit it.

"Here, this should help. Make it last though. I wasn't lying about running low", he said, passing his pipe back to me.

Henry managed to club me across the top of the head as I was taking my first pull on the old pipe, but I didn't mind. The magic calmed my nerves considerably.

We continued out on toward the M4, with Henry's hand swinging a few inches to either side of my face. When his arm started to hurt, I stacked Claire's boxes and a few case files up in the centre of the floor so he could rest it.

"Thanks," he said, with a sigh, sinking lower into his chair. We drove for a full hour along the

M4, passing Hayes, then Slough, without Henry's possessed arm moving much more than an inch or two in either direction.

"Where are we now?" I asked.

"A few miles from Maidenhead", Robert called from the front seat.

"How long do you think the spell will last?" I asked.

"No way to tell."

"We could be driving for hours", I sighed.

"That isn't you talking, my son isn't that negative. Keep smoking."

I returned the pipe to my mouth and did as he suggested, pulling hard and holding the smoke in my lungs before exhaling slowly.

The pipe flew out of my mouth as Henry swiped his hand across my face, knocking it the floor of the cab. He spun around, his arm smacking hard into the window before he managed to contort his body around. He stumbled and fell into my lap groaning in pain and struggling to rub his bruised hand as he continued to point behind us.

"Come off at the next exit." I said, rubbing my face and retrieving my father's pipe from the floor.

CHAPTER 17

"I think he's pointing towards Bray", Robert said, as we peeled off the motorway, crossed a roundabout and doubled back on ourselves.

Henry pointed out the right window as we drove into Bray's town centre. I could see a lake ahead, reflecting moonlight off the dark water. As the cab drew closer, Henry's arm began to swing back to the left side of the car.

"This is it, pull over", I said.

Liv pulled the taxi up on the side of the road and killed the engine. I switched seats to sit beside Henry, resting my head almost on his shoulder and looking down his arm as if I were sighting through a rifle scope.

"He's pointing towards the lake?" Liv said.

"There's some houses up there on the left", I said, squinting through the darkness. "I think he's pointing at one of them."

We sat in darkness for a moment while I pulled on a sturdy pair of walking boots and divided up

Claire's supply of keepsakes with Robert, each of us stuffing our coat pockets. I found six carefully rolled cigarettes in a silver case. The interior was lined with purple velvet and each rollie had a single word carefully written on the side of them like STRENGTH, CALM and CLARITY.

"Well are we just going to sit here? The spell could wear off any moment", Robert said.

Liv looked between us soberly. "This is a bad idea, we should be calling for backup."

"And tell them what? We can't turn back now. Dad's right, he could still be pointing at any one of a dozen houses."

Liv sighed. "Fine, but you all do exactly what I say, when I say it, alright? This is recon. I know you all have a personal interest, but if he is as dangerous as we think he is, our best option is to figure out and protect anyone he is targeting rather than confront him directly. Understood?" She turned to look at each of us in turn.

I nodded.

"No argument here, detective", Robert said.

"Yes, ma'am", Henry said, still sighting down his arm as if it were a rifle.

We left the taxi and formed a loose circle around Henry and his perpetually extended arm as we walked back up the road we had driven down. Henry pointed to the right where the road forked leading up a residential street called Tithe Barn Drive. The houses closest to the main road looked expensive with large gardens and brand new, German made cars parked in most of the spacious driveways. Henry continued to point deeper into the estate, so we continued. The quiet of the estate after the bustle of London was unnerving.

I tried to imagine the kind of killer that could live here in this perfect picture of suburban life. No matter how I twisted the picture, it wouldn't fit with the monster I had drawn in my mind. I thought perhaps this was just somewhere he could lay low and rest after another day of killing. Maybe Liv was right, and the killer was fast asleep. I thought of little Stephie. *No,* a part of me said. *Evil like this doesn't sleep.*

We paused briefly behind a hedgerow while a woman in a dressing gown wheeled a bin out to the end of her driveway before calling a Labrador and heading back inside.

"You're sure about this spell?" I said.

"Not really", Robert said.

"This could fit, you said he would have to be well resourced to acquire so much power?" Liv suggested.

"I suppose. I guess I just didn't picture this", I said, glancing at Liv.

"You'd be surprised", she said.

Once the woman's porch light went out we continued up to the next bend where the concrete fell away into a dirt road, to either side of which stood a stone pillar with a large number 63 chiselled out of the stone.

"That must be it", Liv said, her face illuminated by her phone as she peered down at the map on its display. "It must be that house."

Beyond a thick hedgerow and a smattering of elm trees stood a house visible only as a block of darkness against the clear night sky.

"There's no lights on. If this is the place and he really is asleep, this could be the best opportunity we have to corner him", I said.

"It's too dangerous", Liv said, glancing pointedly at my father and Henry. My father shivered, cupping his hands around his pipe for warmth and Henry had his head pitched to the side and was continuing to peer down the length of his arm.

"What is it?" I asked.

"It's just I'm pointing at the furthest left side of the building. We could walk around to the right to make sure it's definitely the house and not somewhere else on the other side of the lake", Henry said. "If he starts moving, we'll know exactly where he is, won't we?" he said, indicating his still-raised arm.

"He's right", Robert said. "If we leave now we don't have anything to aid your investigation."

Liv was staring at her phone as if she were considering calling it in. I could see her predicament plain enough; there was no evidence, no conceivable reason for her to suspect a man staying in this house. She had no cause whatsoever to direct the attention of the police here. "Fine, we'll do a lap of the house. But any sign of movement and we are gone, alright?"

We all nodded, and started up the path. The crunch of gravel beneath our feet and the sound of our coats flapping in the wind kept me glancing nervously back at Henry every few seconds. I was reassured to see the others were similarly nervous. The dark windows came into view as we wove our way through the trees until the front of the house came into view. There were no cars on the driveway, just two potted ferns framing the front door. My eyes flitted between the windows, looking for any sign of movement, when someone tapped my shoulder.

"I think the front door is open", Robert whispered. "Look there." He pointed.

"Any post?" I said.

"Keep moving, we are too in the open here." Liv said.

We were standing facing the front of the house where a proper paved road separated two lines of trees, which I guessed cut a more formal path back out to the rest of the estate.

"Wait", I said pointing at the heap of post just visible beyond the door. "Look, we are this close to a name."

Liv looked conflicted; bringing civilians clearly didn't sit well with her but these were exceptional circumstances. "Fine, wait for me over there behind the trees. I'll go", she said.

I caught her arm. "Let me help", I said, pulling a wad of napkins from my pocket. It was too dark to make out the words properly, so I just shoved the first one into my mouth and started chewing.

"That's really kind of disgusting", she said.

I nodded, my mouth too full of paper and ash to attempt a reply. I finally managed to swallow some of it without coughing or gagging, letting its power gather. She held out her hand which I pressed between both of mine, and imagining a bubble forming around her entire body, silenced her steps and muted the rustling of her clothes. After a moment, I nodded and released her hand.

She waited until we were hidden amongst the trees, then turned and started walking towards the front door. She looked small beside its grandeur. The lightless windows seemed to stare down at her, both hollow and intimidating.

"You should have gone with her", my father said, repeating exactly what I had just myself realised. She was the detective, meant to serve and protect and bring killers to justice. That was her job, not mine. But then it wasn't her job to deal with rogue mages. It wasn't mine either, but I at least had some defence against magic.

I watched, my heart beating harder in my chest, as Liv climbed silently up the steps to the front door. She squatted down, pausing as she stared into the room beyond. After a few moments she inched closer, reaching for the stack of letters pinned beneath the door. Her fingers closed round the nearest one and I held my breath, watching as she tried to pull it free. The door seemed to have been wedged by the stack of letters. I glanced at Henry who was still pointing unflinchingly at the front of the house.

I looked back at her. She was almost lying down she was so low to the ground, her arm fully extended as she pulled at the letter. I stepped around the tree and started towards her, keeping myself hunched over and low to the ground. I was halfway to her when the letter came free. I heard paperwork spilling across the floor as my foot hit the first step. The door swung wide, paused, then back the other way. Liv threw herself forwards but she was too far away to gain enough leverage to stop it from slamming.

The crash echoed loudly off the stone floor inside

the house, and across the driveway towards where Robert and Henry were emerging from the trees. We turned in unison to watch Henry. His hand was still levelled at the front door. My father had his pipe in one hand and a browbeaten novel in the other as they rushed up the steps to join us. As they did, I noticed Henry's arm lowered several inches until he was pointing squarely at the hip high letterbox.

"Hold on. It isn't moving", I said.

"That noise would have woken the dead", Liv said.

There was a pause as understanding passed between our eyes.

"You think he ended it?" Henry asked.

"Well nobody has come running", I said. "Nothing has burst into flames. Like you suggested, maybe he ended it when he came to his senses. Look where he's pointing", I said lining my finger up with Henry's. "He could be on the other side of that door. This could all be over."

We stood together watching Henry's arm for several minutes. When it didn't so much as twitch, I tried the door. *Locked.* I pulled out my lock picks and started working the lock. I tried for a full five minutes while the others watched Henry, but I was too anxious or the lock too good. In the end, I used a little magic to trip the bolt, pushing the door slowly wide.

"Fin!" Henry said, making me jump. I turned in time to see his arm drop heavy to his side. The spell had finally expired. He looked relieved to have his arm back.

I turned back to the open door and stepped across the threshold, slipping one of Claire's cigarettes to my lips with a trembling hand. I didn't light it, just in case someone was lying in wait, but knowing it was there, ready to draw on at a moment's notice, helped a little. I squinted into the darkness and could see the outline of a sweeping curved staircase to my right and a row of glass doors at the far end of the house. The glass doors led out to a back garden and the lake, which registered only as an expanse of darkness. In the enormous space between the front and rear door, I could make out nothing; no furniture of any kind.

"We need a light?" Henry suggested.

"Alright", I said, "But wedge the door and run like hell if you see or hear anything. Dad and I will take care of the rest". I nodded to my father and we both buried our hands into our pockets, ensuring we were both touching as many keepsakes as possible as Liv and Henry pulled out their phones and cast two narrow beams of light around the room.

"Damnit", Henry said.

"What?" I said, spinning around and looking in

every direction.

"I've only got like eight percent battery left."

I exhaled sharply, turning my attention back to the room. The stone floor looked to be dusty but otherwise completely bare. I walked deeper into the room, the others on my heels moving their light around as we went.

"There's no one here."

"What about upstairs?" Henry said.

"At no point did you point upstairs, Henry", Liv said, a little impatient.

"Oh yeah."

Liv walked towards the nearest light switch and flicked it on. "No power", she said, when the lights failed to come on. "Looks like the owners moved out a while ago. Maybe the killer squatted here for a few days then left. Could the spell have gone wrong?"

"Well magic is hardly an exact science", Robert said. It wasn't the first time I had heard him use the phrase.

"What were the owners called?" I asked, turning to Liv.

"Nelson, Randall Nelson", she said reading off the letter.

"Does the name mean anything to you?" I asked Henry, who had wandered to the end of the room and was peering out into the back garden.

He shook his head then said, "Hey, come look at this". He was holding his light up above his head. "Are those what I think they are?" he asked.

"Jesus", I muttered.

"Are those graves?" Liv said, joining us.

In the distance, just before the garden fell away to the lake, stood two gravestones. I swallowed. "This Randall could be our man", I said, pushing open one of the glass doors that opened out into the garden. A gust of cold wind rushed through to meet us.

"Are you insane?" Henry asked.

"We'll just be a second. Why don't you check out upstairs with Dad."

He didn't seem to like that suggestion either.

"Henry, you were pointing right here, not up there, remember. The killer isn't up there. He isn't here at all", I said, speaking at a normal volume now. "He would have shown himself by now if he was."

"I guess", he said, eying the staircase with trepidation.

"It's fine", Liv said. "We'll just be a second. Help Robert with the letters. See if you can find out who else lived here and when they moved out. There might be some bank statements or requests for overdue rent."

"I'll stay with him", Robert said, his face pale. He seemed similarly reluctant to venture out into the night to look at graves.

Liv led the way across the garden path. She swept her light back and forth across the lawn. A couple of sheds stood next to an industrial-looking barbecue, and to the right was a dense crop of trees leading up to the lake. Nothing seemed out of place.

We stopped in front of the gravestones and read their inscriptions.

Evie Nelson - 21st January 1995 - 25th March 2015

Beloved daughter, our light in the darkness.

The second gravestone looked new, the earth beneath it even looked fresh compared to the first.

Evelyn Nelson - 14th September 1974 - 4th June 2016

"She died barely a month ago", I said.

"But look at the daughter, that ties in with when Henry said Claire went through a difficult time. This must be it. The daughter must have been her patient when she died."

Liv snapped a picture with her phone and stared down at it.

"It must be the husband, Randall. He's the killer."

"Hey!" Henry shouted from the back door, his eyes were as wide as I had ever seen them. "You need to see something upstairs", he said.

We rushed after him and followed him up the stairs. Robert stood in one of the bedroom doorways. He blinked at us, then stepped aside.

"What is it?" I asked, searching his eyes. He didn't speak.

"Take a look for yourself", Henry said. "It's the only room with anything in it." He pushed the door open and shone his light into the room beyond.

"Jesus", Liv said, as she entered.

I stayed put. "Dad, are you alright?"

He swallowed and nodded, finally meeting my eye. "Go on."

I followed Liv into the room. Pink carpet beneath a darker pink rug, soft pink bed linens and a dark pink headboard. Posters of pop heartthrobs I didn't recognise were tacked to two walls and even the desk had a powder pink sheet over it. On the chair sat an electric pink *Hello Kitty* backpack.

"This is the only room like this?" I asked, stepping over to the desk beneath the window and turning back to face the others.

"All the others are stripped completely bare. I'm guessing one of the graves was for a little girl",

Henry said, sounding sick.

"Yes, but the girl was twenty when she died", Liv said.

"Twenty?" Henry repeated. He was flicking through what appeared to be an old romance novel, the cover depicted a moustachioed older man with slick black hair in a passionate embrace with a young woman. The title read, *To Possess A Heart.* I caught sight of highlighted passages and the kind of heavy fanned pages and dog eared corners which suggested it had been read countless times. With a swell of pity, I wondered just what sort of childhood Evie must have had in this house. Even virtually derelict the place was still clinically clean and seemed bereft of any sort homeliness.

"Maybe the parents did it?" Henry suggested, dropping the book down on the chest of drawers.

"I don't think so. Most of this stuff looks brand new, it's like a monument to her. This has been ironed recently", I said, staring down at the cloth covering the desk. I rested a hand against the raised fold in the fabric and was surprised to find resistance from something underneath. I lifted the cover off the desk and felt a chill sweep through the room. Every inch of the desk was blackened as if it had been seared by a grill before being scrubbed clean again. Every inch, except at the very centre where a circle of un-scorched wood remained. Within that circle the word GOODBYE had been scratched into the wood with something sharp.

"She killed herself." I said, reaching my hand towards her final message before Robert caught my arm.

"Don't be careless, son. My guess is every part of that desk had etchings on it. Whoever absorbed the rest of those messages left that word behind for a reason. We have a name, that should be enough to confirm how they both died. Right, Detective?"

Liv nodded. "It's a start."

I continued to stare down at the word. They were right, there was no point in putting myself through that. Knowing the identity of the killer was enough. "If the daughter or wife were a patient of Claire's, perhaps she was killed for some imagined revenge for not being able to help them?"

"Maybe they both were?" Henry suggested. "Ah damnit, my phone is about to die."

I raised my head to look out the window. I saw nothing but my own reflection until the light from Henry's phone abruptly cut out and the garden below came into gradual relief by the shifting moonlight.

My eyes were drawn back to the tombstones as

I pondered how the mother and daughter had died. The part of me speaking in Ryan's voice said, *At least the little girl has her mother now. At least she isn't alone out there anymore.*

He couldn't have been more right. Still not believing my eyes, I reached out a shaking hand and covered Liv's phone, cutting out the last of the light in that strange bedroom.

"Fin?" Liv said, as we stood there in almost total darkness, my night vision gradually returning.

I touched the cigarette still hanging at the corner of my mouth then crushed it on my tongue and started chewing.

Positioned in front of her daughter's grave, staring up at the house through tangled clumps of filthy hair, stood the sinewy corpse of Evelyn Nelson. Her own grave looked sunken and empty by comparison as the month old corpse in the fouled white dress began sprinting towards the house.

CHAPTER 18

"Fin, what the hell...?" Liv started to say, cutting off suddenly when the sound of a glass door exploding reached us.

"What the fuck...?" Henry cried.

I pushed passed him and slammed the door closed, throwing my back against it and bracing myself as she started up the stairs. This wasn't the slow-moving limp of the undead from a George Romero film, however. She made it up the long flight of stairs in four steps, her bare feet hitting the staircase in a rapid hammer blow stride. *Thud thud thud thud.* I used the last of the magic gathered in my belly to strengthen my legs and back just as the creature reached the top of the stairs and threw herself into the door in a primal rage.

"Fuck!" I cried, as my magically-enhanced muscles strained to push back, and were still almost overwhelmed. "Help!"

Henry threw his back to the door beside me as

the thing continued an unrelenting assault to gain entry to the room.

"Jesus Christ, what is that?" Henry cried.

Liv pulled a telescopic baton from her pocket and snapped it open, her illuminated phone raised to her chest in her other hand the only source of light.

"Dad, keepsakes!" I said, pointing to my father's stuffed pockets.

His trembling hands went to his pockets but I could see he was too terrified to make use of them. Liv went to him and started emptying his pockets onto the floor. I clutched the wad of napkins in my pocket, feeling woefully unprepared for this. I took in another hit of magic and slapped my hand against the light switch. The bulb in the pink lampshade hummed to life before fading again. I waited for a break in the pounding against my back and hit the light switch a second time, burning through two more napkins in the process as the power left my fingers in a spark of electric current. It had the desired effect, however. The light came on and the horrible pink decor was suddenly visible.

"I'm almost out", I said, as the door's wood panelling started to crack.

Liv approached me, thrust her hand into my coat pocket and pulled out the silver cigarette case. She cracked it open and pushed the first one to my mouth and lit the end.

I nodded my thanks, and breathed in deeply, hardening my mind. "Alright, we need to make it to the car."

"How?" Liv said.

I looked at my father, and held the cigarette out to him. He took it after a moment and pulled hard on it.

"Flip the bed on its side and drag it over here", I said, noting the sturdy wooden frame and thick mattress. "I'll pin her, and hold her in here as long as I can while you three make a run for it."

"What about you?" my father asked, dropping his side of the flipped bed next to me.

"I'll follow out the window once you have a decent head start."

"Did you hear how quickly she made it up those stairs? No way you can outrun her", Liv said.

"You're forgetting I'm a mage. I'm pretty handy in a scrape", I said, trying to sound confident. "The door is going to cave in any second, we don't have time to argue."

A disembodied arm punched through the door and scratched across my chest before locking around Henry's throat, crushing his wind pipe. The cigarette I had been smoking burst into flames as I heard Henry choke, tearing fretfully at the rotten arm. I caught her around the wrist and pulled with all my strength. I had to leverage my other hand against the doorframe but after a second Henry slipped free, rubbing his throat.

The door burst open in an explosion of splintered debris. The woman stood, her dislocated jaw hung impossibly wide as if she were in a perpetual scream. She stood framed in the doorway for a second as she looked at each of us with those hollow unseeing eyes, before fixing upon me.

My hand closed around the remaining cigarettes and my fist erupted in a ball of fire as I channelled everything into me. She leapt, slashing and clawing at my arms and chest as I held her at arm's length, my hand clasping around her vile, flesh-sagging throat, to stop her teeth from finding me. She drove me backwards with ease, my strength no match for her own. I threw a flaming fist into the side of her head, once, twice, three times, but she was already dead, and the blows only diverted her for barely a second. I channelled more strength and pivoted on my front foot, lifting and throwing her into the desk by the window.

"Run!" I shouted to the others as I lifted the bed and dashed forwards with it like a shield, pinning the dead woman between the desk and window. I kept pushing, hoping to stop her from getting her feet under her. It worked until, in her struggle, she broke two of the legs on the desk and hurled it over my head towards the doorway. Without the desk in her way, the woman regained her footing immediately and started to drive me back across the room, pushing back against the other side of the bed.

I had nothing left to draw from and my strength began to falter.

"Hold on!" Henry shouted, throwing his weight against the mattress on my left.

"I've got a plan", Robert shouted behind me as Liv slammed into the matress on the other side.

Together the three of us managed to hold her in place.

"Are you ready yet?" Liv shouted.

I looked around, pushing my back to the mattress to see what my father was doing. Robert was on his knees with three novels wedged between two shaking hands. He appeared to be muttering to himself.

"Ready", he said, pushing the broken desk aside which had caught in the doorway.

"Alright, give her one last push and then run for the door." Liv said. She hefted her baton, crouched low and braced herself against the bedframe with her free hand, then started swinging at the corpse's knees.

A hellish screech sounded following the crunch of metal hitting rotten bone.

"Now!" she yelled.

I gave one last push with Henry, throwing the woman back towards the window, then the three of us rushed the door, Henry in the lead, then Liv, with me bringing up the rear. I started down the stairs after the others then stopped, looking back at my father who was knelt with his hands pressed to the floor just outside the room.

The undead Evelyn threw off the mattress and got her feet back under her before giving pursuit. She made it halfway across the room before hesitating. Her feet were sinking through the carpeted floor as if it were quicksand. She fought and tore at the ground even as she sank deeper up to her calves. By the time she reached the door she was waist deep, slashing wildly at the door frame for any sort of leverage.

"You did it", I said.

"It should hold her a little while." he said, dusting ash from his hands. I went back and helped him to his feet, watching as the wood solidified around her and started to creak and groan as she struggled to break free.

Liv and Henry were waiting for us at the front door. We helped each other down the stairs, feeling the onset of our overuse of magic settling over us like a storm cloud. We passed the broken desk on the stairs which had lost all four of its legs on its descent, before getting stuck between two of the balusters.

We reached the bottom of the stairs just as the groaning of wood elevated to several loud snaps, and strips of wood the length of my arm dropped to the stone floor beneath the landing. As one we looked up at the flailing legs of the woman's corpse as she wriggled free from her wooden prison.

My pockets empty, the word GOODBYE, flashed across my mind and before I could stop myself, I threw myself back up the stairs just as the dead woman dropped. She landed in a crouch, like a wild animal preparing to make a kill. I slammed my hand into the centre of the broken desk as hatred unlike anything I had ever experienced boiled up in my veins like thick tar. It was suffocating and exhilarating at the same time.

I threw my hand out over the banister as she rushed towards the door. I hurled it at her, every venomous last drop of it. Black flames raged from my hand, erupting over the banister in a gushing fountain of death. She collapsed silently, enveloped in dark flames. I closed my hand, crushing the flames into her bones, I wanted nothing of her left, no part of her to survive, not even her ashes.

I watched as the dark mass within the flames collapsed to the floor; a high-pitched whine followed a series of distinct pops, hisses and crackles as the corpse broke apart.

The rush of power left me as quickly as it had arrived. As soon as it was gone exhaustion crashed over me, and sent me sprawling to the stairs. I gagged and retched, certain that hatred had a physical presence, a cold and clammy weight to it, both heavy and putrid.

It was several minutes before I managed to comprehend that my eyes were still functioning. Evidently, my earlier spell had worn off while I flitted between consciousness and the abyss.

"Son? Can you hear me?" Robert said. He and Henry had each taken an arm over their shoulder and between them were carrying me along a dark street. The cold breeze felt good against the cuts on my arms and chest.

I managed a groan to let them know I understood.

The Austin pulled up in front of us, Liv in the driver's seat. She must have run on ahead. She got out and opened the door for me, pushing the case files and clearing a space for me to collapse into. I embraced the floor of the vintage cab like we were old friends reunited. I was distantly aware of banging my knees and forehead as I hit the deck, but I was too far gone to care.

#

"He doesn't look so good", Henry said.

"He'll be right as rain once we get him to a meeting", my father said.

"A meeting? Look at him, he needs a hospital!"

"Could he be... you know infected? One of *them*", Henry asked.

"One of who?" my father asked.

"You know, the undead. A *zombie*", Henry said, his voice low.

I laughed, or at least tried to. A strange snorting gurgling sound came out of me, which only made me laugh, or in this case gurgle, harder. I had visions of Henry trying to destroy my brain before I took a bite out of him.

"Is he choking?" Liv's called.

"I think he's laughing", Robert said, he sounded relieved.

"Seriously, a zombie?" I croaked, trying to sit up.

"Well I don't know, that's the first zombie I've come across", Henry said.

"She was really more of an enchanted corpse", my father said.

"She was not even remotely enchanting", Henry said.

"Alright, let's go with cursed then", Robert said as I slumped back against the door with a wince.

"How are you feeling?" Liv asked, through the

partition.

"Like a tenderised piece of meat."

"How bad is it?" Robert asked, stuffing a pen and paper into my hands.

"I've been worse. It was more anger than anything."

"What does that mean, exactly?" Liv asked.

"It means it could have been much worse and my son has far more luck than sense. Anger is fleeting, hatred tends to leave a much deeper scar." Robert said.

"Practically, it means if you can get me to a meeting within the next half hour I won't be completely useless for the rest of the week."

My father shook his head and gestured impatiently to the notebook in my lap. I blinked at it and started writing the final thoughts of Evie Nelson. After the expulsion of rage just minutes ago, there wasn't much left I could discern. Flashes of intense frustration hit me in diminishing waves like an aftershock, but they were inarticulate and lacking shape. By no means lacking strength, but insubstantial, like a storm cloud. Nearest I could tell the inscription was made a few days before she killed herself, before the numb melancholy had fully settled over her, and when frustration and anger and a desire to lash out still consumed her. Had she spent longer with the message just sitting at that desk, I would have been able to glean more from Evie. For the remainder of the drive back to the city, however, she remained silent. I had aided her in satisfying her anger, literally destroying her mother in fire, there was little left to be said.

"We are here", Liv called.

"Here?" Henry said.

"It worked at a takeaway place, why not here? Check Amber's list, every meeting on there finished hours ago."

The group fell silent as they dragged me out of the car and carried me across the street towards a bar, where a truly awful rendition of Barry White's *Three Times A Lady* was being butchered by a group of men. It was karaoke night at the *Dog and Duck.* A bouncer at the door watched us coming and made a face.

"You must be joking?" he said.

"It's urgent", Liv said, flashing her Detective's badge. "Move."

"Christ", he grumbled, stepping aside.

The place was busy, but people moved aside quickly enough once they saw me hanging between Henry and my father. Nobody liked being thrown up on, after all. Liv walked ahead of us, jumped up onto a little raised stage, flashing her badge to the DJ who looked completely bewildered, then to the three men still singing.

"Get off the stage", she said, impatiently.

"We weren't that bad!" one of them chided as they left the stage.

I grinned groggily at Liv between the three of them as they pulled me onto the stage and propped me up in front of the microphone. The single spotlight hitting my face and the sea of baffled faces was enough to make me start sweating.

"Couldn't have picked anywhere busier?" I muttered.

"Just get on with it before they start heckling."

I took a deep breath and tried to take a little more of my own weight. "Hi, my name is Fin and I'm an addict", I said into the mic. There were a couple of half-hearted laughs, and a few more when someone shouted out, "You aren't kidding mate!"

I ignored the crowd, focusing inwardly instead, trying to see past my own immediate pains to the one burning away deeper inside of me. To touch that well of hatred once more, to understand and articulate it.

"Tonight I felt blinding anger beyond all reason", I said, quietly. "I would have done anything just to hurt this one person. Just to see them burn, to devastate them utterly. I would have destroyed myself just to have that satisfaction, of having the final word, and to know everything she put me through was repaid tenfold."

My stomach settled as I spoke, the knot gradually releasing its hold, the nausea mercifully subsiding as the numerous cuts and bruises I had sustained rose to take their place. I took a step away from the microphone before turning back. "Oh, and I think I'm in love with a girl from my father's advanced literature class", I added. This earned a few cat calls and even a little applause.

I walked off the stage and went straight to the bar and ordered a round, before turning to listen to my father's confessions. They were much shorter than my own, for he had used much less magic than I had, but he spoke with the same sincerity and grace he always did.

Liv joined me at the bar and helped me carry the drinks over to Henry who had managed to snag a vacant table near the back of the room. I put the drinks down and lowered my exhausted body to the stool.

"Are you sure you don't need a hospital?" Liv said.

"I'm okay. we need to talk about what happened first", I said, downing a third of my pint.

Liv sighed. "Fine, I'll see if they have a first aid kit behind the bar", she said, eying my bloody shirt.

We waited in silence, sipping our drinks. Henry looked appalled after tasting his own. "Shandy?" he said.

"I needed a clear head", I shrugged.

My father joined us at the table and sat down opposite me. He had a cut on his forehead and more along the shoulder of his jacket, and Henry would have a black eye by morning. Liv looked exhausted but appeared otherwise unhurt. She cracked open the first aid kit and set to work cleaning me up.

"You three look a state", I said, smiling, then immediately wincing as Liv pressed something which stung horribly to a cut on my chest.

"You're hardly one to talk. You look like you've been put through a wood chipper", my father said, holding his pint glass to his forehead.

"Are you alright?" I asked.

"I'm fine. After the grave, and then that thing coming out of the ground...I thought it was the girl, I couldn't get the image out of my mind. I just froze,", he said, shaking his head.

"Don't apologise. We all panicked", I said.

"You didn't", my father said. I saw something in his face, but it was too fleeting, and gone before I could make sense of it.

"What happens now?" Henry asked, looking at Liv. "Can you check police files on this guy?"

"If he has a record, I can, for all the good it will do", she said.

"What do you mean?" Henry asked. "You have a name now, surely you can find a current picture of him somewhere? That was a huge house, you don't get money like that laying low."

"Right but what can I do with it even if I do find it? I can't go to my superiors without evidence of any wrongdoing, and aggressively pursuing someone I think is a suspect will only draw unwanted attention to me and more than likely alert *him* that we are on his trail."

"This is so messed up. We know who he is and where he lived, we should have SWAT teams and helicopters hunting him", Henry said, disappointed. "There must be something?"

"I can see if any of them have a police record. Check how the mother and daughter died. If there was any suspicion surrounding their deaths. If there was any suspicion surrounding this Randall Nelson it would help us to at the least get the case reopened."

"Can you check if the house is still registered to the Nelsons?" I asked.

"Yes, why?" Liv asked.

"That place was stripped bare. I suspect he sold everything of value in the house to buy up as many keepsakes as he could."

"Except the daughter's bedroom", Liv said.

"He couldn't bring himself to get rid of anything in that room", Robert said.

"Guilty conscience?" Henry said.

"Or he just missed them too much", Robert said. He sounded tired.

"Are you joking? He reanimated his dead wife", Henry said.

"To protect the daughter's room. She didn't come after us until Fin started messing with her things, remember?" my father said.

Henry looked at Liv. "What do you think? You're the detective."

"I think we still don't have enough information. Every possibility raises a hundred more questions, and none of them are without problems."

"How so?"

"Well it's possible the husband killed them both. Maybe he just likes killing, or maybe he suffered some sort of psychotic break, and the whole mage thing just exacerbated the issue."

"It isn't possible", my father said. "The kind of mental collapse you are talking about would lead a mage to self-destruct."

"Fin said the same thing when we first met, but the fact is, he keeps killing. Perhaps you're wrong?" Liv said, looking to me.

"Assuming it was possible to kill on this scale using magic, the other authors of the keepsakes he is using should have had an impact on him. The conflict between those personalities should have driven him to inaction, or at least made him waver in his conviction", I said.

"Is it possible he is just ignoring those other voices in his head?" Liv asked.

"I don't see how he could. Dad?" I asked.

He shook his head. "I don't understand it either. I've only heard of two murders being committed by a mage. Both crimes of passion and both times the mage in question turned themselves in within a few days. The resources he must be burning through to maintain this level of power defies reason."

"Who cares? Why does it matter now? Maybe the guy lost his mind and killed his wife and daughter, or maybe they were murdered and he's just out for revenge", Henry said.

"It matters because it could help us find him, figure out his next move, who he might target next", I said, shortly. My head was starting to hurt on top of my throbbing cuts, and this wasn't helping.

"What then?" Henry said. He sounded angry now. "Even if we do find him, we almost all died back there and it was just a spell he left behind. We can't beat him, not until he chooses to be beaten. Better to wait and hope he self-destructs sooner rather than later." With that he stood up, leaving behind his ale shandy, and went and found a vacant stool by the bar where he gestured vaguely at the whiskey shelf.

CHAPTER 19

Henry's words seemed to linger in the air even after he left the table.

"He isn't wrong, you know. This man has used more magic in a few days than most of us do in our entire lives. I would call it extravagant if the realities of it weren't so horrifying", my father said. "Animating a corpse is archaic, medieval even, but by all accounts, it shows a callousness I cannot fathom. His own wife? How could he possibly withstand the side effects?"

"I still don't see how it's possible. Is there anything you can think of, any rumours, anything at all, where you heard of magic being used like this?" I asked.

He hesitated.

"Dad?" I prompted as he glanced uncomfortably at Stone.

"I'm going to head into the station and see what I can dig up on the Nelson family", Liv said, standing.

I rose with her. "Alright, I'm going to stick around and go through Claire's patient files. Call me in the morning?"

She nodded, gulping down half a pint before leaving.

"What is it?" I asked, sitting back down opposite my father.

"You need to stop this. Leave it to the police. Please, Fin."

"What about Claire?"

"She's gone. I won't watch you throw your life away too trying to find the one responsible."

"Claire didn't throw her life away, it was taken."

"I didn't mean Claire. When Belle disappeared..." he shook his head. "I went to a very dark place. It might sound absurd given how much we bickered, but us working together, that is what ultimately convinced me to stop searching."

I felt a familiar knife twist in my gut as I recalled the haggard man that had returned after progressively longer and longer stints away. He had travelled up and down the country a half dozen times then across the channel into France before finally giving up. "Right it had nothing to do with you bleeding us dry and those shady looking debt collectors."

"Actually, no, it didn't. If that were the case, why didn't I resume the search after I had repaid them?"

I didn't speak, not having given it much thought before. Never being one to shy away from pressing his advantage, my father continued, "The point is I had reached a fork in the road. Continue, for who knew how long, searching for a daughter who may not want to be found, or return home to my son and our work."

"Your work. It has always been your mission, not mine. I just stepped in when you were away." I said. I felt childish given my father's sincerity but the conversation was scratching at old scars. It was a strange and disappointing thing to receive an answer close to the one you wanted. His work, his mission, had always been the search for the answers to our lost history, to advance our collective knowledge. To my father this had been one of the most difficult decisions of his life, to give up the search for a missing daughter, to resume what he deemed to be his life's work. I respected him for it, and the strength of will it must have taken him then, and every day since to stick with it. The problem was he had a second child. *Me.*"

I looked up, and could see the hurt in his eyes before his face hardened. "We spent three years together working towards finding the truth. You don't mean that."

I sighed, sinking lower into my chair. "I don't

know what I mean, I'm exhausted."

"Don't do that, don't let me off just because you feel sorry for me. You have something to get out, so say it." he said.

"I don't know, it was years ago. You really want to dig it up now?"

"You do know. Tell me?"

"Fine", I took a breath. "Couldn't I alone have been the reason you stopped searching for Belle? *Shouldn't* I have been? Every time you mention that fateful like affirming decision to return home to a troubled teenage son, you find it necessary to caveat it with the need to resume our most important work together. I get that you lost a daughter, but I lost my sister and the better part of a father on the same day and we barely spoke about it. You never told me where you went exactly or what you did while you were gone. Maybe I could have helped."

My father looked lost in the bubbles of his pint. "You don't understand… I was afraid you hated me for abandoning the search."

"I don't hate you for stopping." I said, honestly. The fact was he had spent three long years away from home only returning to replenish lost funds and keepsakes or to recover from long stretches of magic use. I had seen how much it had cost him each time he returned. "I resented you not telling me anything. I still do. What aren't you telling me here? I know you're hiding something."

"Always the investigator," he said. "I thought we were reconnecting for a moment there."

"We were… we did. Now go on."

He rolled his eyes. "Very well, I don't think it has anything to do with the investigation though."

"What does it have to do with Liv? You keep looking at her funny? You two didn't…?" I couldn't help wince.

"Nothing like that." he smiled, clearly flattered by the suggestion. "Nothing quite so interesting. I'm sorry to tell you this son, but I had something of a relapse. She was one of the officers busting an underground card game I was involved in."

"You've been playing again?"

"Just once, I swear. About a month ago. I've not been back since."

"Is that why you're low on keepsakes? You didn't bet a seeker keepsake?"

"No, no. In fact, part of the reason I joined the game was to pre-empt the possibility of one falling into my hands soon and me being tempted to gamble it away."

"Good." I said, relieved. "Then why did you look shifty when I asked about unusual forms of magic?"

"Oh, it just reminded me of something I saw after your detective and her friends detained me. As we each scrambled to put together an appropriate spell or try and talk our way to freedom, I spotted someone walk out, completely unchallenged. He must have passed a dozen officers, including our lovely detective. Even now I cannot fathom what manner of spell he used. I managed to give them the slip but by the time I got out of the building there was no sign of him."

"That's why you looked so anxious when we showed up at your office? You recognised her?"

"I thought she had tracked me down." he shrugged.

"And that your own son was turning you in?"

"farfetched, I realise."

'Not that farfetched." I joked.

He half smiled. "The police know who this Nelson character is, it's time you stepped aside. A week ago I believed myself to be something of an authority on magic. Today I feel like I'm at year one again." he looked over at the bar.

"I'll take Henry home with me. he shouldn't go back to the flat after tonight."

I thought of my own dusty flat and decided I would rather sleep in the back of the taxi.

My father walked me out past the bouncer, four

half pints of ale shandy tucked into our coats, which we then rested on the roof of the taxi. He hugged me when I turned to face him. "I'm okay", I said. He held me at arm's length and examined me, refusing to let me go.

"What is it?" I asked. He had the same conflicted look on his face I had seen in the pub.

"I'm just taking the measure of the man you've become", he said, sighing.

"That bad?" I said.

"I've never seen you so full of purpose." he said. It could have been a compliment but he sounded too disappointed for the statement to land anywhere close. "This..." He looked at the case files in the back of the cab. "This is too dangerous. Please, leave it be. I can't lose another child."

I recoiled a little at that punch to the gut. "I would if I could", I said, and I meant it.

"If not for Claire." he said, sounding tired. I didn't contradict him. "Fin, I'm sorry but if you ask for my help in this again, I won't do it. I'm afraid you are on your own."

"Ever the puppet master." I said, my temper returning.

"I won't be party to you getting yourself killed."

"You know I should have been straight with you when I left the first time. But if it still isn't obvious, I have no plans to ever come back to *our work*." I said, air quoting the final two words.

"Such a waste, you could have been so much more", he said, his face reddening.

"You don't think I'm trying to be? I chose a different path than the one you laid out for me. Don't take that as me being ungrateful, I appreciate it, but you have to know I'm not you. I'm allowed to make my own choice."

"Whatever excuses you need to tell yourself, son", he shot back. "I know you struggled after your friend Ian died, but I could have helped you if you'd just let me. I could have made things easier for you."

"I know you could have, but that isn't what I needed. I was hurting people and I didn't care. I know you've never struggled with the morality of how we live, but I do."

Robert's eyes flashed fury for a moment, before he spoke, his voice low and cold. "You've no idea, son. No idea."

I watched him head back into the pub, letting the chill from the night air wash over me in the hopes it would clear my head for the long night ahead. I didn't blame him, I had almost gotten him killed barely an hour ago. It was a wonder anyone was still speaking to me. I thought of the stacks of files piled into the cabin. Perhaps he was right, they had a name, what more could I do?

It wasn't my job after all, I could just climb in the back and go to sleep. Nobody, not even Stone would blame me for it. If it hadn't been for the case files, I was certain I would have followed through on the idea. I told myself it was simple curiosity but the truth was I missed Claire too much to simply ignore them.

I took a few minutes to get comfortable on the back seat with the cardboard boxes stacked to one side, then relocating the drinks from the roof to the back with me. My initial plan of drinking one pint per box failed at the first hurdle. I'd expected clinical objectivity, something I could mentally detach from the Claire I had known and cared about, but every sentence she had written was so soaked in *her,* she might as well have been sat in the car with me. I was onto the second shandy by the time I finished reading the third file in the first box.

It quickly became obvious these notes were never meant to be anything other than an exercise in cathartic exorcism. More for her own benefit, than for her patients, and certainly not to be seen by anyone else. She never named her patients, but described them briefly, and their reasons for coming to therapy with her. Every word was completely uncensored and often came off as harsh and judgemental.

Depressed male, mid-forties. Possibly bipolar. Resents his wife for their lack of intimacy to cover an affair he had three years ago. - I suspect performance issues in the bedroom though he has yet to confide in me about them, probably because I'm a woman. Trying to figure out if he is more likely to be open with one of the boys. If he doesn't spill the beans soon I will refer him to David.

Depressed female, forties. Extremely reluctant to open up to me about feelings towards her husband. She constantly deflects my questions, making small talk whenever I ask something uncomfortable. She also seems extremely paranoid about being discovered in therapy.

Remember for future sessions - she seems to hate any kind of pity. She reprimands me for showing any sign of sympathy towards her and becomes more distant whenever I do.

Week 2 - Called to cancel.

Week 3-5 - No show (No call either!).

Week 6 - Showed up but barely says two words to me. I've suggested she start keeping a diary and for her to open up into that first then come and see me again. Again she was reluctant, but once I told her she never has to show me, or anyone else the contents, she relaxed. I've suggested we move to monthly visits rather than weekly.

Month 3 - client seems more together. She says the diary is helping. She admits to feelings of anger towards her husband though she volunteered no further details.

Month 4 - Client calls and cancels all future meetings.

Neurotic female, mid thirties. Self diagnosed obsessive compulsive, cleans constantly throughout the day. Symptoms seem more severe since death of her mother. Woman fixated on an argument she had with the mother days before she died. She becomes hysterical whenever I bring the conversation back to this argument.

I read every file cover to cover in the first box before reading only the first few paragraphs alone from each file in the second. Occasionally she had included a copy of a prescription she had written out for one of her patients. Since these were dated, I used them to make a timeline for each box. Most of her patients came to her in three or six month stints after a bereavement or finding out that their partner had been cheating on them for a number of months, years or in one case, three decades.

It wasn't until the third box that I found someone who matched my mental picture of Evie Nelson, and even then I had to read the contents of the first page several times. Claire only ever referred to the girl as E. The picture she described was of a troubled sixteen-year-old girl caught shoplifting and immediately sent for four weeks of psychotherapy with Claire to "fix the problem". Claire had quoted the father directly in one of her early notes.

Teenage girl. Cried throughout first half of session before laughing through most of the second. I think she was actually testing me, to see what she could get away with. Clearly has issues with authority figures, particularly the parents. She claimed to find it amusing that she had been shoplifting for over a year and had only just been found out. She believes parents didn't care until it reflected badly on them with friends and neighbours when she got herself arrested.

After initial meetings, E is reluctant to discuss parents directly though appears to enjoy describing her other misdeeds. Drinking and mild drug use are frequent occurrences. Parents are oblivious. I now believe E to be deeply unhappy. I also believe she is hiding some deep anxiety regarding her own identity.

Father seems to be mostly absent, mother openly refuses to believe her daughter is capable of any wrongdoing whatsoever. This seems to be causing E further anxiety and she complains of tension headaches.

Week 2 - E has broken into several houses with her boyfriend. She takes pleasure in telling me things she knows I cannot tell her parents.

Week 3 - E has started asking for painkillers directly. I'm not convinced she is being truthful regarding her headaches, and never seems upset when I deny her the drugs. This may be another test. She jokes her mother could open a chemist with the amount of drugs in her handbag. I think she may be reassuring herself that I am not her mother. I like her. She reminds me of me a little.

Week 4 - We talk about the future for the first time. She tells me she loves her parents even though they are idiots. E seems different. Content even. I've recommended I see her again next week. She said she would like that but that she would need to talk to her parents first.

Then on the next line, in a different pen, it read, *I should have known what that meant. She wasn't content, she was resigned. She never planned to see me again.*

That was the last time Claire had seen Evie, but the notes didn't stop there. What made up the rest of the pages in Evie's file were disjointed observations with no times or dates. Descriptions of conversations she had initially overlooked or glossed over, looks she had received or phrases she recalled Evie making, all of which were written in the past tense.

I continued to pour over those final pages, they read like the abstract observations of a genius or an insane person. I decided these had not only been written after Evie had died, but that Claire had been using heavily when she made them. I guessed some manner of spell to enhance her recall had been used so that she could relive their sessions over in her mind. It was odd to read what should have been emotive, described in such clinical precision. A by-product of the spell I guessed, like someone describing the geometric and mathematical components of Mona Lisa's smile.

I retrieved the notebook I had started days ago describing the photographs from the crime scene where Claire and the four others had been murdered, and lay it open beside me, noting the similarities between our descriptions.

It was four in the morning when I finally succumbed to exhaustion. I finished the third pint of shandy and sent Liv a text message before letting myself slump back in the chair and sleep. Claire's notes continued to bounce around in my brain like pieces of several different puzzles all muddled together. Each piece had a sense, a logic to it, I just couldn't put it with any others and have them make sense.

#

I awoke with a start to knuckles tapping on glass with the same sort of inconsiderate persistence that a woodpecker might employ against the bark of an old oak tree. I slowly hauled myself into a seated position, and my heavy wool coat which had been pulled up over my head like a blanket fell down, dazzling me with morning sunshine.

"Come on, let me in", Liv said.

I fumbled blindly at the door and popped the lock. "Good morning, Stone", I mumbled rubbing my eyes. "What time is it?"

"Almost eight", she said, sitting down opposite me, careful to evade the spread of paperwork littering the floor. She handed me a coffee which I sipped. "What did you find?"

"Evie was a patient of Claire's, just like we thought. Committed suicide from the sound of it about a month after she started therapy. Claire took it pretty hard, I think she was quite fond of the girl. What about you?"

"Found the police report on the suicide and some other criminal offences prior to that. She sounded like quite a piece of work from what I've read. Multiple B and Es, destruction of property, drug use. The list goes on. Then this", she said, handing me a photocopied picture of the girl's death certificate.

"Overdose", she said.

"Painkillers?" I asked.

"How did you guess?"

"She was asking Claire for them in their last few sessions, though I don't think she ever actually gave her any. I guess she must have gotten them from somewhere else. Probably stole them from her mother, it sounds like she was a bit of a walking lab. Speaking of Evelyn, did you find anything about her?"

"Suicide. Almost identical to the daughter. Overdosed with painkillers, didn't leave a note but the husband's alibi was airtight. Although with mages I guess the term doesn't really apply anymore. Could he have forced them to kill themselves?"

"With the amount of power he's been throwing around, it's possible. But I don't think that's what happened. I think their combined deaths drove him to this. Why target Claire otherwise? He must have blamed her for not stopping this from happening."

"That might fit if the murder happened a year ago and only involved Claire, but this started a year later with eight other victims. Nine including June. I pulled Randall's bank records. He sold his cars, wife's jewellery and everything else from the looks of it after the wife died."

"Evelyn's death must be what tipped him over the edge."

"So, he planned all this, amassed all this power in just one month?" she said.

"I don't know, maybe", I said, unconvinced.

"Possible? Maybe? This is getting us nowhere. We haven't a clue where he is or who he might target next. We are no closer to catching this guy than we were three days ago." She let out a sigh and pinched the bridge of her nose.

"What's wrong?"

"We are almost out of time." She looked at me. "*I'm* almost out of time."

"What do you mean?"

"You didn't see the news? Price woke up last night. He's going to be fine."

"Oh, well that's a relief", I said, swallowing. With everything that had been going on I'd completely forgotten about the injured inspector.

"That's not all. He was saying my name a lot when he came to. The doctor said he was extremely unsettled, so they sedated him. I could be called in for questioning any minute", she said, glancing at her phone.

"You think he remembers what happened? Even if he does, who would believe him?"

"I honestly don't know. If I lie, which I suppose I will have to in order to keep myself out of prison, and he sticks to his story, it would mean the end of his career, mine too probably. They would force early retirement on him."

"Better than you ending up in prison", I said.

"Yes, but Price getting forced into early retirement and never trusting me again is the best case scenario here. If he manages to convince anyone, they might ask me to take a lie detector test just to rule out any involvement on my part."

"They can't force you, though?"

"True, but if I had nothing to hide, then why wouldn't I agree?"

"I guess the best we can hope for is he'll also remember me deflecting bullets out of the air with my mind. Maybe he'll think he was hallucinating. I was there too, remember, I can back up your story."

"Great. I'll pray he doubts his own sanity enough to not mention it then."

"I'm sorry", I said. The fact was there was no perfect solution to this. "If it helps any and he remembers your part he will probably remember mine too. We might even get arrested together."

"Why would that help?"

"Misery loves company?" I shrugged.

Her eyes remained stony but the corner of her mouth quirked a little, though she covered it quickly by sipping her coffee. She passed the police files over to me and I handed her back Claire's notes on Evie.

I was surprised by just how thick Evie's file was. I was onto her third B and E, and fifth destruction of public property report before I looked up at Liv. "How was she not convicted of any of this?" I asked.

"None of the victims ended up pressing charges. If I had to guess, her parents probably talked them round or paid them off. It probably helps if your daddy was a director at a top legal firm too."

"Was?" I asked.

"He took a step back from the company when Evie died. Oh here, I almost forgot", she said passing me a printed A4 picture. The photograph showed an older man, mid stride amidst a spread of other runners, each with a number pinned to the front of their t-shirts.

"It's from the London marathon six months ago. That was taken from the *Times* magazine. I couldn't find much else about him after that."

"He was a runner?"

"Apparently. Doesn't seem very cut up about his daughter does he?" Liv said.

"Not really, although people deal with loss differently. What was the *Times* piece on?"

"Something about how beneficial older workers are to big business. Experience over strength of youth, sixty is the new forty. All that stuff. It's online if you want to read it."

I looked back at the printout and could see why the photo would have been perfect for the piece. A sixty-something man in a competitive business ahead of the teenagers and twenty-somethings struggling to catch up. "You see the badge he's wearing on his collar?"

I looked again, and recognised the emblem but couldn't immediately place it. "What is it?"

"It's for that self-help group Henry mentioned, the Positive Self."

"He was a member?"

"Looks like it. The article doesn't mention it directly, I think his company didn't want to be associated with them since they have a reputation for entertaining a few fanatics. But that might explain why he was at the hotel the other night."

I continued to stare at the picture. "So that's Randal."

"Expecting horns and a forked tail?" Liv said.

"Mm." I grunted. I put the photograph down beside me and continued reading the police report until I noticed Liv watching me. "What is it?"

"I think I figured out something. I'm not sure you'll want to hear it though."

'Is it about Claire?"

"Yes."

"Just tell me." I closed the file and looked at her.

"Claire was the only victim that didn't appear to have been premediated." Liv said. "Claire was never meant to be at the hotel, but what if Doctor June was? In a professional capacity, I mean."

"Claire was standing in for him?" I said. I thought back to the crime scene photos and suddenly it clicked. I had been blinded by the blood matted into the carpet and the spread of dead bodies in the pictures before, but now it seemed so obvious. "It was an intervention."

"I'm sorry."

"Why are you sorry?" I asked.

"Because it means Claire was there by accident. June was the target, not her." I said.

I felt ambushed. I had learned the shape and size of my grief and shoved it productively to one side. In one expression of sympathy Liv had shown me how much more there was that I had previously ignored. Its shape had changed and now I was more painfully aware of how little of it I had yet to process. Claire wasn't even a target, she had just offered to step in for a colleague at the last moment. It all came back to that day, if I hadn't intervened with Greg or if I'd insisted on driving her home or been an ounce more honest or selfish or something, anything! Then she might still be alive.

"If it was an intervention who were the other eight victims?" I said.

Liv wasn't the least bit phased. "When your

father talked about these holidays mages attend, do you think they tell their loved ones where they are going?" she asked.

"Not necessarily. It would depend on the mage in question. I suspect, given what goes on at these events and the stigma attached to it, probably not."

"I thought as much. That could explain why no one has come forward to identify the other eight victims. If they were all here to attend this convention, then the families might not expect to hear from them until after it finishes."

I returned to the file in my lap absentmindedly reading about Evie's past convictions while my mind was still fixed on Claire. I reached the end and backtracked a few pages, certain I must have been paying even less attention that I realised. "There's no mention of shoplifting in here? Claire said their sessions were court mandated, didn't she?" I said.

"No, actually," she said, flipping back a page to the extract I had highlighted. "Claire just says E was sent to four weeks of psychotherapy after being caught shoplifting. Maybe the parents insisted?"

"Doesn't that strike you as odd when she was taking drugs and breaking into people's homes? Shoplifting is a pretty minor offence by comparison, particularly if she wasn't even charged that time."

"It's not impossible the officer who showed up to the scene made a deal with the parents and the shop manager to have the charges dropped if they took her for therapy. Keeps it out of the courts that way."

I felt a chill creep up by spine as I considered this. "Is there a way to check? They could be the next target."

"Not if that officer didn't submit a report."

"Can you at least find out who the officer on the scene was?"

She thought for a moment. "I'll call dispatch", she said, pulling out her phone. She gave the person on the end of the line Evie's full name and the rough period in which the shoplifting must have taken place before hanging up. "She'll call back if she finds anything."

I stared at her phone for a minute, then unable to sit still, I went and returned the pint glasses to the pub, which was just opening. I placed the glasses on the bar and nodded to the bar maid who was reading the newspaper while drinking an espresso. She nodded back looking slightly disapproving. I glanced at the front page of her paper and saw the heading *INSPECTOR WAKES UP FROM COMA*. After visiting the toilets and splashing water on my face, the headline kept returning to me with a deep sense of foreboding.

"Do you remember what the killer told you do to at the hotel?" I asked, as I slipped back into my seat opposite the detective.

"He told me to shoot you", she said, without looking up from her file.

"He said 'shoot them'? Is that all?"

She paused, thinking. "More or less. It's still kind of a blur but I think he told me to kill Price and don't leave any witnesses."

"Did he say 'Price' specifically?"

"I don't remember", she said.

Liv's phone burst into life, and started buzzing on the seat beside her. She answered it and I watched the colour drain steadily from her face.

"It was Price?" I said.

She nodded. "Another officer was called out but Price was just around the corner when she was caught shoplifting. The manager had caught her stealing with a group of friends several times, the others were let off with a warning, but not Evie. Apparently, the manager wanted to press charges against her believing she was the ringleader. Price managed to convince him to agree to four weeks of therapy instead."

"Price wasn't just in the way, he was a target. He's hunting down anyone he thinks is responsible. Randall didn't just go back to the hotel to destroy evidence, he went for Price."

"Jesus, it was in all the papers this morning, we have to get over there", Liv said, swinging the door open and climbing out.

"Wait, I'll drive", I said.

CHAPTER 20

"Bus on the left! Bus on the left!" Liv shouted. She held a phone to her ear in one hand and clung to the dashboard with the other.

"Police business! Get out of the fucking way!" I bellowed out the window, my face inches from an irate cyclist. I put my foot down and forced my way through a red light onto a roundabout to a cacophony of horns and cursing on all sides.

"Yes, this is Detective Stone", Liv was saying down the phone, as the wind whipped her hair. "I need an armed response unit at Ealing Hospital. I have reason to believe the killer is targeting Chief Inspector Price."

There was a pause.

"Better I'm wrong and you send out the unit, than I'm right and you don't. Just get it done", she said before hanging up.

"Was that wise?" I said.

"What other choice is there? We can't go in there alone."

"No I agree, we need all the help we can get. I meant was it wise to piss your boss off like that? He might not send anyone."

"He will, he's too much of a politician not to. If I'm wrong, he gets to blame me, if I'm right, he can still take the credit."

"If you say so. Now keep writing or I'll have nothing to use when we get there." I pointed at the stressed notepad in Stone's lap. Between the phone call and my driving she had barely written a paragraph. I swerved hard around another cyclist and beeped my horn as I cut off a cabbie to my right. I sucked in a little more from the cigarette hanging from the corner of my mouth, my heart racing.

"Chase, if you get me killed in a traffic accident while I'm on duty I swear to god I will end you", she said, returning to her pad. "Jesus, do you even know where you are going?"

"Of course", I said, toking a little harder on my cigarette. "Well this guy does at least." I waved my cigarette at her and turned sharply on the wheel with the other hand.

"I thought you were all out?" she said.

"I am, this guy is basically only good for driving, at least in the magical sense. Very skilled at his job, but not the most emotive of writers. Though I suppose who is when you are talking about driving?"

"So, who is he, a cabbie?"

"And hobbyist rally driver", I said, dropping a gear and flooring it to get ahead of another bus trying to pull out. The driver beeped so I gave him the finger out of my window.

"Must you do that?" she sighed.

"Trust me, love, you want him driving right now, not me."

"'Love?' *Really?*"

"Sorry!" I said, charging through another red light. "I'm almost out, hand me another?"

She passed me another cigarette from the glovebox and I lit it off the first before folding the stub into my mouth and swallowing it. My eyes watered as the hot embers hit the back of my throat, but the sudden clarity of having *The Knowledge* instantly at hand filled me with purpose. "How's it coming?" I asked.

"Not well."

"What's the problem?"

"Well it's not easy writing with you driving like an idiot, let alone the kind of thing you are asking for."

"Such a backseat driver. Just write about anything you've had a strong emotional reaction to. I know it's difficult, but the stronger the feeling, the more you can put into the words, the better chance we have of holding our own when Randall shows up."

"If he isn't already there."

"He still has to find out which hospital Price is being kept at. That isn't public knowledge right?"

"No, they keep information like that under wraps, but I don't see that stopping him, do you?"

"No, but it might slow him down a little", I said, hoping I was right, but putting my foot down all the same. We roared across the city, a speed camera flashing in my rear-view mirror.

"That's three", I said.

"You're keeping score? How the hell do you still have a license?"

I ignored the question, sensing Detective Stone would disapprove of my magically-altered license plate. I waved my hand in front of my face to clear the smoke while the Austin roared up the outside of a long line of traffic before breaking hard and cutting in sharply just before an off ramp.

We headed north on South Ealing road then cut north-west when traffic crawled to a standstill outside one of the University campuses. Finally, after twenty minutes of zigzagging through several backstreets and up the wrong way on a one way street, we made it to Broadway, then pulled left onto Uxbridge where the hospital, with its weathered exterior and blue capped roofs, stood looking like a cross between a run-down factory and a sports centre from the early nineties.

We sped past a concrete ramp which looped emergency vehicles from the street up to the centre of the first floor. I pushed hard on the brake as the Austin bounded up the curb behind the hospital, narrowly evading a sign stating there was no parking. I wrenched up the handbrake and turned to Liv as she held out the single page of sentiment she had managed to get down as we drove. I took it from her and skimmed the contents.

"Is it enough?" she said.

"It will have to be", I said, as I got out and went to the back of the car and popped the boot.

"What are you doing?"

"Supplies."

"I thought you were out?"

"I am, but he doesn't have to know that." I stuffed a pair of shoes and some t-shirts into a bag and pulled it across my shoulders.

She looked tense marching quickly ahead of me towards the entrance. Even the automatic doors of the old building seemed tired, opening only reluctantly when our noses were almost pressed to the glass. Liv headed through the busy foyer and started pushing her way through the sick and injured to the front of the line where she flashed her ID and started speaking with the woman on the front desk and the nurse standing beside her, both of whom wore floral scrubs.

I glanced around at the waiting room occupants half expecting to find Randall among them. En masse they appeared, as disparate and random a collection of people you could possibly gather, but on closer inspection each familial knot had one thing in common. There were solitary wives clinging to handbags too tightly and conspicuous fathers attempting to entertain children too young to understand why they were there. Every one of them was a puzzle with a piece absent, a story without a centre. Nervous, almost guilty glances passed between the fortunate, the ones who knew their loved ones were coming home soon, while others stared at a fixed point ahead of them or at the children reading aloud from the big colourful books from the centre of the visitors' lounge floor. I can't draw magic without the written word, no mage can, but there are some places where the air seems so thick with it I begin to question myself.

Several eyes fixed on me in a glare before someone finally spoke up. "Excuse me, sir? *Sir?* You can't smoke that in here", a nurse beside me said.

"Oh right, I'm sorry", I said, realising I was still

smoking. I looked around for an ashtray.

"Look mummy! That man's smoking" one of the children said.

"Outside!" the nurse said, her face reddening.

"It's alright." I stuffed the cigarette into my mouth and swallowed it. I cringed and coughed one final puff of smoke as the children roared with laughter and the parents looked appalled.

The nurse's mouth hung open for a moment in utter consternation as she tried to make sense of the stupidity she had just witnessed.

"You are standing five feet from the exit", she said, shaking her head and turning away from me to face the seated occupants.

"Mr and Mrs..." she started to say before she was cut off by the fire alarm.

All eyes turned to me for a moment as if they expected to find I had lit up again the moment the nurse's back was turned.

"Chase, move it!" Liv shouted across the room.

We pushed our way through the first set of doors and along a grey corridor, passing a hospital porter pushing an empty wheelchair and several more visitors on their way to or from the hospital cafe which ran the length of the corridor to our left. The alarm continued to ring out overhead as we veered right towards the fire escape and hurried up a flight of stairs against a stream of patients and medical staff hurrying in the opposite direction.

"Price is on the third floor, east wing of the ACU", she said, taking the stairs two at a time.

I pulled gently on some of the cabbie's power to keep up, leaving the rest to pool at my centre, ready to call on at a moment's notice. Every face we passed I stared into expectantly.

"How long until your backup arrives?" I said, as we passed the second floor.

"If they are coming they should be here any minute", she said, pushing the door open onto the third floor to a riot of noise. More hospital porters and nurses stood directing people towards the exits. Liv flashed her badge as a doctor challenged us. He pointed down the hallway towards a second nurses' station at the far end of the room.

We pushed through the crowd gathered in front of the lifts when the lights abruptly went out across the entire floor. There was a scream, then a child somewhere behind us started to cry.

"It's him", I said, looking ahead for the source of the scream.

"You!" Liv said, grabbing a nurse by the arm. "We need to clear this floor right now."

I broke free from the crowd as the emergency lighting cut in, casting the scrubbed floor ahead of me in dull green. As I reached the second nurses' station I came to a stop. Two men in police uniforms lay sprawled in the middle of the corridor, one on top of the other as if they had been dropped there like unwanted toys.

"Jesus", Liv said, rushing forwards towards the nearest officer and checking his pulse. "He's breathing. Nurse!"

"Same here", I said, pressing my fingers into the throat of the second.

We were surrounded by a doctor and three nurses a second later. "Don't move them", the doctor said, her fingers moving deliberately down the first man's neck. "Doesn't appear to be broken."

"Where is Price's room? The officer you had in here, which room is he staying in?"

"Room seventeen", one of the nurses said, pointing ten paces up the corridor. A white glow rolled beneath the doorframe.

"You need to move them now", I said, looking towards the closed door beyond the doctor. "Get them away from here, drag them if you have to." I grabbed a canister of pepper stray from the officer's belt and moved towards the door.

"Do it", Liv said, moving beside me and snapping her telescopic baton open.

I stepped up to the door, watching the light move

as I retrieved Liv's letter from my pocket. It was too dark to make out any of the words but I stared at the green tinted paper for a moment anyway.

"Are you sure you are up to this?" Liv whispered, pausing by the doorway.

As I drew in power from her letter, smoke billowing from my hand, I hoped my anger would outweigh the fear pressing down on me once the door opened and I finally faced Claire's killer. I thought of the bloody corpses and wondered just how much more of a fight I could possibly offer Randall. In seconds the paper was ash at my feet and I felt my entire nervous system twitching with electric energy. It wasn't just power Liv had given me though, she had leant me her courage too. I felt the cabbie bravado retreat as Liv's spirit came to the fore, determined and unwavering.

"I'll try and draw him out, you get Price out of there", I told her.

Liv nodded, stepping to the side of the door, her back pressed to the wall. I pushed the door open a fraction and froze.

Randall stood over the still form of Inspector Price. He was staring down at Price with a hateful sneer as he idly rolled something silver between his fingers. Price's face was stricken, eyes wide in shock as his bandaged body lifted slowly up from the bed and was pushed back into a seated position against the plastic headboard.

The flash of silver caught my eye a second time before seeing that it was a scalpel rolling between his fingers. Randall made no effort to move closer to the bed, the inspector pinned upright against the headboard as if an invisible hand had him by the throat.

Price's mouth moved but no words came out, I felt Liv beside me peer in through the crack in the doorway and stiffen as Randall casually tossed the scalpel. I flinched, pushing the door open another few inches, but there was no magic behind the throw – it landed harmlessly in Price's lap.

Price watched in horror as his own hand reached tremulously for the knife and Randall's expression changed to one of pleasure. Perhaps it was the context with which it was being used, but I found the indulgent, almost catlike expression to be unnatural on his ruddy, bearded face. As Price picked up the scalpe, Claire's crumpled and lifeless body flashed through my mind.

I quickly scanned the room for any cover, but there was nothing except a chair in the far corner and the single bed holding Price. I gripped the mace tighter in my hand then let some of the electricity rocketing through my veins pour out through my palm. My grip slackened, and the canister rose steadily into the air before my face. I raised it up to the ceiling, cupping my hands together in front of me to visualise its path across the room. I dropped my hands a little as Price started to scream. Price's shaking hand brought the blade to his own throat.

"Hey!" I shouted, into the room, my open hands closing in front of me before pulling them violently apart. The canister of mace exploded above Randall's forehead just as he turned, fireball in hand. I dove headfirst into the room as the fireball tore across the room and exploded into the wall where my head had just been. Randall screamed, tearing at his face. Along with the blinding gas, shrapnel from the canister had found its mark, with small quarter inch pieces of aluminium protruding from his cheeks and forehead. Liv rushed into the room, ducking as a vase exploded behind her head.

Randall shoved his hand into the depths of a satchel at his hip.

"Quick!" I said, rushing forwards and throwing up a shield of air and binding it to my forearm as projectiles bombarded me from Randall's side of the room. I felt Liv fall in at my back looking for an opening as we pushed on through the storm of possessed belongings. A belt buckle, broken glass and a fire extinguisher soon joined the hurricane, colliding with the walls and ricocheting off my shield. The scalpel, which Price had tossed aside the moment he had regained control of himself, span in vicious blind circles above my head.

Liv shot out from behind me and lashed out at Randall's knee. The possessed objects in the room fell instantly still. The scalpel dropped blade first into the floor beside my foot. I flinched away from it as Randall collapsed sideways. Liv advanced on him, and the man cowered back from her.

"Fin!" Liv cried.

I looked down as my feet sank through the floor, Liv was already up to her knees, swinging her baton uselessly in Randall's direction as he scurried to the far wall clutching his satchel. As his hand touched whatever was inside, his face hardened, all fear wiped away as power flooded to take its place. His face started to heal, the swelling immediately starting to ease around his eyes as each scrap of shrapnel was forced free by his skin's rapid healing. I felt my heart start to hammer as Randall's eyes locked on Liv. She screamed, clutching her legs, as the floor flowed inwards, crushing her.

I snatched up the scalpel, focused my magic and will into the blade's edge, then hurled. The blade landed true, spearing Randall's satchel and pinning the bag to the wall.

"I'll kill you for that", Randall snarled as he tore at the bag's straps and on the few remaining inches of scalpel still visible.

"Just like you killed Claire?" I spat back, my rage boiling over. I was so busy scouring the room for anything I could reach, anything I could use to hurt this monster, that I almost missed Randall's reaction. I'd expected him to laugh or snarl back some insult, anything I could use to fuel my hatred. Instead he started, and looked back at me. That moment of hesitation lasted only a moment, before the scalpel came free from the wall in a spray of brickwork. He raised his hand and spread his fingers, his entire arm suddenly engulfed in flames which stretched to the ceiling.

"Here!" a voice called.

Price lay against the wall beside the bed to my left, his neck and chest a mess of fresh blood. He looked deathly white but his jaw was set. He lifted the fallen fire extinguisher into his lap and threw it with surprising strength into the air.

"LIV, DOWN!" I shouted as the red canister arced towards me. I folded every last drop of magic I had into my arm. Liv dropped as low as she could and threw her arms over her head as I swung my arm forwards. My hand struck the extinguisher like a gong, and in an explosion of magic, the red cylinder rocketed over Liv's head towards

Randall. I watched it bury into his sternum with a sound like a cannon ball striking a brick wall before a flash blinded me. I recoiled, throwing myself to the side as best I could with my feet still trapped within the molten floor.

Panicked, I rubbed at my eyes frantically trying to restore my vision, expecting the final death blow to take me any moment. When my vision returned Randall was gone, however, and with him half of the exterior wall. The two-panelled window was now reduced to a single pane swinging in place by what little remained of the brickwork and the upper bracket of the frame. Through the crumbling hole a second crack like a gunshot rang out in the distance and a cloud of white foam showered across the car park.

CHAPTER 21

My vision swam as my head hit the floor. I collapsed awkwardly, my legs still bound. I tried to roll onto my side and to check on the others but my shoulder throbbed horribly when I tried to move it. I glanced down at my arm and could see something was very wrong with the way it was positioned beside me, as if my shoulder had somehow dropped several inches. I fought back a wave of nausea and looked away.

"It's just dislocated", Liv said. "Inspector, are you alright?"

"I'll live", Price said. "We are in here!" he added, as heavy footsteps filled the hallway outside.

I heard a sharp intake of breath as nurses and police filed into the room and started tending to the three of us, starting with Price. To my amazement, the man was still conscious and continued to issue instructions to his officers even as he was lifted onto a hospital gurney and wheeled out of the room.

"Do a sweep of the car park. Find the body." He spoke quietly but evenly, as if he needed to get the words out before he passed out completely. I was amazed he was still conscious.

"He had a bomb?" someone asked, as Price was wheeled out. I didn't hear Price correct whoever had asked the question.

The pounding in my shoulder grew worse, I tried to cradle it but hands stronger than my own pushed me flat and told me to keep still. The voices grew hazy and muddled as they asked me questions about my levels of pain, and even asked me to rank each injury out of ten. I told them I was quickly losing feeling in my toes.

Someone told me to lie still as they shone a light in my eyes and clicked their fingers in front of my face. I tried to roll away from them but they persisted and I lacked the strength to put up any more of a fight. The magic-sickness was settling in. They repeated that they were trying to get me free, but I needed to lie still in order for them to do that. For the most part I ignored them and let them talk amongst themselves. A pinch in my arm arrived not long after. A sedative, I guessed, given how heavy my eyelids felt. My body felt like it was drifting, which brought to mind the cloud of foam dropping on the wind.

The last thought that came to me was that Randall was dead and that I had killed him. It occurred to me with the same level of alarm one might feel when recalling a forgotten lunch appointment. Perhaps it was the sedative or the fact I had Liv's detached pragmatism floating around my brain, but I couldn't muster even a shred of pity for the dead man in that moment. I just felt a deep, bone weary relief.

#

When I next awoke, my father and Henry were sitting on either side of my hospital bed. I looked between them, trying to fight off the effects of whatever drugs I had been dosed with.

"He's waking up."

"Finally", Henry said.

"What time is it?" I asked.

"Early", my father said, his voice pitched low, soothing.

I gave my head a shake, I didn't want to be soothed. My left arm was in a sling across my stomach and my shoulder looked to be back in its regular position.

"They relocated it while you were out", Robert said.

"Early? Jesus, what day is it?" I said, looking around the room groggily and trying to sit up. "Are Price and Liv okay?"

"Both are doing well. Liv was a bit banged up

but she's fine. She came by to see you earlier but couldn't stay. They gave Price some more blood and he's awake and doing much better."

"And it's Saturday", Henry added.

I saw my father frown across the bed at him. I studied him closely for a minute as my brain lurched slowly into motion. I pushed the tucked covers off me, located the bed controls and held one of the buttons until I was sitting more or less upright. The room was near enough identical to the one Price had occupied, minus the torn out wall and the implements of death flying about the place. I stared at the little TV set mounted on the wall in the corner by the door. It struck me as strange that it would be turned off, particularly as my father and Henry looked to have been with me for some time.

"Tell me what happened?" I said, forcing my eyes open wide and over-enunciating each word in an effort not to slur.

My father hesitated, sharing a glance with Henry before he spoke. "Official line is, Randall placed a bomb in Price's room. It's the only thing they could think of that would explain the damage."

"What about Randall? How did they explain his body making it all the way out into the carpark?" I asked.

Robert swallowed. "There was no body."

"What?"

"He got away, Fin", Henry said.

"What?" I demanded, kicking the covers off and wincing as pain lanced up through the middle of my shoulder like a hot blade. I froze, halfway to the floor, as something tugged at my wrist. I was handcuffed to the bed. I looked between my father and Henry.

"Who the hell arrested me?"

"Shh!" they said in unison before my father continued.

"If they realise you are awake they will come in and take a statement. Liv said there was enough suspicion surrounding your involvement that they could detain you, though what they would convict you with, I can't possibly imagine. I told you to stay away from this."

"I need to get out of here."

"Son, you almost died", he said, his voice uncharacteristically stern. "What more can you do, beaten up and without magic? The police have it in hand. They know exactly what the killer looks like and what his name is. Think, in order to survive what you did to him, he must have used an enormous amount of his remaining power. Henry?" Robert said, pushing me back as I tried to get out of bed.

"Fin, look", he said, clicking the remote at

the TV. It came to life on a woman standing outside Ealing Hospital. Over her left shoulder a gaping hole was visible on the third floor with lines of police tape stretched across the gap and surrounding a pile of rubble on the grass directly below. Police in hi-vis jackets stood sorting through the rubble. In the bottom right hand corner a picture of Randall enlarged to fill the screen, a phone number printed across the bottom. The TV was muted but I picked out a few choice phrases from the way the news anchor's lips rounded out the words. 'Extremely dangerous' and 'call this number immediately'.

"I can't just sit here and do nothing", I said, irritably.

"Then don't", Robert said. "Explain what happened. Let's figure out why he is doing this and perhaps we can understand what his end game could be."

"What's left to figure out?" Henry said. "He's on some insane revenge mission."

"It's not that simple though, is it?" Robert said, directing the last question at me.

I rattled my handcuffed wrist in frustration then sighed and sat back in bed. "Liv told you what we discovered about Inspector Price?"

"He was the officer on the scene when Randall's daughter was caught shoplifting. I'm surprised someone of his rank would be involved in something so trivial, though."

"I don't think he was on duty, exactly. It sounded like he was already there and got involved to try and dilute the situation."

"So, Randall blames Price for arresting his daughter and getting her sent to therapy with Claire", Henry said. "He killed Claire because he doesn't think she helped her in therapy, and tried to kill Price for getting Evie sent there in the first place?"

"It looks that way", I said, though my voice lost conviction as I spoke. Something in the back of my mind, a part I attributed to Liv, objected to the simplicity of the explanation. "But why not the friends she was caught shoplifting with or the manager who threatened to press charges? Why not any of the other police officers who arrested her for that matter before then?"

"My thoughts exactly", Robert said. "If he's been planning this since Evie died, then why these targets and not the others? As a revenge motive it seems oddly specific."

"He could just be ticking the names off a list. He probably plans to get to the others, but hasn't got round to them yet."

"But his second target was someone high up in the police force? Why start there, surely Evie's friends and the manager would have been easier targets. Why not start with them?" Robert said.

"Is it possible he did and they just weren't made public?" Henry asked.

The three of us fell silent. I didn't think it was likely; while a single shop owner might be easy enough to disappear, a large group of young friends suddenly vanishing would certainly be newsworthy. "Where is Liv?" I asked.

"She had to go back to work", Henry said.

I nodded, glancing back to the TV. "What's that?" I asked, as the image switched back to the hotel where Claire had been killed. They showed a sweeping shot of the blackened outside of the hotel's upper floors. It was the first time I'd seen the hotel since the dragon incident and the damage was nowhere near as bad as I would have expected. A crowd had gathered outside and armed police stood around the entrance.

"Oh, they've been repeating the same two segments over and over all morning", Henry said. "The conference starts today so they have added a load of extra security just in case Randall shows up. As if he would be that stupid."

"It's just to make the guests feel safe", Robert said.

"And to give the news teams something to talk about. Makes them look like they are in control", I said.

"Delicately put", Inspector Price said from the

doorway. A nurse wheeled him into the room, an IV bag followed not far behind carried by a hospital porter. Both the nurse and the porter avoided looking at me. Price on the other hand didn't even blink, his gaze fixed on me.

"Thank you, Karen", Price said as his wheelchair came to a halt beside my bed. "Would you all please give us a minute."

I nodded to my father as he and Henry filed out with the nurse. The porter lingered a moment to hook the IV bag onto the wall above Price, then hurried out of the room, leaving us alone.

"They are a little afraid of you", Price said. "Truth be told, I'm wondering if I should be too."

"Well, once they see me walk to the bathroom with my arse hanging out of my hospital gown, I'm sure that'll put their fears to bed", I said, watching him. "Assuming you uncuff me of course. Sir." I blinked, realising the *sir* was thanks to the part of Liv I was carrying around with me.

Price's mouth quirked a little at the corners.

"Are you going to be alright?" I asked, glancing at the IV and the bandages beneath his chin where Randall had forced Price to press a scalpel into himself.

"I'll live. Looks much worse than it is."

"And what about Liv?"

"She's fine. Back at the station debriefing Riley as

we speak. If Riley takes my advice they will be heading up the manhunt together shortly. Now we know the killer, we should be able to get a good idea where he might go next."

I thought of the bulldog-like man, the part of me still harbouring a part of Liv thought his "debrief" would probably be indistinguishable from his interrogation. "I hope so", I said.

Price studied me for a minute then said, "So, forgive the bluntness but, what exactly *are* you?"

I blinked. "What do you mean?"

"I think you know exactly what I mean."

"Liv didn't tell you?"

"She told me she trusted you, and that you might be able to find Randall before he does any more harm. Under normal circumstances that might have been enough, but after what I saw last night, not to mention what I *think* I saw in that lift back at the hotel, I'll need a little more to go on."

"How much do you remember?"

"Enough to think I hit my head much harder than the doctors were willing to admit."

I thought for a minute, my eyes fixed on the handcuffs as I tried to figure the quickest way to get myself free, and what lies would get them to release me without throwing Liv under the bus.

"You know I don't ever remember a time when telling the truth required me to think quite so hard", Price said, watching me. "Perhaps it would put your mind at ease to consider that I'm not here in any official capacity. I'm off active duty, will be for months I expect, if indeed they take me back at all. Besides, who would believe me?"

"At a guess, the psychiatric ward?" I said, though I didn't really believe it. My natural inclination was to hide everything about that part of myself, particularly from the police, but there was someone else standing in the wings of my mental theatre. *Liv.* She trusted this man completely, and the part of her I carried, though small, was unwavering. Price was both friend and father figure to her, a fact I was stunned she had managed to keep hidden from me. She had put her feelings aside, it was the only way she could hunt the man responsible for this.

"You are already handcuffed to a bed. Try me", Price added.

"Alright. What you remember, every last weird and impossible thing, was real. Liv wasn't in control of herself though, she was forcibly compelled to shoot at us, so don't hold it against her."

"How?"

I hesitated. "Magic."

"Huh."

"*Magic*", I repeated.

"Oh, I heard you", he said.

I waited while his eyes drifted away from me for the first time as if he were performing some complicated mathematical puzzle in his mind.

"So, you can do magic?"

"Right."

"Like a wizard?"

"Sort of."

"Like Ha...?"

"Not exactly." I cut him off. "And before you ask, no, I can't show you."

"Convenient."

"I mean I could, but I used up the last of the power I had on me last night, saving your life and all."

"Hence why you're still in handcuffs?"

"More or less, and frankly it's exhausting."

"I can imagine", he said.

"I can't tell if you believe me or if you are just teasing?"

"No, I believe you. I've seen enough, felt enough, demonstrations to last me a lifetime." Price's face paled and his eyes glazed over for a moment.

"I'm sorry that was your first experience of

magic. I've never seen anyone use it the way Randall has. It shouldn't be like that."

"In my experience, any form of power can be used to do harm. But anyway, I'm not here for a metaphysical debate, we need to find him before he hurts anyone else."

"That's what we've been trying to figure out", I said. "I don't understand why he is picking the targets he has. Maybe he is just insane." I sighed.

"You would know better than I would. I was asleep for most of this investigation. But, if you ask me, the man I saw last night didn't look insane. Determined and sadistic maybe, but not insane."

"How can you say that? He just tried to kill you because you *almost* arrested his daughter once."

"Well for one, he left when I was still breathing. He could have killed me while you and Stone were fighting him off. All those things flying around the room, none of them came within three feet of me. If you ask me, you spoiled it for him. Why else would he wait until I woke up before coming to find me? He wanted me conscious, so he could look me in the eye when he killed me."

"Which means what? He's even more depraved that we first thought?"

"It means it's not just about revenge, he wants

to punish his victims, make them suffer and humiliate them. Liv is like one of my own. Perhaps it wasn't coincidence he chose her to pull the trigger."

I thought for a moment, not having considered that. "He came back to the hotel after the first murder. I thought the fire was to destroy any evidence he might have left behind, but what if it was to humiliate you and make the police look incompetent? If he had succeeded in killing you and leaving Liv burned alive, eventually forensics would have figured out she had shot you."

"Quite the scandal", Price said, bobbing his head. "There's one more thing you should know. After the shoplifting incident Randall and I kept in touch, just emails back and forth really. I took a gamble with convincing the shop owner not to press charges so I wanted to make sure I did the right thing. After Evie committed suicide I didn't expect to hear from him again, but a month or two after she died he reached out to me, thanked me for trying to help her and asked about some volunteer programs. We even met up once to talk about them. That's when I mentioned my promising young protégé."

"Liv?"

He nodded.

"Why are you telling me this?" I said.

He slipped a hand into his pyjama pocket and withdrew a key. "Because I can't go with you and if he's as dangerous as I think he is you might be the only one who can stop him."

I continued to stare at him as he inserted the key into the handcuff lock and they clicked free.

He pocketed the handcuffs and the key, then met my eye. "I know you are capable of killing him, you proved that last night", Price said. "If I was in your shoes I might want him dead too, so I'm just reminding you he lost his wife and daughter and he wasn't always like this. If the police find him before you do, they will most likely shoot him on sight now that they think explosives are a possibility."

"Quite the pep talk", I said.

"Mm", he grunted. "I can't do much to help you while I'm in here but I'll do my best to keep you out of prison, assuming nobody has shot you by then."

"Right, thanks", I said, sitting up too quickly and grunting as my shoulder throbbed painfully. I sat back again, gingerly lowering my left arm back to my chest.

"Hurts, doesn't it? Dislocated my knee once", he whistled like a cowboy. "Now, I'm not entirely sure why, but Liv asked me to give you this." He held out a gold wedding ring on the palm of his hand. "She said to use it if you had to."

I stared at it for a moment before taking it from him and slipping it onto the little finger of my right hand.

He frowned, opened his mouth then closed it again and said, "Nevermind. I won't ask".

I stared at the ring on my little finger, the temptation to draw from it to fix my shoulder was tempting, but what then? I still didn't know where Randall was.

CHAPTER 22

"Everything alright?" Robert said from the doorway.

"Yes, come in. Thanks for waiting", Price said, turning around in his wheelchair and wincing.

Henry and my father filed in. They were each carrying a stack of gift cards. Henry tossed his pile into my lap as my father moved to the window.

"Bloody thing, sorry son. It's sealed shut", Robert said.

I grimaced but opened the first card and read the contents.

Dear Tommy,

I am really sorry you are poorly. Get well soon. We mist you at football.

love,

James

James' use of capital and lowercase letters seemed entirely random, each letter shaped with trembling lines as if it had been written on a rollercoaster. Henry and Robert watched me expectantly.

"You stole these?" I asked, not hesitating before stuffing the first into my mouth.

"From the bins. *Mostly*", Henry said. He seemed rather pleased with himself.

I swallowed with difficulty and stuffed another piece into my mouth as Henry handed me a glass of water. I gulped half the glass then continued eating, Inspector Price watching with a mix between fascination and concern.

I grunted through the wad of cardboard and waved to get my father's attention. I pointed to the clipboard at the end of the bed.

"Ah, yes", he said, squinting down at the doctor's handwriting. "Significant swelling, *blah blah blah*, painkillers, anti-inflammatories..." He shrugged and dropped the clipboard at the foot of the bed.

"Mhmm", I grunted, feeling the steady release of power gathering at the pit of my stomach. I directed it across my chest to my shoulder, focusing on reducing the swelling. I imagined the muscles and tendons surrounding the joint repairing and growing stronger.

After ten minutes of constant chewing on the waxy cardboard my jaw ached more than my shoulder. As long as I didn't move it too much or too quickly the pain was reduced to a distant throb. I raised my left arm out of the sling and cautiously turned it back and forth. Price was staring at me while my father, bored with my slow improvement, watched the news. The two segments had expanded to a third in which the hotel manager was being interviewed by a reporter in front of a long queue littered with police.

Henry breezed into the room holding up three more get well soon cards, which he tossed onto the pile on the bed. "I managed to get a look inside the room on the third floor. Some forensics types were just going in when I passed."

"That was fortunate", Robert said.

"I know, I only had to make five passes before someone went in. The place was in tatters, the floor was all torn up. Looks like you went at it with a sledge hammer. Think your insurance will cover all that?" Henry said, biting his lip a little to stop himself smiling.

"That was all the police", I said, between mouthfuls.

"The police tore up the floor?" Henry said, clearly unconvinced.

"Randall sunk us through the floor the same way Dad did at the Nelson house. Police probably had to tear most of it up to get Liv and I free. Now are you going to help me come up with a plan for finding him before he does any more damage? I'm about as good as I'm going to get."

Henry nodded firmly, dropping back into a chair and leaning forwards. My father's face was turned towards the window.

"Olivia had some suggestions on that matter actually", Price said, drawing my attention away from Robert.

"Mmm?" I grunted, having just started on another mouthful.

Price slipped his hand into his robe and pulled out a little plastic evidence bag and held it out to me.

I took the bag and stared down at the contents. The bag contained two small corners of paper, one slightly larger than the first. The larger piece had a narrow line in dark blue ink which looked to form the bottom part of a 'T' or an 'L'. As I realised where it must have come from I immediately tossed it to the far side of the bed.

"Jesus, what is it?" Henry said, jumping to his feet.

"It's part of whatever Randall has been drawing from." I felt my skin crawl as if a bag of spiders had just been emptied down the back of my hospital gown.

"How did you get that?" I asked, looking at Price.

"Liv passed it to me earlier. She said she pocketed it last night while they were still pulling you out of the floor."

I recalled Randall ripping the scalpel free where it had impaled his bag, pinning it to the wall.

"If it belonged to Randall you can use it to find him, right?" Henry said.

"Maybe. Dad?" I said, looking to him.

Robert was on his feet beside me looking at the forensic bag with the same cold trepidation. "I don't know."

"Stone and I agreed, if there's even a slim chance of it working we need you to take it. The longer he is out there, the more likely it is he ends up hurting more people. I'm sorry to put you in this position, but if he can cause as much damage as Detective Stone suggests, I don't see we have a choice", Price said.

"The spell failed last time and it almost led us to our deaths. I suppose it could work if we had another suitable keepsake, but without knowing why it failed the first time it's not worth the risk", said Robert.

"Wait, if the spell failed why did it still take us right to Randall's house?" Henry said.

"Who knows, perhaps our meaning was off, or our intentions conflicted. Perhaps he was there but left when he saw us bumbling through the trees." Robert said.

"Have you ever had a location spell fail like that before? Still taking you to a location related to what you were hunting?"

"No, never. If it fails, it would usually fail completely, pointing in random directions or nowhere at all."

I sat in thought for a moment when it clicked into place. It was the combination of Liv's analytical mind with my own knowledge and experience of magic. I looked at my father. "What if it didn't fail? What if the spell did lead us straight to the killer, we were just too preoccupied to realise?"

"He can't have been there, there was nowhere to hide, and why would he bother? Randall is basically a walking killing machine", Henry said.

"I'm not thinking of Randall."

My father's eyes widened. "Evelyn."

"The zombie wife? Are you fucking kidding?" Henry said.

"Inspector, you said Randall seemed to be dealing with his grief and that he never showed any sign of blaming you for what happened to his daughter?" I said.

"That was my impression, yes."

"What about Evelyn? Did you spend any time

with her?"

He thought for a moment. "No, I don't believe I ever saw her again after that first meeting when Evie was caught shoplifting."

"Right, and the killer, at least to our knowledge, has never gone after any of the other officers that arrested Evie before that point, most of which led to actual convictions."

"I'm struggling to see how you are making the jump from that to dead zombie wife?" Henry said.

"My point is, the targets don't make sense. Why target Price, who got the shop owner to drop the charges, and not the shopkeeper who wanted to convict her in the first place? Why target Doctor June? What have they all got in common?"

"They all tried in some way to help Randall", Robert said.

"Exactly, but they didn't just try, I think they succeeded. This isn't about hurting those that failed Evie, this is about punishing Randall."

"How though? She's dead, right?" Henry said, uncertain.

"Hate", I said, looking at the end of the bed where the evidence bag still lay containing the two scraps of paper. "She wrote a diary, pouring every hateful feeling into it. The better Randall seemed to be doing, the more she hated him for it, the more powerful her words became."

"She left it for him knowing he would end up consuming it", my father said sounding disturbed. "I can't imagine what a year's worth of resentment and hate would do to a mage. It must have completely overwhelmed him." He sounded sickened.

"What about Claire?" Henry asked.

"My guess is Evelyn felt betrayed. When I went through Claire's files there was one I think was about Evelyn."

"You think?" Henry said.

"I don't know for sure, I was looking for the daughter's file, not the mother's, at the time. Anyway, her notes described a woman having problems with her husband and refusing to open up about it. She even suggested she started writing in a diary if she couldn't open up to Claire."

"So, that probably describes half of everyone in therapy? Plus, you know what Claire is like, she probably asked everyone to start keeping a diary", Henry argued.

"I can't remember her exact wording, but Claire definitely described her as paranoid about being discovered as someone who went to therapy."

"She sounds like a proud woman, but that hardly makes her a killer."

"True, but let's say I'm right and it was Evelyn. Knowing Claire, she might have offered to be part of the meeting at the hotel as a kind of intervention or support group for Randall when she heard that Evelyn had committed suicide."

"So?" Henry said.

"So, it wasn't Randall at all, it was Evelyn, or at least the worst parts of her poured into Randall's body. She was suddenly forced into this group setting, seeing a bunch of Randall's friends all sympathising with *him* and trying to help *him* while she had to sit there and watch them all looking at her. The file said something about her hating being pitied. Maybe that's why she killed them the way she did."

"You're sure it was Evelyn's notes?" Henry asked.

"There weren't any names. But I read every one, and that's the only one I can think of that felt like her", I said, a little breathless. "Have you got my phone?"

Henry pulled my phone from his jacket pocket and handed it to me. I started dialling Liv's number but my father's hand pressed over my own and gently closed it. "You can't, son."

"What? Why not? If he isn't in control it's not his fault. Liv has to know so she can..." I blinked, as the truth of the situation settled over me. The emotions of the half dozen children I had just consumed cried out in frustration, unable to comprehend what the wiser parts of me already knew but didn't want to accept. It didn't matter who was pulling Randall's strings, he was still hunting and killing people. He had to be stopped. The last thing Liv needed going up against someone so powerful was doubt. Telling any of this to Liv would only put her in more danger.

I felt my eyes sting in the corners. My father patted my knee sympathetically. "We need to get you clean."

I looked at Price who was studying me with intense curiosity before looking away as my eyes started to water.

"You're awfully quiet?" I said, defensively.

"I've learned there are two types of men in my position; those that have worked all their lives to reach it, and those that end up there. I find the latter to be the more effective leaders."

"And which are you?" Robert asked.

"The first, but it's never too late to start trying to be the second. Learning that this is real is a good motivator to shut up and listen", he said. "Now, your father is right. We cannot tell the wider police force anything; no one would believe us with perhaps the exception of Olivia, and telling her might put her in more danger. And that's assuming of course your suspicions are correct."

"It's the only thing I can think of that fits", I said,

sniffing a little as I struggled to get my emotions under control.

"Still we need something more to back up your theory. Where are these files you mentioned?"

I frowned. "In the taxi. I double parked, it's probably been towed by now." I glanced around at the bedside table. "Keys?"

"Liv took them. She needed a ride", Henry said, shrugging.

I sighed. "Even if I am right it wouldn't make any difference to how the police deal with him, would it?"

"The man seen leaving a bomb inside a hospital? I'm afraid not. If there's even the slightest possibility he is carrying any explosives they will shoot to kill."

I stared down the length of the bed, my eyes coming to rest on the little evidence bag with the two fragments of paper inside it. There was only one way to know for sure if my theory was right. I stared at it for a long moment then turned to Price and Henry on my right. "Could you contact Liv on the radio and find out where my car is?" I asked, nodding to the officers standing outside the door. Henry immediately rose to push Price's wheelchair for him. "Henry, can you call Amber and tell her to pick up the taxi wherever Liv left it and get over here? We might need to move in a hurry." Henry made a face so I added, "Tell her I'll pay her, just get her here."

I walked them to the door, handing Henry my phone. I started to turn back into the room, but Henry lingered by the door looking uncomfortable. "Everything okay?"

He glanced over my shoulder and seemed to relax as Robert disappeared into the bathroom and closed the door. "I don't know if it's important, but I remembered where I heard about that group, The Positive Self? It was at your dad's place."

"Are you sure?"

He nodded. "He had there flyer on his desk a few weeks ago."

"Maybe he just forgot?"

"Maybe, but he was a bit off when I mentioned it at the time. I dunno, you are probably right."

We shared an uncomfortable look between us, neither one of us entirely convinced, before he turned and headed off up the corridor.

I closed the door behind me and turned back into the room.

"Dad?" I said, as a crackling sound emanated from around the door.

"Adam, you are still wearing the Detective's wedding ring aren't you?" he said.

"Dad…? What are you doing?" I said, panic rising

in my chest. "Don't do this." I said, noticing the plastic bag and its contents were gone from the bed.

"Do what you were just planning to do? You're my son, I can always tell what you are thinking." I could hear the smile in his voice. "Don't hold back, son. Do whatever you have to do to stop me", he said, his voice shaking. The empty plastic bag slid beneath the door followed by a single tendril of grey smoke.

"No!" I shouted.

I threw myself to the side of the door just in time. The door exploded off its hinges, slammed into the end of the bed before flipping over and landing between the mattress and the far wall. I squeezed my fist closed, drawing a little magic into my muscles, and threw my fist into my father's stomach as he stepped out of the bedroom. My father hadn't exercised since our bike rides when I was ten, but he barely flinched as my fist made contact.

"Step aside", he snarled, his voice unfamiliar and cold. He didn't wait for me to comply, throwing me backwards into an armchair. I threw myself out of the chair after him. I rushed him and rugby tackled him into the wall before he threw me off again and turned back to face me.

I ducked under his backhanded fist, dropping to the floor and sending magic into the white aerial cable that had come free with the wall. It shot around my father's ankles as he grabbed me by the collar and lifted me one handed onto my tip toes.

He tried to take a step and dropped to his knees. I threw myself immediately onto his back, my hands trapping his arms in a headlock I suspected was all Liv's doing. He growled and began tearing at the wires with his bare hands, snapping the cable before reaching for me.

"Get off me. I'll kill you if I have to." he said, coldly as I struggled to keep hold of him as he rose easily to his feet even with my full weight on his back.

"I don't believe you. You're not capable of murder."

"Fool, you have no idea." he said, gripping my injured shoulder until I screamed. The next thing I knew I was hurtling across the room. My back struck the arm chair which toppled onto its side with me still in it. I watched my father's advance toward me before he stopped abruptly mid step.

"Dad?" I said, cautiously getting to my feet.

"Adam, you were right, it's her", he said.

"Evelyn?" I said, still keeping my distance.

He nodded, his eyes filling with tears as he dropped to his knees clutching his face. "Oh god."

"Dad, who is her next target?" I asked.

He blinked, looking slowly around the destroyed room. His eyes came to rest on the snowy picture on the TV. "The convention", he said in a small voice.

I felt the bottom drop out of my stomach. "Who? Who at the convention?"

"All of them."

CHAPTER 23

"Jesus!" Henry said, as he was finally permitted back into the hospital room to see us. My father occupied the bed, looking pale, and did not look up when Henry entered. I had insisted he use Price and his entourage of police and nurses to confess and get clean, and though Evelyn's immediate presence was gone from my father's mind, I could still see the taint of that contact hanging over him like a dark cloud.

Price sat in his wheelchair giving out instructions to his officers, and though he had no official power, his men clearly respected him enough to take him at his word and accept his version of events. The official line was my father had had some sort of episode, though no one seemed particularly curious about the specifics of how or why the room had been destroyed.

"I'm alright, son." he said, catching me watching him.

I leaned in closer to him so we wouldn't be overheard. "Do you remember what you said to me?" I said, trying to keep my voice level.

He glanced around the room nervously. "It's a blur, I can't remember much. I'm sure I said some awful things. Sorry."

"You said... It doesn't matter, you weren't yourself. We'll talk about it later." I said, unable to stop myself from noticing the look of relief on his tired face. The Liv at the back of my mind bristled with irritation, but I didn't have the heart to press him on the details of what he had implied he had done. With an effort, I pulled myself away from my father and turned to Henry as I dressed.

"Did you speak to Amber?"

"Hm?" Henry said, staring at the cracked TV screen. "Oh, she's already here." I slipped on my trousers under my hospital gown. Several officers continued to stare at me as I pulled on the rest of my clothes.

"Henry, can you stay with Dad?" I said.

"Of course. Good luck", he said, handing me back my phone.

"Fin? Be careful, son", Robert said from his handcuffed position in bed. He looked as though there was more he wanted to say, but couldn't, not with a room full of police officers. Instead I found his hand and squeezed it before following Price as he was wheeled back out into the corridor.

"Mr Chase, what I said before stands, I'll do what I can to keep you out of prison when this is over, but I can't make you any promises."

"I know", I said. "What about my father?"

"This is a hospital, he's a patient who didn't have his medication. Hardly a police matter", he shrugged.

"Thank you."

"Oh and Mr. Chase, you know why I love that old film?" he said.

I had to think for a moment what he was referring to. "*The Good, the Bad and the Ugly?*" I said.

"Mm", he nodded. "Those characters, at the end of the day there really isn't a whole lot of difference between them."

I nodded farewell and headed for the exit. It didn't take me long to locate Amber. She was double parked right outside the main visitor's entrance.

"You're really here?" I said, unable to contain my surprise as I slipped into the backseat.

Amber looked at me coolly in the rear-view mirror as she blew on fresh, raven black nail polish.

"Some of us show up on time", she shrugged.

The scent of acetone was so heavy inside the car that I opened the windows on both sides a couple of inches. "Uhuh", I grunted. "How long have you been waiting?"

She continued to stare at her nails, her lips pressing into a tight line.

"You do care", I said, unable to help myself.

"Where to, dick?" she said, starting the engine.

#

"I'm sorry, it's life or death", I said, pushing my way to the front of the queue and sliding my bank card into the cashpoint. I withdrew a hundred pounds, stuffed the cash into my pocket and sprinted the length of the street. I arrived back at the charity shop and dashed inside. When the same woman asked me if she could help me find anything, I was forced to take a moment to recover my breath. I ended up miming the shape of the bag and pointing towards the till where she had kept the stack of books with inscriptions.

She nodded knowingly. "Ah it's you. Must have changed your mind eh?" she said, slipping behind the till and placing a Sainsbury's bag-for-life onto the counter.

"Is this all of them?" I asked.

"That's the lot", she nodded.

"How much?" I said between gasps.

She hesitated then said, "Ninety pounds, I've added a few more to the pile."

I rolled my eyes but put the money down onto the counter and hurried out with my overpriced merchandise. The Austin was waiting for me outside the door, Amber having followed me up the street from the cashpoint. I climbed into the back and we sped away.

"I don't think I've ever seen you run", Amber said. She actually sounded concerned.

"Desperate times", I said, dialling Liv's number.

"Hi, it's me. Where are you?" I said, as soon as she picked up.

"At the Marriot, overseeing this dog and pony show. How are you?"

"What? Price said you were back on the investigation with Riley?"

"Technically, I am. He's just got me doing this to keep me out of his way. Why?" she said.

"He's coming after everyone at the convention. Anyone attending is going to be a target."

She hesitated. "Are you sure about this? We have a dozen armed officers checking everyone as they come into the hotel. Nelson's picture is everywhere, how does he expect to get away with this even if he does manage to get inside?"

"I don't think he plans to get away at all. He'll

take his revenge then kill himself."

I heard Liv grunt down the phone line. "So what, you think he'll set fire to the place like he did before? Seal the exits and trap everyone inside?"

"I don't know." I said.

"Christ, how do I deal with this? I can't call the fire department without a fire."

"We are here", Amber called, from the front seat.

I sat forwards and peered out through the windscreen where two police officers were immediately identifiable by the increased bulk afforded by their dark tactical vests and sidearms. They walked calmly along the pavement, their semi-automatic carbines held snuggly across armoured stomachs. Locals and tourists alike gave the pair a wide berth as they cut through the crowd on their way back towards the Marriot.

"Where are you?" I said, into the phone.

"I see you. Wait there", she said, before hanging up.

I closed my flip phone and pulled the lid off the first box of Claire's files. At least a dozen were missing.

"Here", Amber said, handing them back through the partition to me, the contents fanning wide.

"What were you doing with these?" I asked.

"That detective started going through them after she picked me up. I got bored waiting at the hospital", she said, dismissively.

"Find anything?"

"Nothing you don't already know."

I looked at the other boxes and realised they had all been disturbed. "But you went through all of them?"

"I was bored", she said, defensively.

"We'll make a PI out of you yet." I said, watching her face drop. I had said the wrong thing. "But that isn't why you've stuck around is it?" I asked, the realisation slowly dawning on me. "You… you're a.. are you..?" I said, before stopping myself. There wasn't time to voice my suspicions. I gave myself a shake and cleared my throat. "Go home. Take care of the Austin. If things don't go well, consider it payment for your time."

She looked at me through the rear-view mirror as the car behind started honking. She opened her mouth to say something, her face uncharacteristically softening. Whatever she had been about to say was cut off as another horn joined the first. She pursed her lips and stuck her middle finger out the window at the driver behind.

I climbed out of the cab and met Liv on the curb,

watching Amber drive away. Liv looked tense. "Well? Where is he?" she said, expectantly.

"We didn't use a location spell", I said, as we started walking back towards the hotel entrance where the largest knot of police officers stood.

"Then how do you know he is coming here?"

"Robert absorbed the paper fragments you found."

"Is he alright?"

"He'll recover", I said, my throat restricting a little as I spoke.

"Is that why you trashed another hospital room?"

"He was trying to reach Price. I had to keep him there until he used up the last of his magic, hence the trashed room. Anyway, Robert saw the only place he would come next was here. My guess is, he waited until a week ago to start killing so he could end it all here."

"It doesn't make sense. I've been taking statements all morning from members who knew Randall from these conventions. Every one of them said the same thing."

"He wouldn't do this", I said, watching the final stragglers outside the hotel make it past security and disappear through the double doors.

"Exactly. Are you certain about this? The other

victims I can understand, but I just don't see the motive here."

"There's more I haven't told you. It complicates things but I think you need to know." I stopped and turned to face her. "Randall might actually be innocent", I said, just as sirens blared into existence at the opposite end of the street.

"What did you say?" Liv asked, her voice raised over the sound of the sirens.

Five police cars and two riot vans pulled up, their lights flashing, cutting off any more conversation. More armed police piled out of one of the vans and Riley stepped out of the passenger side of one of the police cars. He issued instructions to his officers and they quickly set up a roadblock at either end of the street.

Riley spotted us and marched in our direction.

"Don't say anything", Liv muttered.

"What the hell is he doing here?" Riley growled.

"I'm just out for the day shopping", I said, lifting my orange shopping bag up to show him. "What are you doing here?"

For a second I thought he was going to hit me, then he turned abruptly to Liv. "You are walking on very thin ice, Detective."

"Why *are* you here? The extra units are just going to make people nervous", Liv said.

"They should be nervous. Nelson was spotted on CCTV. He's coming this way."

"What?" I said, looking around. "Why would he show himself now?"

"Who knows, perhaps he's decided to turn himself in. Whatever the reason, we are going to be ready for him and *anything* he might be bringing with him", Riley said. "Stone, keep him out of the way. We'll talk about your future with the Metropolitan Police once Nelson is in custody."

Riley's radio crackled to life. *"Sir, we have eyes on Nelson. Repeat. We have eyes on Nelson. North side of the street."*

Riley hurried off up the street as the majority of the other officers spread out around the police barrier.

"You think he's actually turning himself in?" Liv asked.

"It's possible if his power finally expired, but if he was, why do it here and run the risk of getting shot?"

The crowd of pedestrians that had gathered along the police barrier to watch what was happening parted, and five police officers emerged, escorting a man through the crowd and across the police barrier.

"That's him. They actually have him", Liv said.

I stood on tiptoes, eager to get a look at him. Randall was keeping his head down, his face obscured by his hair, at the centre of the procession.

"He's in cuffs", Liv said, as the group stopped in front of Riley, barely twenty feet from where Liv and I were standing.

"I don't like it", I said.

"Did he have anything on him?" Riley asked.

"Just this", the lead officer said, raising a leather-bound notebook with a hole through its centre.

I caught Liv's arm and pulled her behind the nearest riot van. "We have to get inside the hotel now."

"He's in custody?" Liv said.

"No, he isn't, he's just acquired himself an armed entourage. He's going to make the police do it."

"How do you know?"

I pointed at the officer holding the notebook. "Because that keepsake he brought looks as though it still has at least half its pages. If my father was happy to flatten me to get to Price on a couple of torn corners; I don't see him giving up."

I could see her thinking fast. "The CCTV footage, he showed himself deliberately to draw more police here", she said, shaking her head. "We need to send them away. If we can convince Riley to..." she stopped watching as Riley stepped in beside Nelson and led him towards one of the police cars. He stopped abruptly after a few steps and reached for his radio as the police procession reformed around the pair.

"Quick give me your radio", I said, grabbing the first book out of my bag-for-life and absorbing it in a flurry of smoke and ash. I took the radio just as Riley's voice cracked from the speaker. "All units..."

"*Ymyrraeth*", I murmured. The radio hissed then started to smoke. I could see several others doing the same, as the hissing spread across all the other radios in the vicinity.

"Chase", Liv said, warningly. I cast a glance behind me as two armed officers approached.

"Everything alright over here?", one of them asked.

"We're fine", Liv said.

"I saw smoke."

"Yes, filthy habit", I said, turning and making a show of tripping over my bag. I threw an arm out for support at each officer.

"Easy", the larger one said, helping me to regain my footing.

"Oh sorry", I said, then in a quieter voice, "Egwyl", as my fingers glanced off the carbines strapped across their chests. The pair gave me an odd look and moved off to meet Riley who was waving emphatically at his men.

"What did you do?"

"Hopefully stopped their guns from firing. Come on, we need to get inside", I said.

"Wait", Liv caught my arm. "If he sees us, we are dead, right? Randall will make them open fire on us."

"Pretty much. What better way to humiliate the London police force?" I said, glancing through the side window of the van. Another three armed officers surrounded Randall; he wasn't even bothering to hide it as he touched a hand to each of the newcomers. It was terrifying how easy it was, a simple touch of an arm or shoulder and one by one they each succumbed.

Liv pulled open the door of the van and reached inside and released the handbrake. "No keys. Push!" she said.

I put my hand through the loop in my shopping bag, stepped to the back corner of the van and started pushing. With Liv's help the vehicle slowly started to roll across the street towards the hotel doors. I used a little magic to urge the van faster.

Shouts went up across the street and I pushed Liv forwards. "Get inside, I'm right behind you", I said. She ran ahead of the van and through the double doors as I took her place by the open passenger door and urged the van faster, my muscles straining. It bounced up over the curb and crashed through the centre pair of doors in a shower of broken glass.

I reached into the bag and ripped a dozen pages from the first book and stuffed them into my mouth, hurrying around the car and squeezing myself through the gap to join Liv in the hotel foyer.

"...need to clear this area now! Get them out by the fire escape on the far side of the building or have them wait in the upper floors." The concierge's expression abruptly changed as the sound of gunfire filled the air and a volley of bullets collided with the back of the van.

"CLEAR THE AREA, NOW!" Liv shouted, pushing guests away from the entrance before throwing herself down beside me. My hands pushed into my Sainsbury's bag mainlining magic, an ashen novel in each hand. My eyes watered with the sudden rush of power.

"They are coming", Liv shouted, collaring me and pushing me deeper into the hotel.

An idea struck me as we crossed the massive red and gold rug which ran the length of the foyer. I stopped beside the concierge desk and pressed my hand down into carpet, driving magic down into the floor.

"Fin!" Liv dragged me to my feet and pushed me up the stairs towards reception, bullets ricocheted off the staircase behind us as we reached the top and came face to face with a panicked group of tourists.

"Fin, they are already inside", Liv said, looking down the corridor. "He must have sent more around to the other entrances."

I stepped in front of the family and raised my hands in submission. The air began to shimmer before my eyes, obscuring the officers and their carbines which they kept levelled on us.

"He's got a ticket", the lead officer said, then he pulled the trigger. A spark of fire lit the end of his barrel as a bullet slammed into the wall of air I had thrown up in front of me. The officer didn't get another shot off, as Liv fell upon them. She slammed her baton across their armoured bodies in a flurry of rapid blows striking knee, helmet, wrist, or ankle. In seconds the two men slumped to the floor.

"Can you bring them back?" Liv asked, her chest heaving as she caught her breath.

I looked at the fast-depleting bag of keepsakes and shook my head. "I can't spare the power. The more Randall uses up keeping them under his control, the better off we will all be. Sorry", I said, to the injured men. I stepped forwards and laid a hand on their firearms fusing triggers, blocking clips and crippling them in a half dozen other places so they had no hope of being fired again.

The lift doors swung open behind me and the family piled in. Liv reached in and pressed the top floor. "Knock on every door until someone lets you in, then hide", Liv said, as the doors swung closed on their terrified faces.

"We should cuff them", Liv said, turning back to me as I finished with the officers' sidearms.

"Good..." I started.

Her eyes drifted over my shoulder then she launched herself forwards, pulling me to the ground as fire ripped open the lift doors exposing the redbrick beyond.

"Stay low!", Liv cried.

We crawled on our stomachs towards the doors as more bullets ricocheted off the walls and what remained of the lift doors above our heads. In the pauses between spurts of gunfire, I could hear them shouting as glass crunching underfoot marked the arrival of several more police.

"Stay back! Something is wrong with the floor, go around the other side."

We crawled through the first set of double doors before rising to a crouch and continuing along the corridor. We passed the service elevator and a string of identical hotel room doors before two more police officers turned and raised their weapons at us. They had been pounding on the door to the conference hall.

"Are you here for the convention?" the first officer called.

"No, we're guests", Liv said immediately, her hands raised in surrender.

"She's lying, that's the detective." the second officer said. I threw up a shield of compressed air in front of us, but the gun didn't fire. As he turned his gun on its side and tried to clear the jammed chamber I spotted the line of grey ash on the man's vest where I had marked him.

"Shoot them", the second officer said to the first.

I sidestepped in front of Liv as the first officer's gun roared. My shield caught every round but I could feel my power draining with every piece of lead it deflected.

"You still have your baton?" I asked.

I heard the *snap* as it sprang open. She placed her hand on my shoulder and launched it. It struck the firing officer in the helmet, cracking his visor and diverting his aim.

I pushed my shield out and caught the baton as it fell, visualising a whip-like arm stretching from my hand to its handle. The two officers hesitated, staring at the baton suspended impossibly in mid-air between them. I threw my arm out to the left and then to the right smacking into each man's helmet in rapid succession. I continued to flick my hand back and forth until both men were on their knees with their guns on the floor beside them.

Liv rushed around me, retrieved their weapons and snapped a set of handcuffs between wrist and ankle.

She tossed the broken weapon aside and pushed on the door to the conference hall. "Locked", she said, banging on it. "Please let us in."

"Step back", I said, glancing up and down the corridor, expecting a dozen more guns to come bearing down on us any moment. I reached into my shopping bag for the next book on the pile.

"Please, my husband is hurt", Liv said, catching my hand.

After a moment, a bolt shifted and the door opened.

A panicked face appeared around the door. His eyes came to rest on my shopping bag and some of the tension seemed to leave him. "Hurry", he said, swinging the door wide.

CHAPTER 24

"What's going on out there? We heard gunshots?" the hotel manager said as he bolted the door shut behind us.

"Is it terrorists?" asked a skinny boy, I guessed to be around Amber's age.

Liv ignored both questions. "We need to get everyone out of here. They are targeting anyone coming to the convention."

"Who?"

Liv hesitated.

"Men dressed like police", I said, using a little more magic to seal the doors on the pretext of checking the deadbolts were secure.

"Is there another exit? Another route out of the hotel?" Liv asked.

"There's a fire exit next to the stage which leads straight out onto the road", he stammered. "Our security guard, Colin, went to find out what was going on when the shooting started."

"Show me", Liv said, marching down the centre aisle between banks of chairs facing a raised stage at the far end of the room. Hundreds of heads turned to look at us as we entered, every face a mixture of hope and fear. The only vacant seats I could see were where their occupants had filed out to stand in the aisle.

"There he is", the hotel manager said, as we arrived at the glass doors.

Colin, a stocky, ruddy-faced man with a shaved head and a tight red shirt came into view around the corner of some industrial-sized bins. He was jogging, his arms swinging at his sides. The hotel manager fumbled with the keys looped onto his belt when the glass shattered from its frame, and blood spurted from the manager's chest. The gunshot registered a fraction of a second after the fact. I glanced at Colin, but he was just as shocked as the rest of us, turning to look back up the alley behind him before throwing himself with surprising speed under cover against the bins. I followed a beat later, ducking down behind the stage.

Liv grabbed the hotel manager by the legs and dragged him away from the doors as he cried out, clutching his bloodied arm. Someone handed Liv a wad of napkins which she stuffed under the manager's shirt against the wound. He let out a cry.

"Must be a sharpshooter on the roof", Liv said. "Why only the one shot though?"

"She just wants to keep us pinned down here", I said.

"She? What are you talking about? You said before Randall might be innocent, what aren't you telling me?"

"It's not Randall doing this, it's Evelyn. It's been Evelyn all along, working through Randall. The slaughter at the hotel, Doctor June, Price. None of them were targeted because they failed to help Evie, they were targeted because they succeeded in helping Randall. This is Evelyn's perfect revenge. The location spell pointed us straight to Evelyn's grave. I should have realised sooner. You saw the diary he was carrying?"

"She wrote it?" Liv said. "It doesn't change anything. He... they will kill everyone in this room unless we stop him. Can you do anything?" she asked, looking down at my diminished supply of keepsakes. "Jesus, is that everything?" she said, without waiting for me to reply.

"Why doesn't he just storm in here himself?" Liv asked.

"She wants spectacle. Forcing the police to hurt civilians... it's all part of her twisted revenge. If they shoot even a handful of these people it will be in the news for years. It would be like a terrorist attack."

"Why the hell are you smiling?" she asked.

"That means he won't be coming in himself, he'll just be sending those armed units in here to do his dirty work."

"And that's better?"

"Better for us", I said, turning my back to the stage to take in the banks of seats and their desperate occupants. I turned back to the stage, looking up into the rafters from which hung a heavy stage curtain. "We need to move everyone we can backstage."

"They can't stay here, Fin. We need to get them away from the hotel."

"No, that's what she wants. That's why they haven't stormed in here yet. She wants to make it public, she wants spectacle. Police gunning down civilians in the street. She them to make a run for it. We have to force them to come and get us."

Liv looked across at the injured manager. He was propped up against the stage, being tended to by another hotel employee and a woman from the convention who I guessed had medical training.

"What about the rest? They won't all fit back there."

"We need to get them to lie down in the middle rows. The chairs will give them some cover", I said.

"Are you sure about this?" she said, looking tense.

"You really want me to answer that?" I said.

She shook her head and stepped up onto the stage and began issuing instructions to the audience. Faster than I would have believed possible, the crowd filed down onto the stage and filled every conceivable space beyond the heavy curtains. I could think of nothing to comfort them with. "Try and stay as quiet as you can", I said to the front row. I turned and nodded to Liv. After a moment, the crimson red curtain swept across the stage like a dark cloud, pitching row after row of anxious faces into darkness.

I moved to the centre where the two halves met and retrieved two more books from my bag and consumed them, crumbling the ashen pages between my fingers before pressing them against each half of the curtain, willing the fibres to strengthen, to be impervious to even the slightest rip or tear.

A minute later I stumbled to the edge of the stage and hung my legs over the edge, clutching at the Sainsbury's bag as I struggled to retrieve my next fix. I stuffed more pages into my mouth. My vision steadied and the sickness left me after a few seconds of steady, laborious chewing. I watched as Liv divided the remaining audience members into five rows at the centre of the room. I could see many of them were trembling and crying as they folded themselves down onto the floorSeeing them like that, I would have killed Randall if I had the strength to. I considered using a little magic to calm my nerves, but stopped myself with one look at Liv. She had just asked these people to lie down and trust her, knowing what was about to happen.

"Can you do anything for them?" she asked, her voice sounding small. I looked down at the last stack of books in my shopping bag and Liv's wedding band around my finger. The weight of magical potential called to me. I closed my fist and let the metal dig into my flesh and felt myself teeter on the brink of taking it all into myself, to meet the imminent threat of violence with an equal force of my own, but it wouldn't be enough. Worst, I didn't trust myself to even attempt it. I would lose myself in so much power and end up hurting the wrong people and playing right into Evelyn's hands.

"No", I said finally, just as a heavy rhythmic thud started at the far end of the room.

I met Liv's eye and for the first time since I had sat across from her in that interview room, she did not look away. I braced for the aftershock, but the expected angry cries from her mother and grandmother for Liv to flee this life she had foolishly chosen never arrived. For an instant I thought their echoes might have left me for good, but they were still there. Quieter than before only… different.

Liv nodded slowly as if she'd expected as much.

"But you can", I said slipping the ring off my finger and taking Liv's hand.

She tried to pull away. "You'll need it!"

I shook my head. "It's no use to me in this fight. There is no violence in them. Not that I could find, anyway."

She snorted as if she found that hard to believe. "What is there then?"

"Acceptance…" I swallowed and took a deep breath as I slid the ring onto her finger before gripping her hand tightly in both of mine. "Pride…" Smoke starting to billow out from between our fingers as I drew more heavily from the ring letting the magic flow through me as I folded it back into Liv. She closed her eyes as a stream of energy flowed into her. "And above all, a desire to protect what they love most." I willed her muscles to be quicker, her skin to be as strong as steel, her reflexes sharper. Whatever would keep her safe. Liv's eyes shot open as the door at the far end of the room groaned in protest as it was finally ripped free from its hinges.

She pulled away as the first gunshots sounded, and started running so fast around the outside of the room I only located her once she cleared the back row and was cutting left towards the men pouring into the room. The first to clamber over the broken door scanned the convention hall, a shotgun coming to rest on me. Liv's baton cracked into the side of his weapon sending his aim wide, the shotgun round hitting the curtain in a crackle of magic.

My skull throbbed horribly, all I wanted to do was crawl under the nearest chair and curl into a ball but I wasn't quite done yet. When the nausea subsided, I found myself on my knees still clutching the bag of overpriced bestsellers. I glimpsed Liv disappear among the dark uniforms, her enhanced figure a blur of rapid blows, weaving between their clumsy forms like a dancer. It was both thrilling and terrifying to behold. She pushed herself into the centre of their group, forcing them to abandon their firearms in order to avoid shooting one another. They may have been compelled to fire on anyone attending the conference but that didn't include their own people.

I hobbled to the edge of the tiered seating where the outer wall lay bare the brickwork which ran the full length of the theatre. I picked a brick at random, one with a slightly yellow tinge and pressed my first novel against it.

"Torri!", I muttered, focusing on the wall. The

book disintegrated instantly, the full force of it hurled into that single point. "Torri!", I said again, a crack forming beneath my palm as another book dissolved in a cloud of smoke. "Break!" I repeated, the crack widened and split off in several more directions.

"Torri." Debris and dust rained down from the wall as if it had been struck by a hammer. Behind me, the second half of the unit stormed into the room from the alleyway. I threw my hands into the air, a paperback in each hand, as a rifle was levelled in my direction. "I'm not attending the conference!" I called, glancing in Liv's direction where her baton was darting between armoured bodies with violent speed. "I work with Detective Olivia Stone! I am not attending the conference!" I repeated as two of the armed officers continued towards me while the remaining four peeled off up the aisle.

"On your knees!" The first one shouted. He sounded confused, his weapon swinging between me and the battle raging at the back of the theatre.

"They are just paperbacks." I said, calmly.

"Drop them!" The second officer said, stepping around behind me.

"On your knees!" He gripped my shoulder and started to shove me down. "We should check backstage. They could be…"

"Everyone escaped", I whispered, lacing the words with magic as the first paperback dissolved in my hand.

"How?" The one opposite asked.

"Through this hole in the wall." I said, gesturing to the cracked brickwork beside me.

"What?"

"You should probably *report back.*" I said, laying a little more force into the words.

"I better report back!" The man behind me hurried down the steps and out the way he had come.

"What? Carter? Carter!" He sounded desperate as he turned after him.

I lunged for him but he was too quick. The sudden flash as the paperback dissolved in my hand made him turn. The butt of his rifle caught me on the chin and send me reeling back against the wall. He must have struck again because the next thing I knew I was on the floor and my leg felt like a knife had been slashed across my shin. I threw out a hand but I was too disorientated.

"Fin!" Liv cried, from somewhere nearby. It sounded like she was still giving them hell.

I waited but no follow up swing came. The wall, with a crack running across three bricks swam into view. I dragged the Sainsbury's bag towards me and dug out another paperback.

"Torri." Another paperback.

"Torri." Another. A shower of brick dust and smoke filled my vision.

"Let go of me, John." Liv's voice.

"You aren't going anywhere until I get some fucking answers", John said.

"Torri!"

"What the hell is he..." John's voice was cut off with a grunt of pain.

The crack widened and split off in several more directions. I turned my head aside as chunks of brickwork fell away from and showered me in debris. I coughed through the smoke and saw Liv was standing protectively behind me.

"Liv, he's coming. You need to hide." I said, stacking the last three paperbacks and placing them at the foot of the wall.

"What the hell is this, Stone?" John said.

"Here," Liv said, dropping down beside me and forcing her ring back onto my little finger. It felt pathetically thin now. A skinny band of gold, almost a mockery of heavy band it had been just moments before.

"Go!" I said, turning back the wall.

I heard hurried footsteps as Liv rushed up the

aisle. Out of the corner of my eye I saw her duck down in the middle rows. Strong hands collared me and tried to drag me to my feet. I cried out as my knee protested, but kept my watering eyes focused on the crumbling wall as John forced me to stand.

"*Torri!*" I cried, for a final time. A section big enough to crawl though fell outwards into the car park beyond.

"Stone, what...? I don't...?" John turned me bodily round and held me by the collar. "What is this?" I saw the almost deranged look in his eye then. He looked terrified. Terrified of what he had seen, of what he had been compelled to do and the knowledge that he would do it.

"Sorry about this", I grimaced, getting my good foot under me and gripping his wrist. "*Lie down and play dead. Tell your men to do the same.*" I said, using the last embers of my magic. It wasn't much. Certainly not enough to compel anyone to do anything against their will, but Evelyn's grip on them had faded and he was grateful for any alternative.

"Lie down and play dead. Now", John said, turning to the other sticken, beaten and baffled looking officers. Half of them were down due to injury, but the others gradually lay down.

Once they were all looking suitably dead, I hopped to the front row, lowered the nearest seat and dropped down into it with a deep, bone-weary sigh. I stretched my good leg out and ran a hand down my throbbing shin. Finally, I slipped Liv's ring off my little finger and dropped it into my jacket pocket as the crunch of glass underfoot marked the arrival of Evelyn Nelson.

CHAPTER 25

"Hello Randall", I said, looking up. He stepped cautiously in front of me, hesitant eyes casting about for any signs of a trap. Once he seemed satisfied, he stepped a little closer, his eyes on me. The pressure of his magic against me felt like a physical weight. I fanned my hands out to show they were empty, wincing against the layers upon layers of protective magic he had so carefully thrown over himself in such an extravagant display of power.

"You helped them escape", he said, his voice waspish and cold.

I cried out as an invisible hand gripped my wrist and squeezed.

"Yes! I did. I took out all your puppets too. Sorry about that, Randall", I said, blinking as the nausea of magical withdrawal settled unpleasantly between the pain in my shin and the agony shooting up through my wrist.

"They must have escaped through here, sir", a

voice said from my left. I turned bleary eyes in that direction and could see the officer I had compelled standing in front of the break in the wall.

"Any sign of them?"

"No, sir. Should we pursue?"

"Don't bother", he said. "Put your pistols in your mouth instead."

"Yes, sir."

I heard the distinct sound of sidearms being drawn from hip holsters. Not everyone obeyed. Most simply drew or put a hand to their sidearm. Randall grimaced his frustration. *"All of you!"*

Some shook as they brought their weapon to their lips but anyone conscious who hadn't been disarmed, obeyed.

"Good." he smiled. "Now,"

"Randall, wait", I said, before he could speak. The use of the name Randall made his eye twitch. "Why are you doing this? The Randall I've read about would never…"

He snorted. "Why? Revenge, obviously." He turned back to the police.

"Oh no, you misunderstand." I choked out a small laugh in an attempt to gather my courage. "I get your motives, you are insane. What I want to know, is why you waited a year? Were you really planning all that time? You must be livid now I've stopped you."

"Stopped me?" he scowled. "You've barely slowed me down. You were a minor inconvenience. An annoyance, that is all. I could crush you right now. You are completely spent. I can tell, while I have all of this", he said, showing me the leather-bound notebook tucked protectively under one arm.

I switched tack, eying the notebook. "Impressive what bags of money can buy isn't it? I saw your house. Once your wife took the coward's way out, I guess you were living pretty lean eh? What, did you sell the Jag on the way back from her funer..." I choked off suddenly, my throat constricting as that same invisible hand closed around my throat. It held me for a few seconds then released, leaving me gasping for air.

"You really have no idea do you?" she said, real pleasure in Randall's voice. "You've been stumbling after me all week trying to figure things out, and you still have nothing."

"What do you mean?" I said, slipping uncertainty into my voice. I kept my eyes fixed on Randall, determined not to give Evelyn the slightest cause to return her attention to the police.

"The hotel? Price? The occupants of this ridiculous convention? You, a fellow mage, no less. Such a shame", Evelyn said, the voice an amused taunt.

"Like you said, it was revenge for your daughter", I said, letting my voice waiver.

"Poor thing."

"Why Claire?" I asked.

Randall glanced at the limp forms on the floor, then spoke in a low tense voice. "That, wasn't meant to happen. *She* shouldn't have been there at all."

"Is that why you killed her? Because she hosted an intervention for you?" I said, forcing myself to snort with derision. I tasted blood and immediately started coughing.

"I arranged a distraction for her to keep her away from that fucking *support* group." She sounded disgusted. "If people spent more time home with their family, and less time listening to the problems of scum like that, my baby girl might still be alive."

"A distraction?" I said, not having to hide my surprise then. "Greg? You arranged that?"

"Just a little nudge. Addicts are normally so easy to manipulate", he said, genuine sadness creeping into his voice. There was something else too, a feminine fluttering of eyelids which didn't fit at all with the man standing before me. He sighed. "I liked Claire, she tried so hard to help

Evie get back on track."

I croaked out a laugh. "So, it wasn't revenge at all? It was because she showed up unexpectedly? Pretty sloppy, given all this preparation, eh Randall?"

The face Evelyn wore hardened. "No, she died because she threw her lot in with those brainwashed idiots. He was never the same after they got their hooks into him", she said grimacing as she turned to the banner above the stage. She stared at it for a moment then snapped her fingers and the words *The Positive Self* burst into flames.

"Who?" I asked, frowning with confusion. "Who was never the same?"

She turned back to me, rolling her eyes theatrically. Now that I knew to look for it, all the mannerisms must have been Evelyn, they had just been shoehorned into Randall's body. "You still have no idea? How is it you of all people came the closest to stopping me? Just lucky I suppose. Still, all you've cost me is a little time. But I'm not an impatient person and the best punishments are the ones that last. How does it feel knowing you were completely outmatched from the start? I hope it offers you some satisfaction knowing that you could never have beaten me", she said, raising her hand in front of her, as if her fingers were closing around my throat. I cried out as she dragged me into the air, my battered and broken body hanging limply in her grip.

I tried to push the pain and nausea aside, knowing I was moments away from death, my heart thrumming like a jackhammer in my chest.

"Not so relaxed now, I see?" she said, the pressure easing around my throat and jaw. I opened my mouth ready and more than willing to beg for my life, but that was exactly what she wanted to hear before she ended it, I could see the anticipation in her eye. The glee.

"Actually, you were right before", I said, feeling the pressure increase against my chest as if a boa constrictor was slowly tightening its coils around me.

"Oh?" she asked.

"It is satisfying to know I could never have beaten you, Randall." I placed the tiniest emphasis on the name, the slightest of provocations.

She pushed his lips into a thin irritable line, then my arms were being pulled out to the sides, my recently relocated shoulder screaming in agony. I bit my lip, squinting against the pain. Crying out would only bring her the satisfaction she wanted. I stared at her mouth, my own teeth digging into my bottom lip as she finally said the words, "Silly boy, it was me all along. *Evelyn*".

The world seemed to stop. It was only a second but the momentary reprieve from the agony I had been feeling a moment before made me wonder if I had actually died and somehow missed the occasion. I was weightless, suspended momentarily in a bubble of air, as if the world around me had frozen.

Then Randall screamed. It was a horrible soul-rending thing, pulled deep from somewhere dark and hopeless. The ghost of his dead wife had left him. I dropped to the floor, my feet buckling beneath me. Randall tossed aside the black diary he had been clutching and wept his face buried in his hands.

"*I'm sorry, I'm sorry, I'm so sorry...*" he repeated, hysteria crashing into him like an eighteen-wheeler. Police removed the sidearms from their mouths and holstered them with shaking hands.

"It's over, you can get up now", I said. The others were already on their feet, though none of them wanted to approach Randall, who continued to sob on his knees. Crippling nausea hit me as I listened to his sobs, and even the act of sitting up seemed to suddenly require more concentration than I could spare. I slumped onto my side, letting my eyes fall out of focus. Liv's slender, albeit blurred figure, came loosely into view. I listened to her read Randall his rights and snap on a set of handcuffs. The other officers recovered themselves soon after and followed

Liv's example. Grateful, perhaps, to have the routine of their training to fall back on.

"There's a man critically injured on the stage, call an ambulance and start moving these people out into the street. John, secure Mr. Nelson", Liv said. She sounded tired but her voice still held the authority of her rank. Something about that filled me with such pride that my eyes started to water. I searched my mind for the cause and found Liv's mother and grandmother standing arm in arm, beaming at the scene, a dozen or more bewildered men on their beaten backsides looking to her, their little Livvy, for direction. I put my head back and closed my eyes.

#

I opened my eyes and realised time had moved on. I appeared to be outside the rear of the hotel lying on a stretcher next to several parked police cars.

"What's going on?" I asked, trying to sit up but finding my progress impeded by a strap across my chest. My eyes drifted in and out of focus on the swarm of police officers and ambulance workers taking statements and seeing to the traumatised audience members.

"Sit back, you are alright", Liv said from beside me.

"Why are we here?" I asked, thickly. I was too tired to make the words fit the questions I had intended to ask. Liv, to her credit, managed to decipher my meaning.

"The streets are jammed in every direction. Half the country thinks it was a terrorist attack, so people are fleeing the area. The injured are being taken to the hospital in order of severity. Sorry, you didn't make the cut."

"Really?" I said.

"They dosed you up on painkillers and bound your arm and your leg. You'll manage as long as you don't move around too much."

"Randall?" I asked.

"Sitting in a riot van on his own waiting to spend a very long time in prison. That is if we can find anything solid to convict him with."

I took a deep breath and tried to focus on her. "What do you mean?"

"Well there isn't really much evidence to convict him with. Nobody knows how he killed any of these people. The popular theory for today is that he somehow managed to hypnotise the entire unit. Either that or he hired a bunch of mercenaries to dress up like police who vanished into thin air. Unless he confesses, the prosecution will have a tough time." She sighed.

"You heard her in there, it was all Evelyn", I said.

"Mm, that was clever by the way, getting him to confess like that. It only almost cost you your life. How did you know he would fall for it anyway?"

"*He* wouldn't have. But Evelyn wasn't a mage."

"True, but she was married to one for most of her life, she must have known how the whole confession cleansing thing worked?"

"Mm, but knowing about it and having learned to live with it yourself are completely different. I doubt she ever went to a meeting with him. She would have been too embarassed. Evelyn had his power but she didn't have his experience. She felt invincible and never once had to learn her limits."

The crowd parted and two familiar faces pushed their way through the hoard. I raised my hand and waved as Henry and my father faught their way over to us.

"Son, are you alright? Why hasn't he been taken to a hospital? Where are the fucking doctors?" Robert said.

"He's okay, couple of broken bones and a few bruises. He'll be in one of the next ambulances out of here once they arrive", Liv said. "I need to check in with Riley. He wanted to read your statement the moment I had it down on paper."

"I don't remember giving you any statement?"

"You didn't. I finished it while you were asleep. You talked Randall down. Good job", she said, giving me a tired smile.

"Oh, before I forget", I said, wiggling my good arm free from my restraints. Henry and my father took pity on me and unclipped my chest strap so that I could retrieve Liv's ring from my pocket. "Sorry we couldn't save more of it", I said, passing her the narrow band of gold.

She took it and slipped it back on her finger, watching me, her face unreadable. She looked at my leg and then my wrist, opened her mouth then closed it again. "Good work, detective", she finally said, waving her pad over her shoulder as she walked away.

Henry watched her go then beamed at me from the foot of my stretcher. "You did it, you beat him, or her, or whatever. How did you do it? Another Dragon? Fireball? Whirlwind?"

Robert gave Henry a look and he fell silent. "Actually, she beat herself. I got Evelyn to confess. Once she was gone, Randall came back to himself."

"Oh", Henry said, disappointed. He looked at my father. "Well, are you going to give it to him or are you just going to let him lie there and suffer?"

"Yes, I thought before you confessed and got yourself clean you might want to push your healing along a little", he said pulling a crumpled napkin from his pocket and handing it to me.

I read the words on it and pulled him into a one-armed hug. The napkin read simply, *My son.*

"Thank you. I might have another use for it though. Think you can go and borrow a couple of jackets from the ambulance crews?"

"On it", Henry said, immediately disappearing into the crowd as if I'd merely asked him for a glass of water.

"Never changes, does he?" I said.

Robert watched him go; his lips pursed. "He's hurting. He's grateful too for what you did. Once he starts talking about it all he'll find it difficult to stop, though. Anyway, that can wait. What are we stealing these jackets for?"

#

"Coming through!" Henry called over my head. He and my father kept their heads low as they wheeled my gurney through the crowd. Nobody raised so much as an eyebrow as we weaved through the ranks of police. We pulled up beside the riot van where two officers stood guard at the rear. The truck had been positioned among other vehicles so the rear doors were hidden from the rest of the street and the assembled TV crews.

"Shit!" Henry said, as the gurney took a sharp turn to avoid the officers and I rolled off the bed onto the street. The two officers dropped immediately to assist me back onto the gurney.

"Thank you, boys", Robert said, tapping the first on the arm and muttering. "You look tired, *why don't you have a little sleep?*" Henry and I both stifled yawns. It wasn't a command but a suggestion, albeit a forceful one but nowhere near strong enough to break his will. Still, it sent a shiver down my spine.

I leant heavily on the second guard, as the first slipped onto the gurney and Henry threw a blanket over him, covering his uniform up to the neck. Robert reached for the second officer and shook his hand firmly once I was back on my feet.

"Constable! *It's been too long! how is the family?*" he said, a broad welcoming smile across his face as smoke puffed out of his mouth. Again, from simple proximity Henry and I cracked a smile too.

The officer blinked confused then after protracted and tense moment, his face split into a grin and he started telling Dad about his kids. I gently slipped the key from his belt and unlocked the door to the back of the riot van. With Henry's help, I hopped past the now sleeping guard, and climbed up into the van. "Make it quick", Henry said, before closing the door, leaving me alone in semi-darkness with Randall. He sat handcuffed to a seat on my left.

"I'm ready to confess."

"Randall?" I said, keeping my voice even, hopping to the bench opposite him and sitting down.

"Oh, it's you. Have you come to finish it?" he asked, he didn't sound concerned by the idea.

"Is that what you want?" I said.

"It doesn't matter now. Thank you for stopping her. For stopping me."

"You saw everything that happened?"

He nodded, his eyes gazing blindly into the floor. "I can't stop."

"That wasn't you."

"Yes, it was. My body, my senses, my mind. It was just her in control. She did all that, killed all those people just to punish me? She thought I didn't care, but Evie... How could she think that? All the charity work, everything I did, was to try and make up for my mistakes. I had no idea. A year... she never said a word."

"That thing wasn't Evelyn", I said.

"She said so herself, it was Evelyn. How could she...? How could I not know?"

"It was Evelyn, but not all of her. All her doubts, her second thoughts, her love for you, that she must have held back or buried elsewhere. It's probably why it took her so long to write. That diary was the darkest parts of her soul."

He met my eye for a moment then looked away.

"So, what happens now?" I asked, "Confess to crimes you didn't commit and go to prison for a very long time?" I withdrew the napkin from my pocket. "You don't belong in prison."

"Just get it over with", he said with a deep, bone-weary sigh. "Take justice for your friend. It would be a mercy."

I pushed myself off the bench and hobbled forwards. The napkin flared like flash paper, and I was nearly floored by the sudden flood of emotion. My father had managed to pour so much pride into those two simple words, I almost doubled over with the weight of it. I had always known my father loved me, but to feel the evidence of it coursing through my veins was something else entirely. He had watched on the news as reporters described the scene and gunshots sounded in the background; each one had hit him like a punch to the heart. I had only ever felt fear like it once before, in fact. The panic and uncertainty, the possibility that he might outlive both his children. Tears ran hot down my face as I felt the well of power gathering like a bonfire in my stomach.

I lowered my hand to his forehead. He accepted it unequivocally and without hesitation.

I focused on the contours of his face, the shape of his peaked hairline and the colour of his beard. It was the face of the man that had caused so much slaughter, the face that had taken Claire from me.

Gradually the beard lengthened into a month's growth and his short crop of dark hair turned chestnut. The changes were slight but notable. Just enough to cast a flicker of doubt into the mind of any eyewitness. It wasn't much but I didn't think I could spare any more power given what was to follow. I gripped his forehead tight in my hand and concentrated on the last terrible four weeks of Randall Nelson's life and muttered a single word as the rush of power pooled briefly in my palm before flaring and filling the van interior with a flash of blue light.

"Forget."

EPILOGUE

"We're here." Amber called, cutting through my stupor as the cab pulled to a stop. I awoke and sat up to perform an awkward one armed stretch. After the incident at the hotel the doctors had told me I had dislocated my shoulder a second time. That, coupled with the assortment of other bumps and bruises, meant that I was spending as much time as possible asleep when I wasn't at a meeting or dealing with my new protégé. My shoulder flared up every time I moved but pain relief was out of the question. I was an addict after all.

"Good, seems to have quietened down a bit." I said, peering out the window. The news vans were long gone. All that remained were a couple of kids on flashy bikes from the estate daring one another to ride closer and closer to the police tape. Britain's finest weren't taking any chances though, they had taped off the entire house as well as the spacious driveway and gardens just to be sure. Two uniformed officers stood with their hands tucked into their vests against the chill. During my week of recovery cooped up at Henry's place I had apparently missed the final days of summer. My father had offered to take me in, but I felt that was probably a bridge too far. As nice as his place was I dreaded to think what our latest exploits – or heroics, as he put it - would have done for his popularity around campus, and besides, I felt my presence was better served keeping Henry out of trouble.

"Want to run a little interference for me?" I asked, looking at Amber through the rear view mirror.

"Can I use magic?" she asked, her voice eager.

"That depends. Do you need to use magic?" I watched her glance out at the police officers, both of which were male and both of whom carried the slumped shoulders and general disposition one might associate with a shift not even halfway through guarding an empty house from children.

"No." she sighed, opening her door.

"Hold on", I said, suppressing a smile. "Might as well make this a teachable moment." I dug into my tobacco pouch and searched the contents for a suitable quote. When I looked up Amber was turned all the way round in her seat to watch me.

"Seriously? You'll let me use magic on them?"

"Lord no. What is the first thing you have to learn about being a mage?"

"Control." she recited instantly, her tone bored.

"Good. Now show me how much control you have. Smoke this while you distract them, make it last as long as you can. Take in the power but don't use it, just hold it there ready."

"What's the point in that?"

"Because I'm your master, and you do as I say, young apprentice."

"Sounds boring."

I frowned. "Just trust me. You don't need magic to distract them, but you do need to master some control. If you manage to hold it until I get back, then I'll teach you a spell."

"What kind of spell?" she asked, taking the cigarette from me and looking suspicious.

"You can pick. Anything you like, within reason." I waited a moment as she considered this. "Well you have a think about it and let me know?" I said.

She nodded, not really paying attention.

"Draw them away to the left if you can so I can slip in around the back."

"Right." she nodded, and got out of the car. I watched her go from the back seat. She crossed to the pavement in front of the house then turned and walked the length of the yellow tape, passing the two policemen as she went. She paused a little to their left and the two men idled over to her and quickly started up a conversation.

I got out, stuffed my tobacco into my coat pocket and walked swiftly across road and under the police tape. The children on bikes whooped as I crossed the line but thankfully this must have been a fairly regular occurrence since nobody raised the alarm.

I felt a chill as I entered the back garden and saw the two graves, but didn't linger for more than a few seconds over the disturbed topsoil. The broken patio doors at the rear of the house had been taped up and with minimal effort I squeezed through and made it inside the house. The place was deserted so I headed towards the stairs giving the scorched patch of hardwood a wide birth. The smell of charcoal had an undertone of sweetness like old meat left too long on a barbeque. I could hear Amber and the police officers, and a playfulness to her tone I found both reassuring and a little disconcerting. A charming Amber and the smell of barbequed corpse was a little more than I could deal with. I shook off the thought as I cautiously made my way up the stairs by the light from my Motorola.

I stepped over the gaping hole in the floor where Evelyn's corpse had briefly been contained and searched inside what remained of Evie's bedroom. It had largely been stripped except for the posters, the bed and most of the larger furniture. Price had told me that the item I was looking for had not made it into evidence so unless someone had deliberately removed it, it was still within the house. After checking all the obvious places, I mentally re-enacted the night in question, physically walking my way through my movements, then Stones, then Henry's, and finally my father's, as best as I could recall them.

I had a genuine and unaided, eureka moment as I lowered myself onto my knees beside the bedroom door just as my father had. I crawled on my knees towards the hole and dropped to my belly, peering down between the joists and the floorboards for what I sought. It was no wonder the police had missed it. Hanging by the corner of its dust jacket at the very edge of my grasp was the novel Henry had briefly glanced at and disregarded the night Evelyn had risen from her grave. It must have slipped through the floor when Evelyn's corpse had. Carefully, I tore the book free as close to the floorboard as I was able. It came away intact for the most part, with just the top corner of the first few pages still buried within the wood. The cover read:

To Possess A Heart

John D. Lacey

I shivered as the more sinister meaning of the title struck me. Even the image of a couple in the throes of passion did nothing to appease the thought. The woman seemed too vulnerable, her head thrown back and her eyes closed in a semblance of death, the man too entitled, his hand held possessively over her heart. I extracted myself from the floor and hurried out the way I had come. I made my way across the street and back to the car and slumped down into the back seat. I flicked through the pages of the book stopping when I came to a passage highlighted using a yellow marker and started reading.

He smiled companionably to his cohorts over his brandy, pausing only to savour the scent of chestnut and honey. 'Surely you must know?' He laughed at the hopelessness of them as they continued to stare open mouthed at his boldness.

'It is not unlike the taming of a wilful stallion, batter them down and break their will. Do so and the soul will welcome you with open arms. Once accepted, they are yours to direct as if you stood yourself in their shoes.'

'And how should one approach this undertaking?'

'Whether passing fling or something greater, words spoken truly and from the depths of the soul must be exchanged. I find a letter or conveniently left diary

to be the keenest approach. This is not to be tried on a whim, of course. The target must be suitably receptive and your message must be unwavering. I find it best to work oneself up into an appropriate state of singlemindedness. Where the mind leads, the heart will follow.'

'Such a bother, surely this could take weeks?'

'Longer still, I should say. One must sacrifice to truly possess the heart.'

THE END

Finley Chase will return in...

Blood Bonds

THE MEMORY MAGE

Strange Addictions

After an investigation goes sideways, private eye and functioning mage, Finley Chase becomes embroiled in the search for a serial killer.

The only problem is he's addicted to magic. He can't trust himself to get behind the wheel or ride the underground without the emotions of the other passengers getting the better of him. It doesn't help that half the Metropolation police consider him their only lead.

Discovering one of the victims is an old friend and convinced the murders could not have occurred without magic, Fin has no choice but to hunt down the killer and clear his name.

finding the killer will require every last scrap of magic from his dwindling bag of tricks. if he could just convince the other personalities bouncing around his head to shut up and help...

Printed in Great Britain
by Amazon